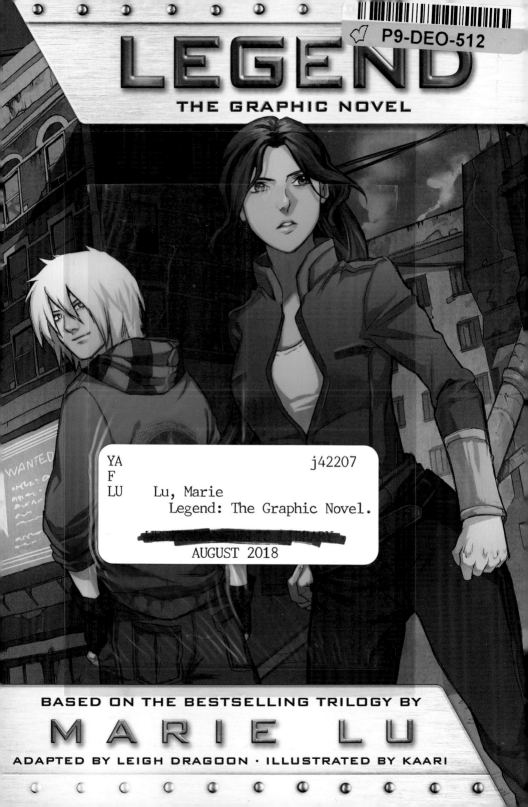

LEGEND

THE GRAPHIC NOVEL

BASED ON THE BESTSELLING TRILOGY BY

MARIE LU

ADAPTED BY LEIGH DRAGOON · ILLUSTRATED BY KAARI

G.P. Putnam's Sons
An imprint of Penguin Group (USA) LLC

Published by the Penguin Group
Penguin Group (USA) LLC, 375 Hudson Street, New York, New York 10014, USA

USA | Canada | UK | Ireland | Australia | New Zealand | India | South Africa | China

penguin.com
A Penguin Random House Company

Text copyright © 2015 by Xiwei Lu.

Photo credits: cover and page 1: (steel) © iStock/Thinkstock.
Illustrations copyright © 2015 by Penguin Group (USA) LLC.

Library of Congress Cataloging-in-Publication Data is available.

Penciled by Kaari
Colored by Kaari, Kate Yan, Angie, and Julia Laud of Caravan Studio
Cover design and lettering by Ching N. Chan
Printed in Canada

ISBN 978-0-399-17189-5

3 5 7 9 11 10 8 6 4

LOS ANGELES, CALIFORNIA
REPUBLIC OF AMERICA
POPULATION 20,174,282

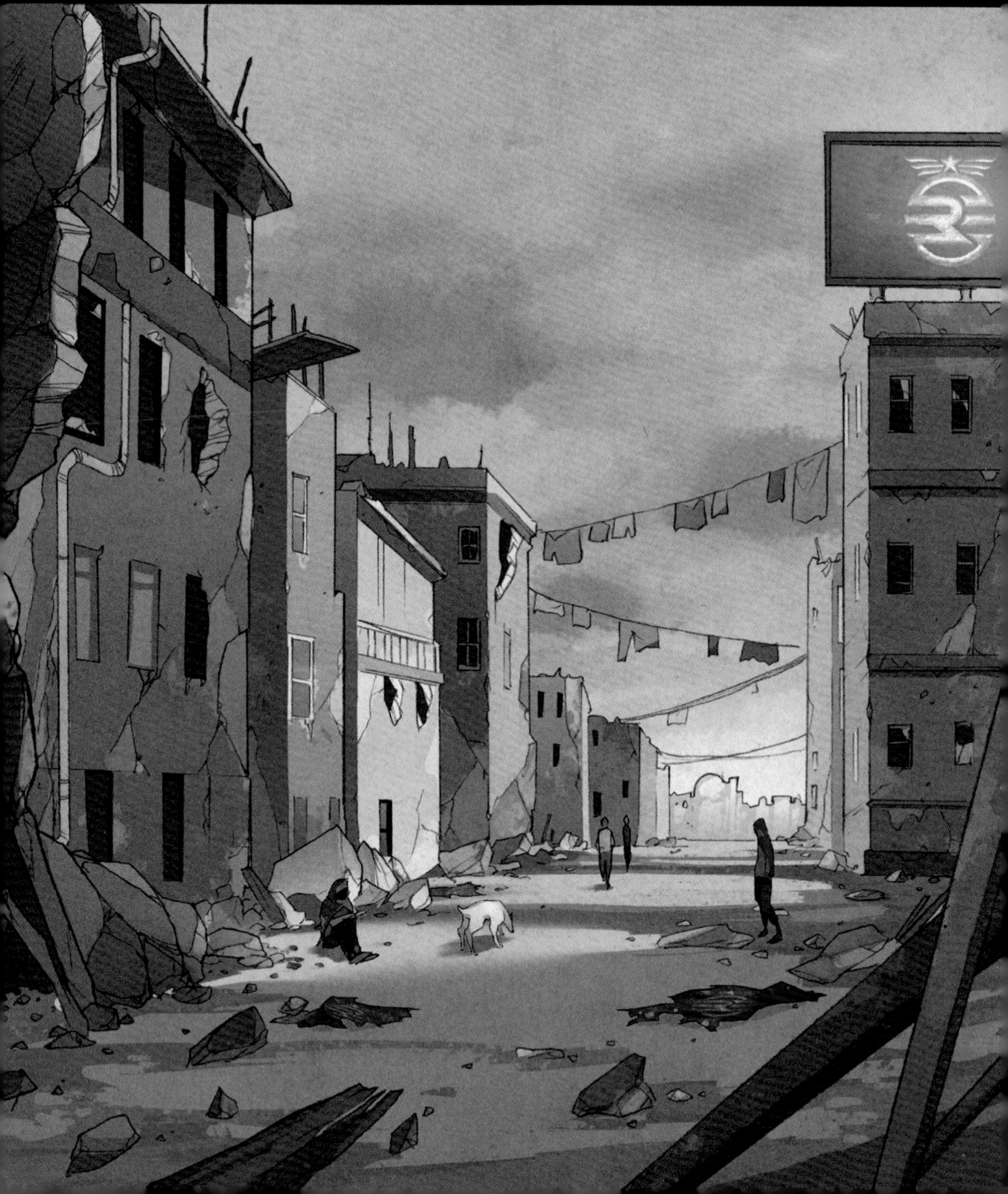

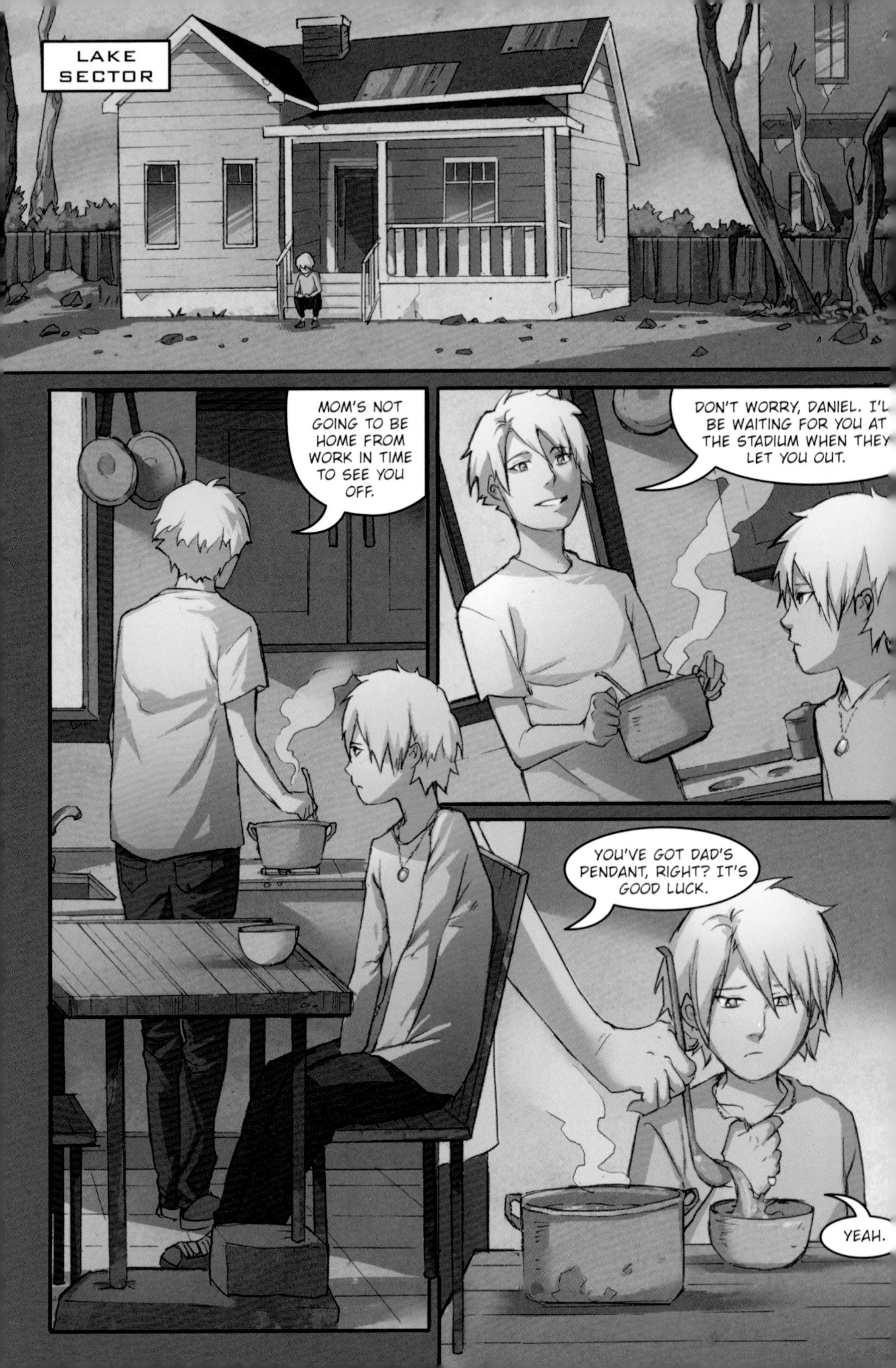
LAKE SECTOR
MOM'S NOT GOING TO BE HOME FROM WORK IN TIME TO SEE YOU OFF.
DON'T WORRY, DANIEL. I'L BE WAITING FOR YOU AT THE STADIUM WHEN THEY LET YOU OUT.
YOU'VE GOT DAD'S PENDANT, RIGHT? IT'S GOOD LUCK.
YEAH.

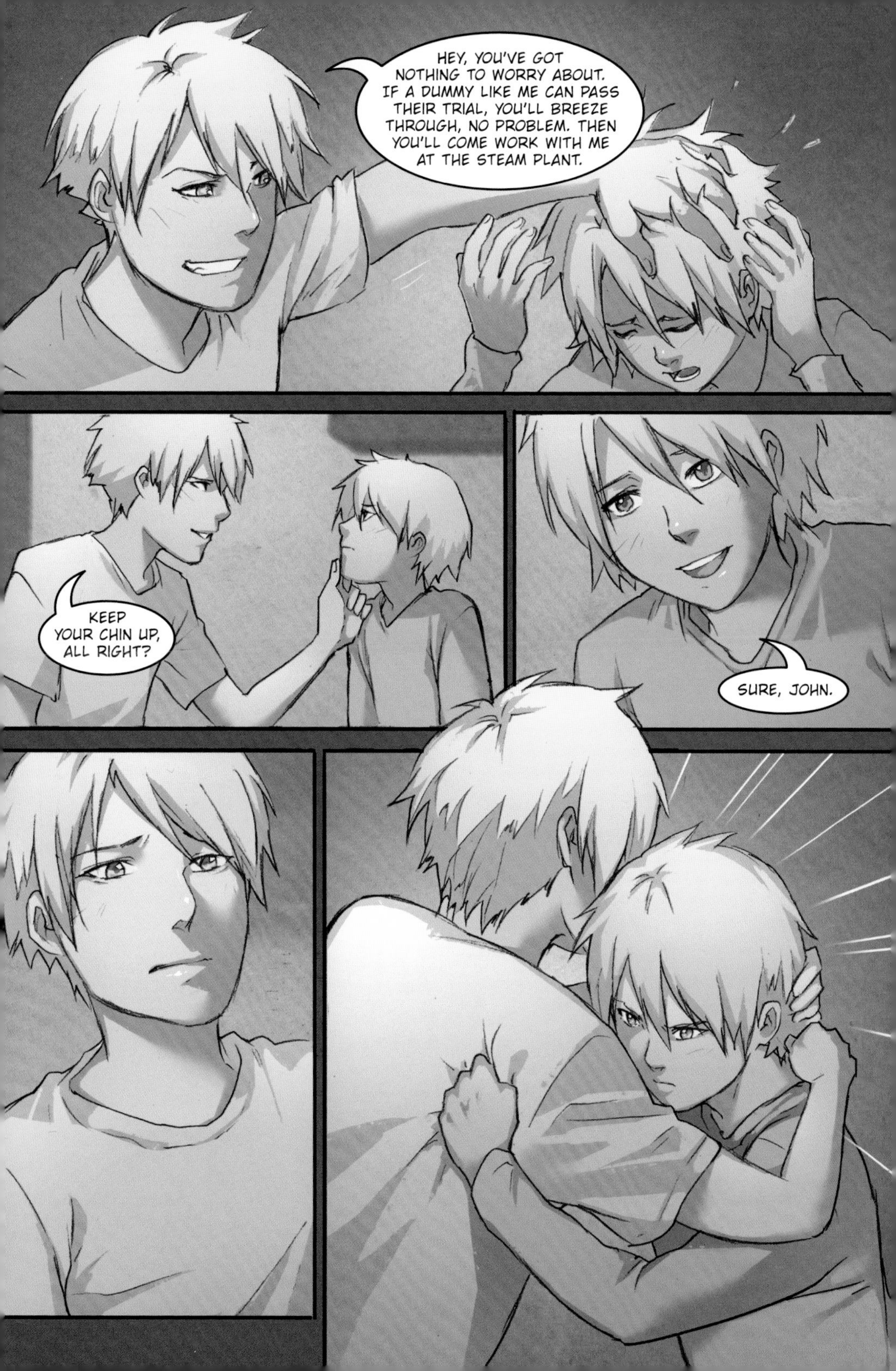
HEY, YOU'VE GOT NOTHING TO WORRY ABOUT. IF A DUMMY LIKE ME CAN PASS THEIR TRIAL, YOU'LL BREEZE THROUGH, NO PROBLEM. THEN YOU'LL COME WORK WITH ME AT THE STEAM PLANT.
KEEP YOUR CHIN UP, ALL RIGHT?
SURE, JOHN.

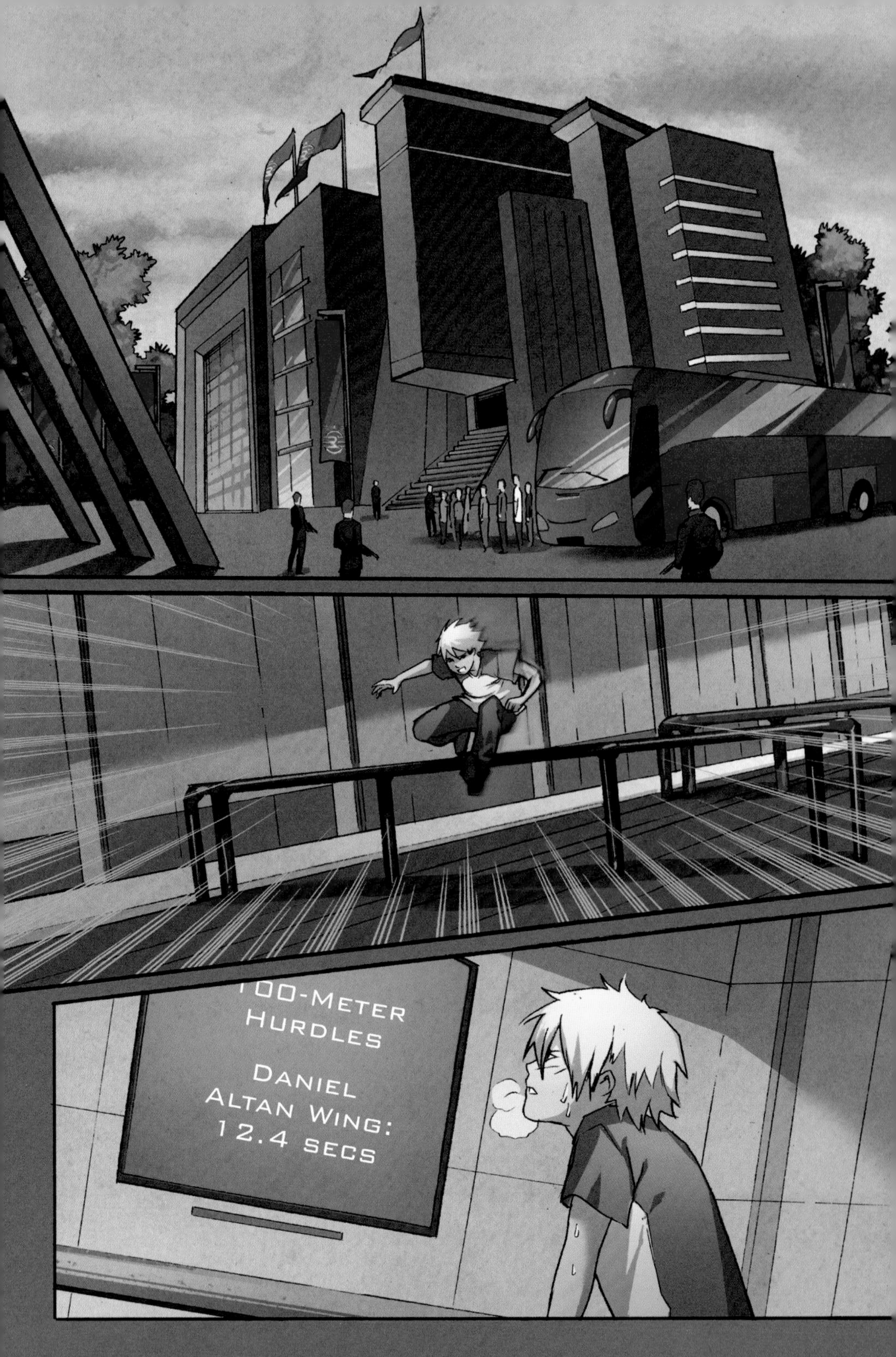
100-Meter
Hurdles
Daniel
Altan Wing:
12.4 secs

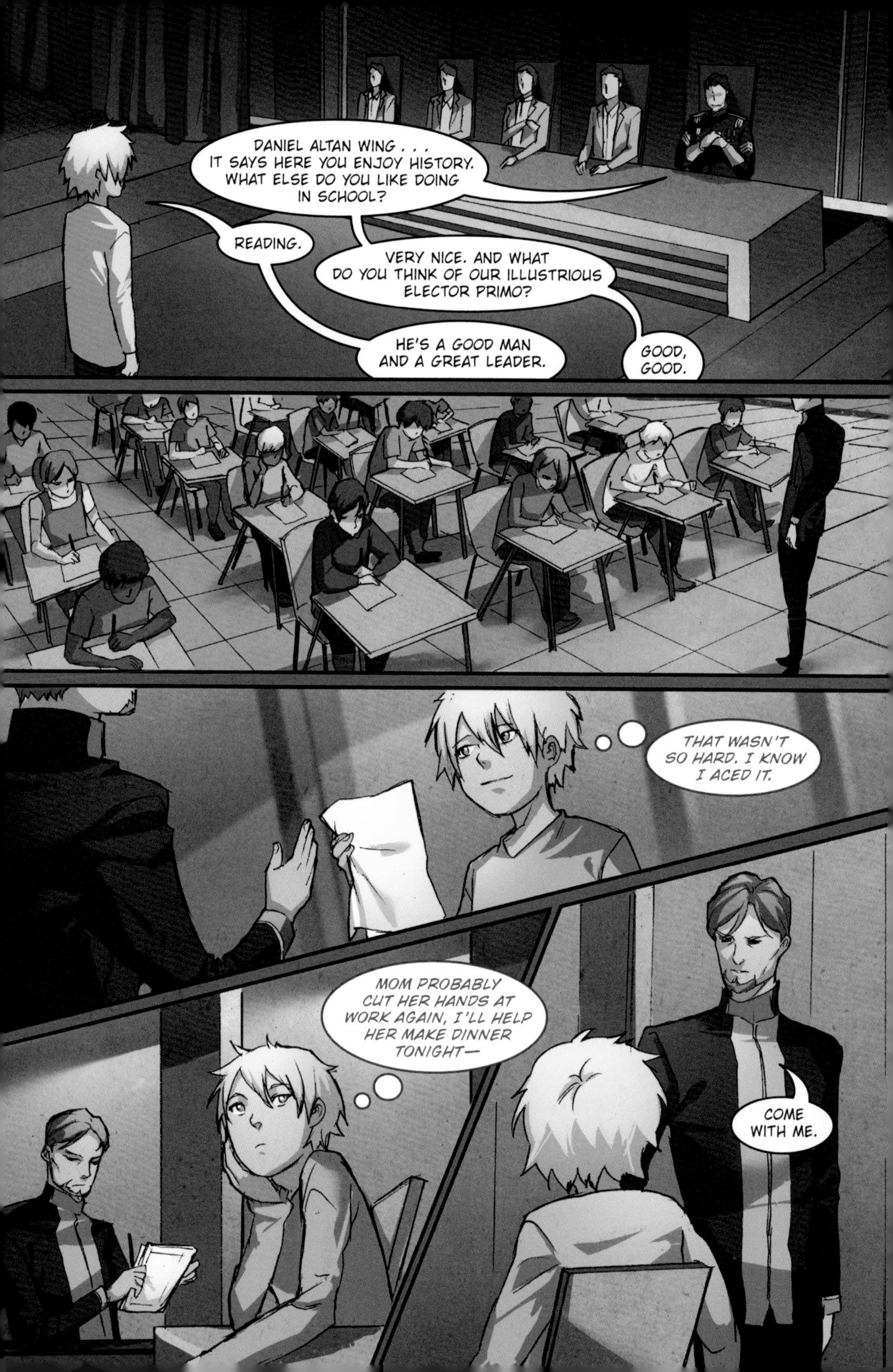
DANIEL ALTAN WING . . . IT SAYS HERE YOU ENJOY HISTORY. WHAT ELSE DO YOU LIKE DOING IN SCHOOL?
READING.
VERY NICE. AND WHAT DO YOU THINK OF OUR ILLUSTRIOUS ELECTOR PRIMO?
HE'S A GOOD MAN AND A GREAT LEADER.
GOOD, GOOD.
THAT WASN'T SO HARD. I KNOW I ACED IT.
MOM PROBABLY CUT HER HANDS AT WORK AGAIN, I'LL HELP HER MAKE DINNER TONIGHT—
COME WITH ME.

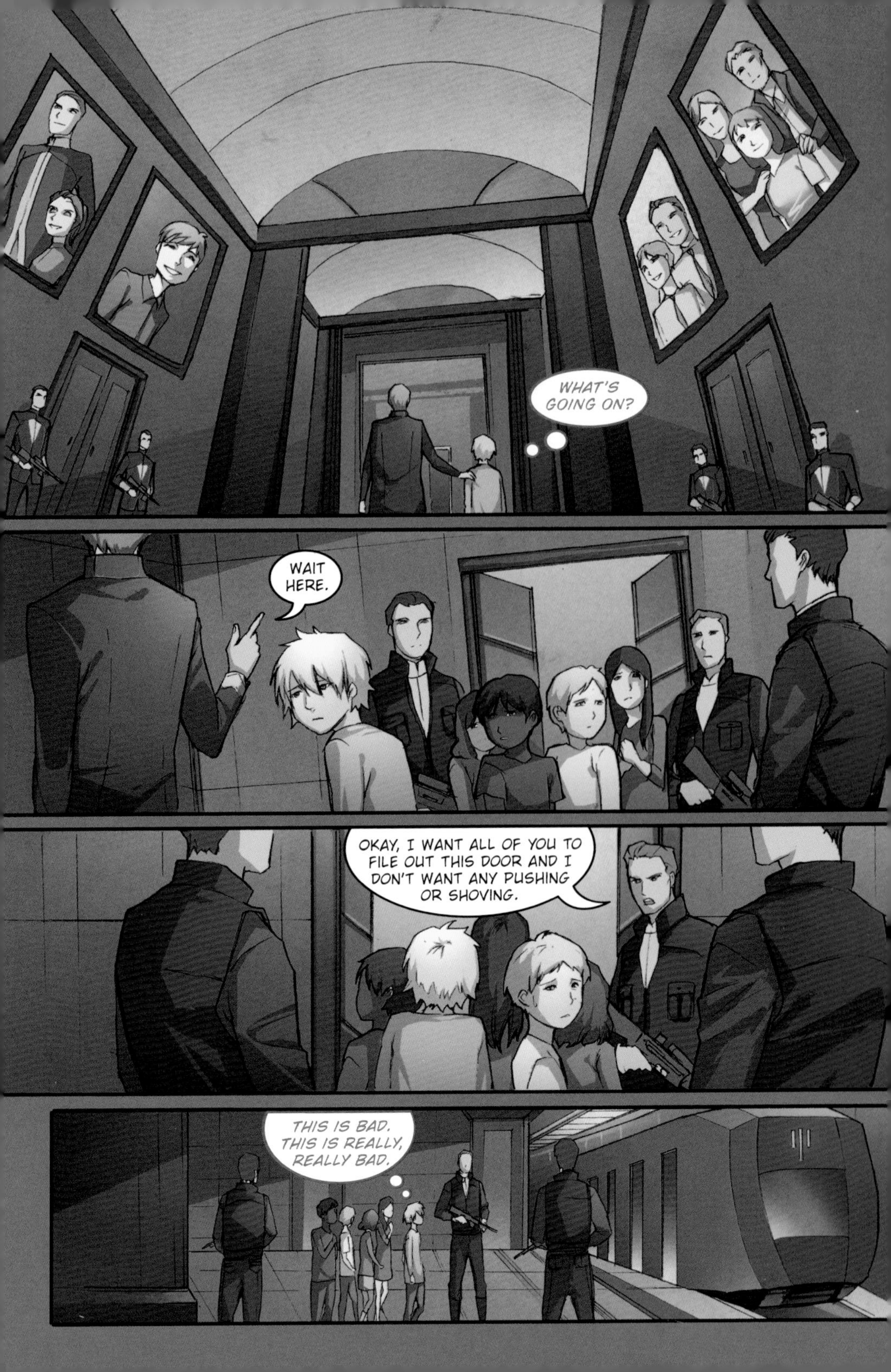
WHAT'S GOING ON?
WAIT HERE.
OKAY, I WANT ALL OF YOU TO FILE OUT THIS DOOR AND I DON'T WANT ANY PUSHING OR SHOVING.
THIS IS BAD. THIS IS REALLY, REALLY BAD.

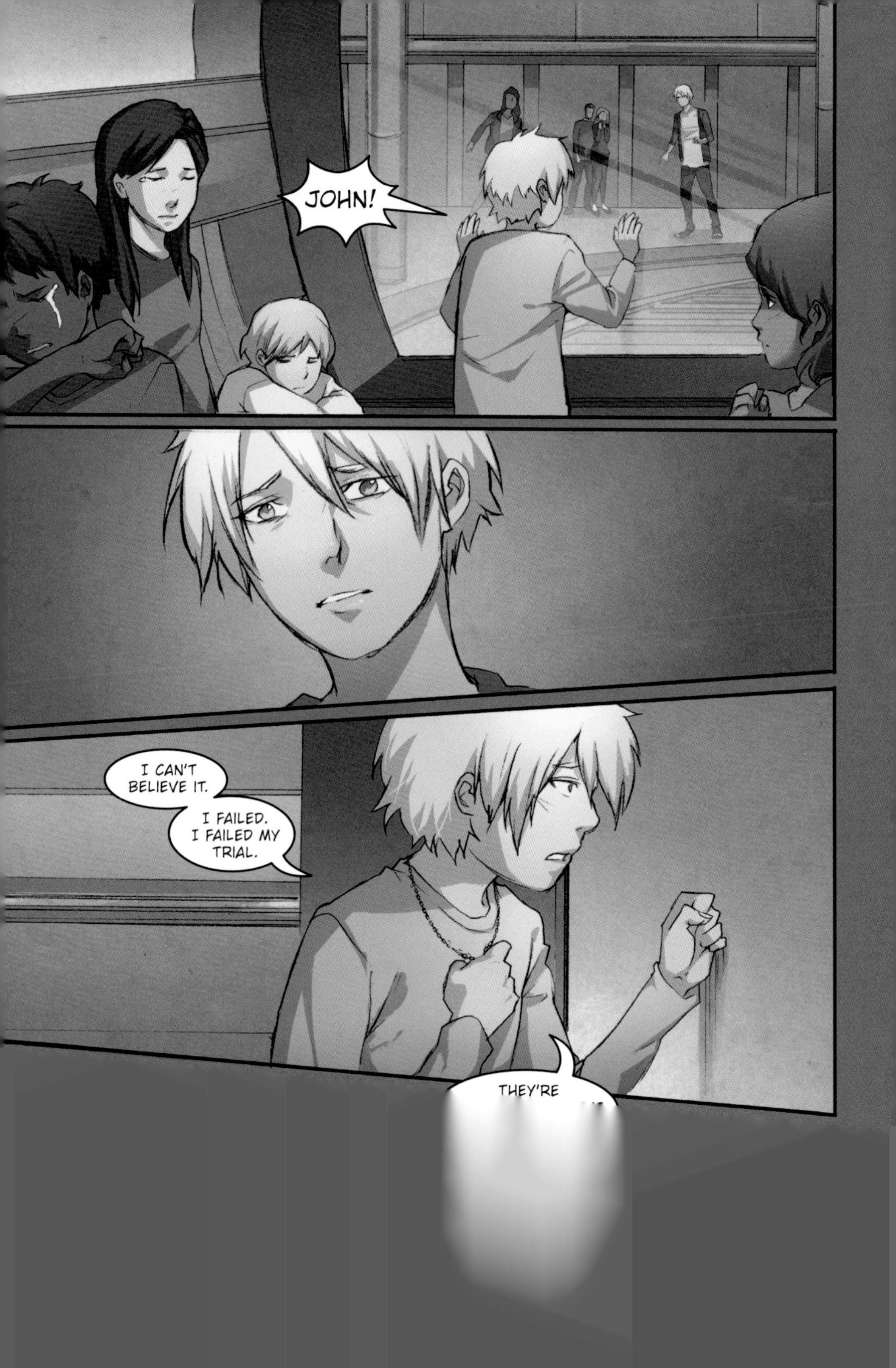
JOHN!
I CAN'T BELIEVE IT.
I FAILED. I FAILED MY TRIAL.
THEY'RE

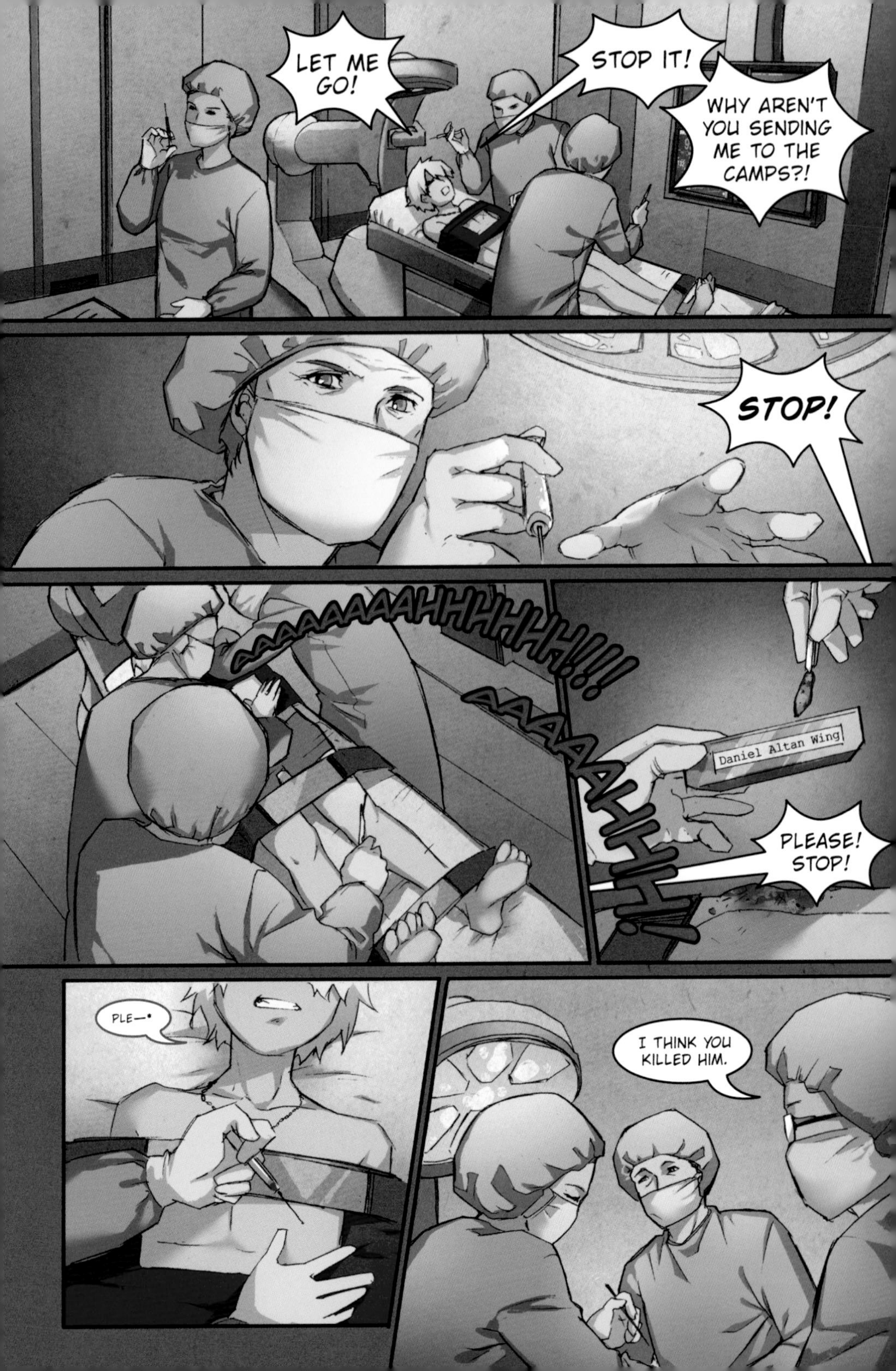
LET ME GO!
STOP IT!
WHY AREN'T YOU SENDING ME TO THE CAMPS?!
STOP!
AAAAAAAAHHHHHH!!!!!
AAAAAAHHHH!
Daniel Altan Wing
PLEASE! STOP!
PLE—•
I THINK YOU KILLED HIM.

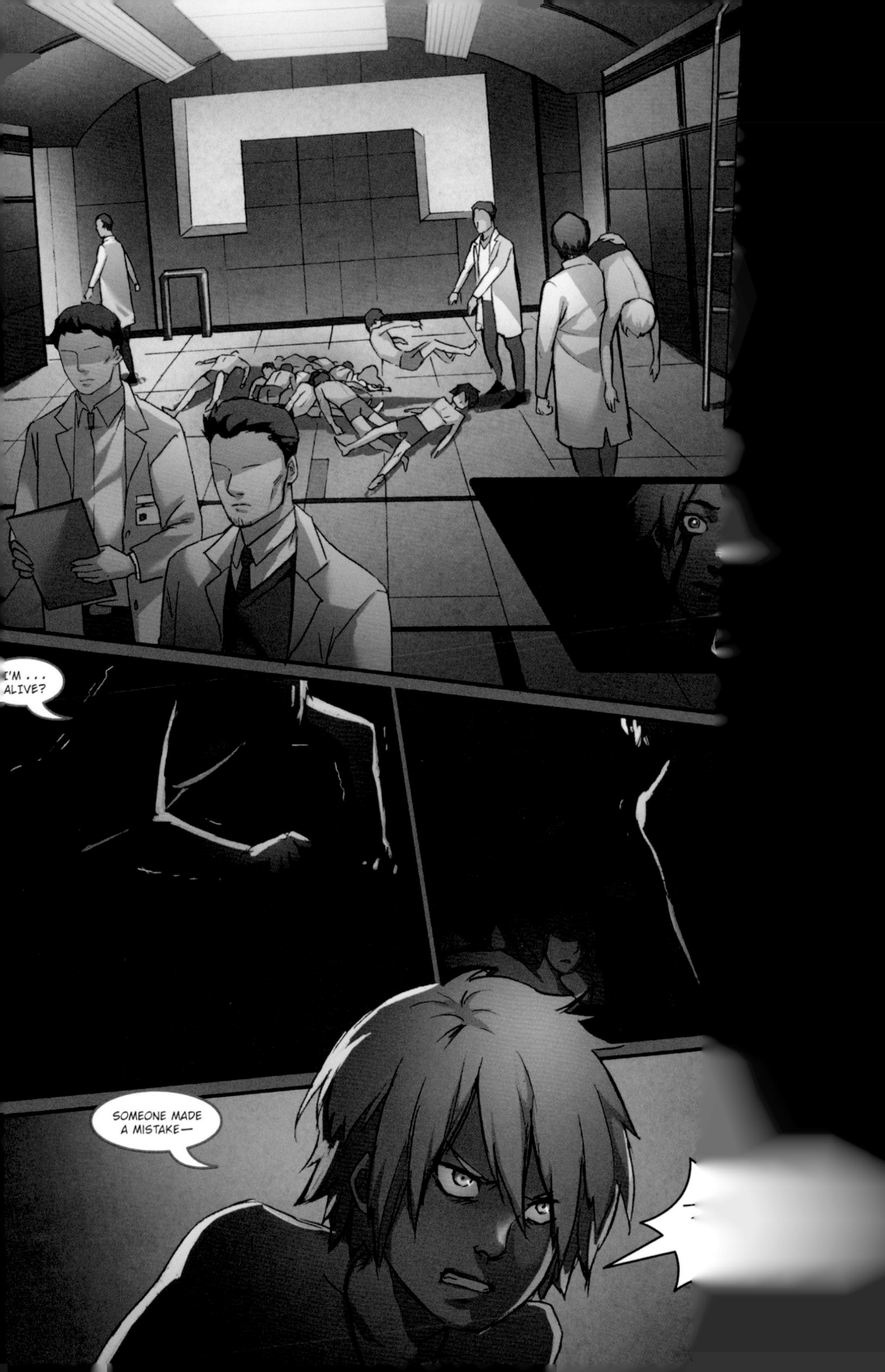
I'M . . .
ALIVE?
SOMEONE MADE
A MISTAKE—

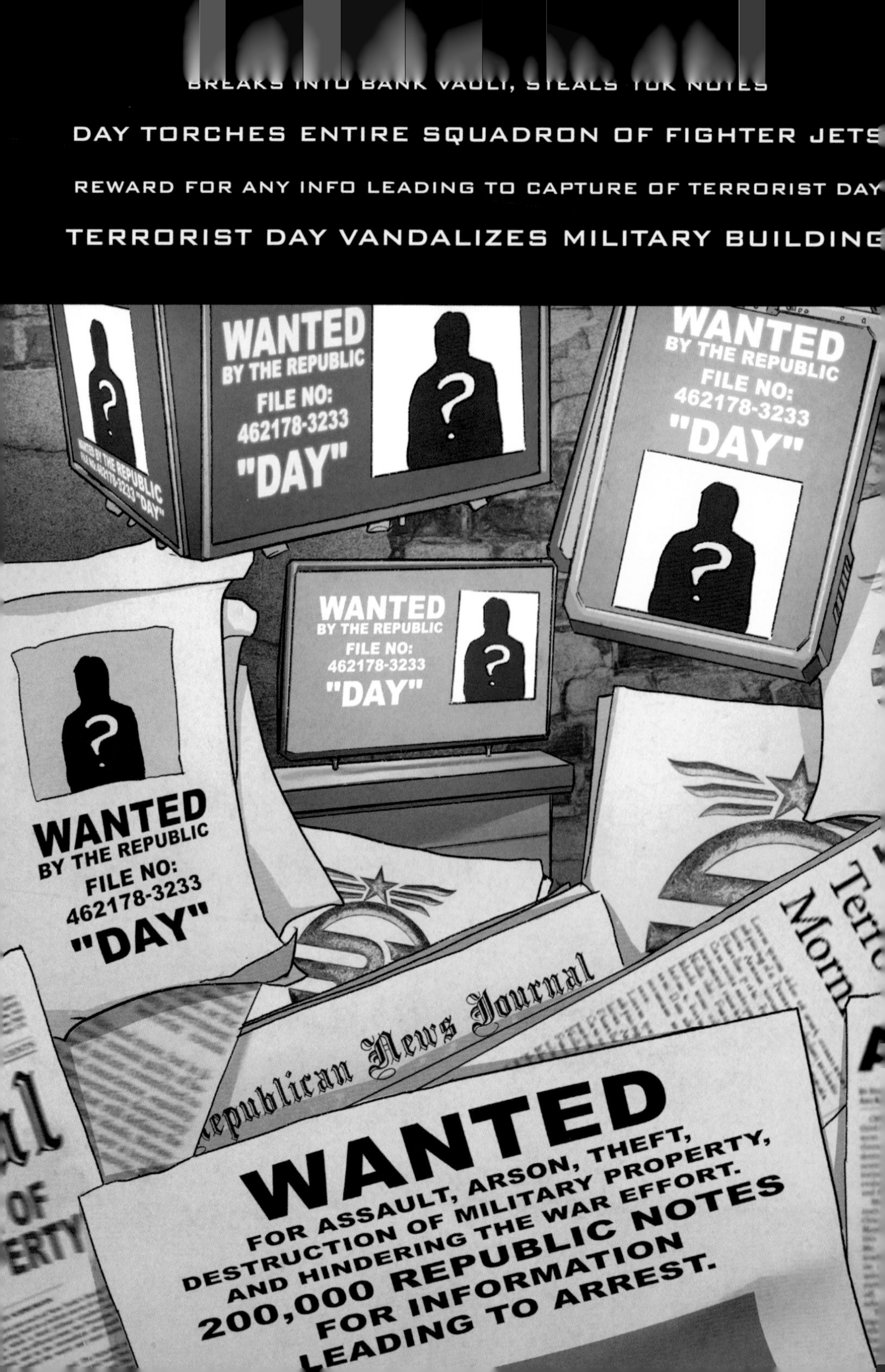

DAY TORCHES ENTIRE SQUADRON OF FIGHTER JETS
REWARD FOR ANY INFO LEADING TO CAPTURE OF TERRORIST DAY
TERRORIST DAY VANDALIZES MILITARY BUILDING
WANTED BY THE REPUBLIC FILE NO: 462178-3233 "DAY"
WANTED BY THE REPUBLIC FILE NO: 462178-3233 "DAY"
WANTED BY THE REPUBLIC FILE NO: 462178-3233 "DAY"
WANTED BY THE REPUBLIC FILE NO: 462178-3233 "DAY"
WANTED BY THE REPUBLIC FILE NO: 462178-3233 "DAY"
Republican News Journal
WANTED
FOR ASSAULT, ARSON, THEFT, DESTRUCTION OF MILITARY PROPERTY, AND HINDERING THE WAR EFFORT.
200,000 REPUBLIC NOTES FOR INFORMATION LEADING TO ARREST.

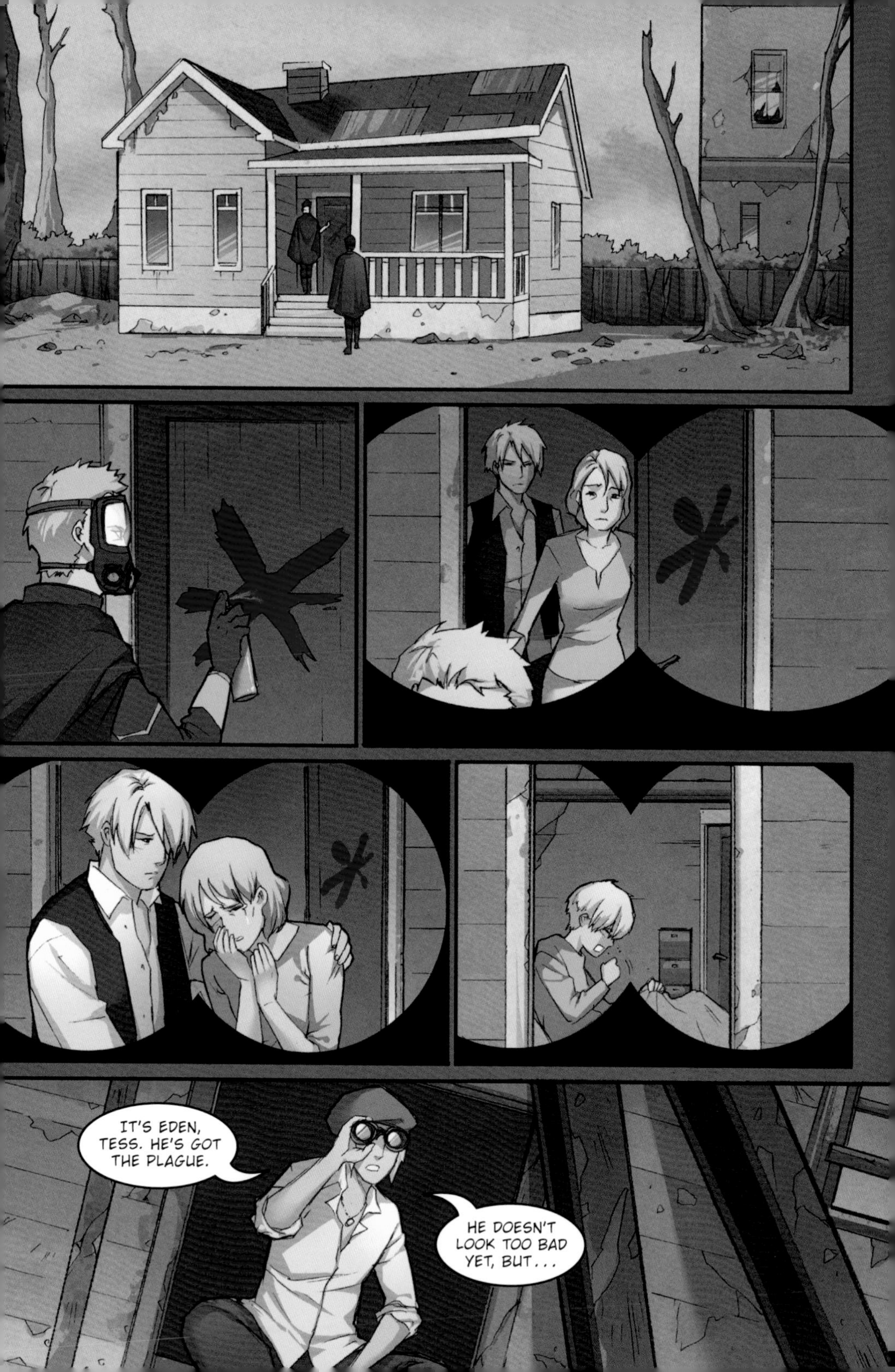
IT'S EDEN, TESS. HE'S GOT THE PLAGUE.
HE DOESN'T LOOK TOO BAD YET, BUT . . .

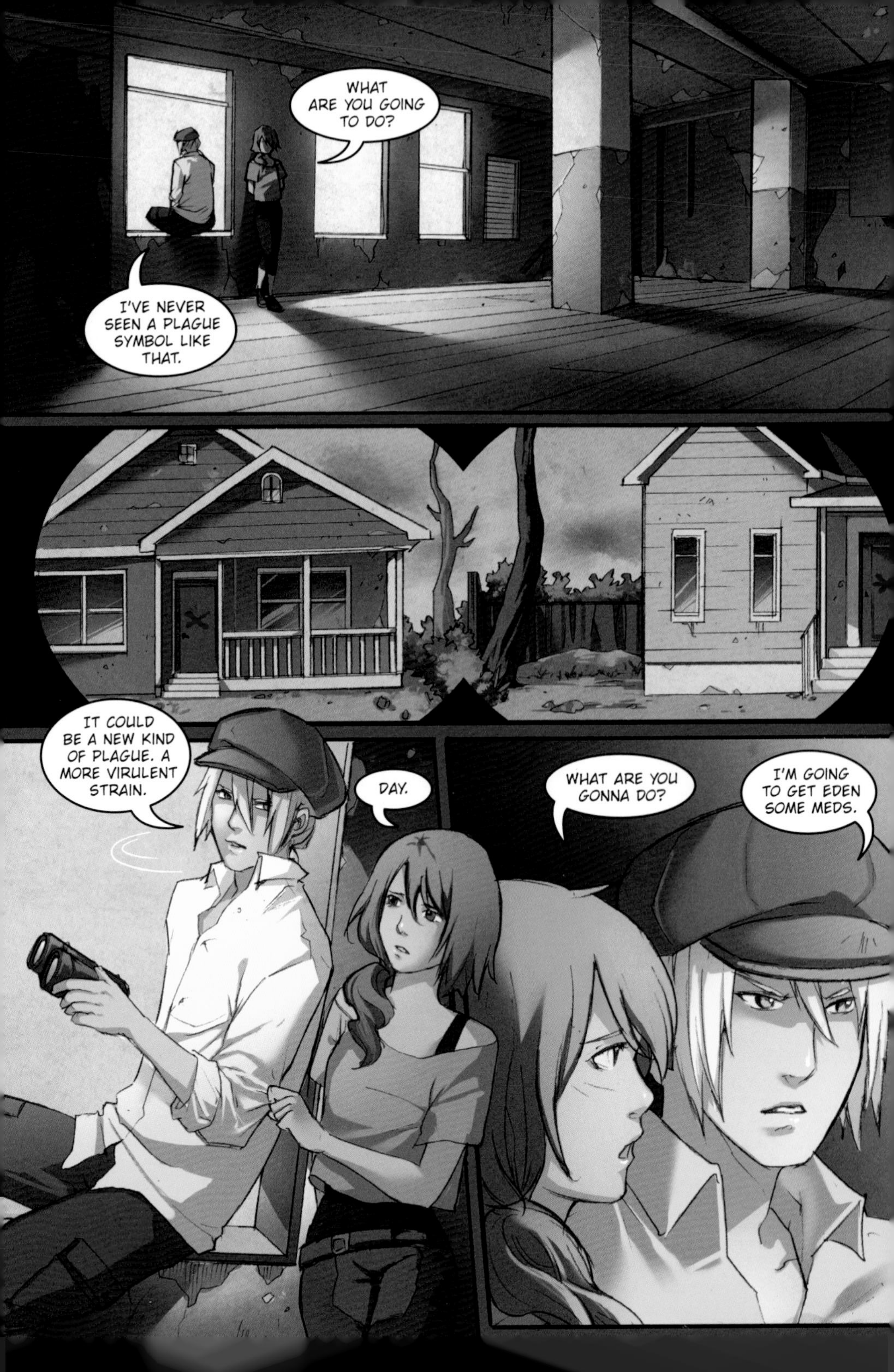
WHAT ARE YOU GOING TO DO?
I'VE NEVER SEEN A PLAGUE SYMBOL LIKE THAT.
IT COULD BE A NEW KIND OF PLAGUE. A MORE VIRULENT STRAIN.
DAY.
WHAT ARE YOU GONNA DO?
I'M GOING TO GET EDEN SOME MEDS.

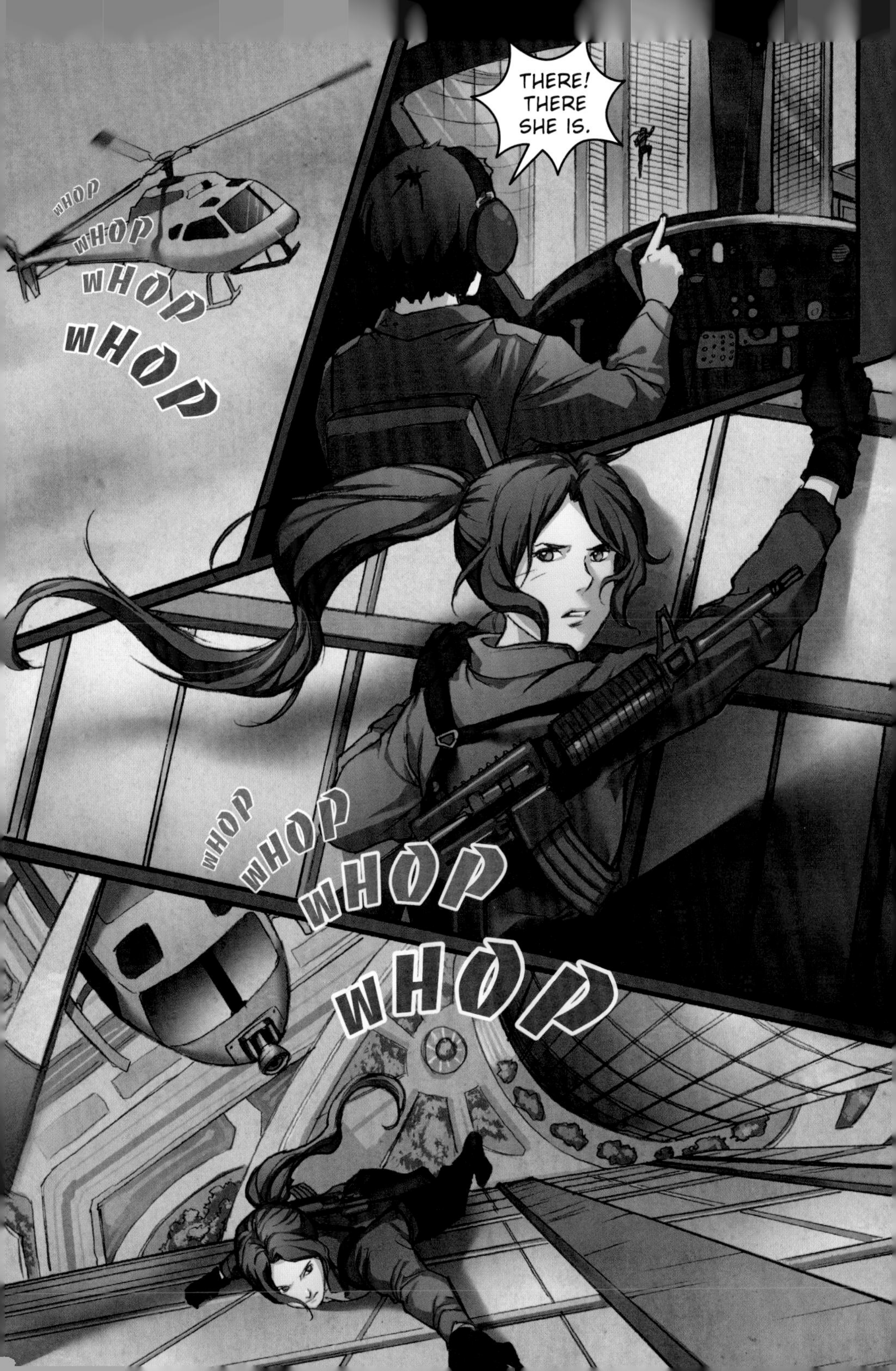

THERE! THERE SHE IS.
WHOP WHOP WHOP WHOP
WHOP WHOP WHOP WHOP

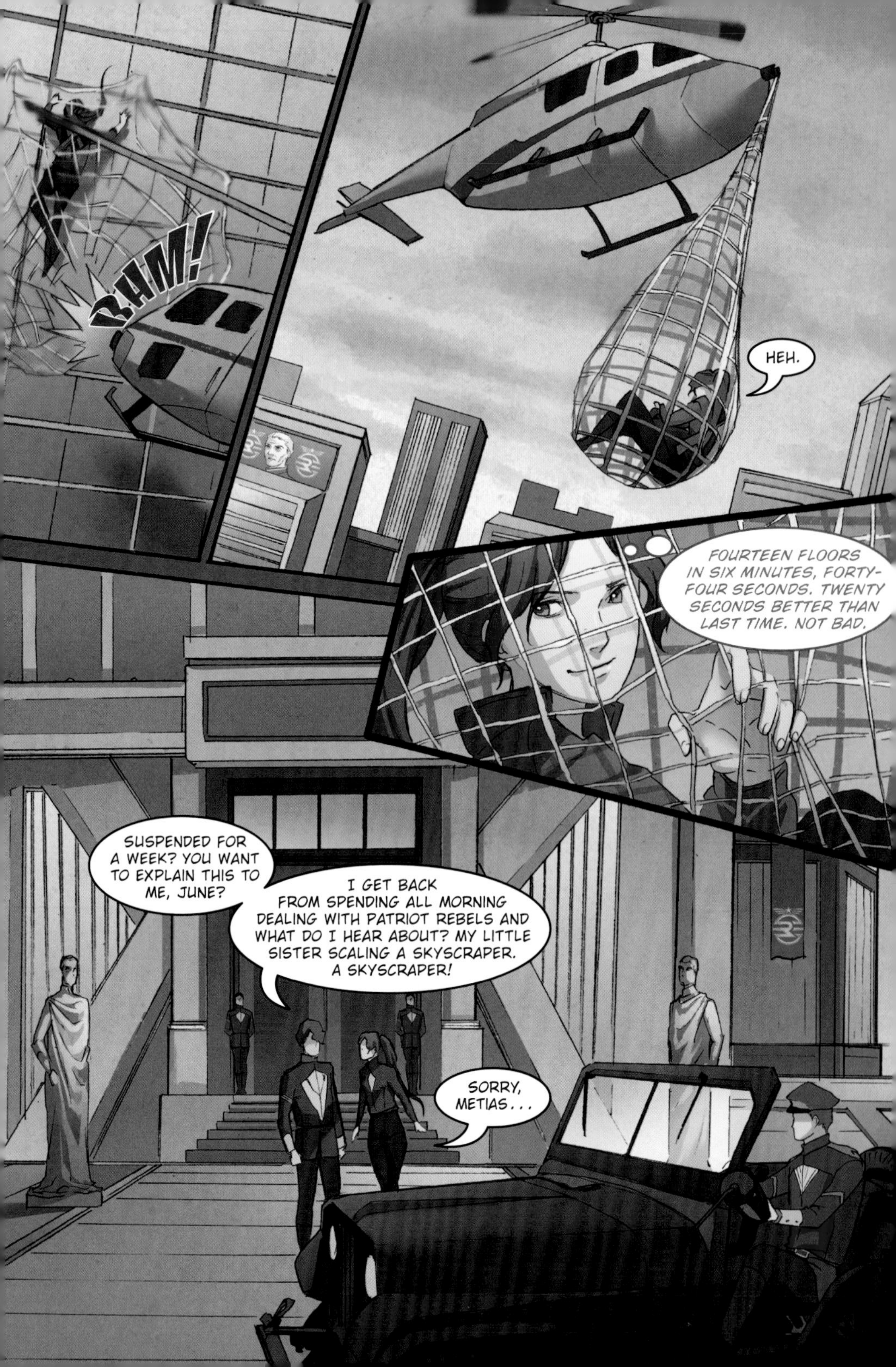
BAM!
HEH.
FOURTEEN FLOORS IN SIX MINUTES, FORTY-FOUR SECONDS. TWENTY SECONDS BETTER THAN LAST TIME. NOT BAD.
SUSPENDED FOR A WEEK? YOU WANT TO EXPLAIN THIS TO ME, JUNE?
I GET BACK FROM SPENDING ALL MORNING DEALING WITH PATRIOT REBELS AND WHAT DO I HEAR ABOUT? MY LITTLE SISTER SCALING A SKYSCRAPER. A SKYSCRAPER!
SORRY, METIAS . . .

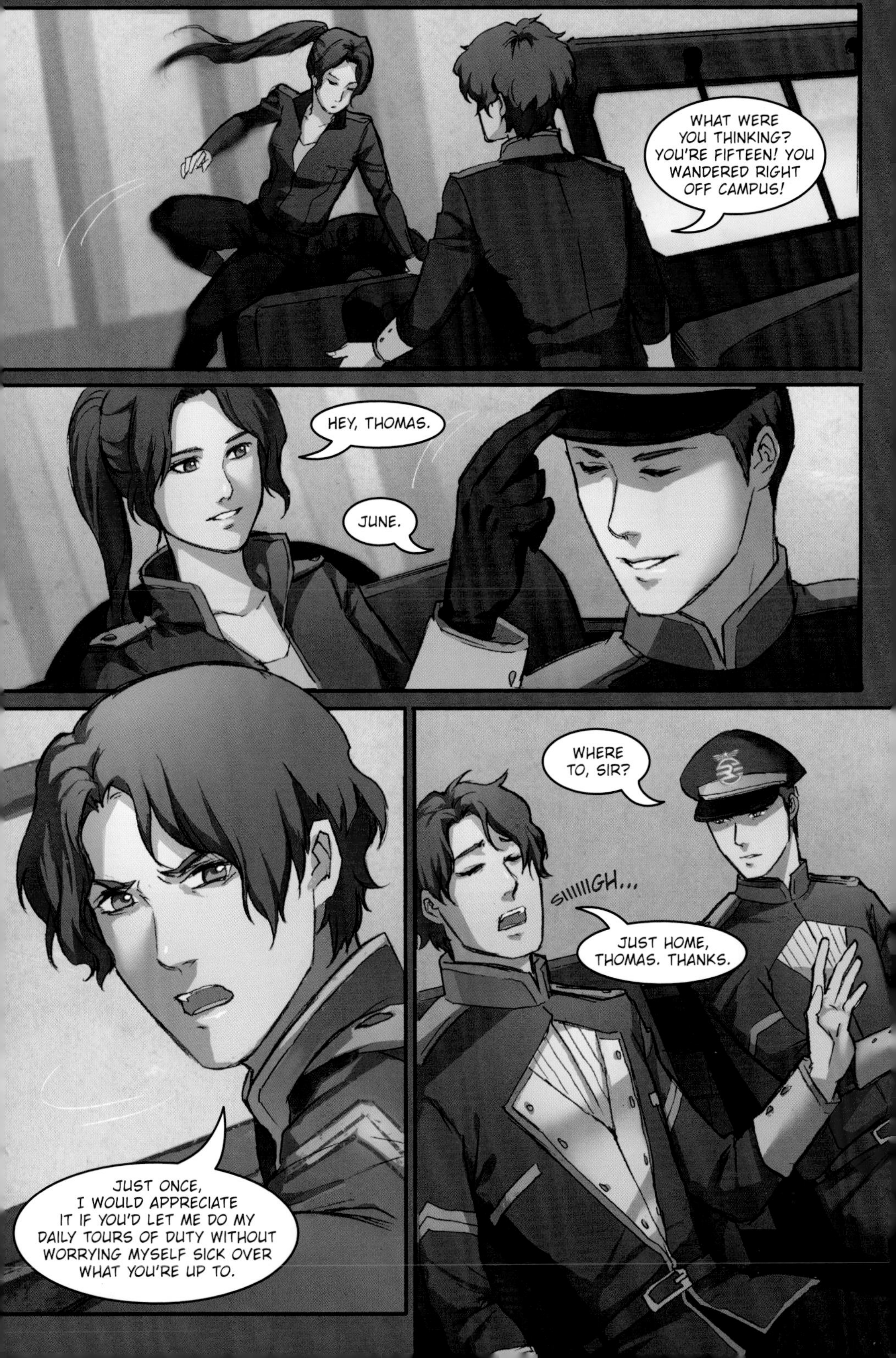
WHAT WERE YOU THINKING? YOU'RE FIFTEEN! YOU WANDERED RIGHT OFF CAMPUS!
HEY, THOMAS.
JUNE.
JUST ONCE, I WOULD APPRECIATE IT IF YOU'D LET ME DO MY DAILY TOURS OF DUTY WITHOUT WORRYING MYSELF SICK OVER WHAT YOU'RE UP TO.
WHERE TO, SIR?
SIIIIIGH...
JUST HOME, THOMAS. THANKS.

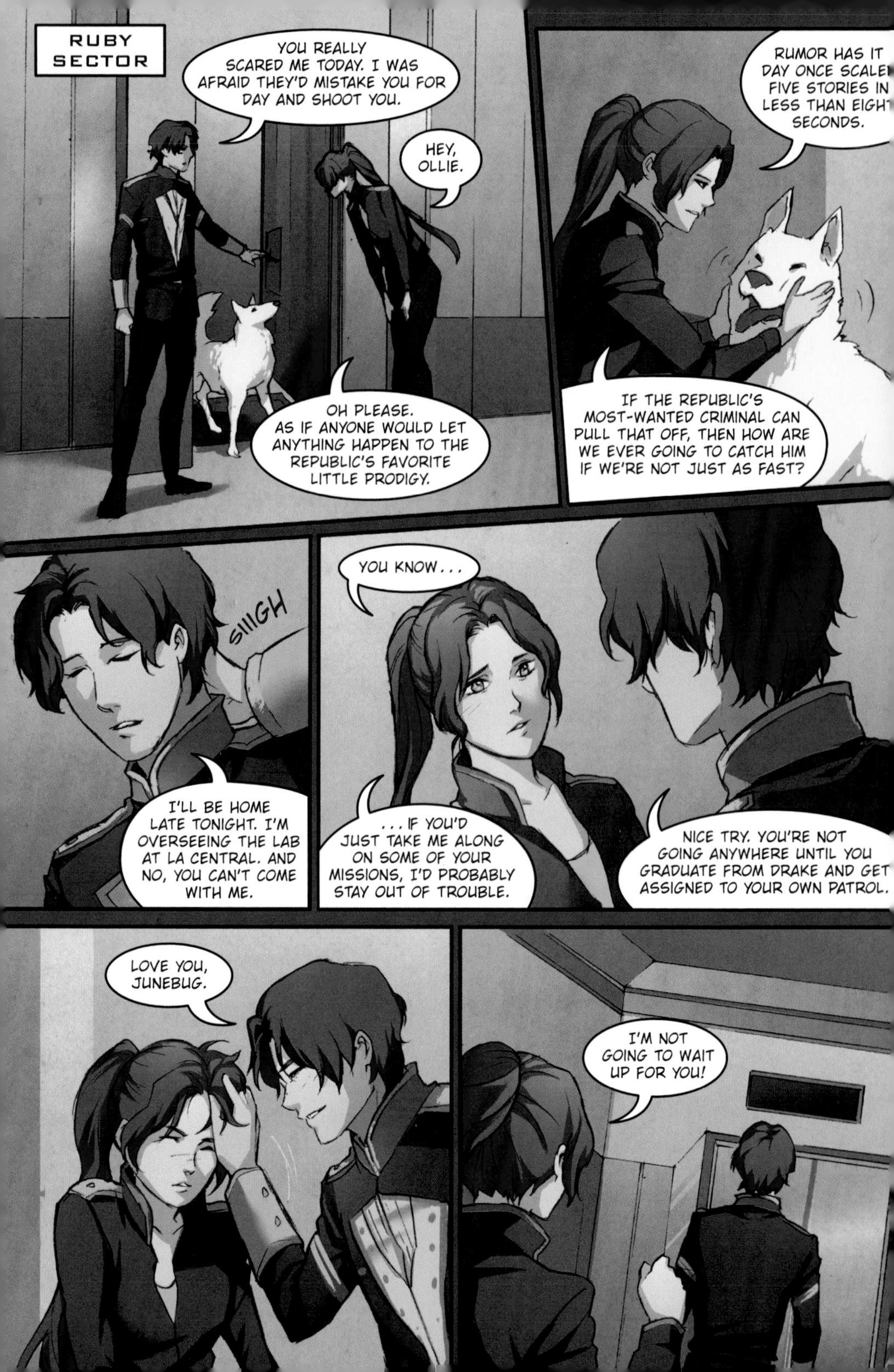
RUBY SECTOR
YOU REALLY SCARED ME TODAY. I WAS AFRAID THEY'D MISTAKE YOU FOR DAY AND SHOOT YOU.
HEY, OLLIE.
OH PLEASE. AS IF ANYONE WOULD LET ANYTHING HAPPEN TO THE REPUBLIC'S FAVORITE LITTLE PRODIGY.
RUMOR HAS IT DAY ONCE SCALE FIVE STORIES IN LESS THAN EIGH SECONDS.
IF THE REPUBLIC'S MOST-WANTED CRIMINAL CAN PULL THAT OFF, THEN HOW ARE WE EVER GOING TO CATCH HIM IF WE'RE NOT JUST AS FAST?
SIIIGH
I'LL BE HOME LATE TONIGHT. I'M OVERSEEING THE LAB AT LA CENTRAL. AND NO, YOU CAN'T COME WITH ME.
YOU KNOW...
...IF YOU'D JUST TAKE ME ALONG ON SOME OF YOUR MISSIONS, I'D PROBABLY STAY OUT OF TROUBLE.
NICE TRY. YOU'RE NOT GOING ANYWHERE UNTIL YOU GRADUATE FROM DRAKE AND GET ASSIGNED TO YOUR OWN PATROL.
LOVE YOU, JUNEBUG.
I'M NOT GOING TO WAIT UP FOR YOU!

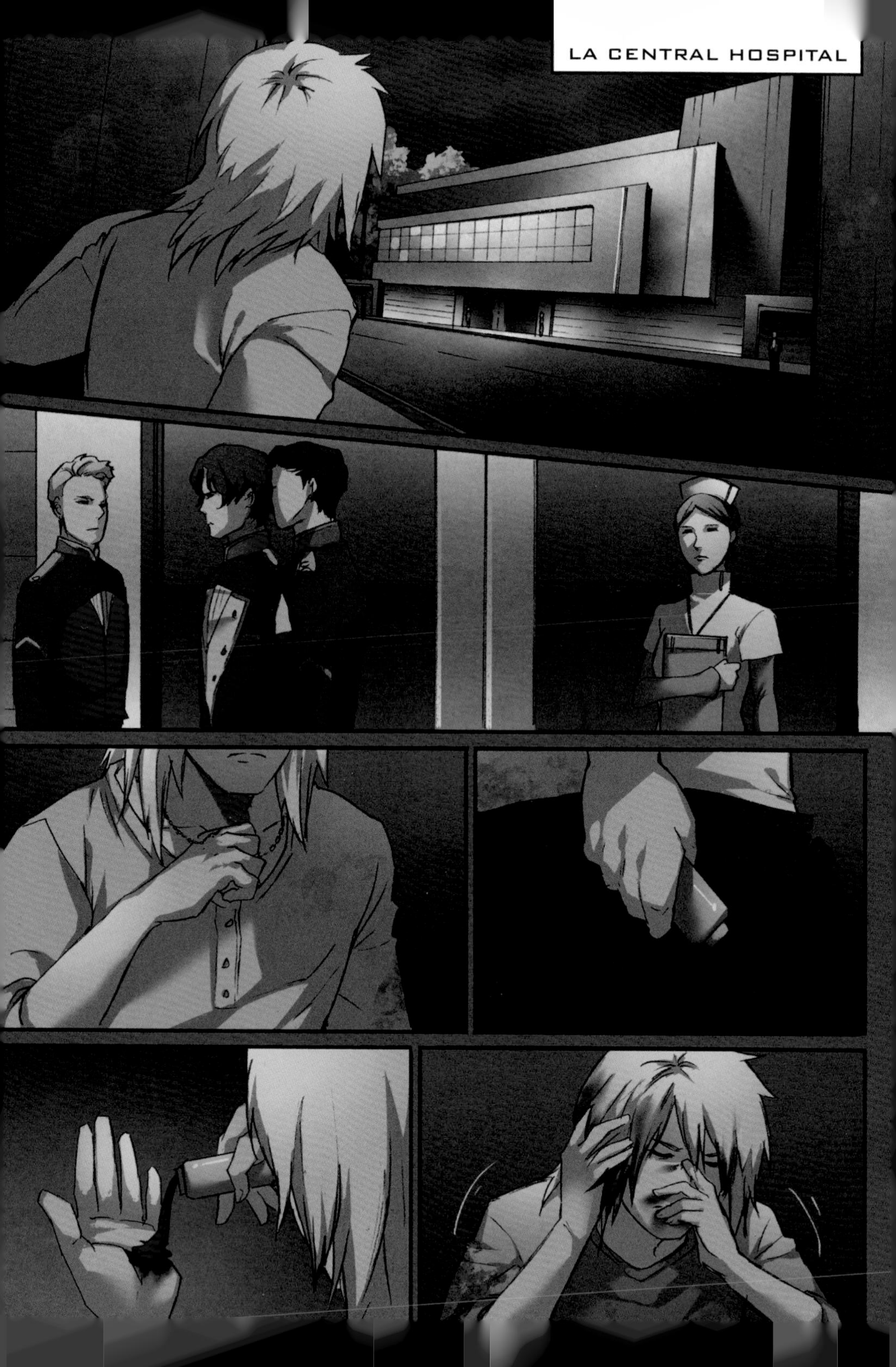
LA CENTRAL HOSPITAL

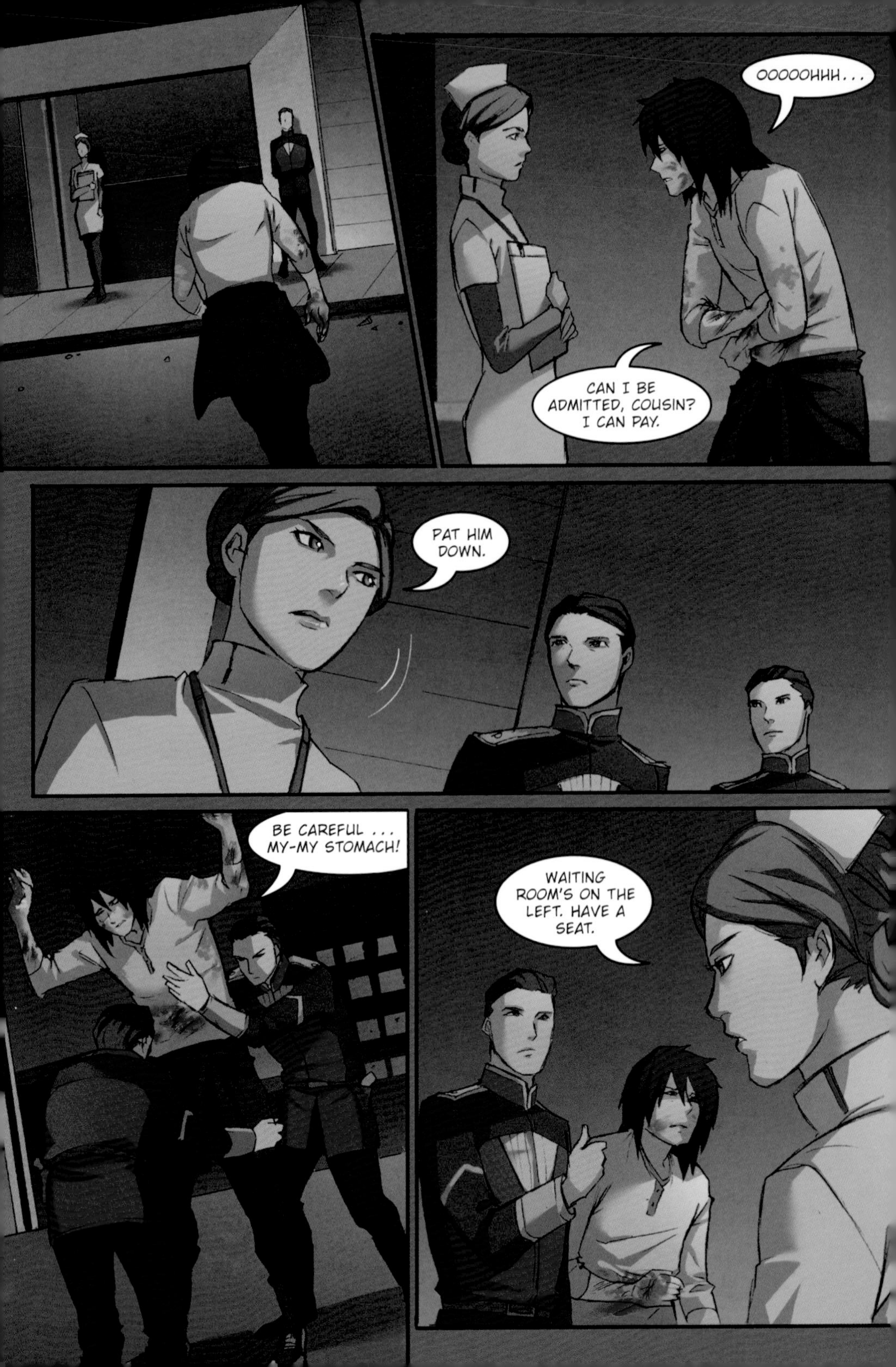
OOOOOHHH . . .
CAN I BE ADMITTED, COUSIN? I CAN PAY.
PAT HIM DOWN.
BE CAREFUL . . . MY-MY STOMACH!
WAITING ROOM'S ON THE LEFT. HAVE A SEAT.

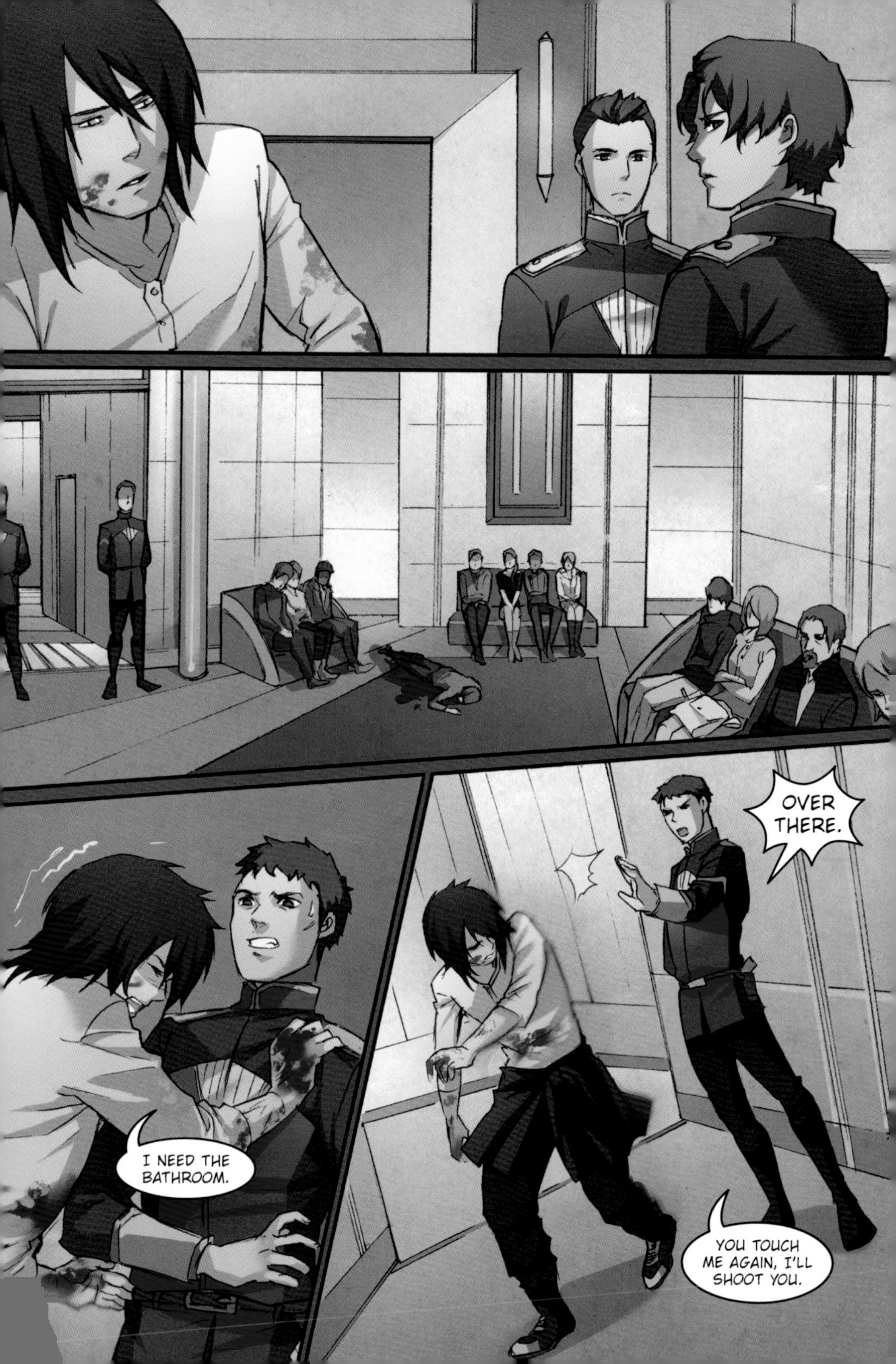
I NEED THE BATHROOM.
OVER THERE.
YOU TOUCH ME AGAIN, I'LL SHOOT YOU.

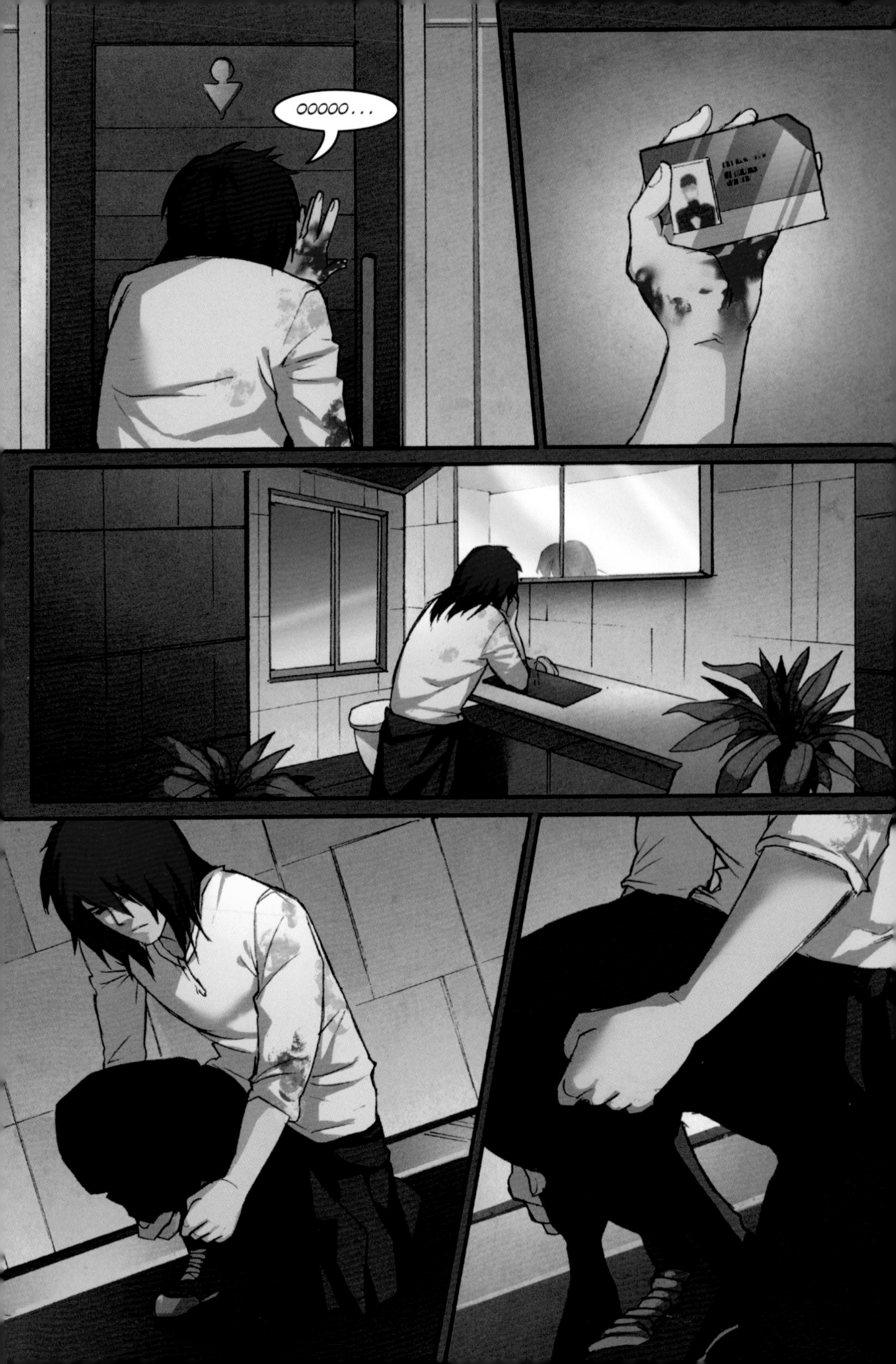
OOOOO . . .

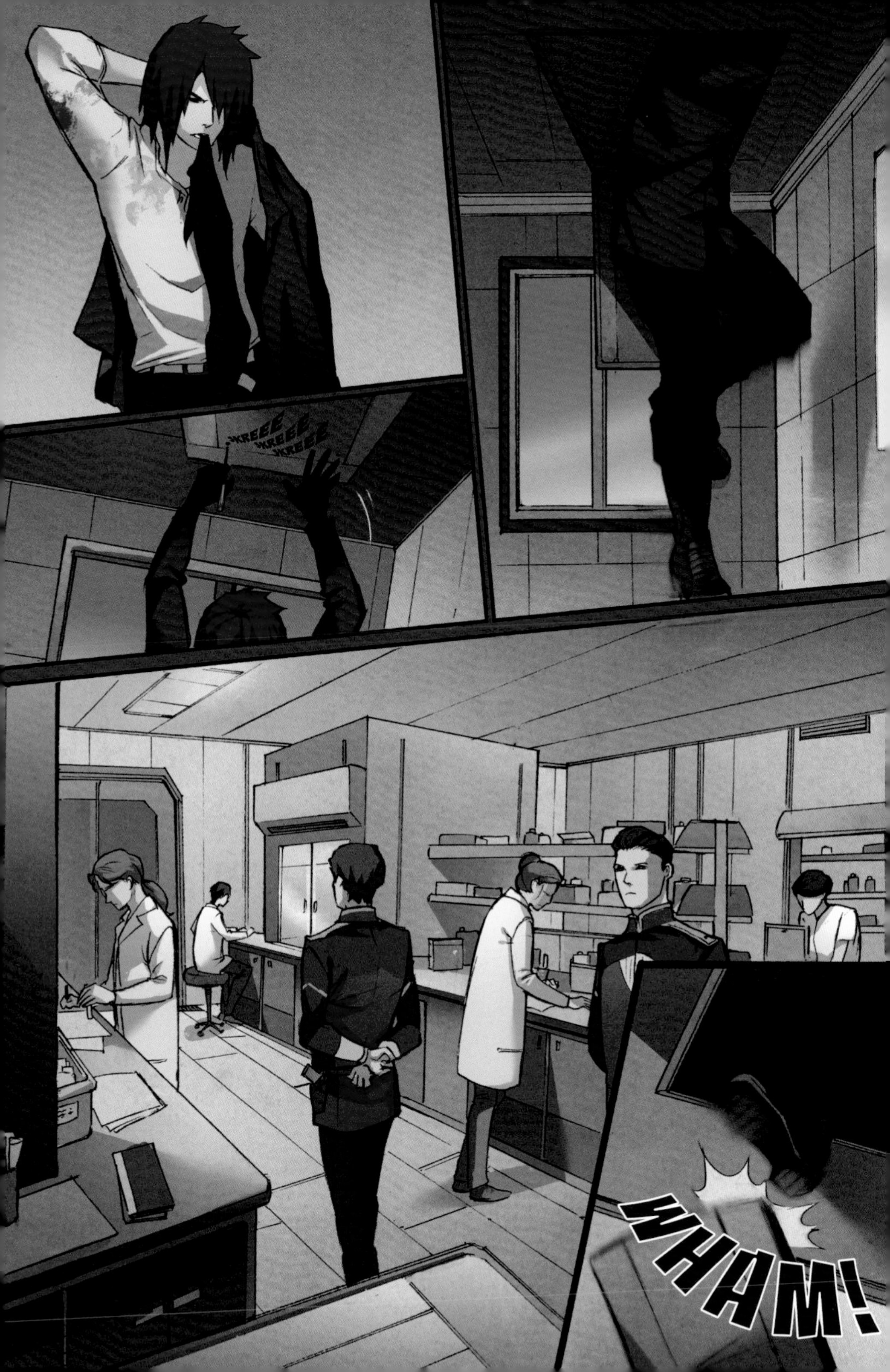
SKREEE
SKREEE
SKREEE
WHAM!

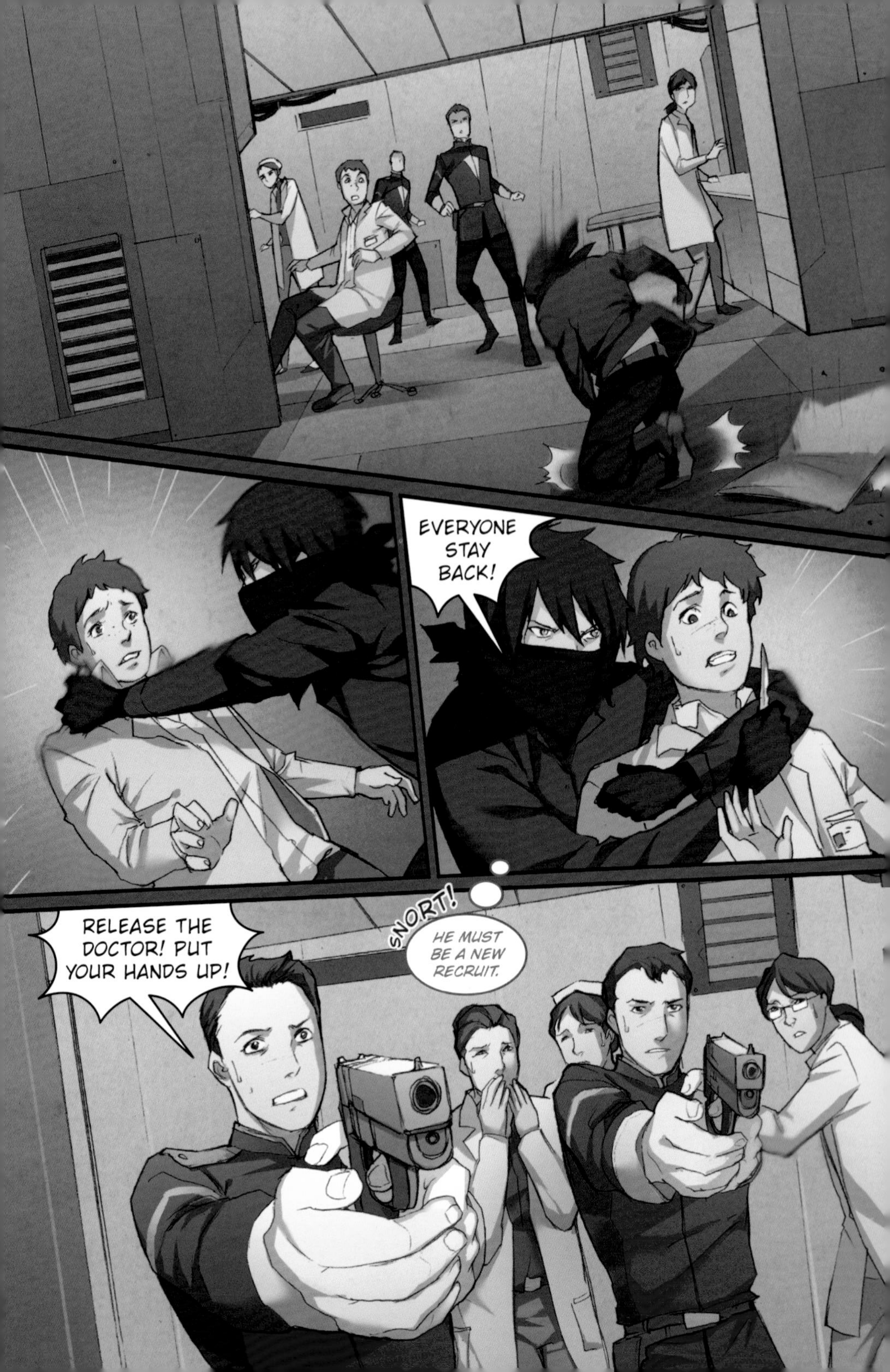
EVERYONE STAY BACK!
RELEASE THE DOCTOR! PUT YOUR HANDS UP!
SNORT!
HE MUST BE A NEW RECRUIT.

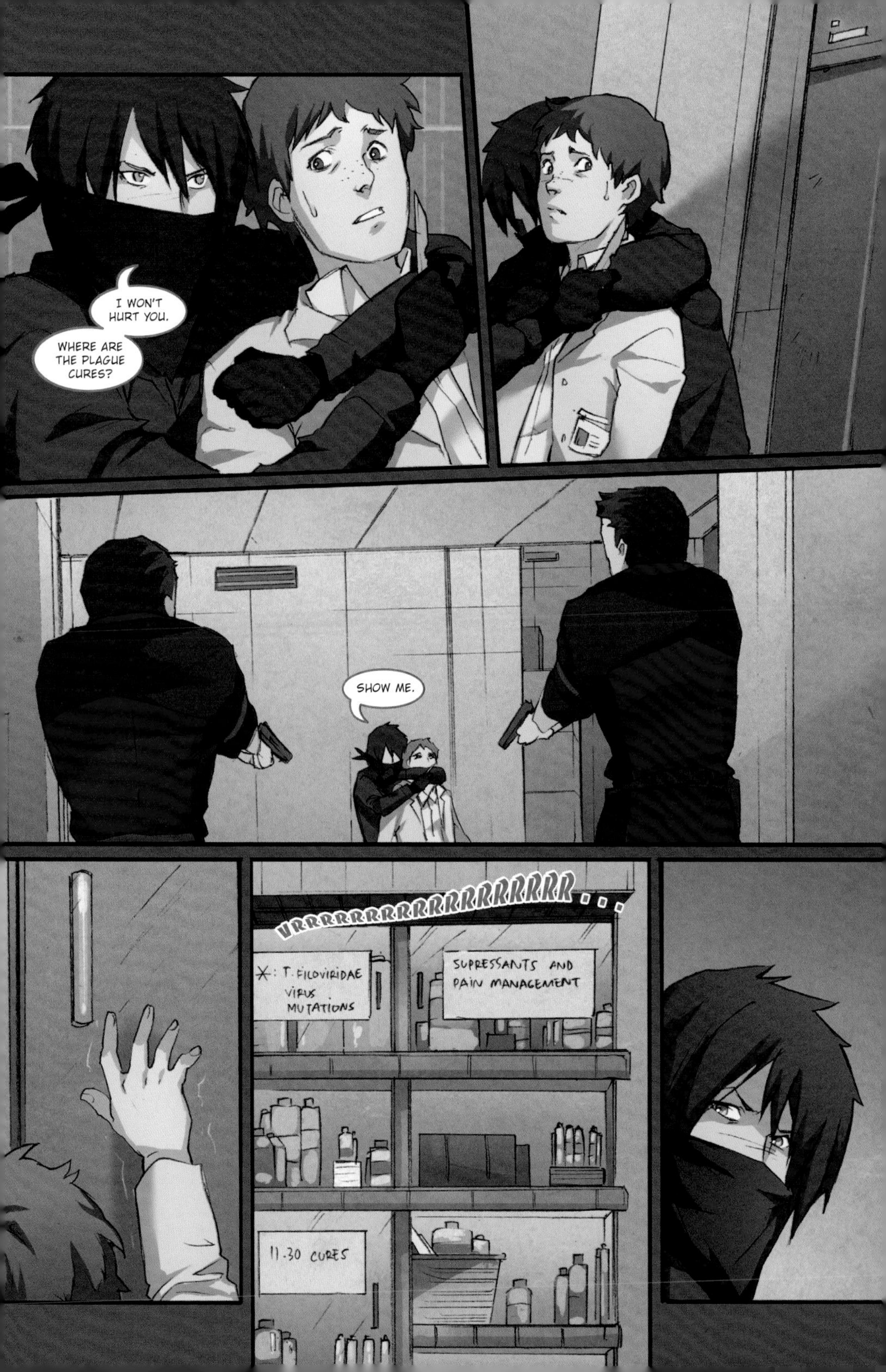
I WON'T HURT YOU.
WHERE ARE THE PLAGUE CURES?
SHOW ME.
VRRRRRRRRRRRRRRRRRRRRRR...
*: T. FILOVIRIDAE VIRUS MUTATIONS
SUPRESSANTS AND PAIN MANAGEMENT
11.30 CURES

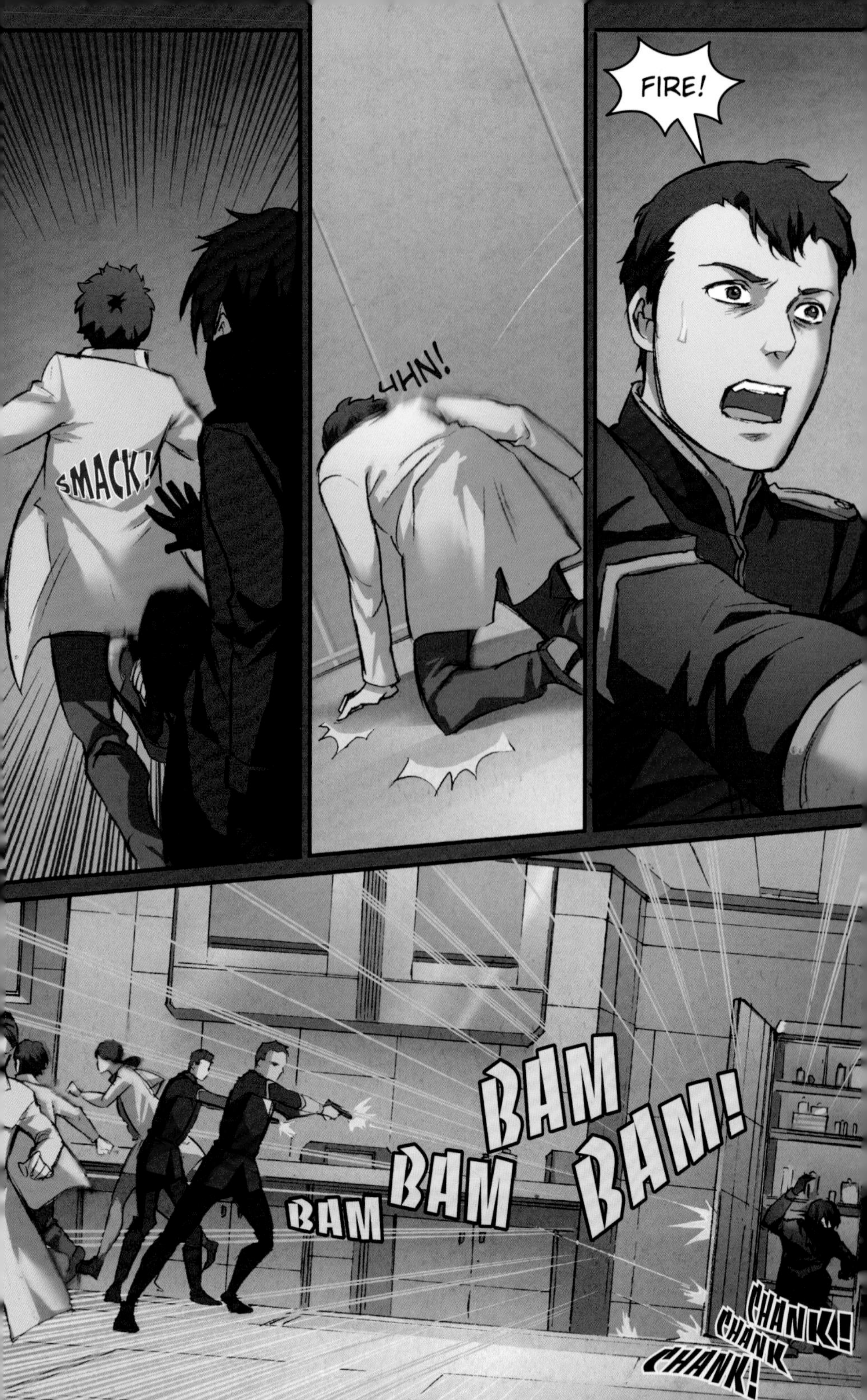
SMACK!
UHN!
FIRE!
BAM
BAM
BAM
BAM!
BAM
CHANK!
CHANK
CHANK!

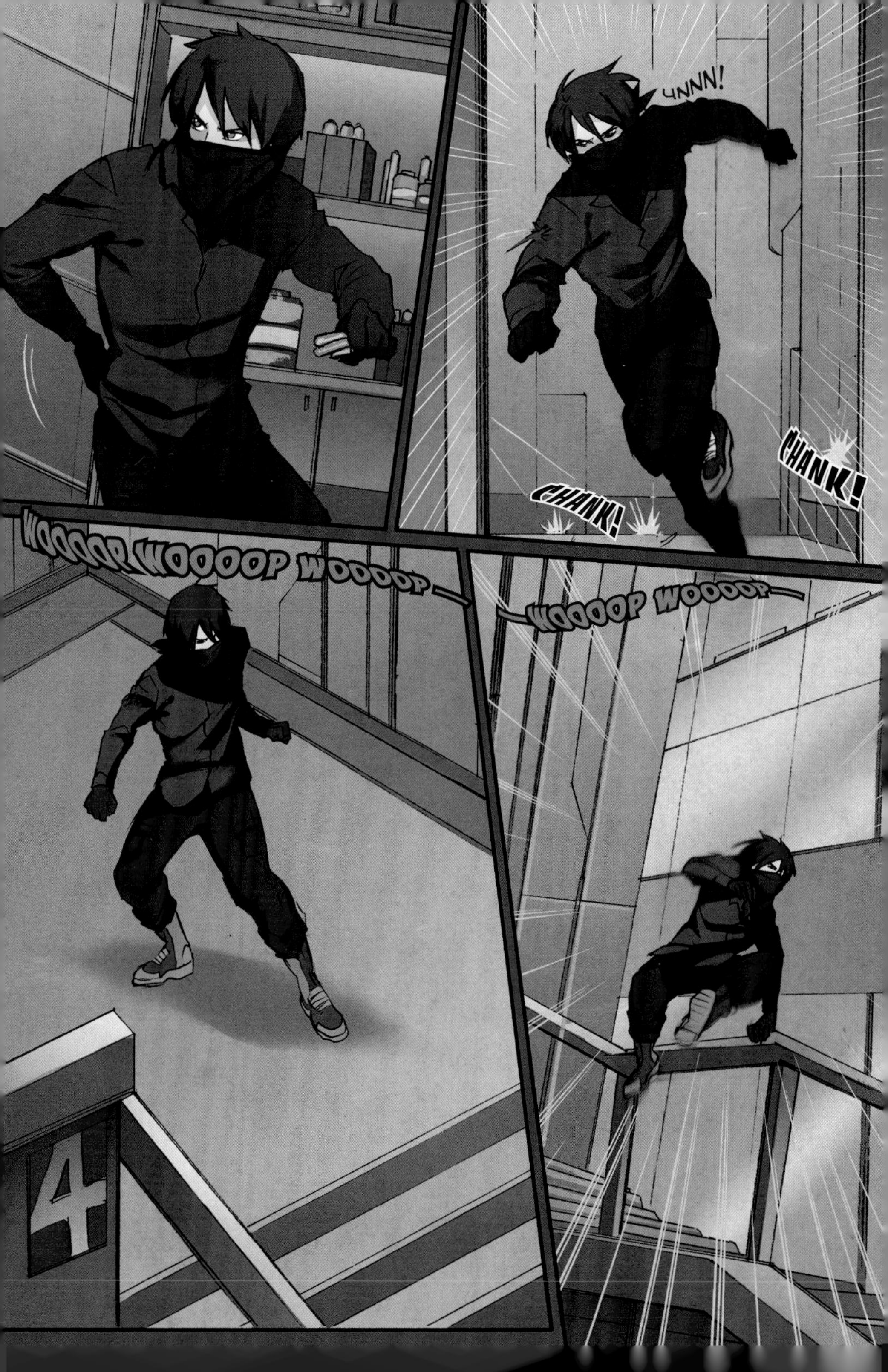
UNNN!
CHANK!
CHANK!
WOOOOP WOOOOP WOOOOP—
—WOOOOP WOOOOP—

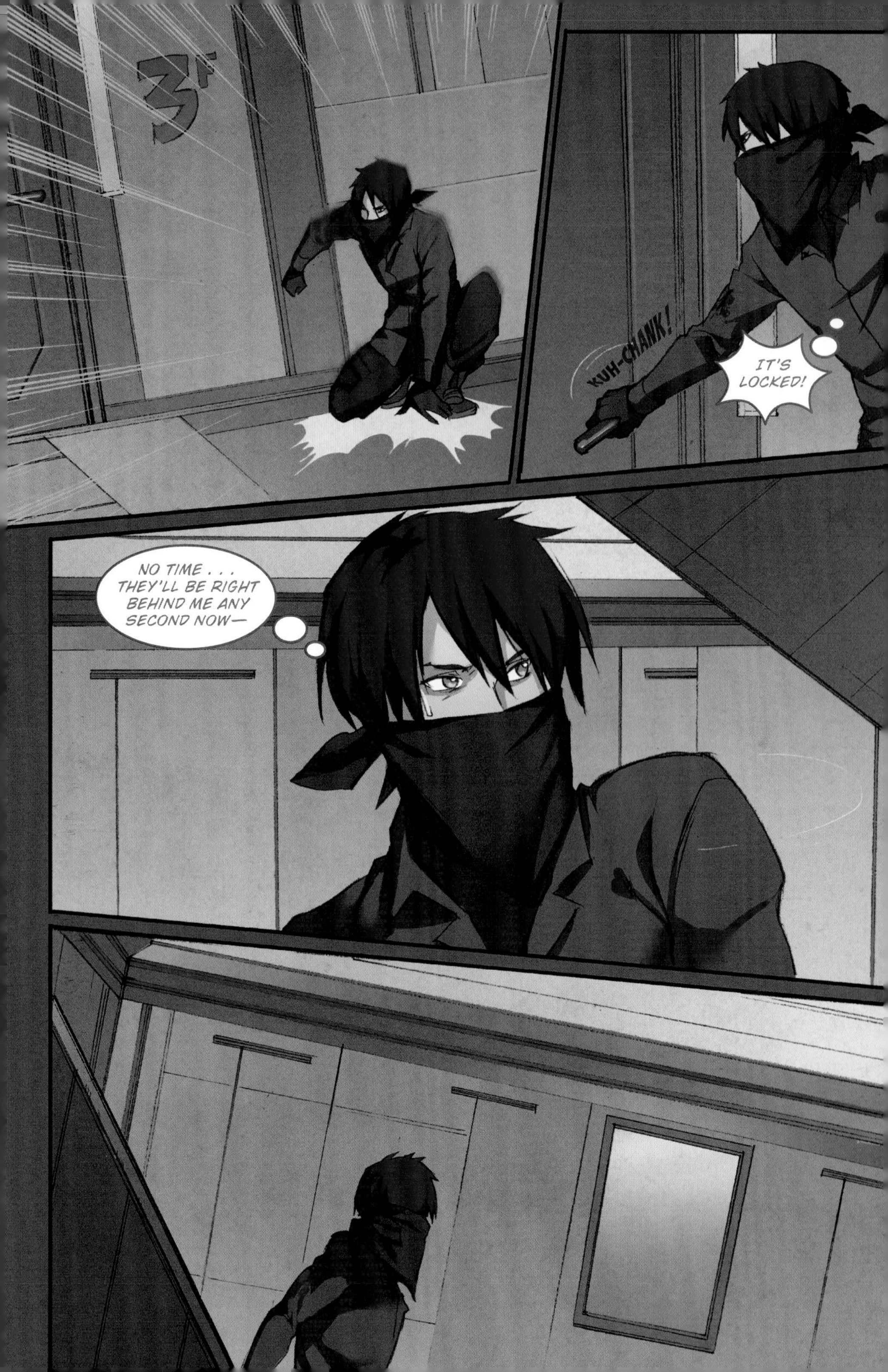
KUH-CHANK!
IT'S LOCKED!
NO TIME . . . THEY'LL BE RIGHT BEHIND ME ANY SECOND NOW—

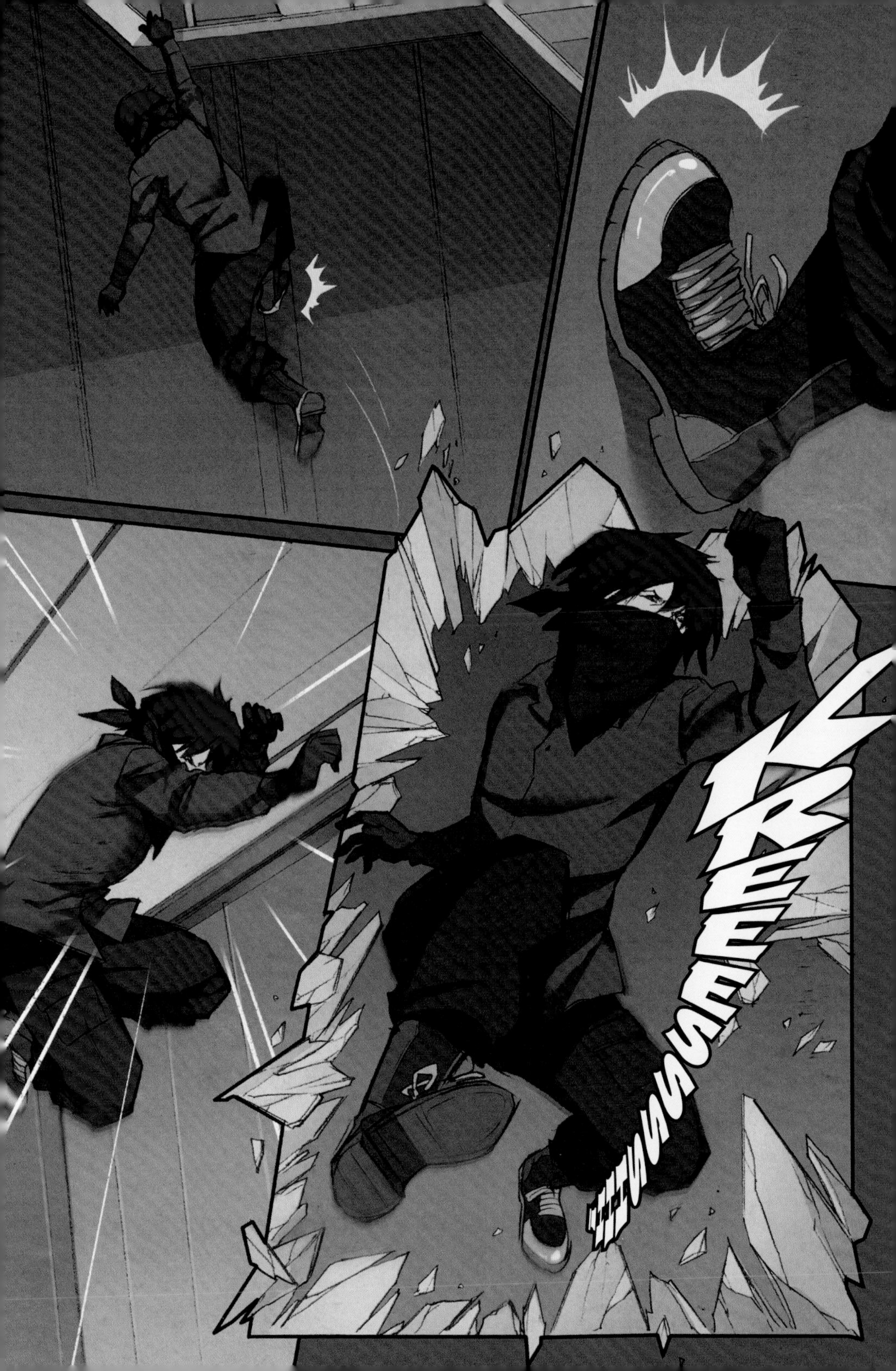
KREESSSSH

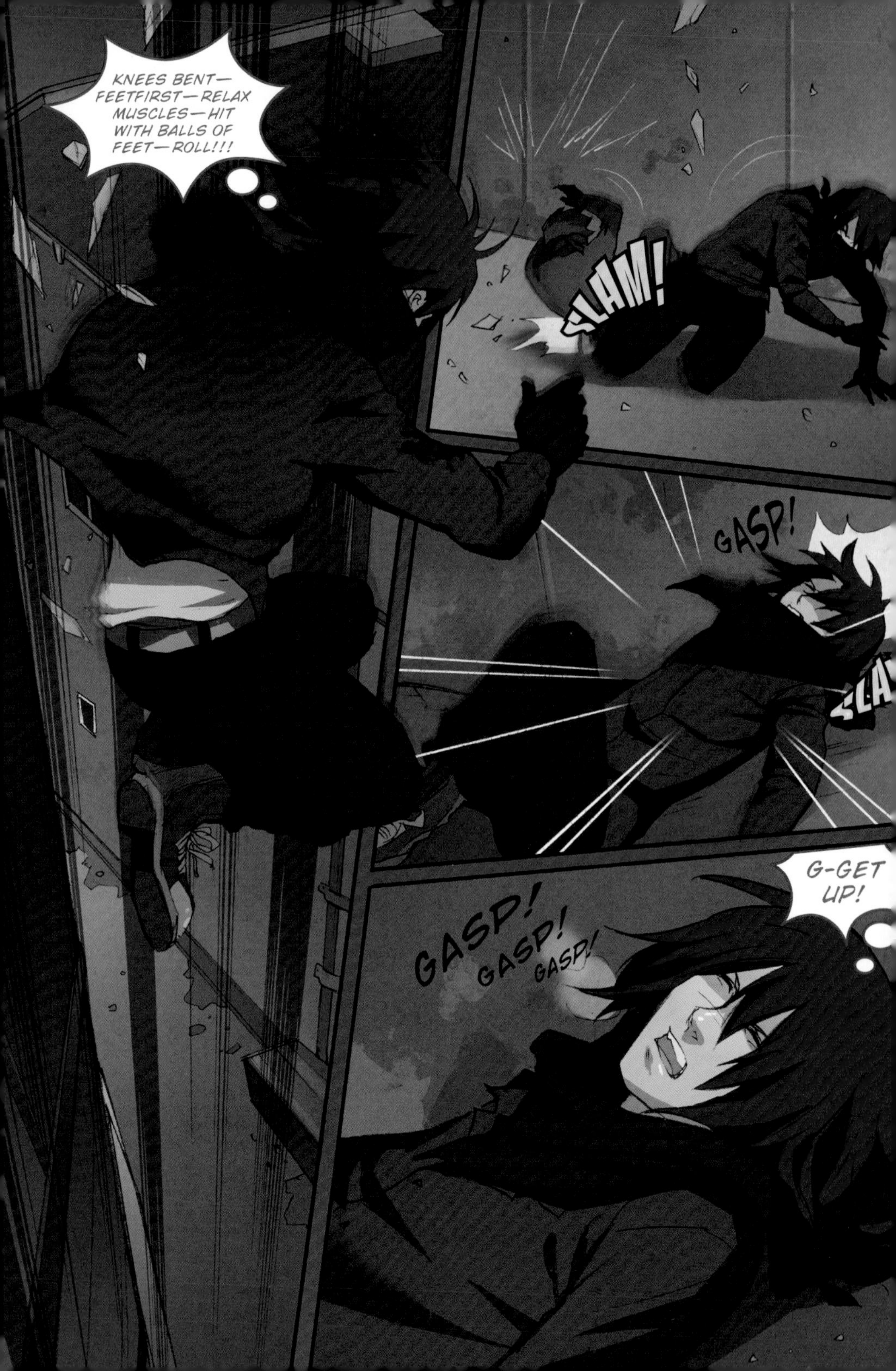
KNEES BENT—FEETFIRST—RELAX MUSCLES—HIT WITH BALLS OF FEET—ROLL!!!
SLAM!
GASP!
GASP! GASP! GASP!
G-GET UP!

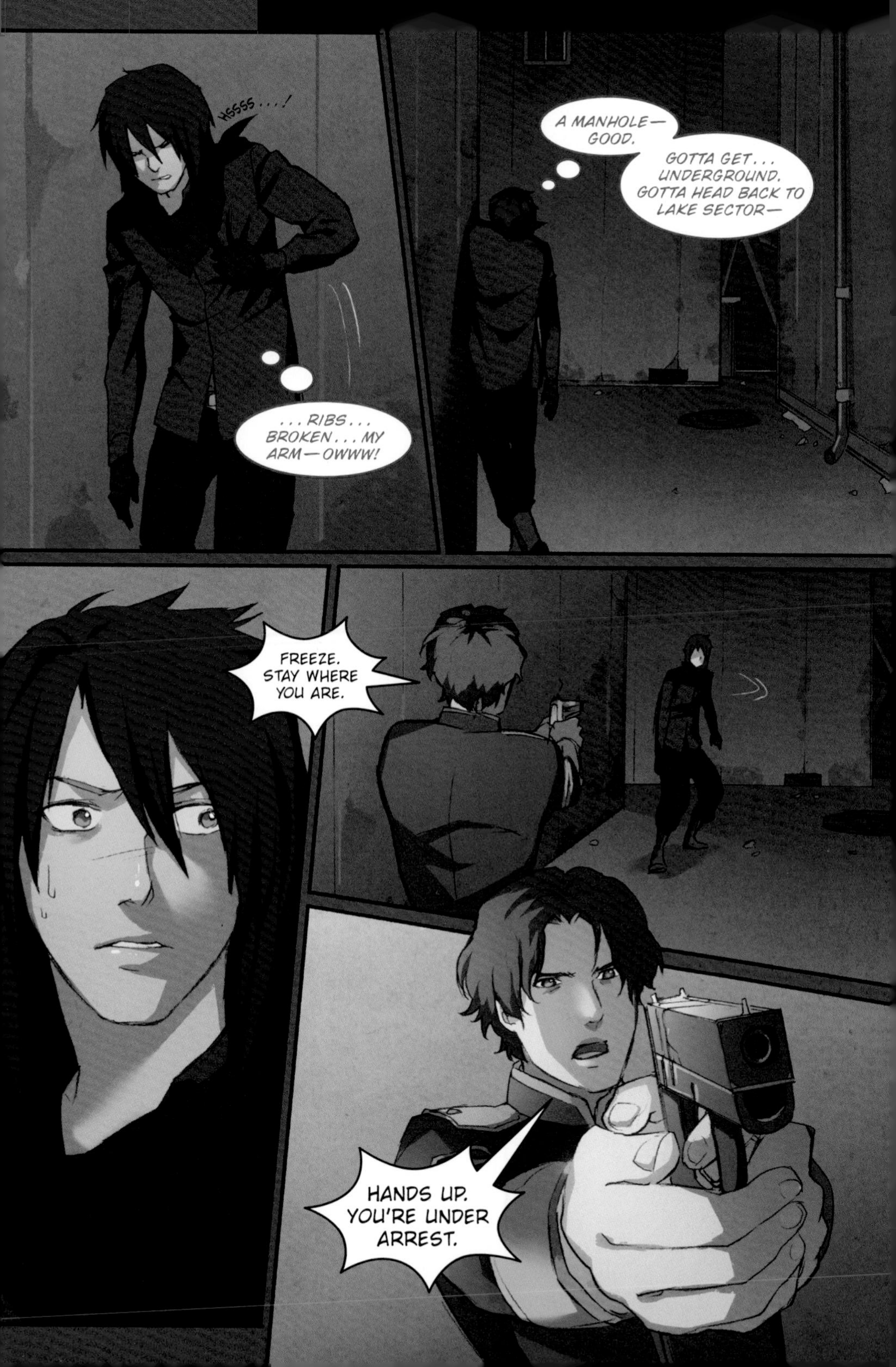
HSSSS . . . !
. . . RIBS . . . BROKEN . . . MY ARM—OWWW!
A MANHOLE—GOOD.
GOTTA GET . . . UNDERGROUND. GOTTA HEAD BACK TO LAKE SECTOR—
FREEZE. STAY WHERE YOU ARE.
HANDS UP. YOU'RE UNDER ARREST.

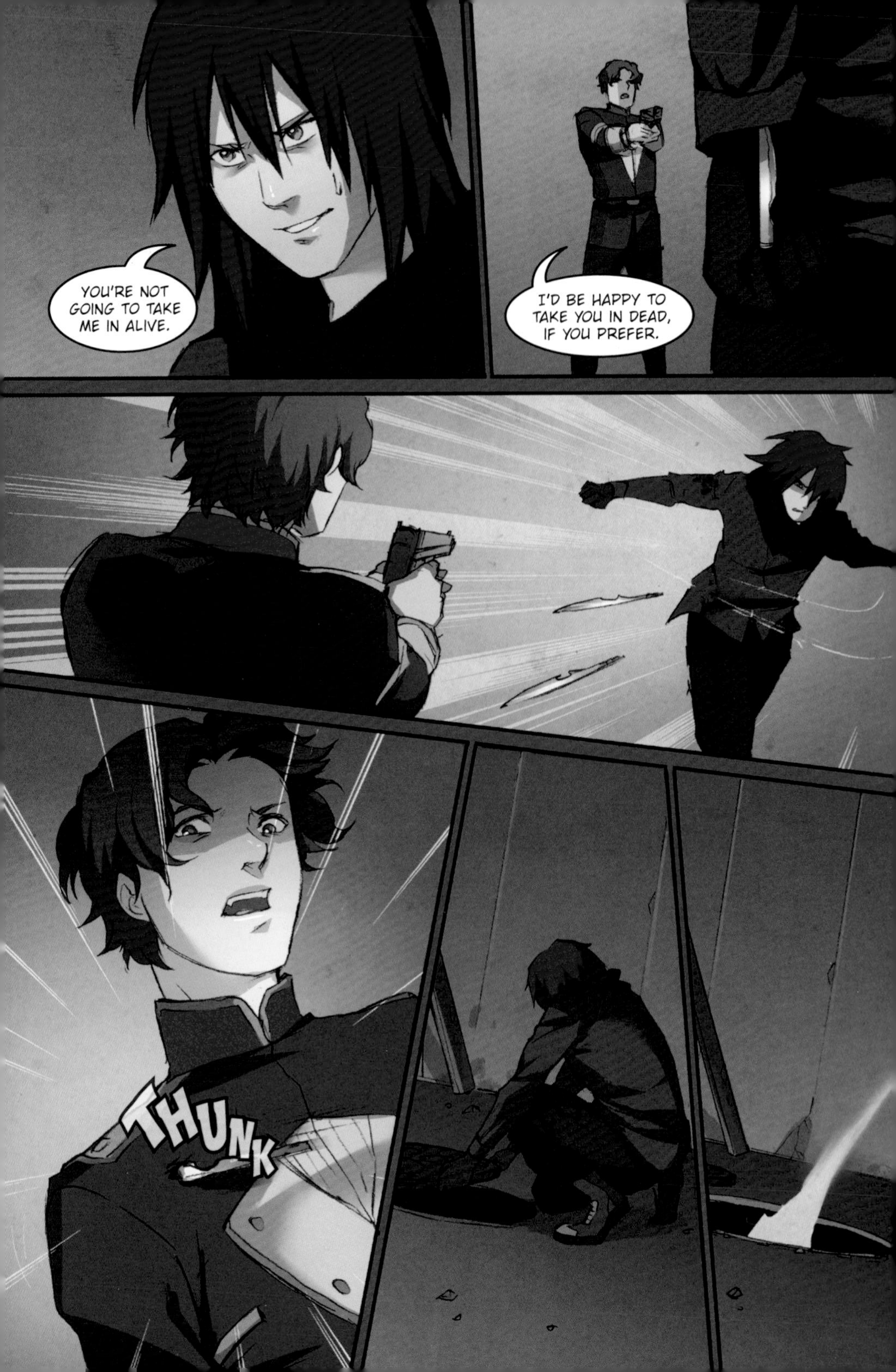
YOU'RE NOT GOING TO TAKE ME IN ALIVE.
I'D BE HAPPY TO TAKE YOU IN DEAD, IF YOU PREFER.
THUNK

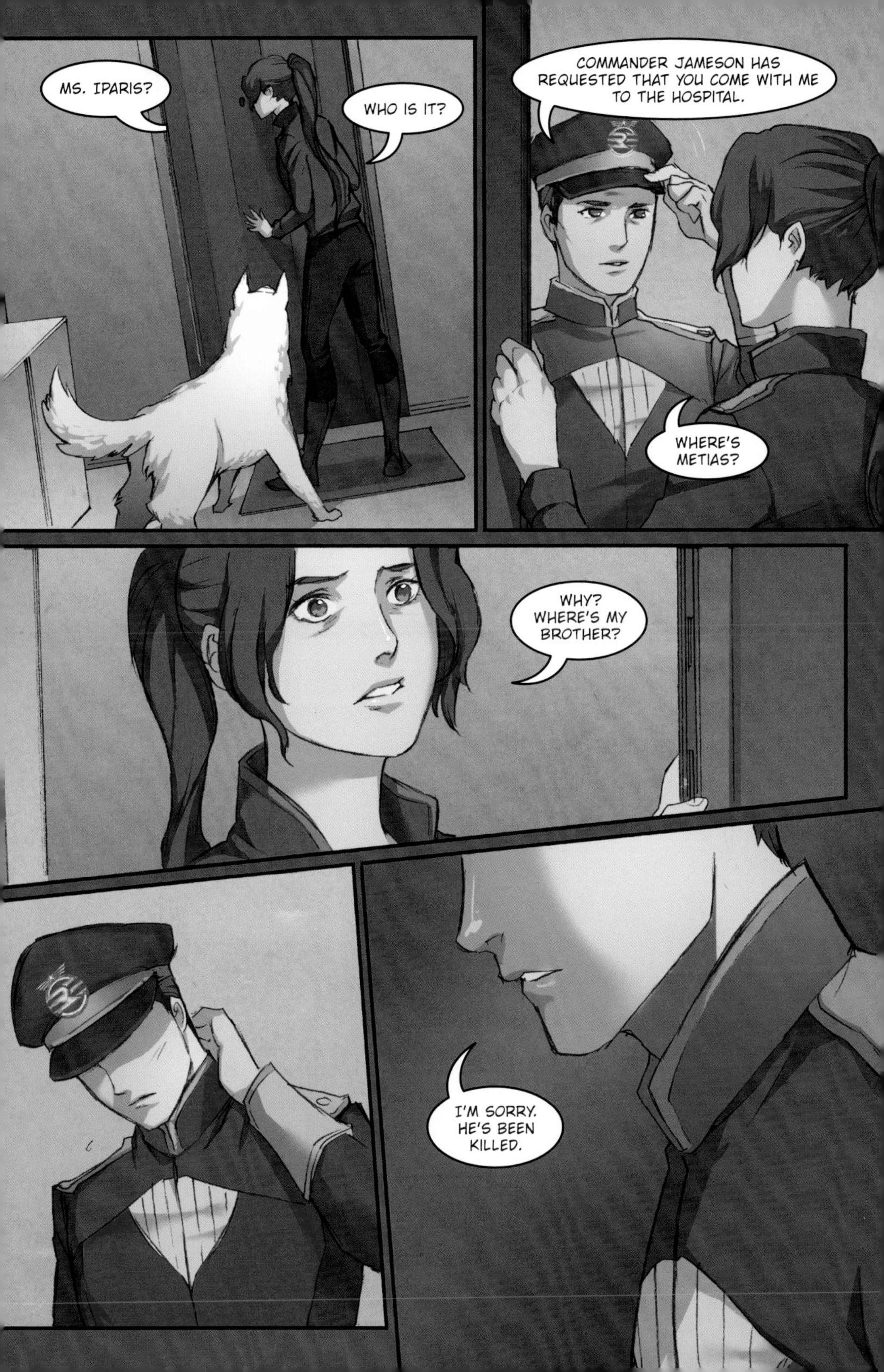
MS. IPARIS?
WHO IS IT?
COMMANDER JAMESON HAS REQUESTED THAT YOU COME WITH ME TO THE HOSPITAL.
WHERE'S METIAS?
WHY? WHERE'S MY BROTHER?
I'M SORRY. HE'S BEEN KILLED.

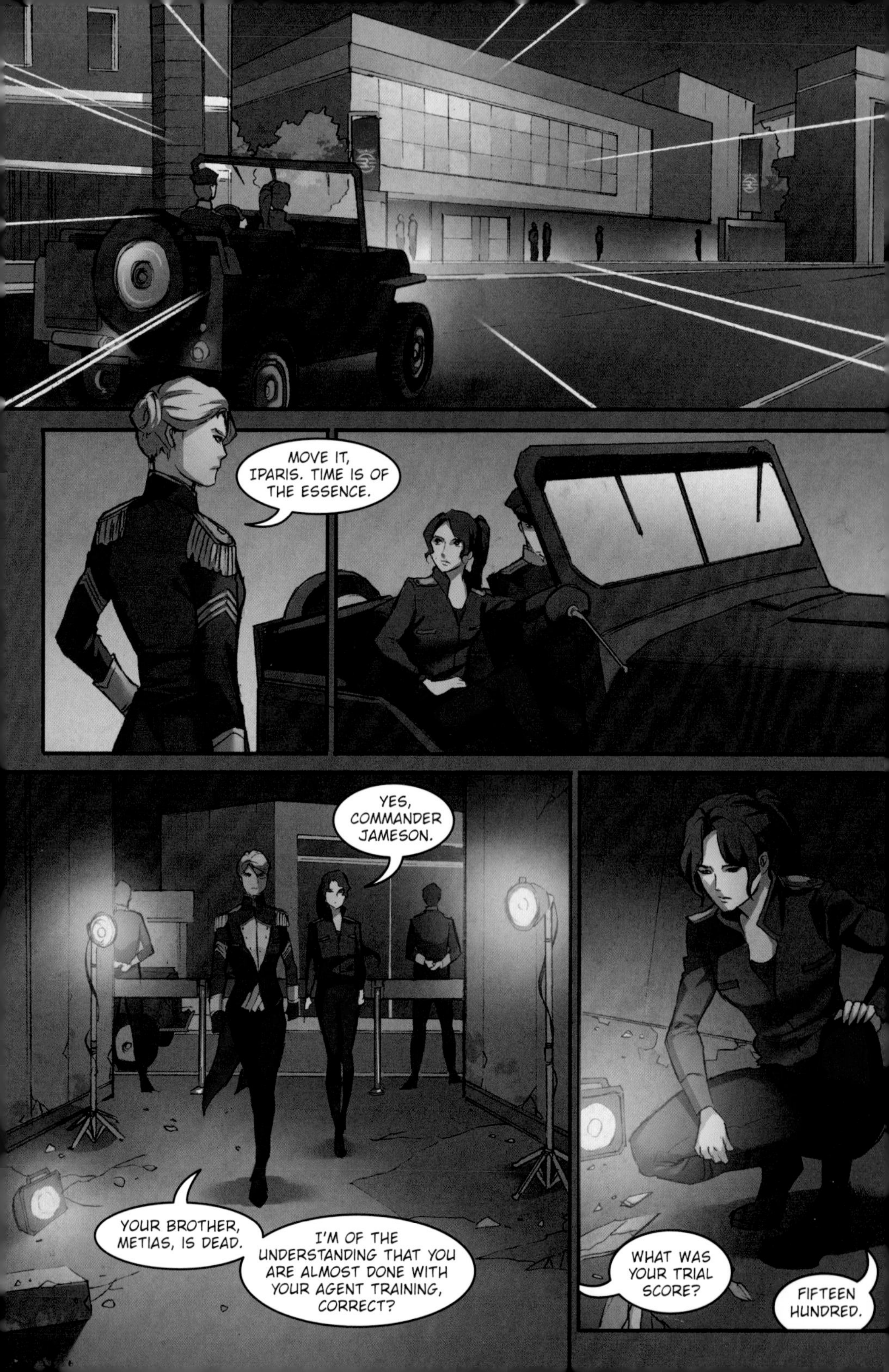
MOVE IT, IPARIS. TIME IS OF THE ESSENCE.
YES, COMMANDER JAMESON.
YOUR BROTHER, METIAS, IS DEAD.
I'M OF THE UNDERSTANDING THAT YOU ARE ALMOST DONE WITH YOUR AGENT TRAINING, CORRECT?
WHAT WAS YOUR TRIAL SCORE?
FIFTEEN HUNDRED.

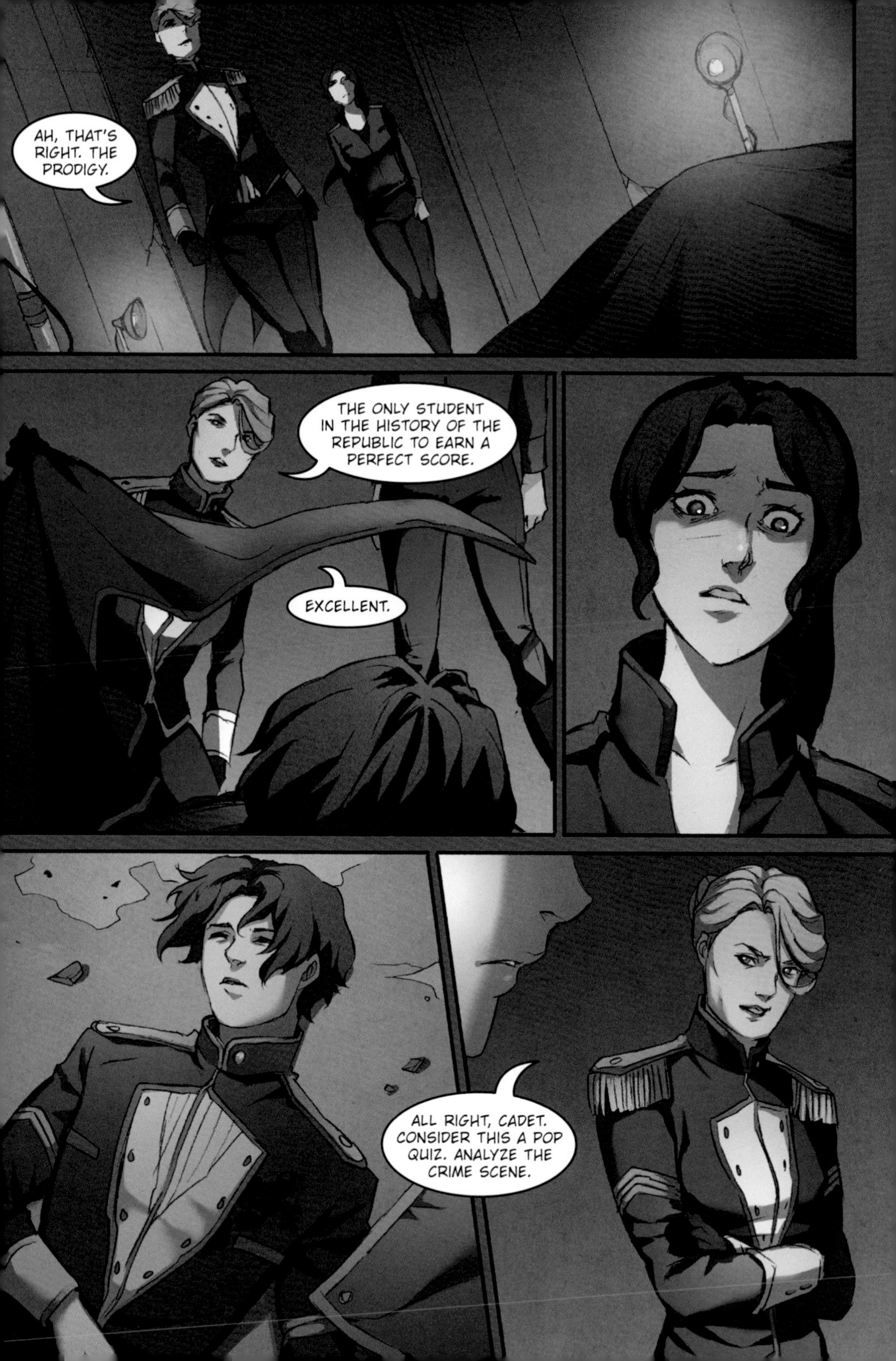
AH, THAT'S RIGHT. THE PRODIGY.
THE ONLY STUDENT IN THE HISTORY OF THE REPUBLIC TO EARN A PERFECT SCORE.
EXCELLENT.
ALL RIGHT, CADET. CONSIDER THIS A POP QUIZ. ANALYZE THE CRIME SCENE.

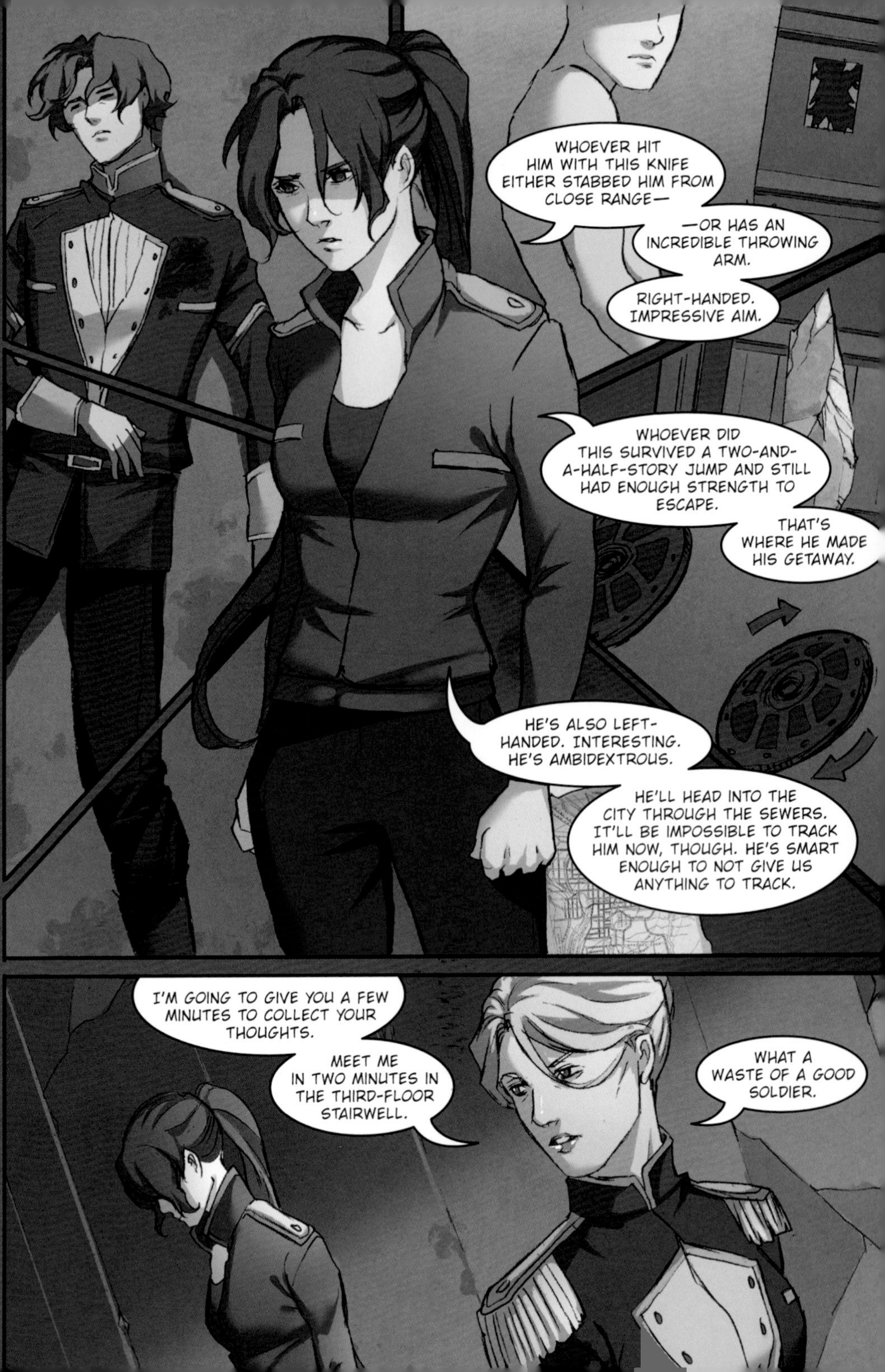
WHOEVER HIT HIM WITH THIS KNIFE EITHER STABBED HIM FROM CLOSE RANGE—
—OR HAS AN INCREDIBLE THROWING ARM.
RIGHT-HANDED. IMPRESSIVE AIM.
WHOEVER DID THIS SURVIVED A TWO-AND-A-HALF-STORY JUMP AND STILL HAD ENOUGH STRENGTH TO ESCAPE.
THAT'S WHERE HE MADE HIS GETAWAY.
HE'S ALSO LEFT-HANDED. INTERESTING. HE'S AMBIDEXTROUS.
HE'LL HEAD INTO THE CITY THROUGH THE SEWERS. IT'LL BE IMPOSSIBLE TO TRACK HIM NOW, THOUGH. HE'S SMART ENOUGH TO NOT GIVE US ANYTHING TO TRACK.
I'M GOING TO GIVE YOU A FEW MINUTES TO COLLECT YOUR THOUGHTS.
MEET ME IN TWO MINUTES IN THE THIRD-FLOOR STAIRWELL.
WHAT A WASTE OF A GOOD SOLDIER.

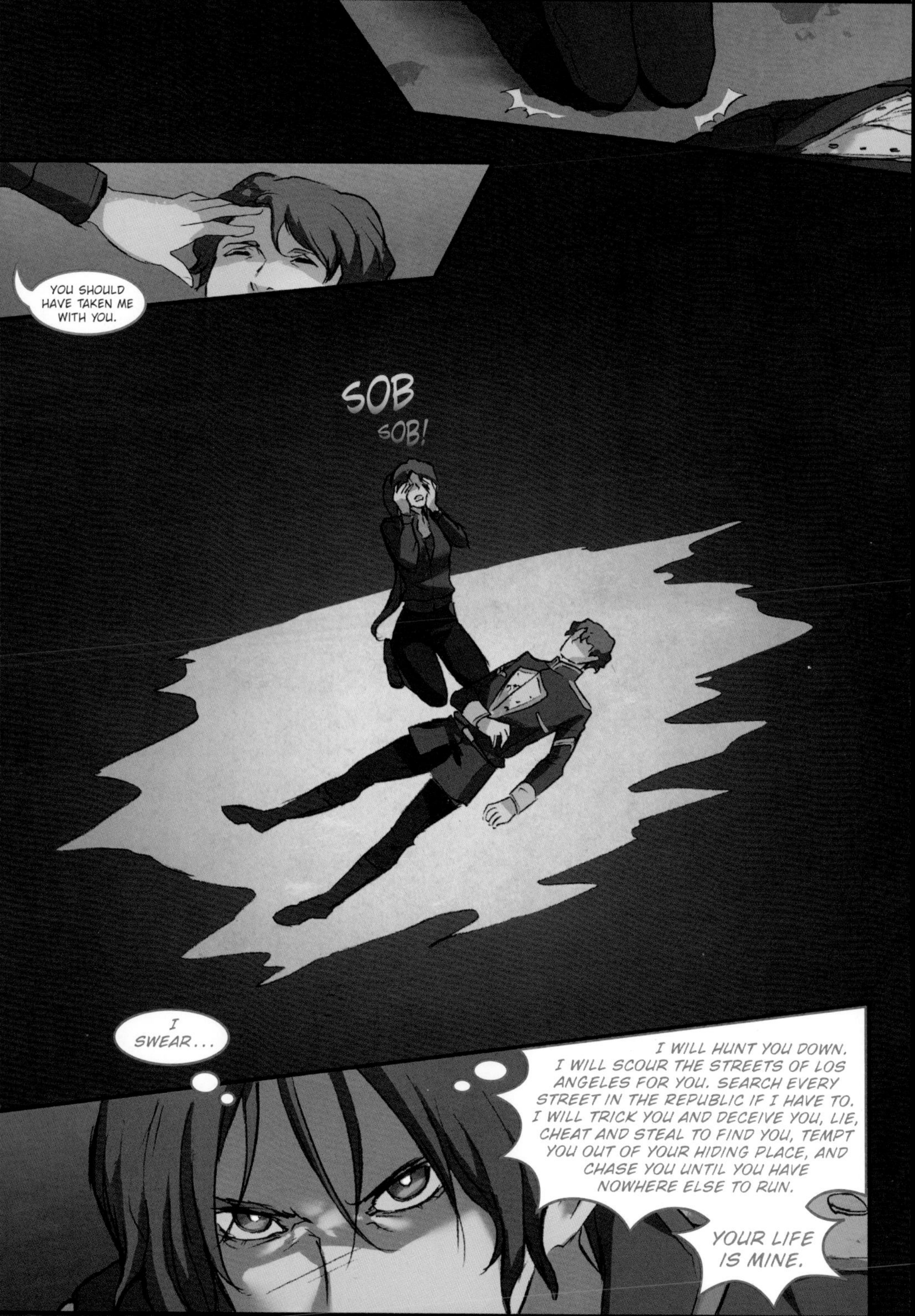
YOU SHOULD HAVE TAKEN ME WITH YOU.
SOB
SOB!
I SWEAR...
I WILL HUNT YOU DOWN. I WILL SCOUR THE STREETS OF LOS ANGELES FOR YOU. SEARCH EVERY STREET IN THE REPUBLIC IF I HAVE TO. I WILL TRICK YOU AND DECEIVE YOU, LIE, CHEAT AND STEAL TO FIND YOU, TEMPT YOU OUT OF YOUR HIDING PLACE, AND CHASE YOU UNTIL YOU HAVE NOWHERE ELSE TO RUN.
YOUR LIFE IS MINE.

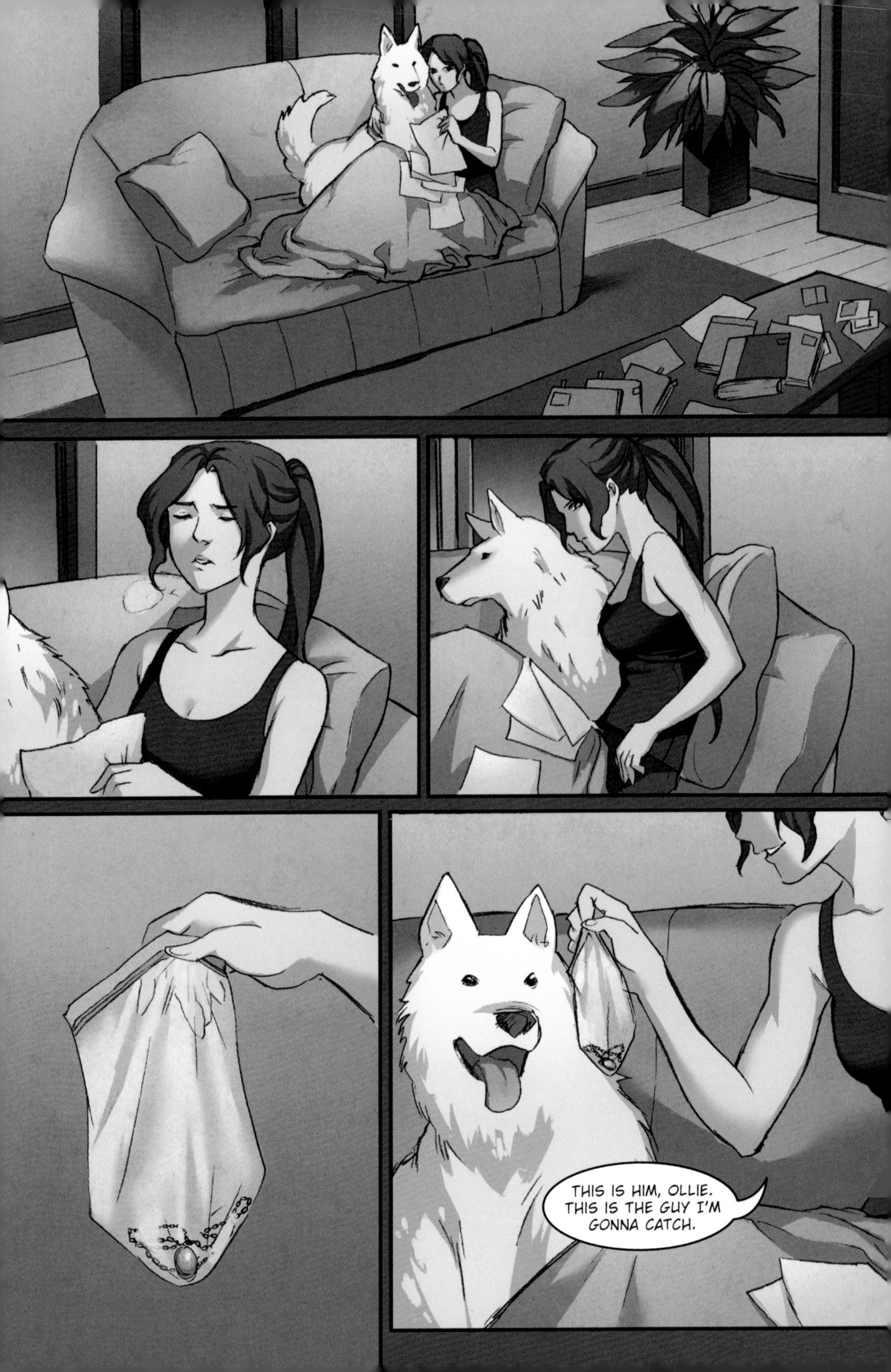
THIS IS HIM, OLLIE. THIS IS THE GUY I'M GONNA CATCH.

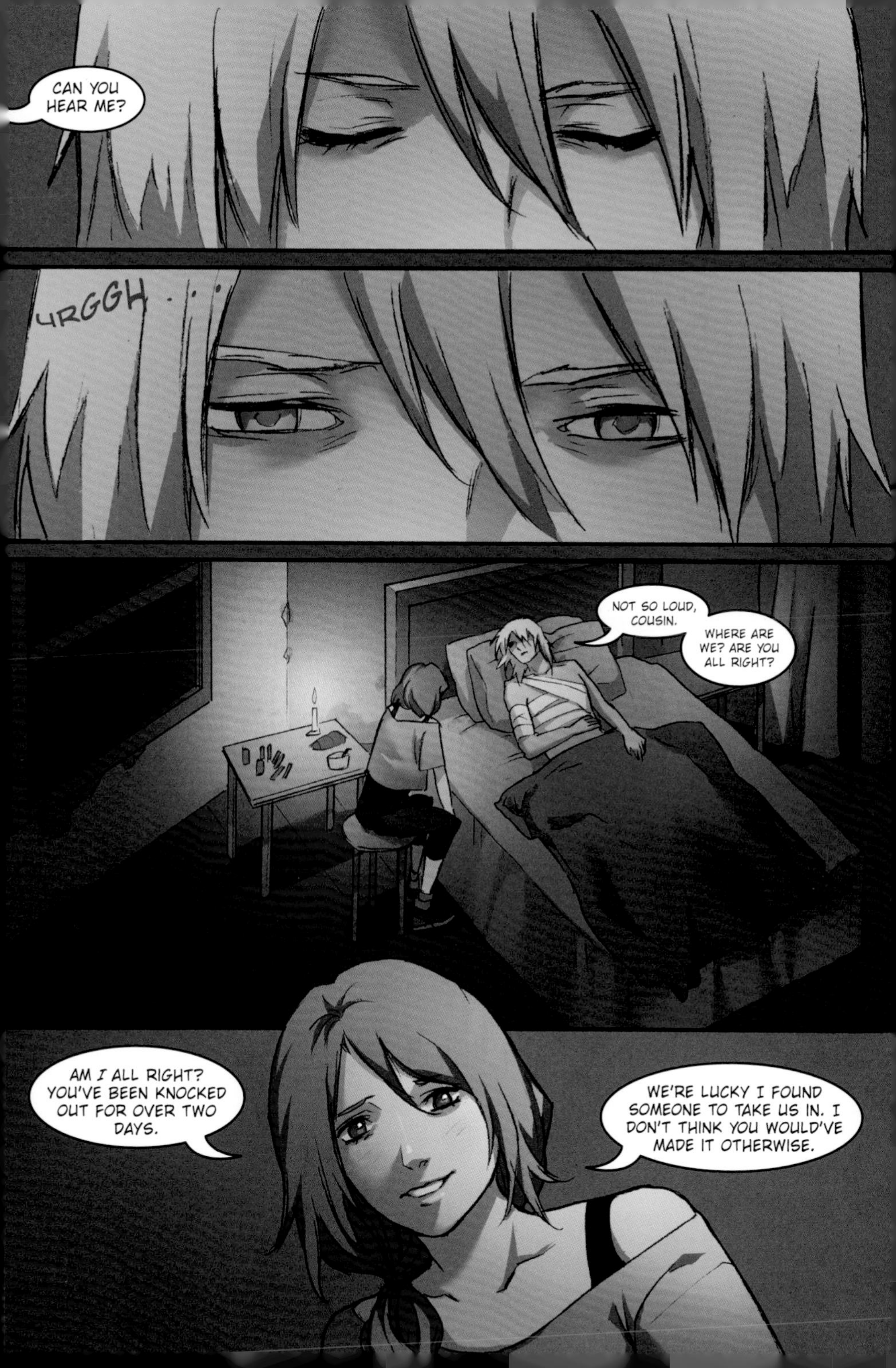
CAN YOU HEAR ME?
URGGH...
NOT SO LOUD, COUSIN.
WHERE ARE WE? ARE YOU ALL RIGHT?
AM *I* ALL RIGHT? YOU'VE BEEN KNOCKED OUT FOR OVER TWO DAYS.
WE'RE LUCKY I FOUND SOMEONE TO TAKE US IN. I DON'T THINK YOU WOULD'VE MADE IT OTHERWISE.

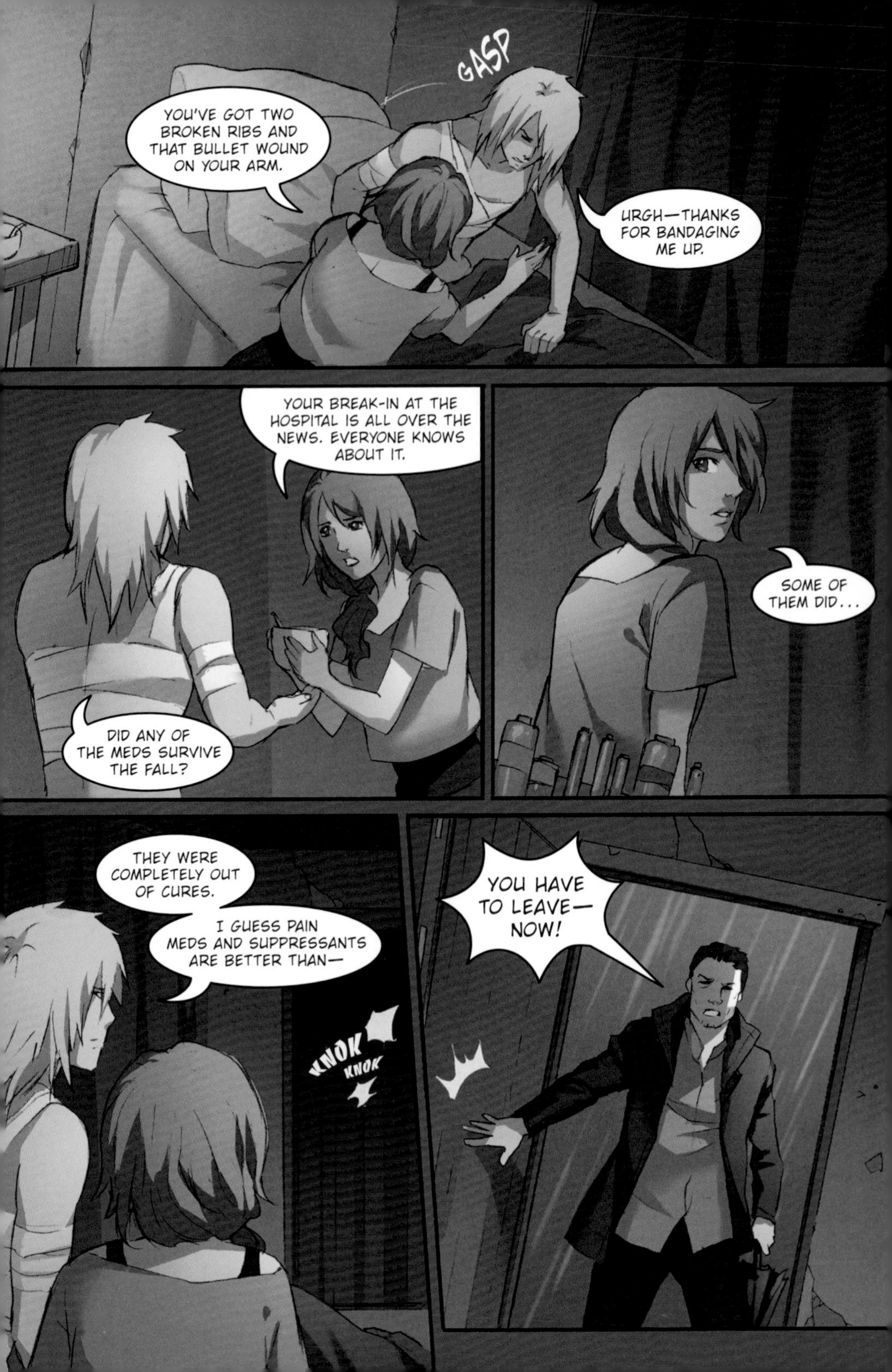
GASP
YOU'VE GOT TWO BROKEN RIBS AND THAT BULLET WOUND ON YOUR ARM.
URGH—THANKS FOR BANDAGING ME UP.
YOUR BREAK-IN AT THE HOSPITAL IS ALL OVER THE NEWS. EVERYONE KNOWS ABOUT IT.
DID ANY OF THE MEDS SURVIVE THE FALL?
SOME OF THEM DID...
THEY WERE COMPLETELY OUT OF CURES.
I GUESS PAIN MEDS AND SUPPRESSANTS ARE BETTER THAN—
KNOK KNOK
YOU HAVE TO LEAVE—NOW!

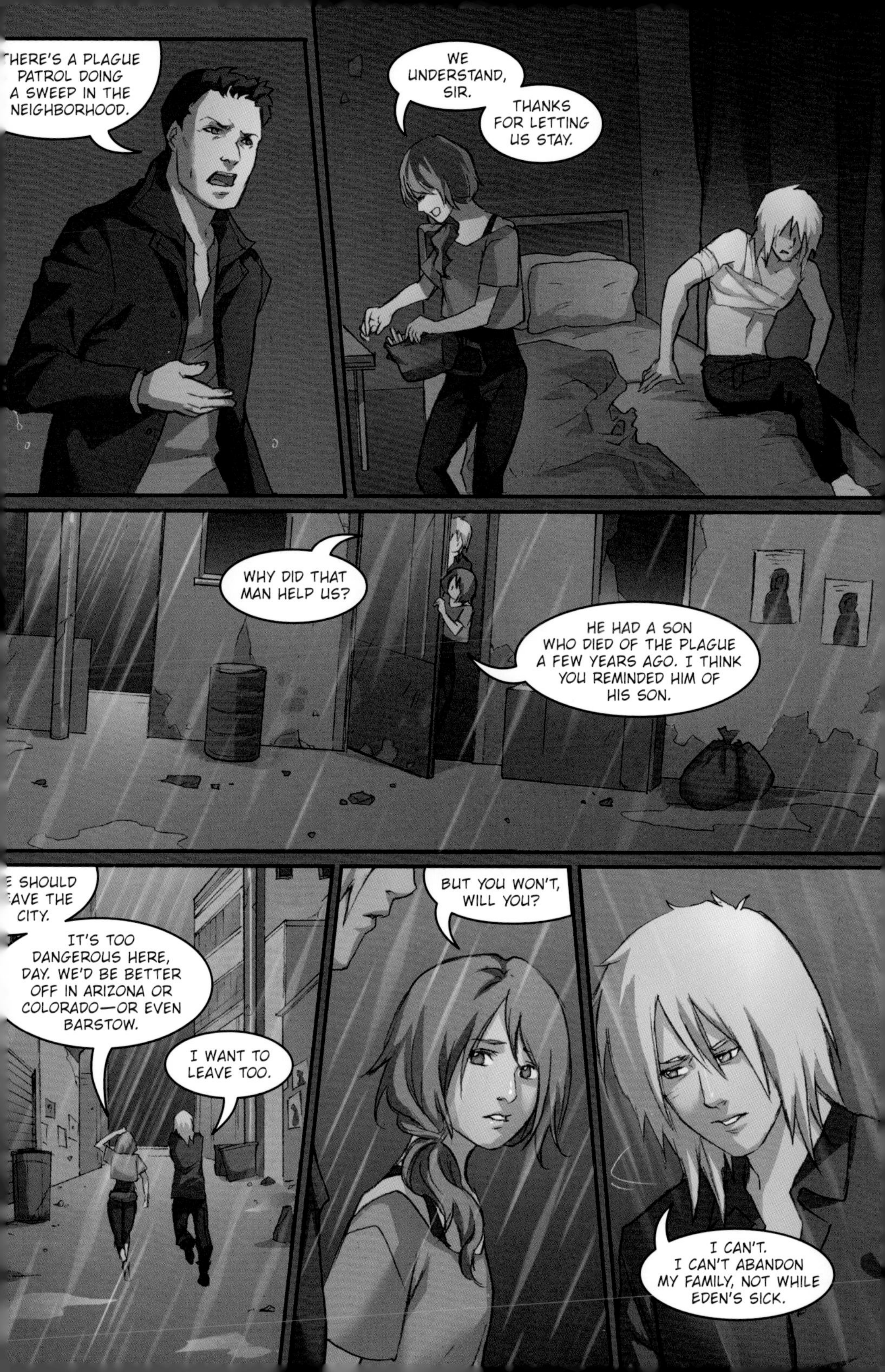
THERE'S A PLAGUE PATROL DOING A SWEEP IN THE NEIGHBORHOOD.
WE UNDERSTAND, SIR.
THANKS FOR LETTING US STAY.
WHY DID THAT MAN HELP US?
HE HAD A SON WHO DIED OF THE PLAGUE A FEW YEARS AGO. I THINK YOU REMINDED HIM OF HIS SON.
E SHOULD EAVE THE CITY.
IT'S TOO DANGEROUS HERE, DAY. WE'D BE BETTER OFF IN ARIZONA OR COLORADO—OR EVEN BARSTOW.
I WANT TO LEAVE TOO.
BUT YOU WON'T, WILL YOU?
I CAN'T. I CAN'T ABANDON MY FAMILY, NOT WHILE EDEN'S SICK.

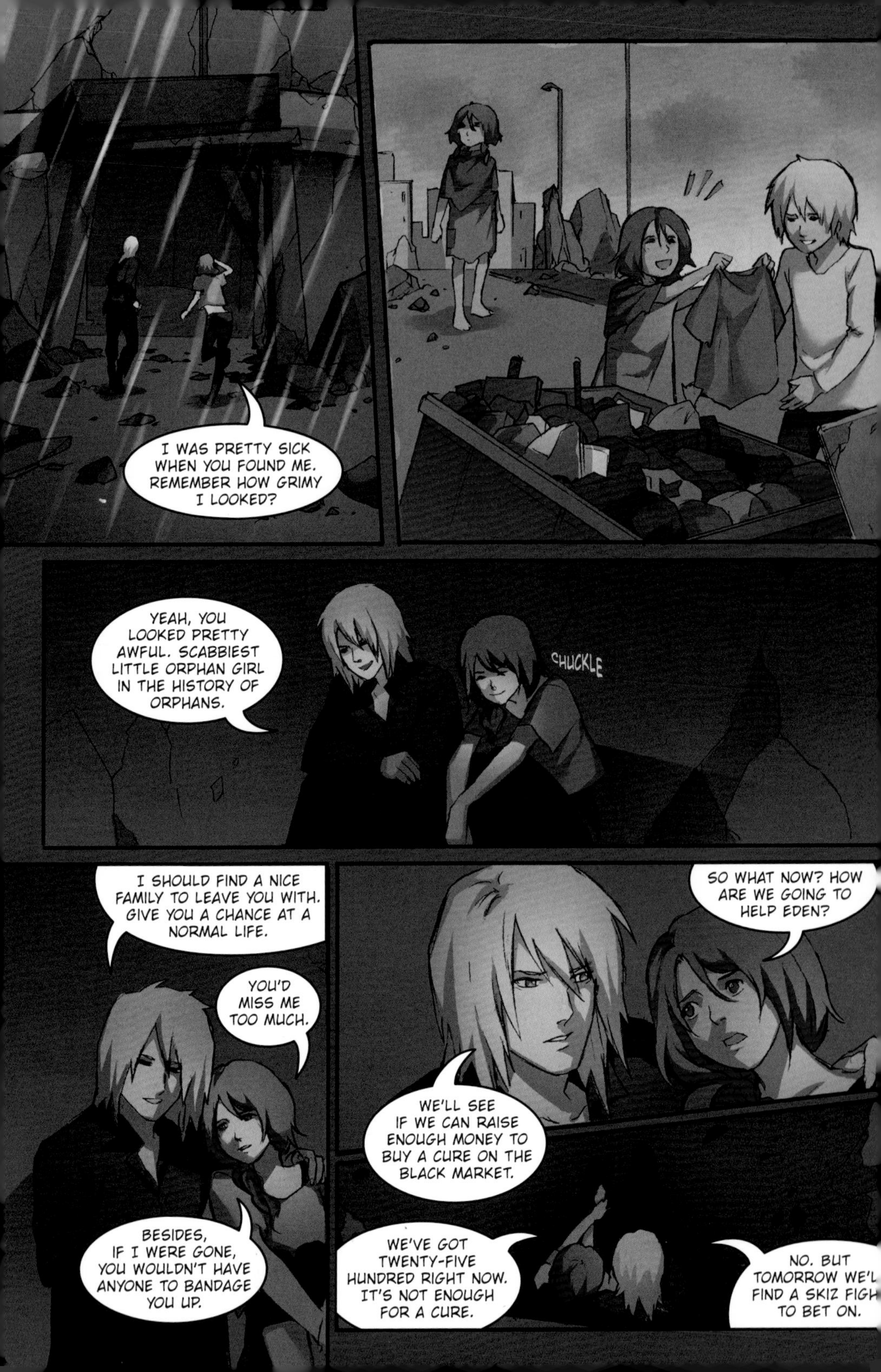
I WAS PRETTY SICK WHEN YOU FOUND ME. REMEMBER HOW GRIMY I LOOKED?
YEAH, YOU LOOKED PRETTY AWFUL. SCABBIEST LITTLE ORPHAN GIRL IN THE HISTORY OF ORPHANS.
CHUCKLE
I SHOULD FIND A NICE FAMILY TO LEAVE YOU WITH. GIVE YOU A CHANCE AT A NORMAL LIFE.
YOU'D MISS ME TOO MUCH.
BESIDES, IF I WERE GONE, YOU WOULDN'T HAVE ANYONE TO BANDAGE YOU UP.
SO WHAT NOW? HOW ARE WE GOING TO HELP EDEN?
WE'LL SEE IF WE CAN RAISE ENOUGH MONEY TO BUY A CURE ON THE BLACK MARKET.
WE'VE GOT TWENTY-FIVE HUNDRED RIGHT NOW. IT'S NOT ENOUGH FOR A CURE.
NO. BUT TOMORROW WE'L FIND A SKIZ FIGH TO BET ON.

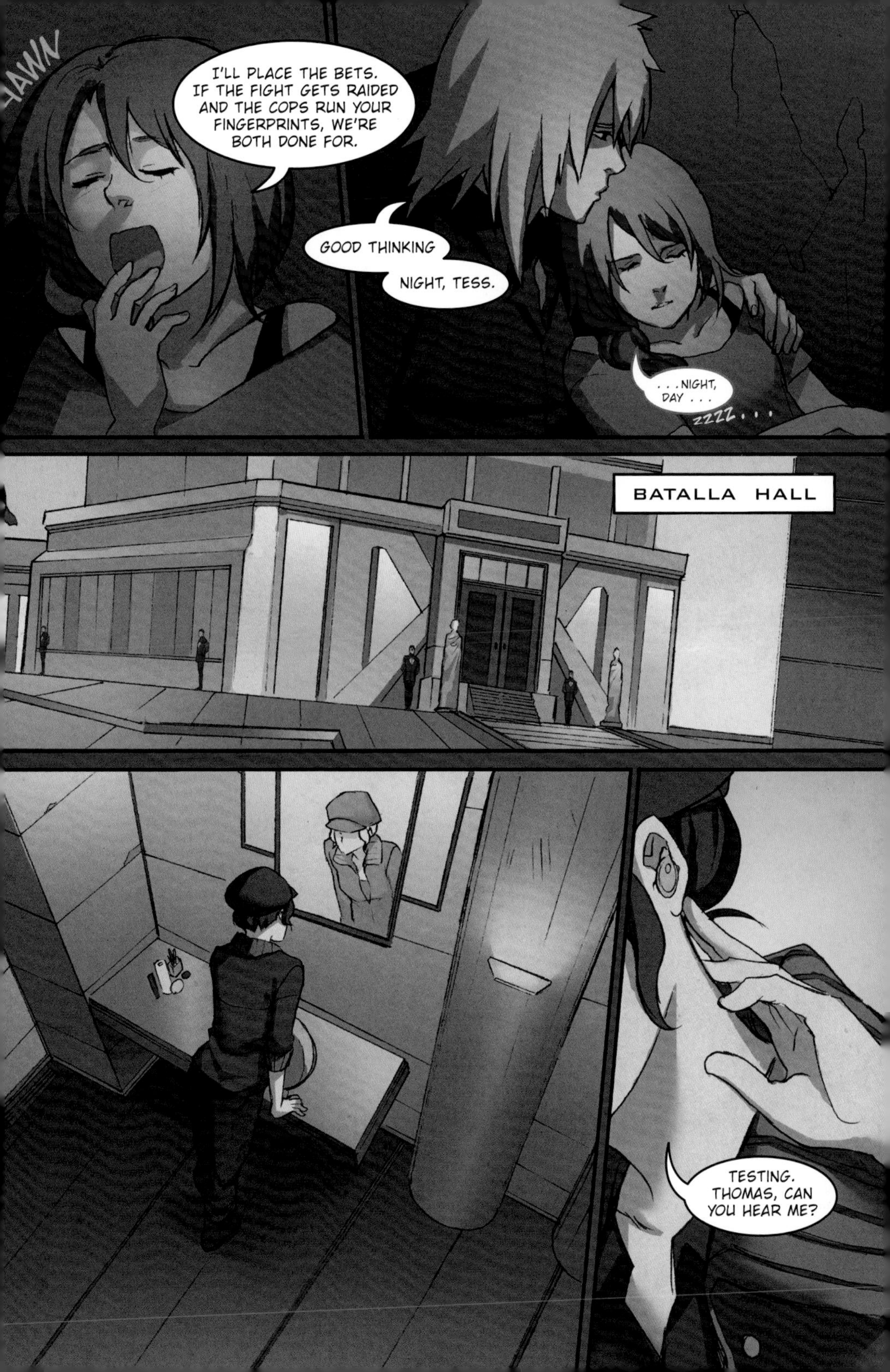
I'LL PLACE THE BETS. IF THE FIGHT GETS RAIDED AND THE COPS RUN YOUR FINGERPRINTS, WE'RE BOTH DONE FOR.
GOOD THINKING
NIGHT, TESS.
. . .NIGHT, DAY . . .
ZZZZ. . .
BATALLA HALL
TESTING. THOMAS, CAN YOU HEAR ME?

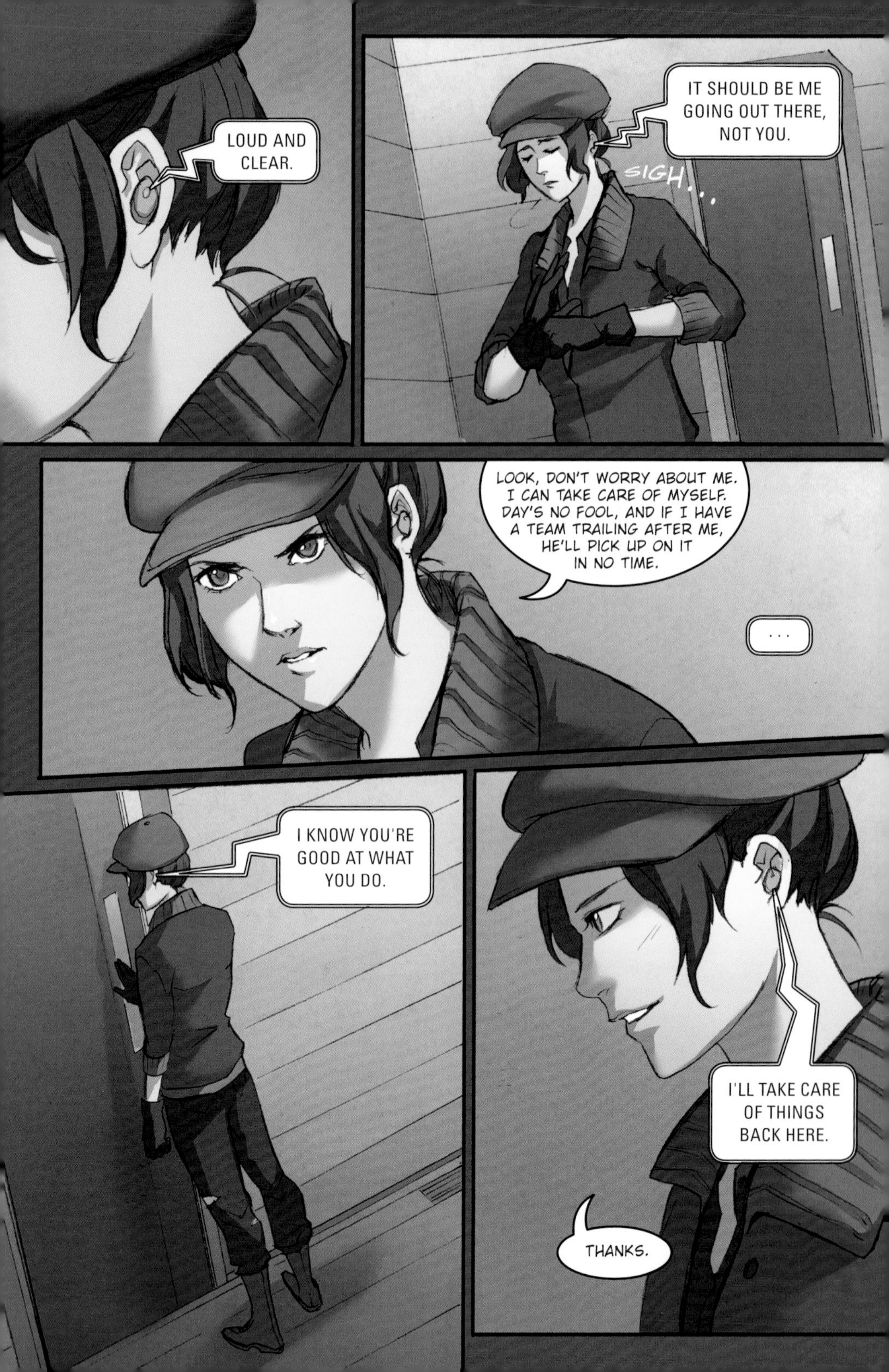
LOUD AND CLEAR.
IT SHOULD BE ME GOING OUT THERE, NOT YOU.
SIGH...
LOOK, DON'T WORRY ABOUT ME. I CAN TAKE CARE OF MYSELF. DAY'S NO FOOL, AND IF I HAVE A TEAM TRAILING AFTER ME, HE'LL PICK UP ON IT IN NO TIME.
...
I KNOW YOU'RE GOOD AT WHAT YOU DO.
I'LL TAKE CARE OF THINGS BACK HERE.
THANKS.

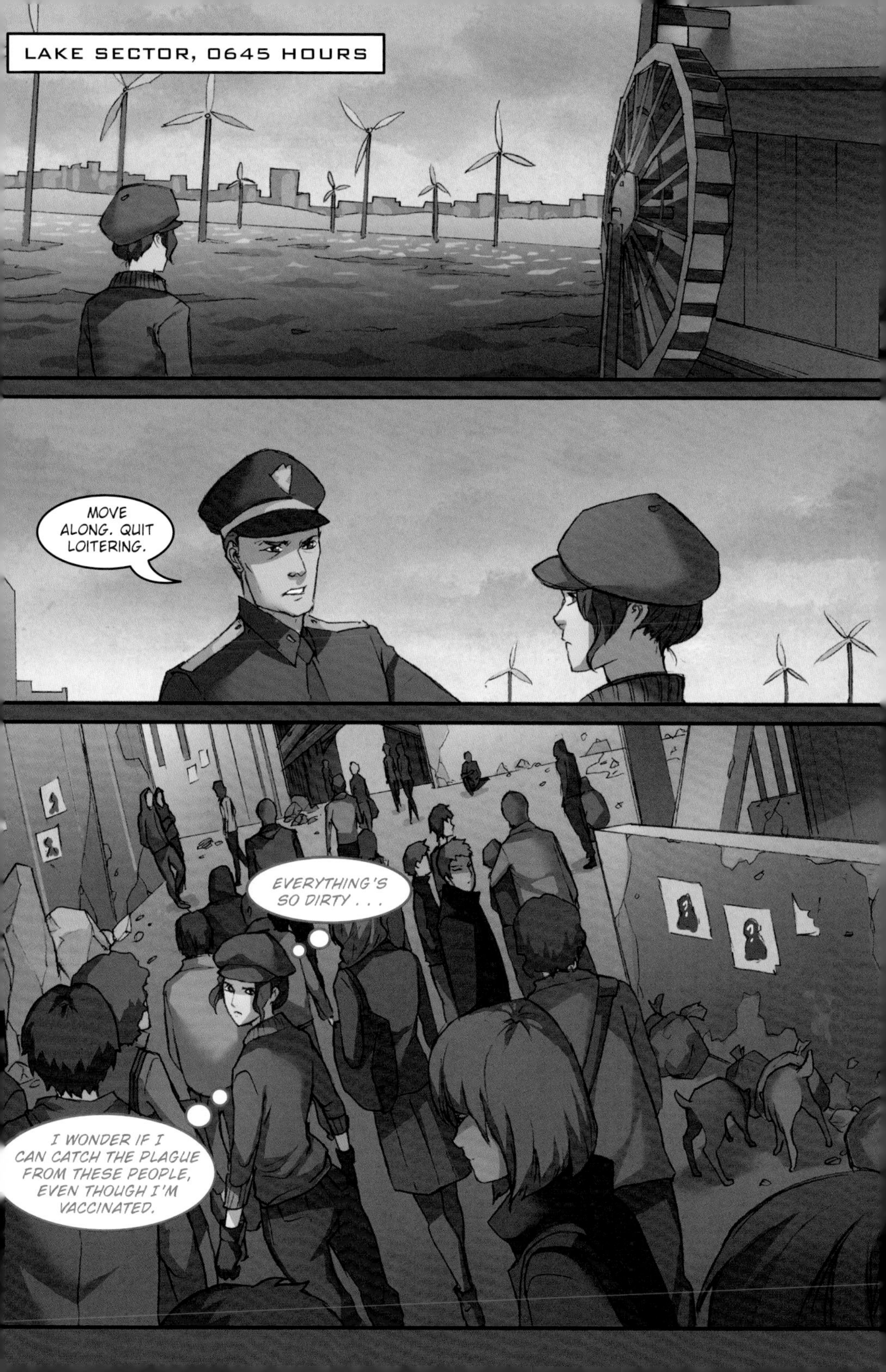
LAKE SECTOR, 0645 HOURS
MOVE ALONG. QUIT LOITERING.
EVERYTHING'S SO DIRTY . . .
I WONDER IF I CAN CATCH THE PLAGUE FROM THESE PEOPLE, EVEN THOUGH I'M VACCINATED.

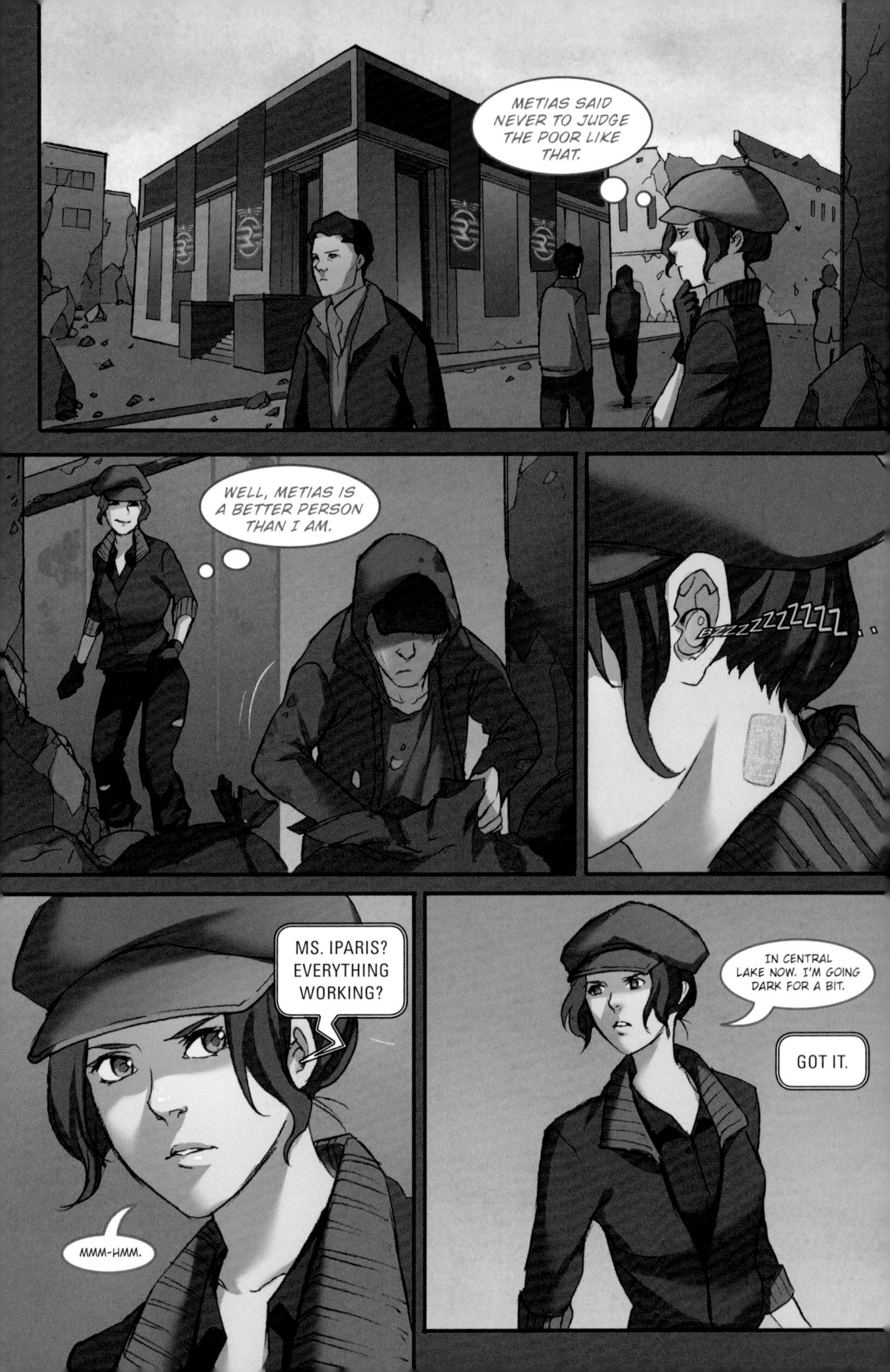
METIAS SAID NEVER TO JUDGE THE POOR LIKE THAT.
WELL, METIAS IS A BETTER PERSON THAN I AM.
BZZZZZZZZZZZ. . .
MS. IPARIS? EVERYTHING WORKING?
MMM-HMM.
IN CENTRAL LAKE NOW. I'M GOING DARK FOR A BIT.
GOT IT.

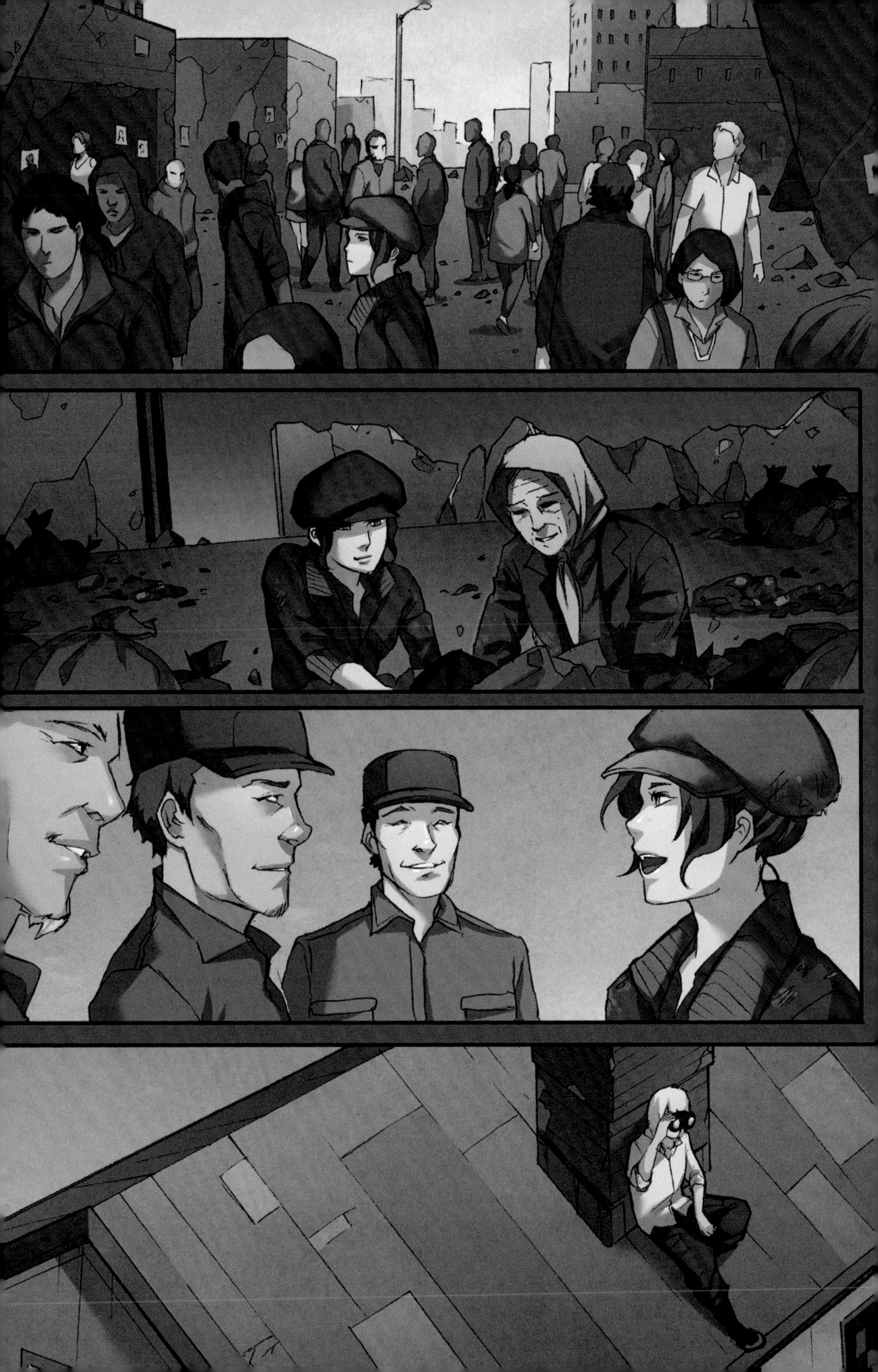

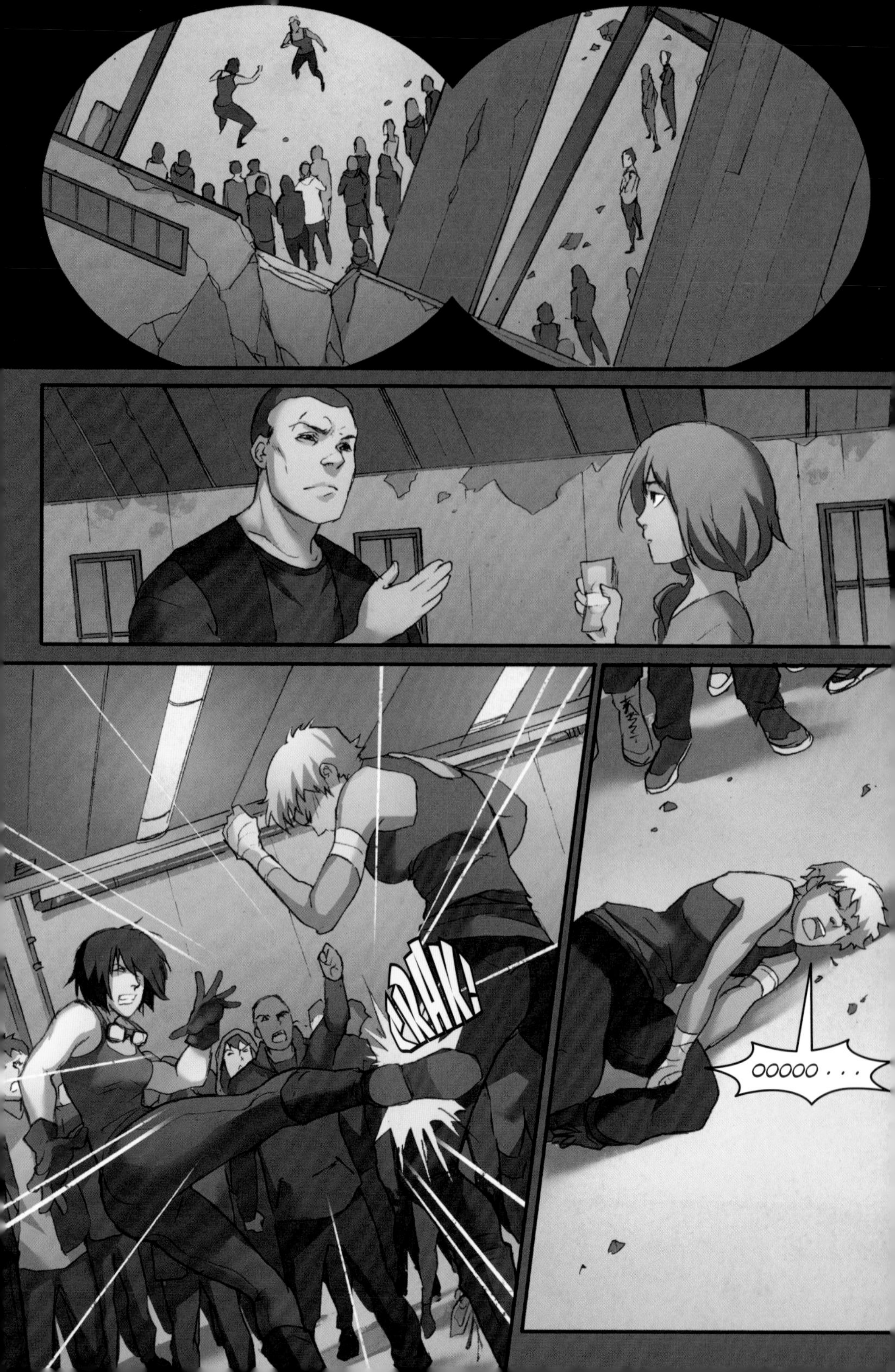
KRAK!
OOOOO . . .

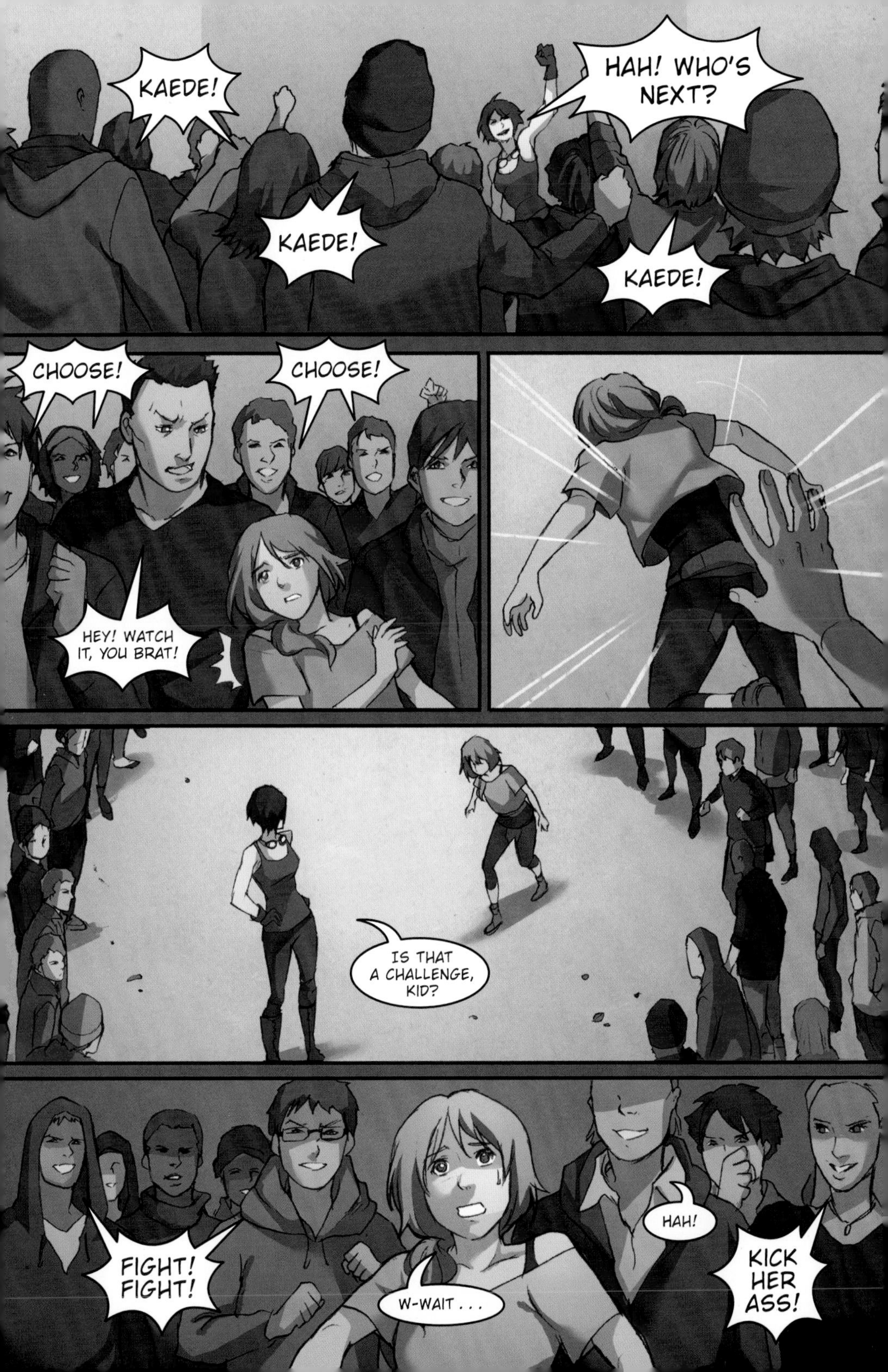
KAEDE!
HAH! WHO'S NEXT?
KAEDE!
KAEDE!
CHOOSE!
CHOOSE!
HEY! WATCH IT, YOU BRAT!
IS THAT A CHALLENGE, KID?
FIGHT! FIGHT!
W-WAIT . . .
HAH!
KICK HER ASS!

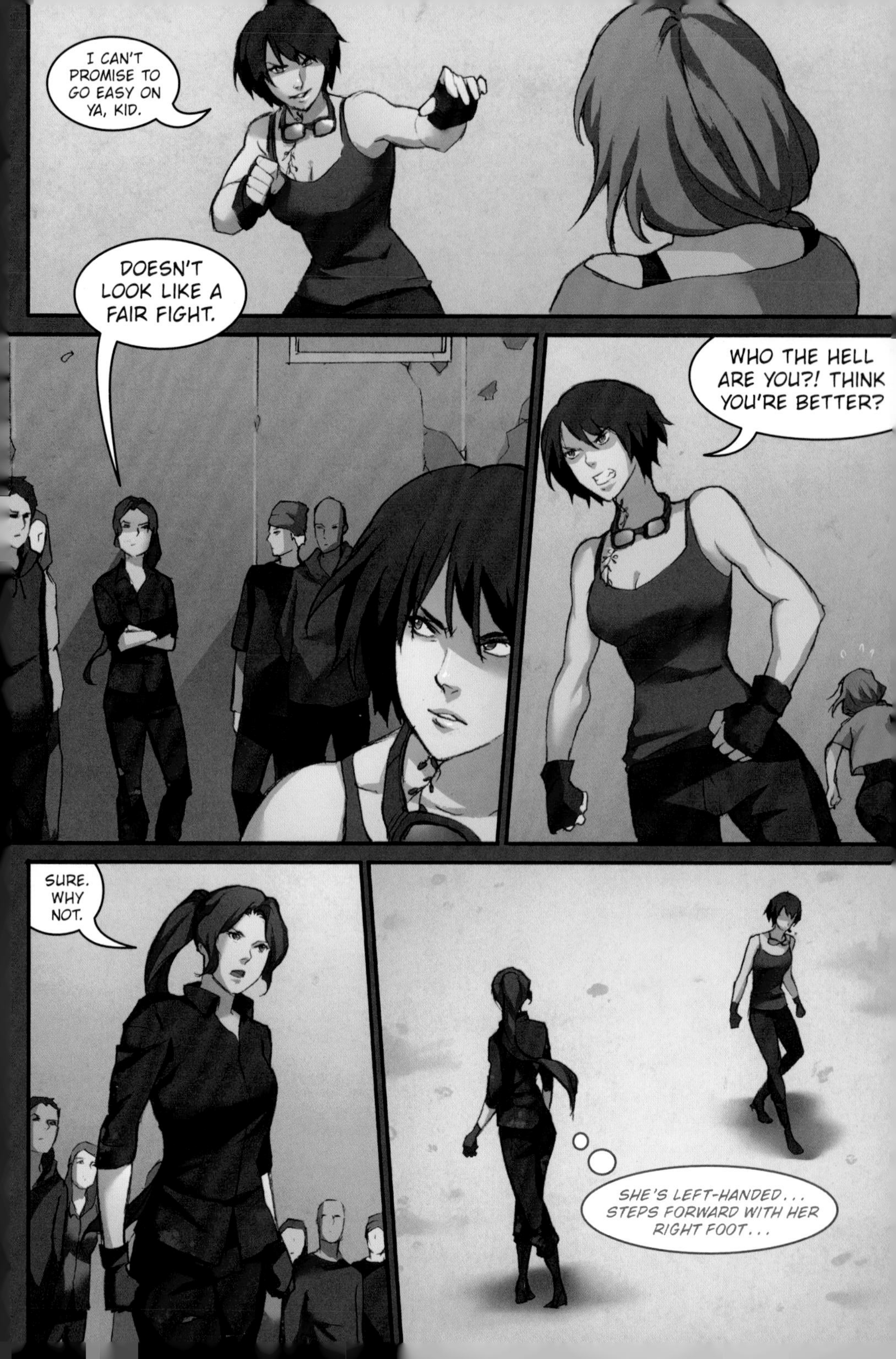
I CAN'T PROMISE TO GO EASY ON YA, KID.
DOESN'T LOOK LIKE A FAIR FIGHT.
WHO THE HELL ARE YOU?! THINK YOU'RE BETTER?
SURE. WHY NOT.
SHE'S LEFT-HANDED... STEPS FORWARD WITH HER RIGHT FOOT...

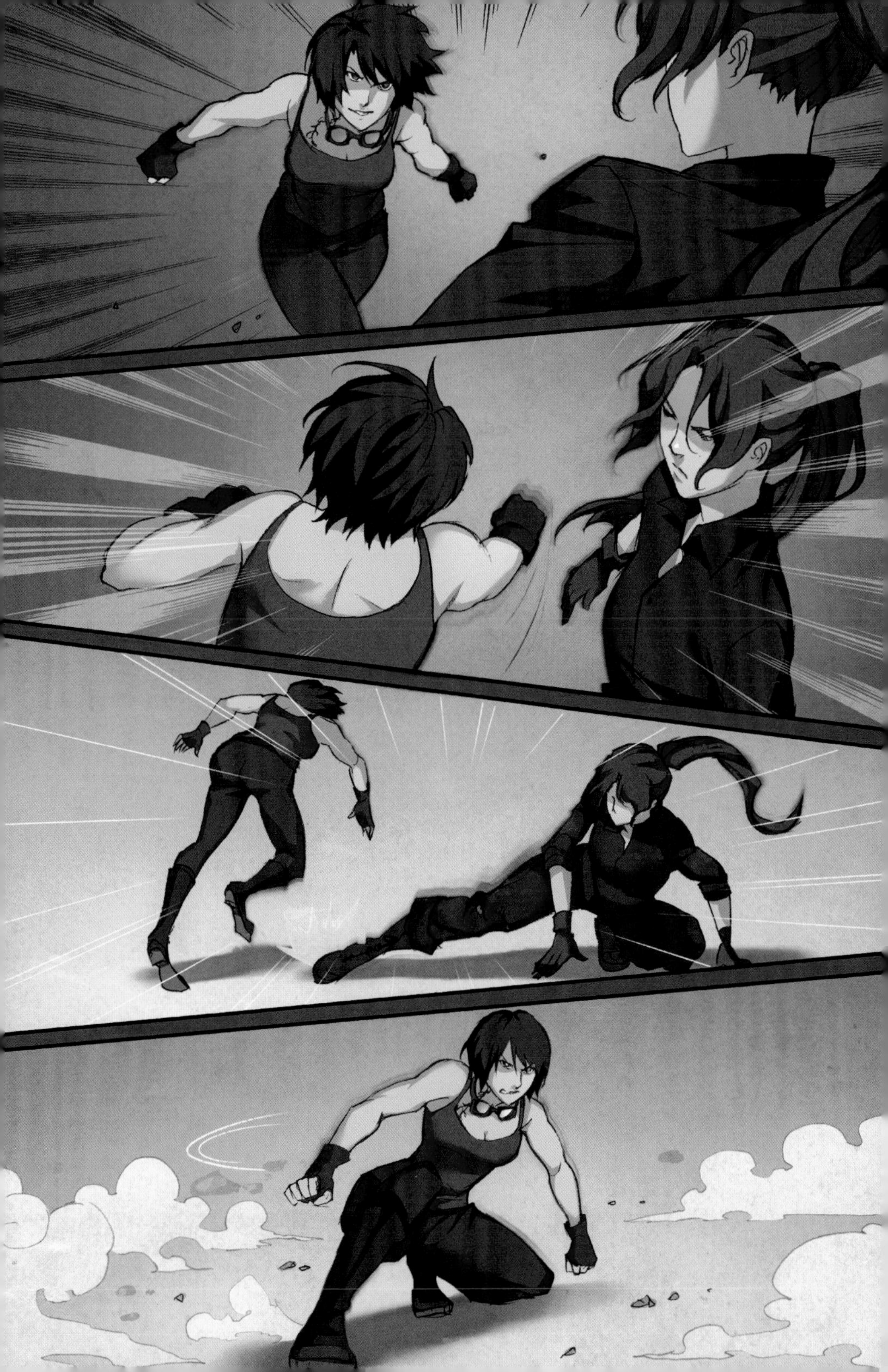

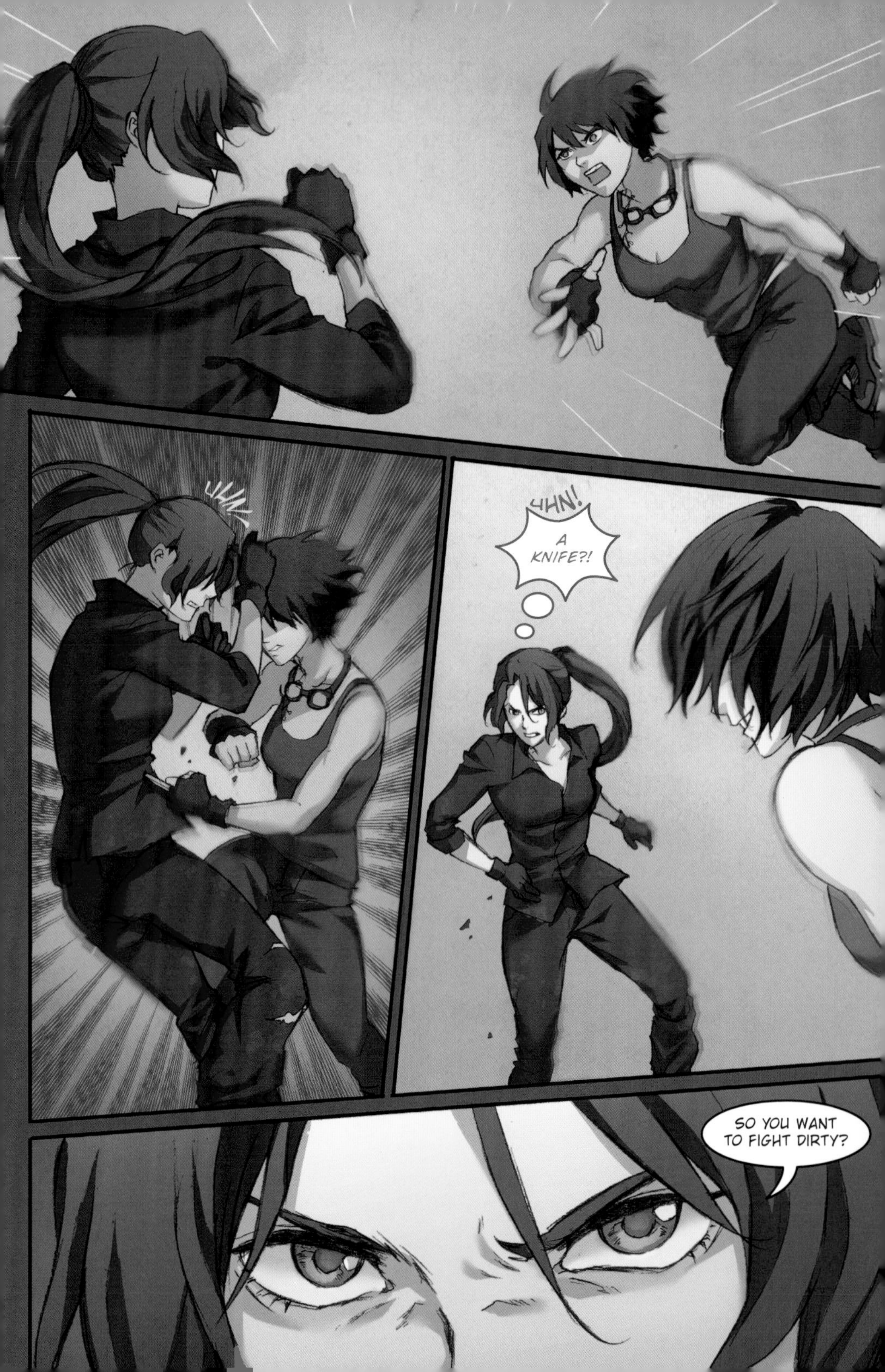
UHN
UHN!
A KNIFE?!
SO YOU WANT TO FIGHT DIRTY?

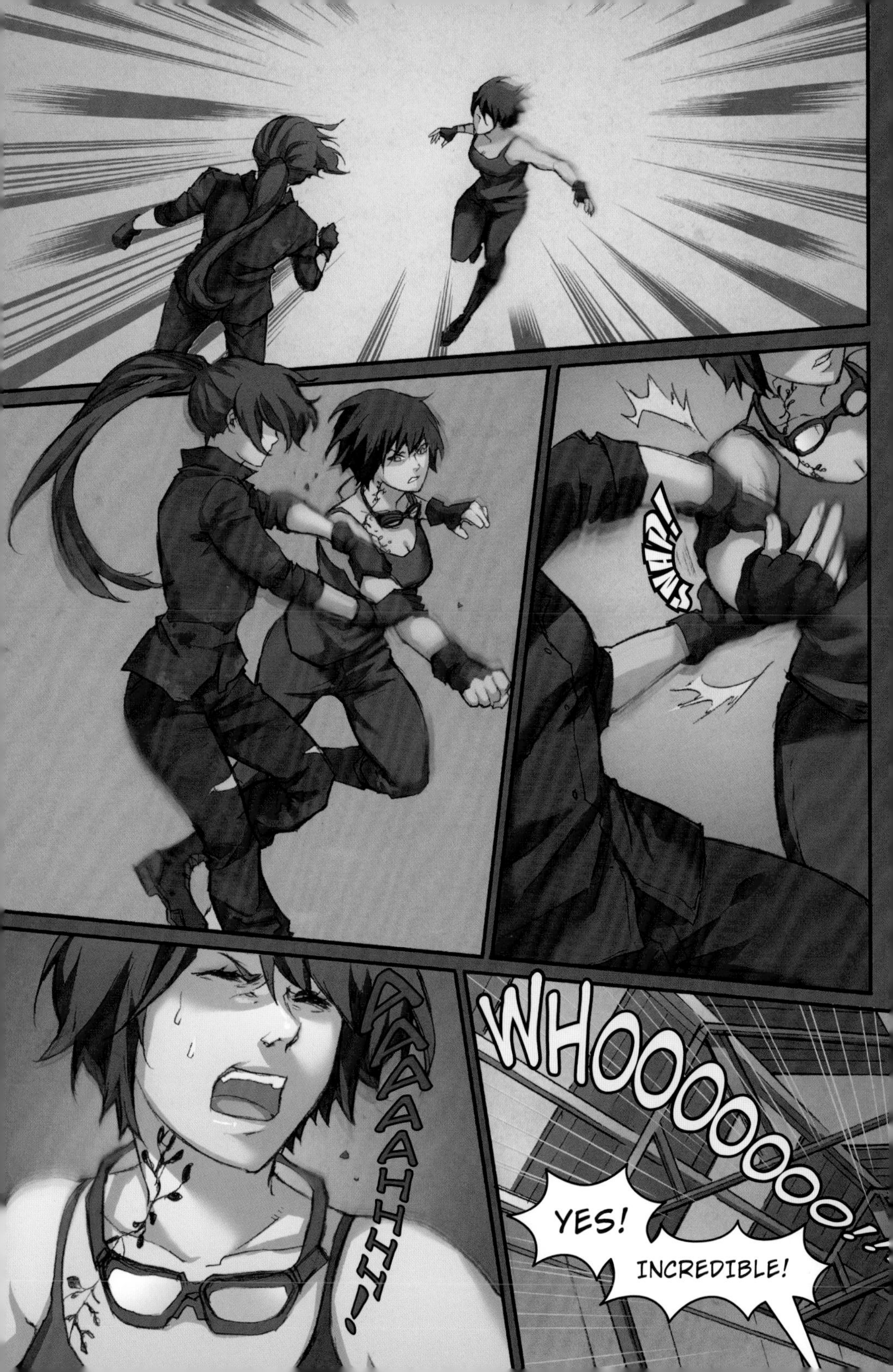
SNAP!
AAAAAHHHH!
WHOOOOOOOO!!
YES!
INCREDIBLE!

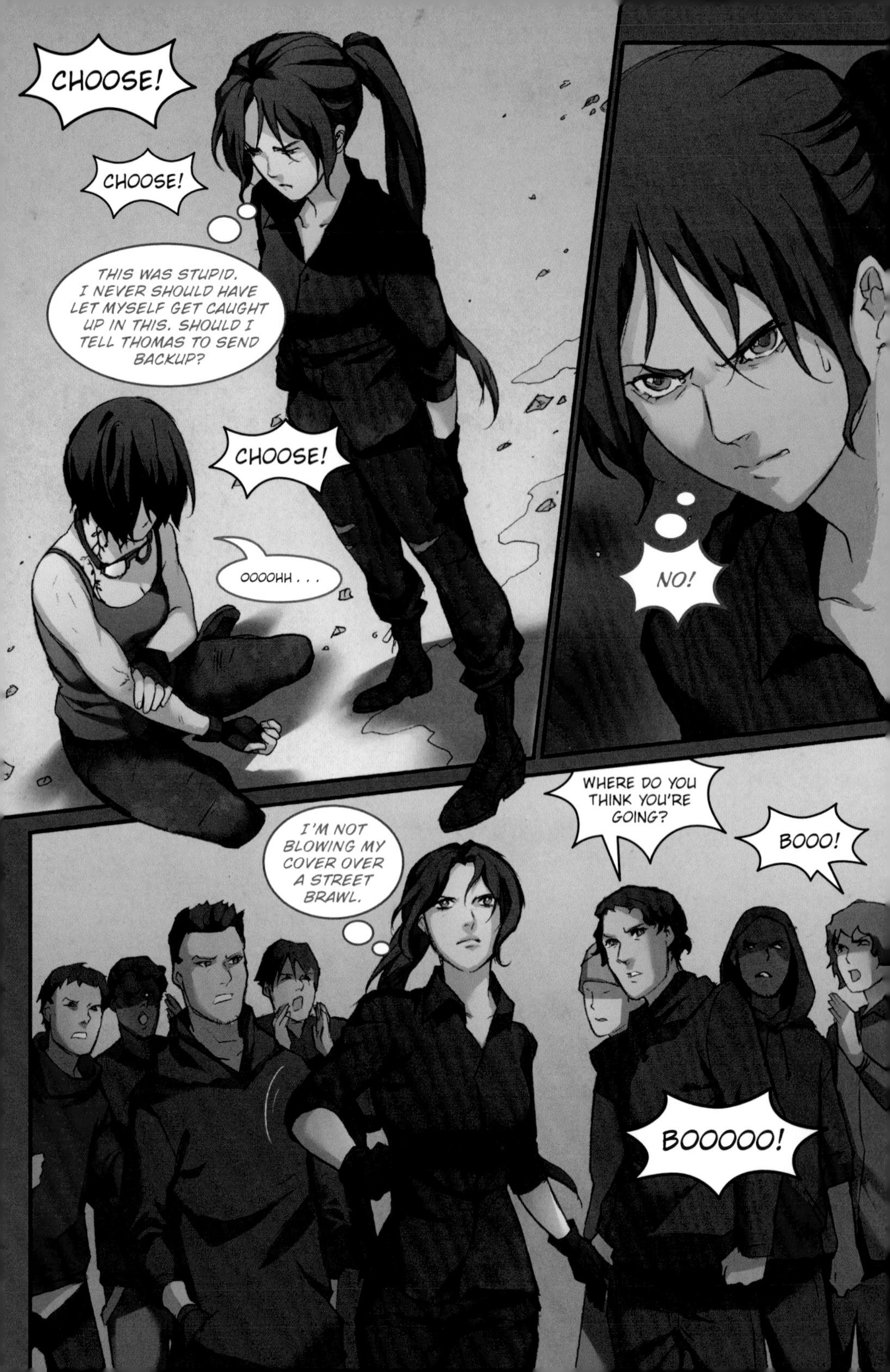
CHOOSE!
CHOOSE!
THIS WAS STUPID. I NEVER SHOULD HAVE LET MYSELF GET CAUGHT UP IN THIS. SHOULD I TELL THOMAS TO SEND BACKUP?
CHOOSE!
OOOOHH . . .
NO!
I'M NOT BLOWING MY COVER OVER A STREET BRAWL.
WHERE DO YOU THINK YOU'RE GOING?
BOOO!
BOOOOO!

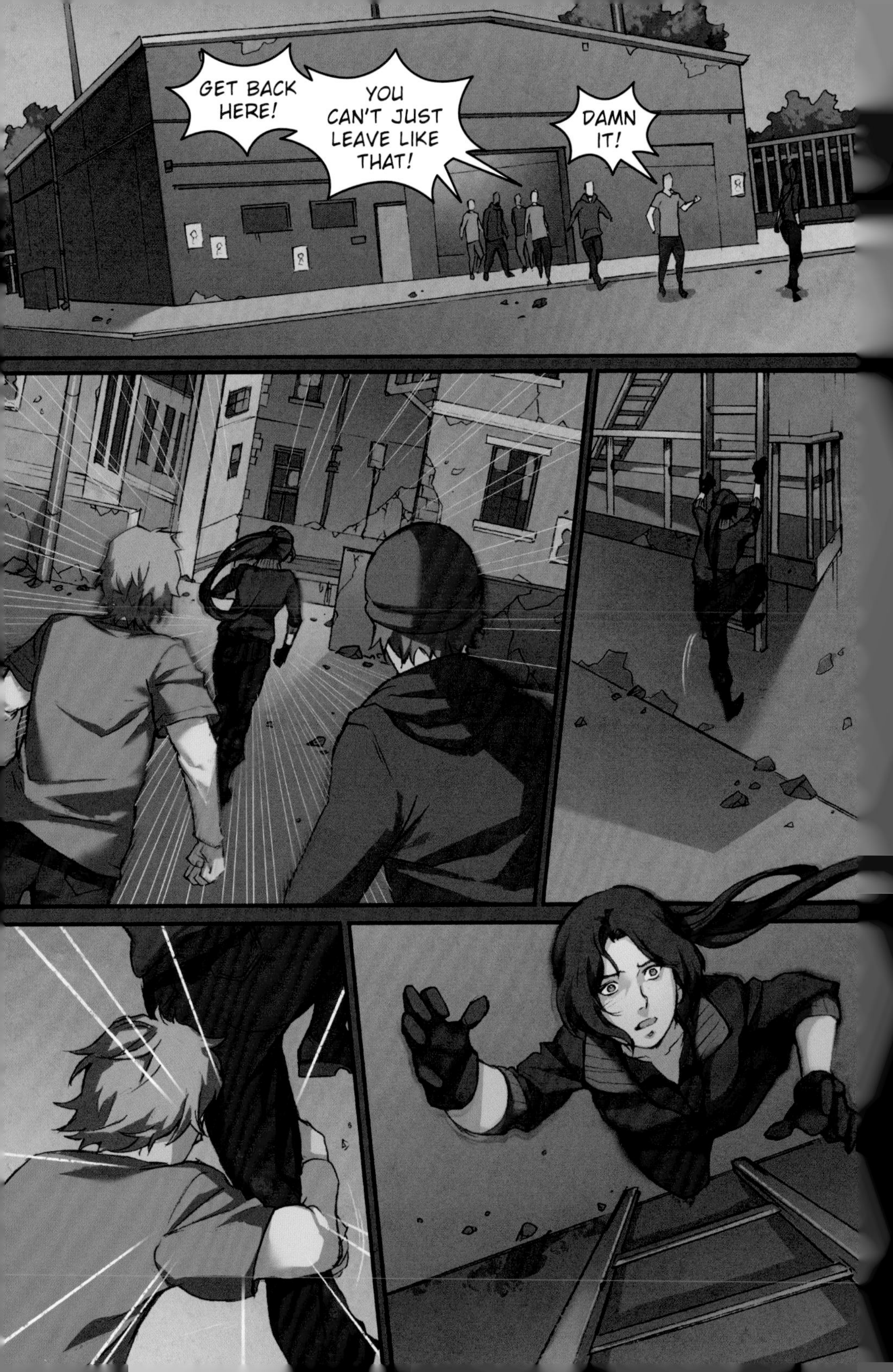
GET BACK HERE!
YOU CAN'T JUST LEAVE LIKE THAT!
DAMN IT!

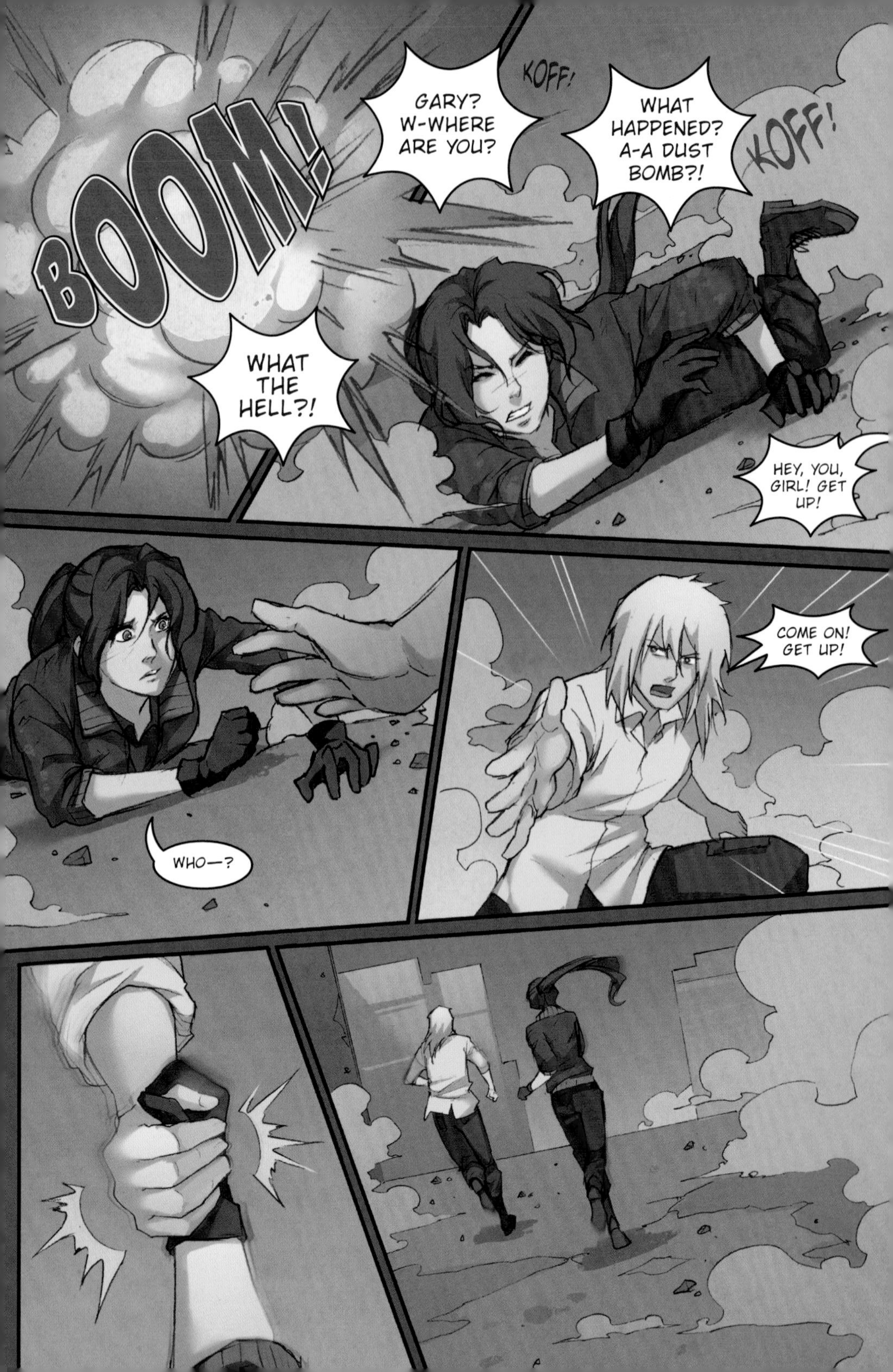
BOOM!
GARY? W-WHERE ARE YOU?
KOFF!
WHAT HAPPENED? A-A DUST BOMB?!
KOFF!
WHAT THE HELL?!
HEY, YOU, GIRL! GET UP!
WHO—?
COME ON! GET UP!

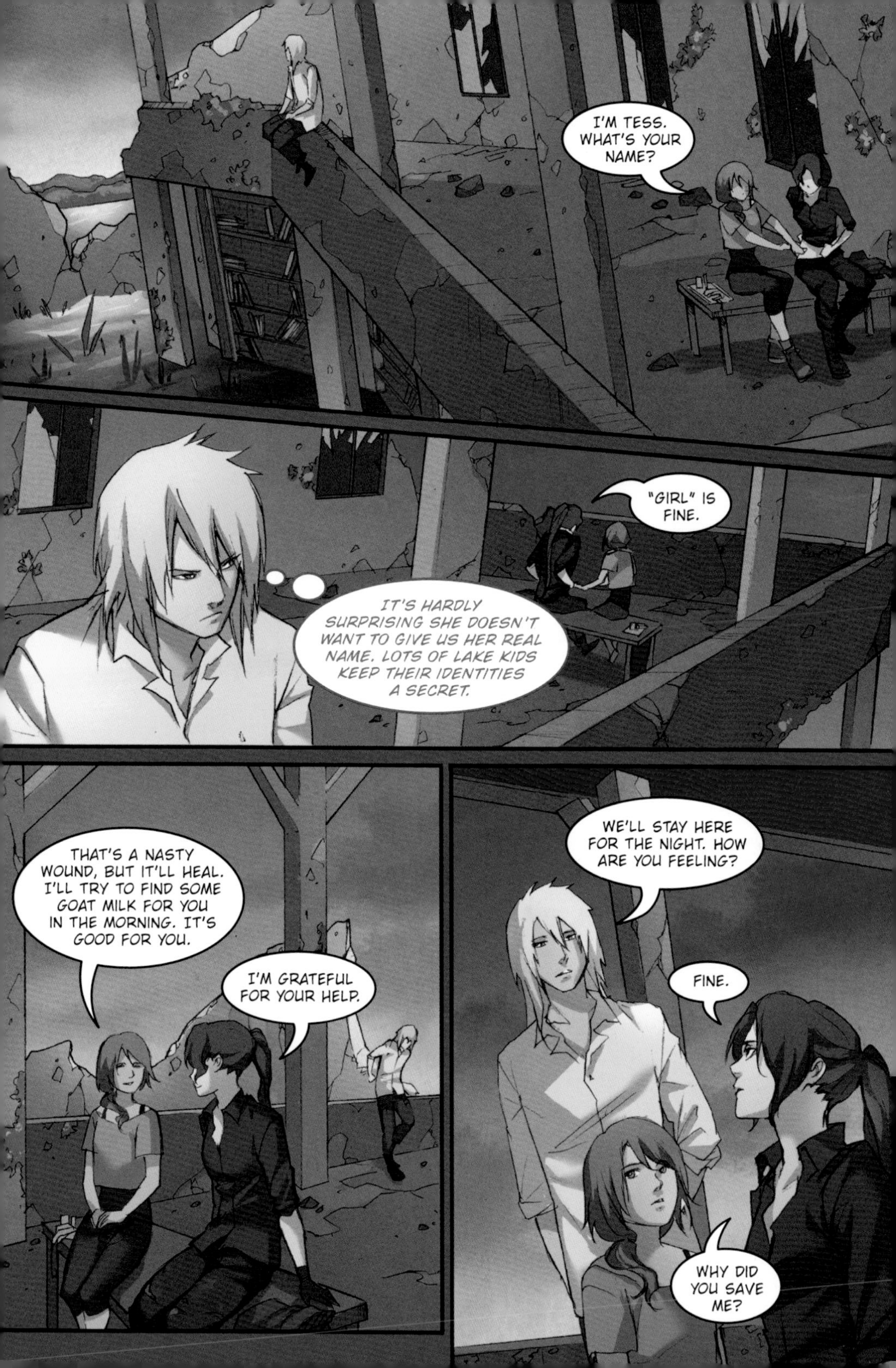
I'M TESS. WHAT'S YOUR NAME?
"GIRL" IS FINE.
IT'S HARDLY SURPRISING SHE DOESN'T WANT TO GIVE US HER REAL NAME. LOTS OF LAKE KIDS KEEP THEIR IDENTITIES A SECRET.
THAT'S A NASTY WOUND, BUT IT'LL HEAL. I'LL TRY TO FIND SOME GOAT MILK FOR YOU IN THE MORNING. IT'S GOOD FOR YOU.
I'M GRATEFUL FOR YOUR HELP.
WE'LL STAY HERE FOR THE NIGHT. HOW ARE YOU FEELING?
FINE.
WHY DID YOU SAVE ME?

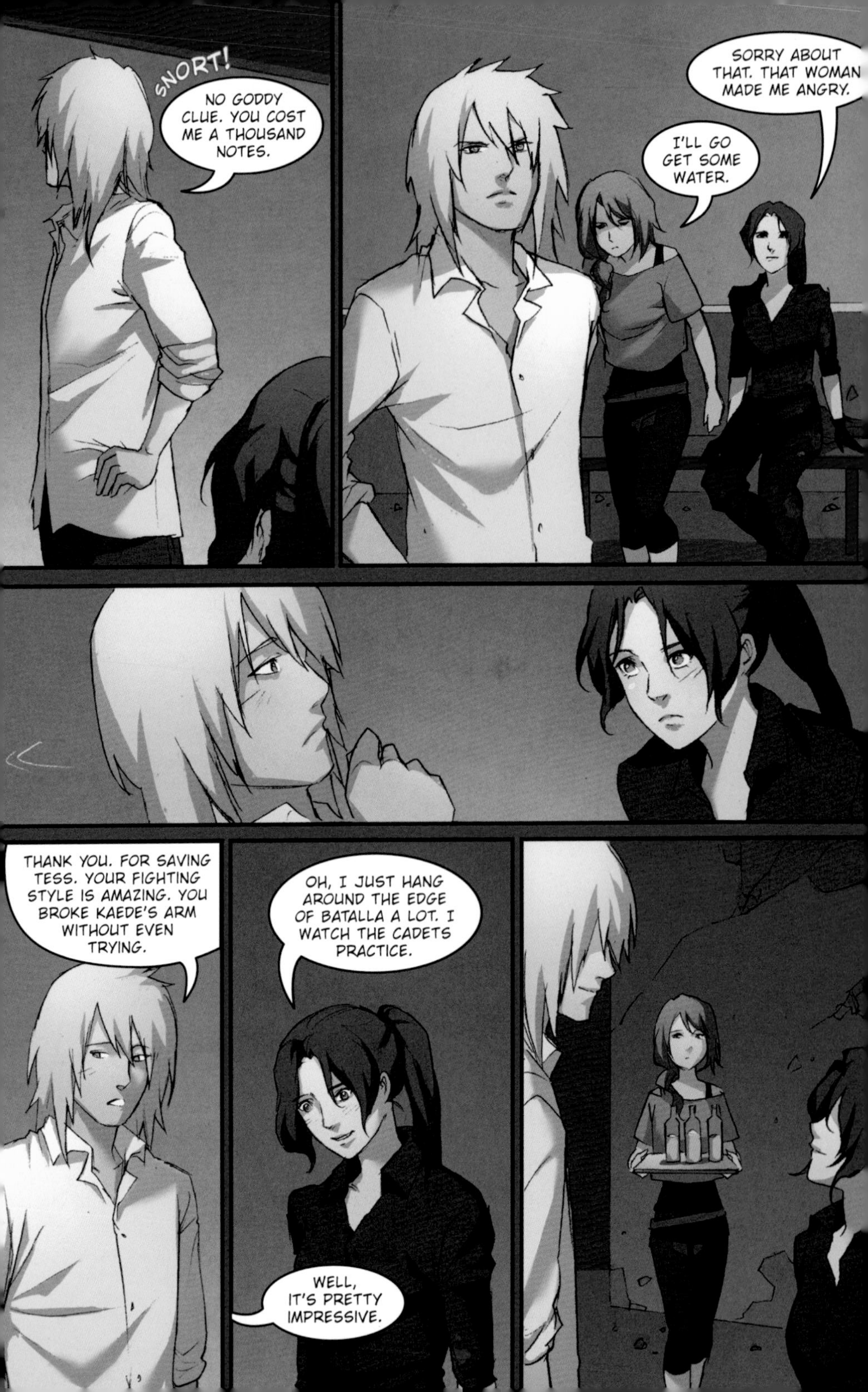
SNORT!
NO GODDY CLUE. YOU COST ME A THOUSAND NOTES.
SORRY ABOUT THAT. THAT WOMAN MADE ME ANGRY.
I'LL GO GET SOME WATER.
THANK YOU. FOR SAVING TESS. YOUR FIGHTING STYLE IS AMAZING. YOU BROKE KAEDE'S ARM WITHOUT EVEN TRYING.
OH, I JUST HANG AROUND THE EDGE OF BATALLA A LOT. I WATCH THE CADETS PRACTICE.
WELL, IT'S PRETTY IMPRESSIVE.

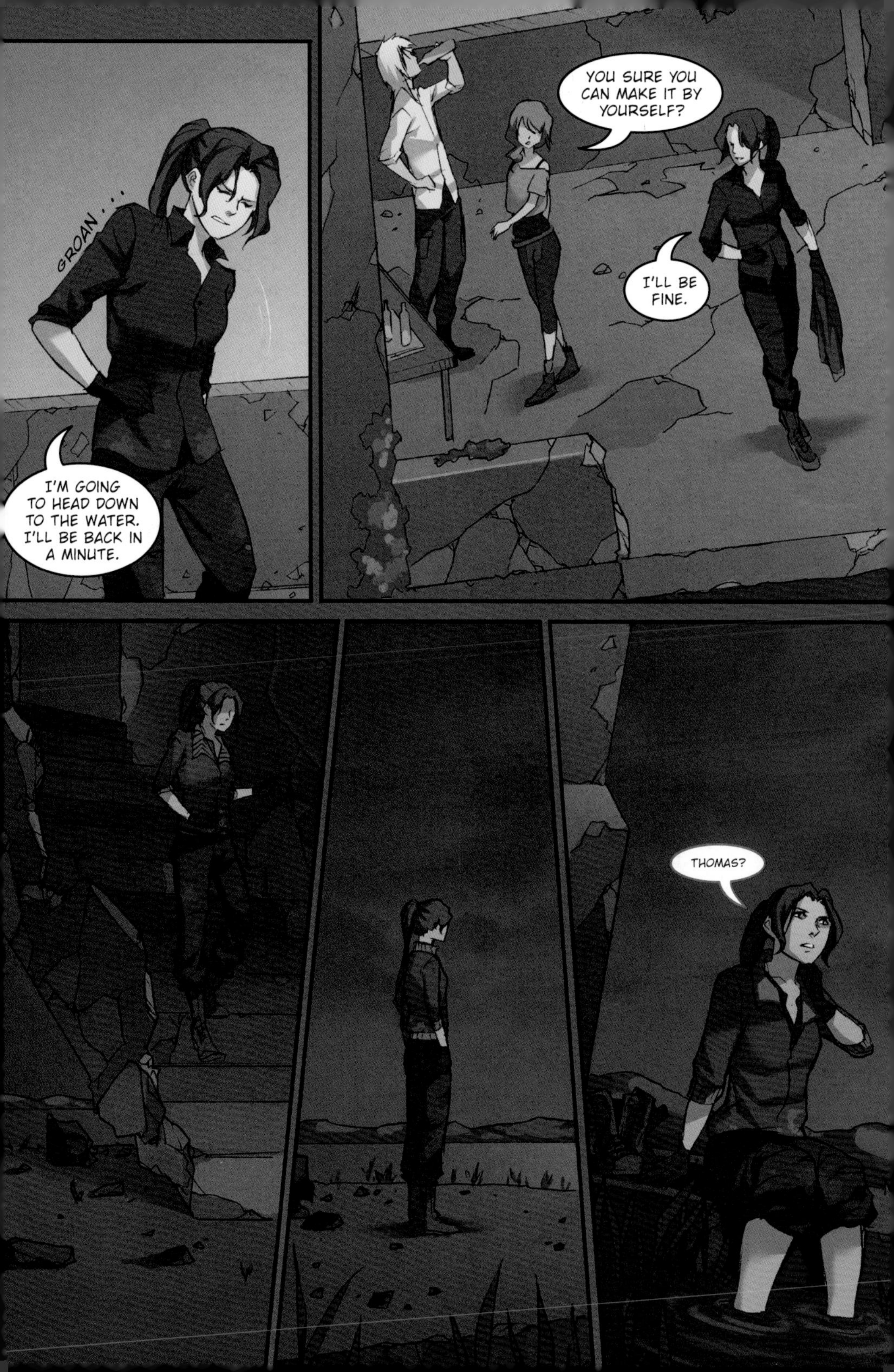
GROAN . . .
I'M GOING TO HEAD DOWN TO THE WATER. I'LL BE BACK IN A MINUTE.
YOU SURE YOU CAN MAKE IT BY YOURSELF?
I'LL BE FINE.
THOMAS?

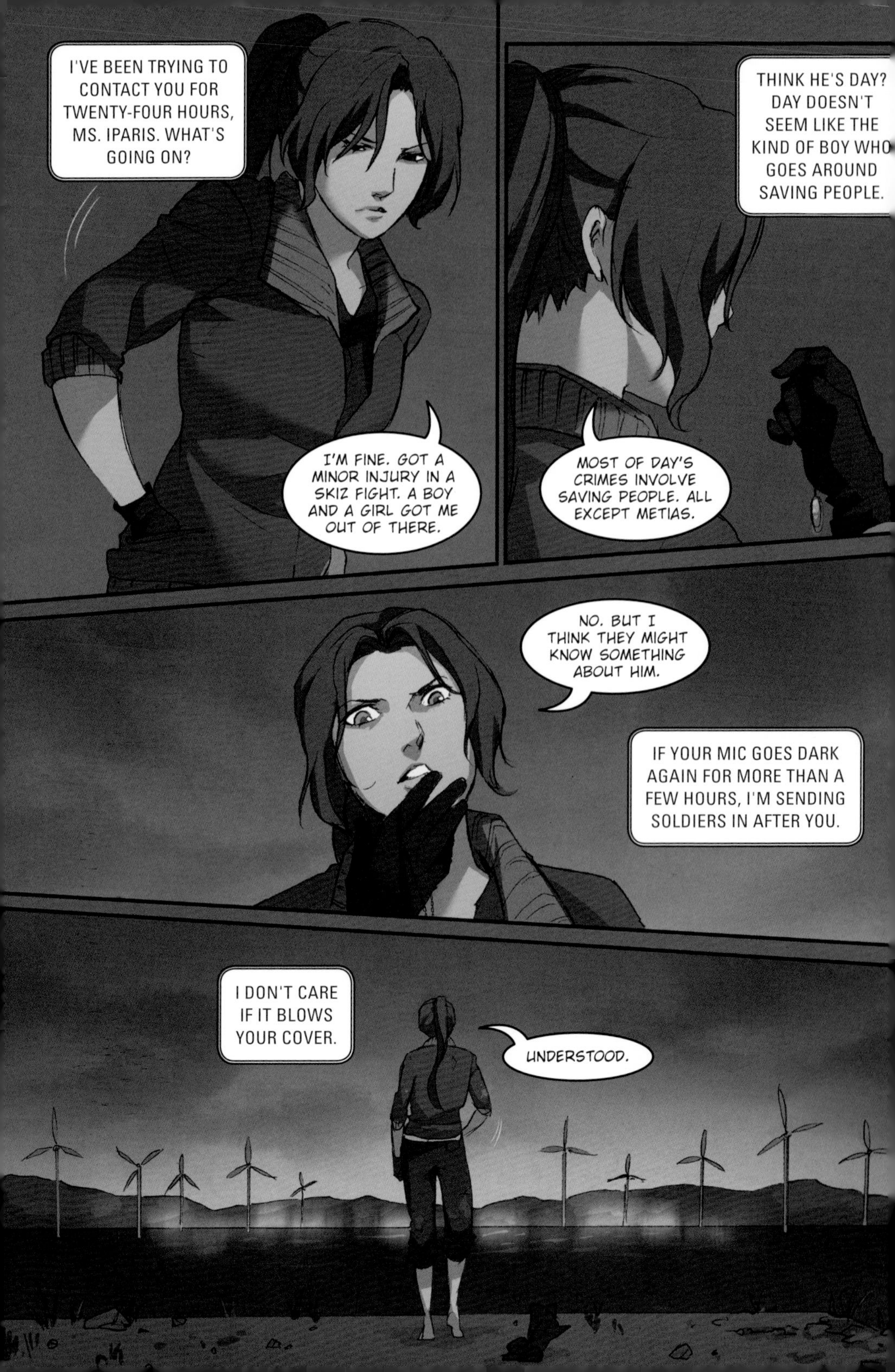
I'VE BEEN TRYING TO CONTACT YOU FOR TWENTY-FOUR HOURS, MS. IPARIS. WHAT'S GOING ON?
I'M FINE. GOT A MINOR INJURY IN A SKIZ FIGHT. A BOY AND A GIRL GOT ME OUT OF THERE.
THINK HE'S DAY? DAY DOESN'T SEEM LIKE THE KIND OF BOY WHO GOES AROUND SAVING PEOPLE.
MOST OF DAY'S CRIMES INVOLVE SAVING PEOPLE. ALL EXCEPT METIAS.
NO. BUT I THINK THEY MIGHT KNOW SOMETHING ABOUT HIM.
IF YOUR MIC GOES DARK AGAIN FOR MORE THAN A FEW HOURS, I'M SENDING SOLDIERS IN AFTER YOU.
I DON'T CARE IF IT BLOWS YOUR COVER.
UNDERSTOOD.

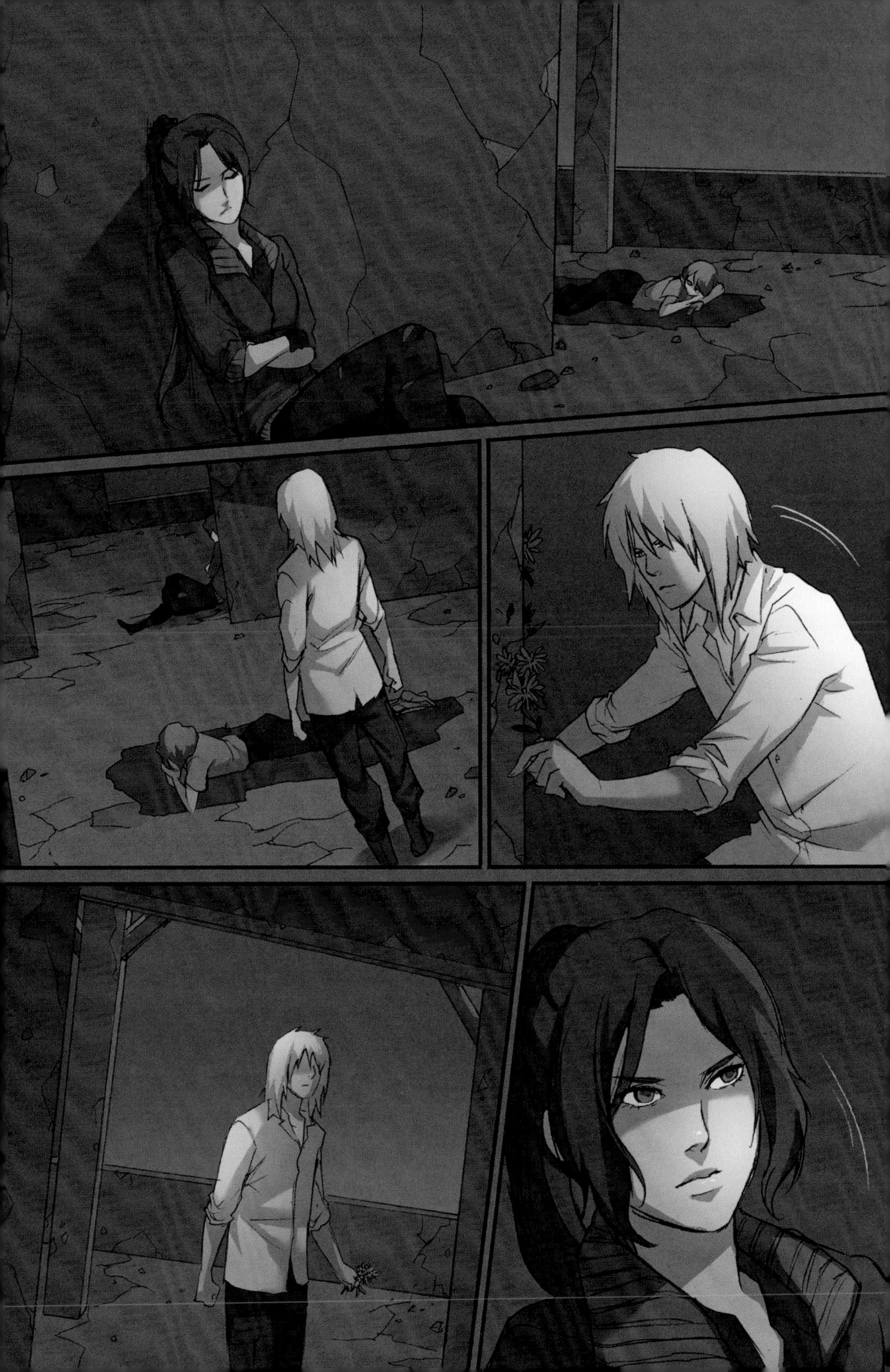

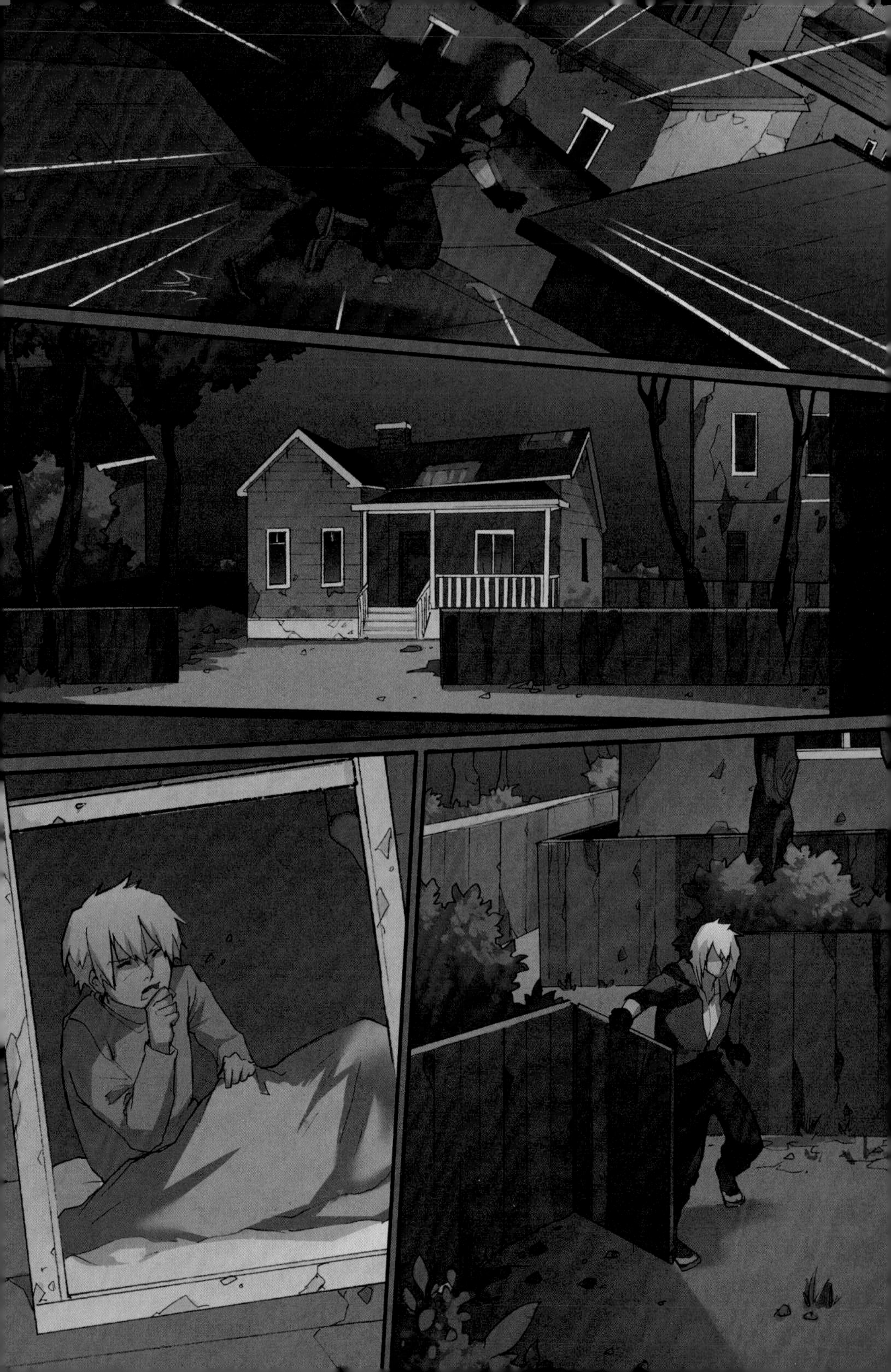

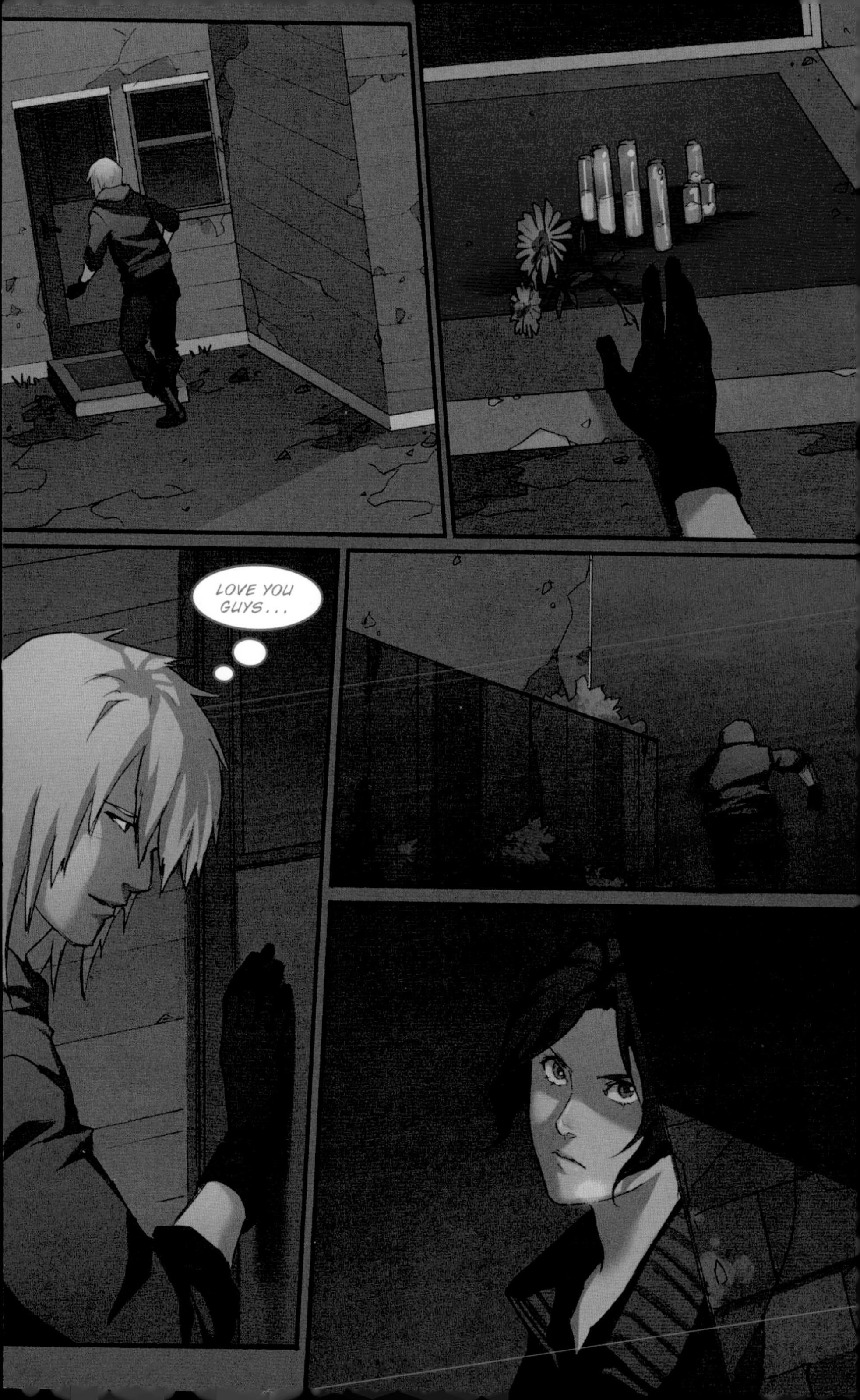
LOVE YOU GUYS . . .

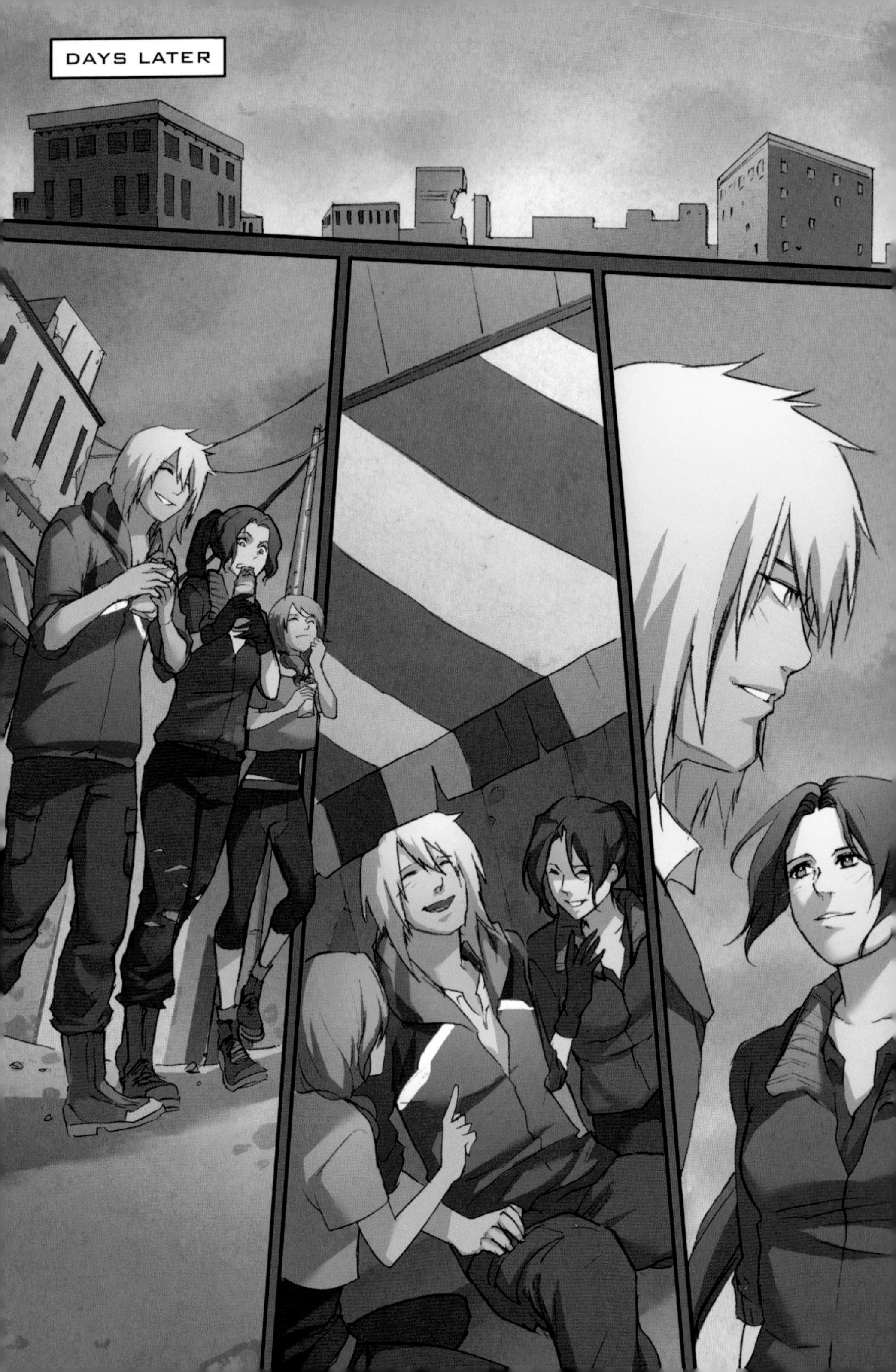
DAYS LATER

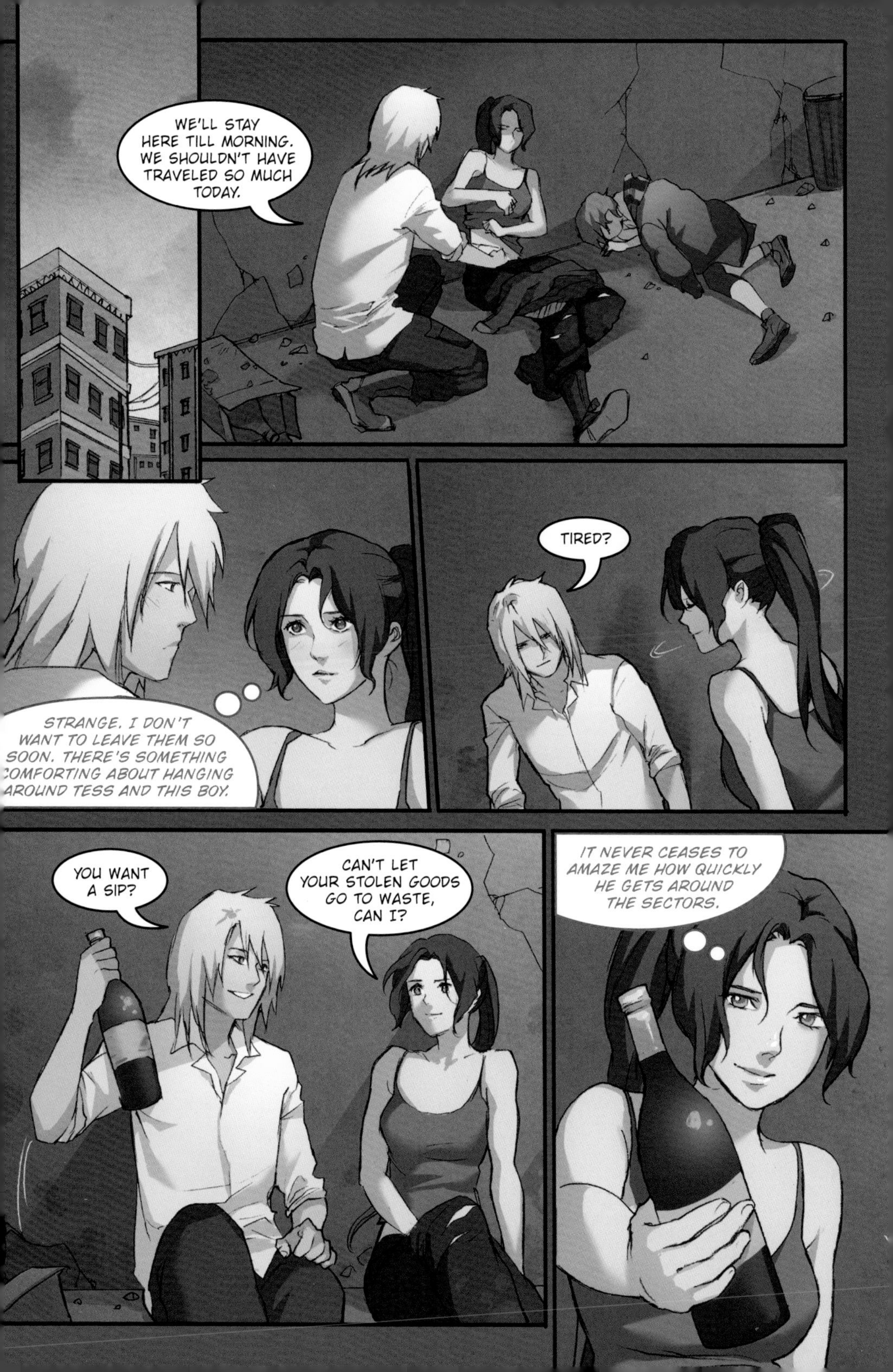
WE'LL STAY HERE TILL MORNING. WE SHOULDN'T HAVE TRAVELED SO MUCH TODAY.
STRANGE. I DON'T WANT TO LEAVE THEM SO SOON. THERE'S SOMETHING COMFORTING ABOUT HANGING AROUND TESS AND THIS BOY.
TIRED?
YOU WANT A SIP?
CAN'T LET YOUR STOLEN GOODS GO TO WASTE, CAN I?
IT NEVER CEASES TO AMAZE ME HOW QUICKLY HE GETS AROUND THE SECTORS.

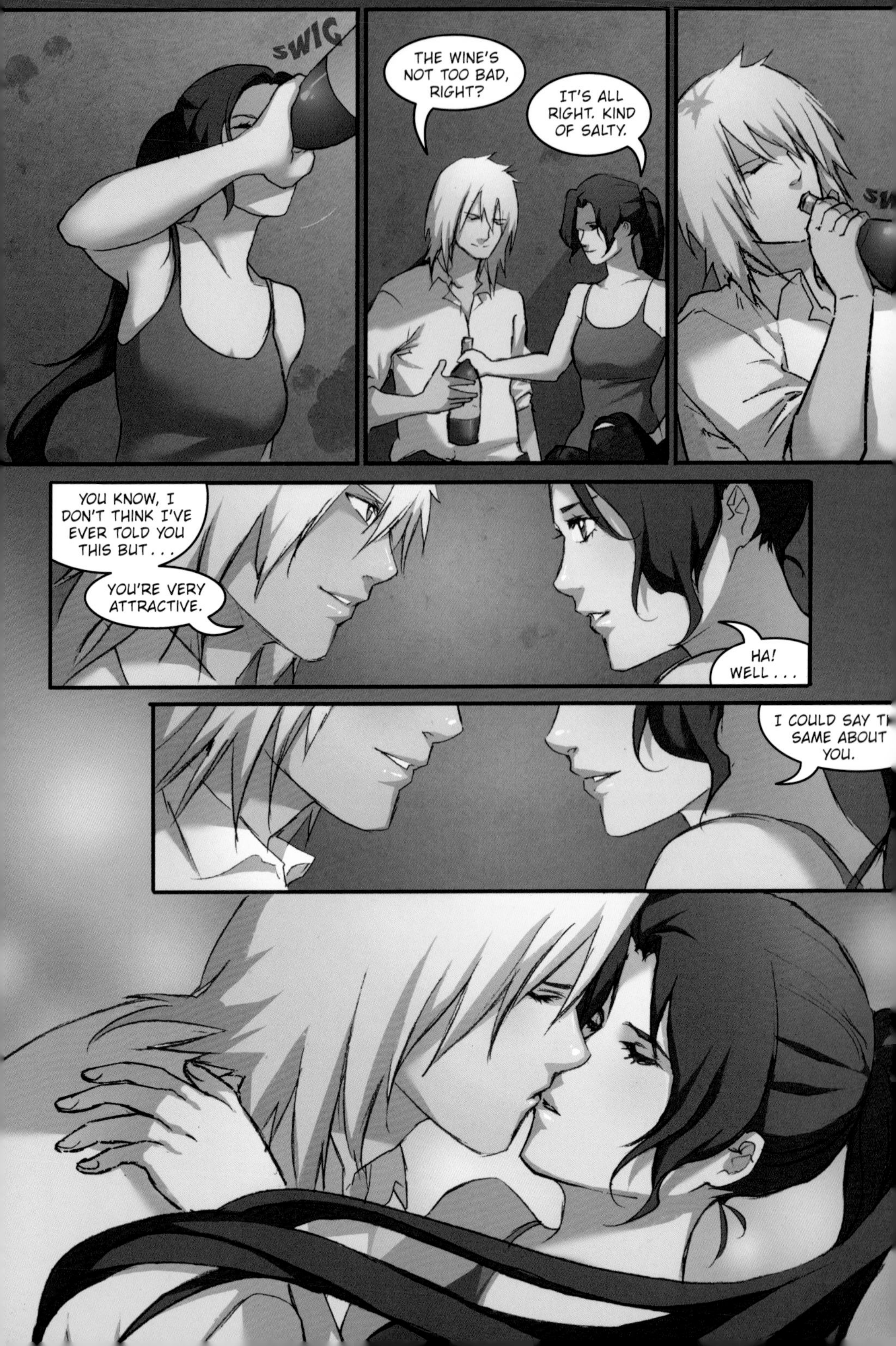
SWIG
THE WINE'S NOT TOO BAD, RIGHT?
IT'S ALL RIGHT. KIND OF SALTY.
SWIG
YOU KNOW, I DON'T THINK I'VE EVER TOLD YOU THIS BUT . . .
YOU'RE VERY ATTRACTIVE.
HA! WELL . . .
I COULD SAY THE SAME ABOUT YOU.

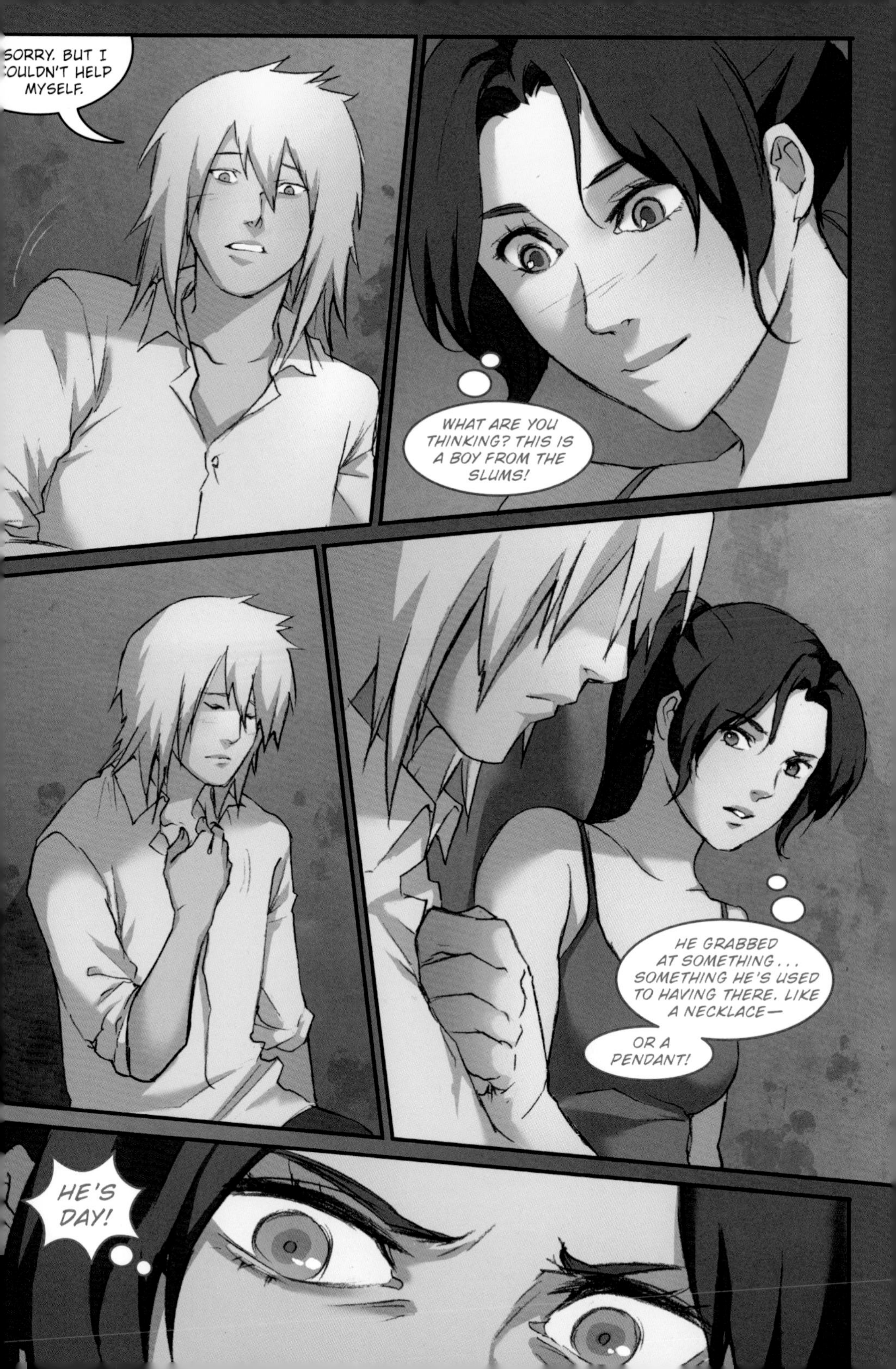
SORRY. BUT I COULDN'T HELP MYSELF.
WHAT ARE YOU THINKING? THIS IS A BOY FROM THE SLUMS!
HE GRABBED AT SOMETHING . . . SOMETHING HE'S USED TO HAVING THERE. LIKE A NECKLACE—
OR A PENDANT!
HE'S DAY!

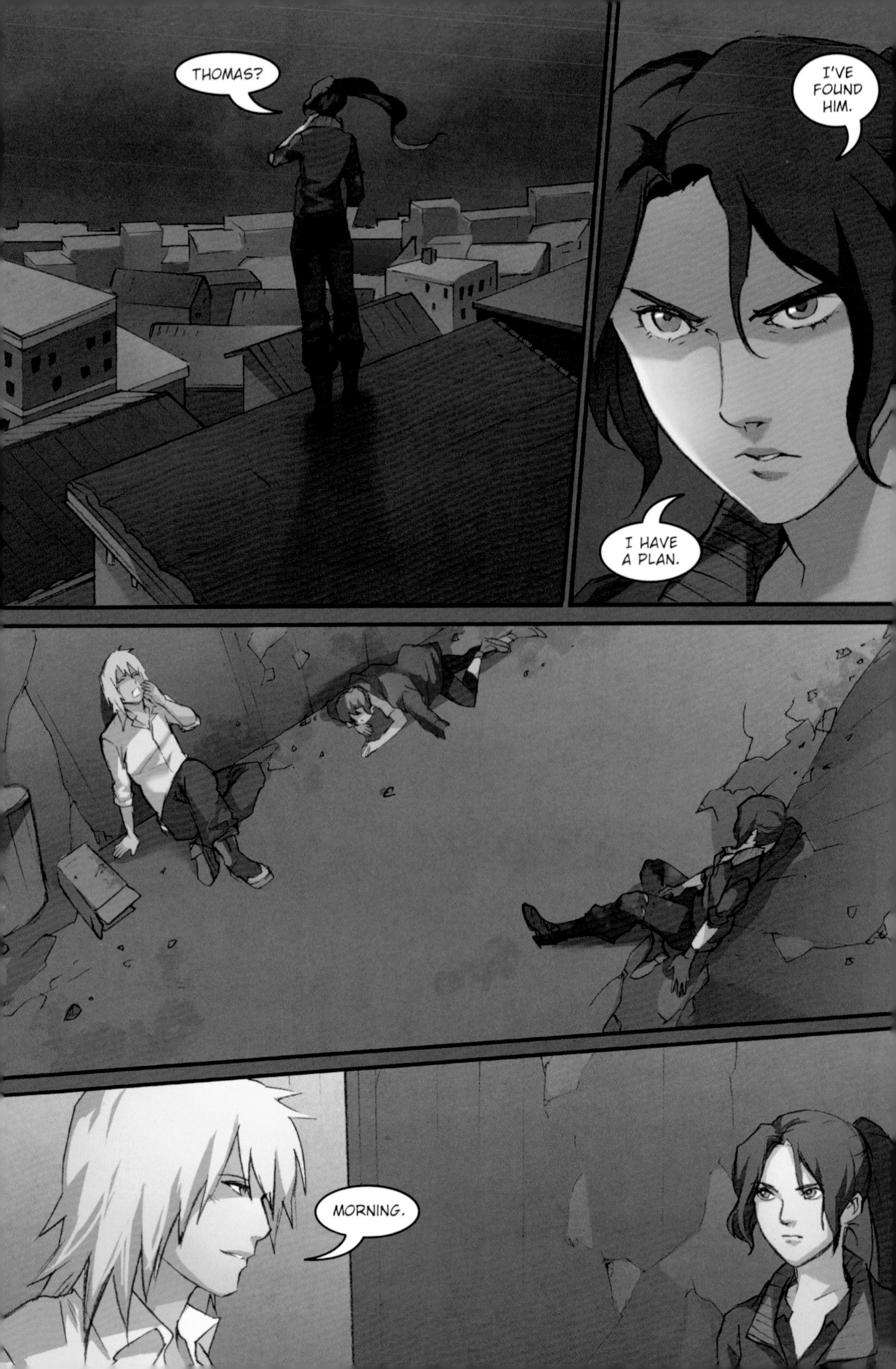
THOMAS?
I'VE FOUND HIM.
I HAVE A PLAN.
MORNING.

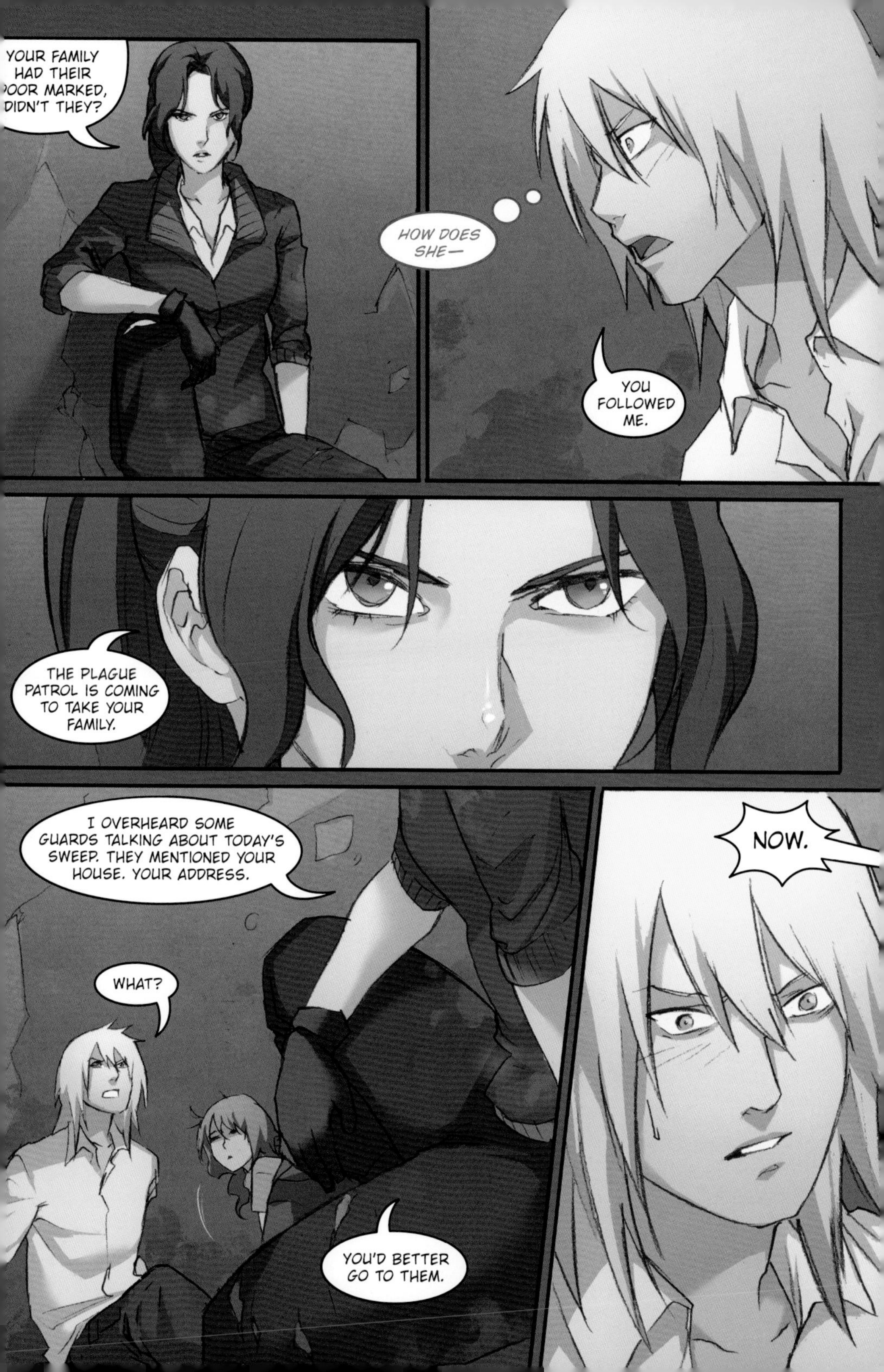
YOUR FAMILY HAD THEIR DOOR MARKED, DIDN'T THEY?
HOW DOES SHE—
YOU FOLLOWED ME.
THE PLAGUE PATROL IS COMING TO TAKE YOUR FAMILY.
I OVERHEARD SOME GUARDS TALKING ABOUT TODAY'S SWEEP. THEY MENTIONED YOUR HOUSE. YOUR ADDRESS.
WHAT?
YOU'D BETTER GO TO THEM.
NOW.

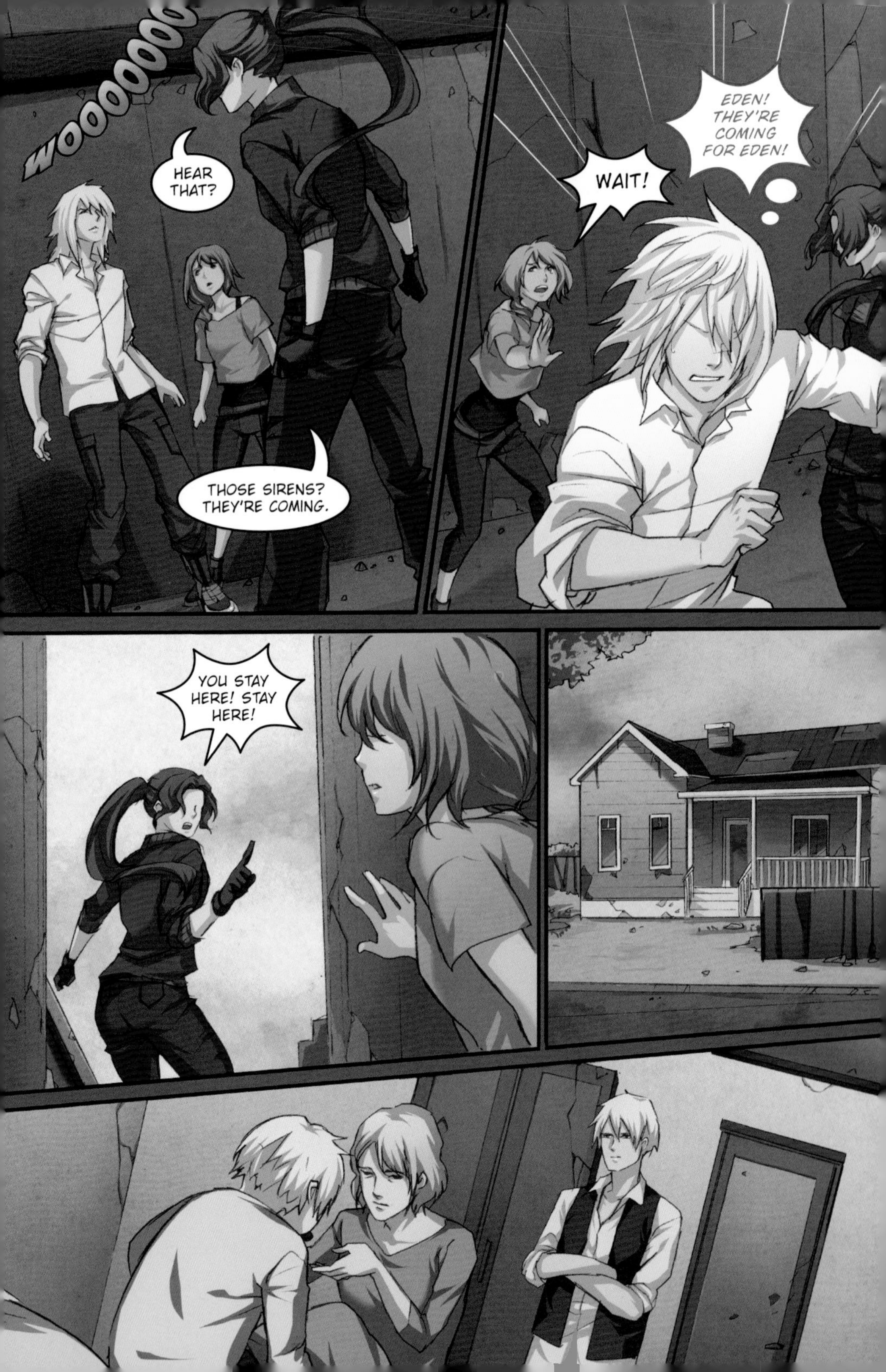
WOOOOOOO
HEAR THAT?
THOSE SIRENS? THEY'RE COMING.
WAIT!
EDEN! THEY'RE COMING FOR EDEN!
YOU STAY HERE! STAY HERE!

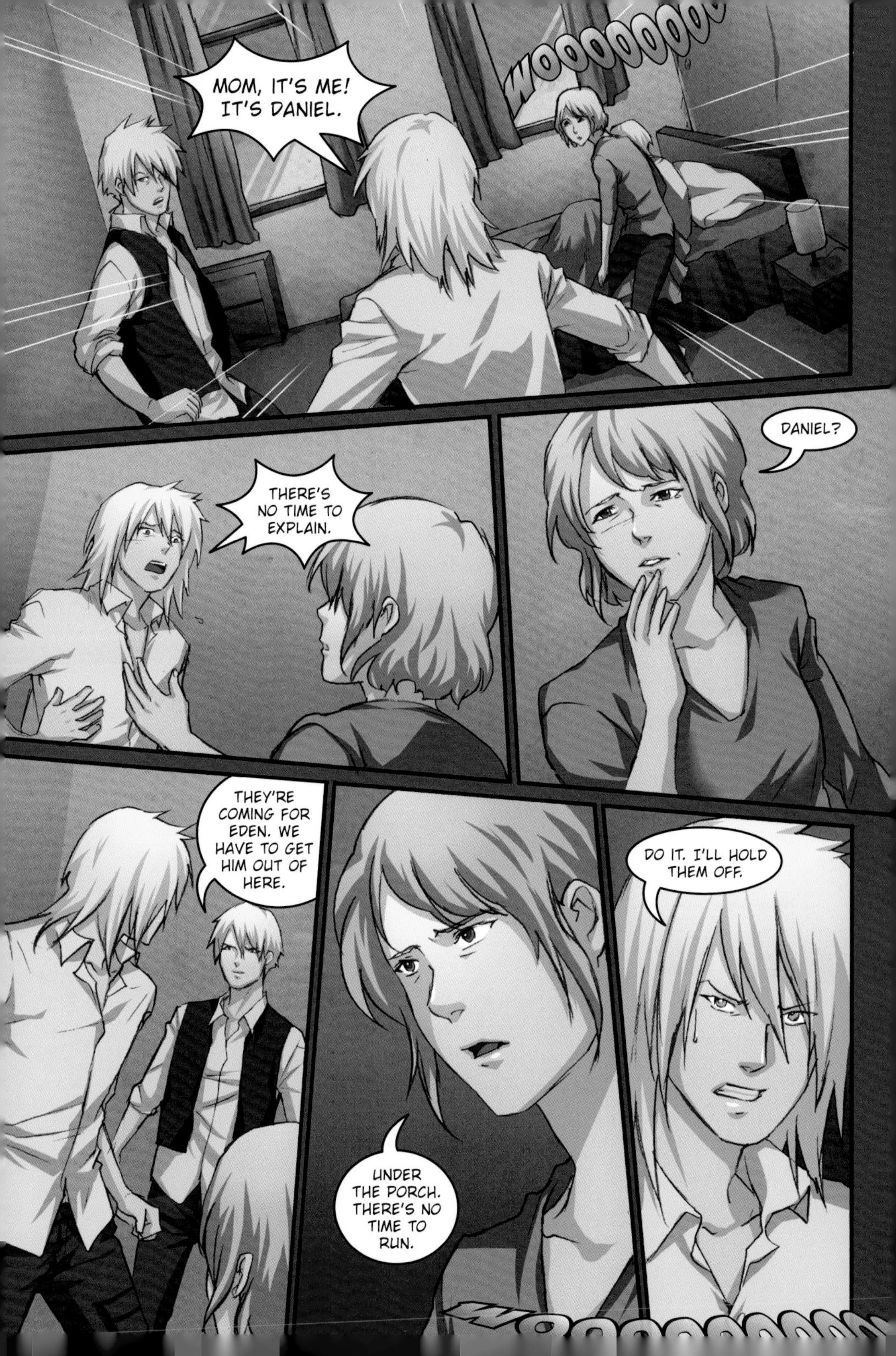
MOM, IT'S ME! IT'S DANIEL.
WOOOOOOOO
THERE'S NO TIME TO EXPLAIN.
DANIEL?
THEY'RE COMING FOR EDEN. WE HAVE TO GET HIM OUT OF HERE.
UNDER THE PORCH. THERE'S NO TIME TO RUN.
DO IT. I'LL HOLD THEM OFF.
WOOOOOOOOO

NRREEEEEEZZ

KRAK!

CRASH!

DAMN!
WHAT THE
HELL—

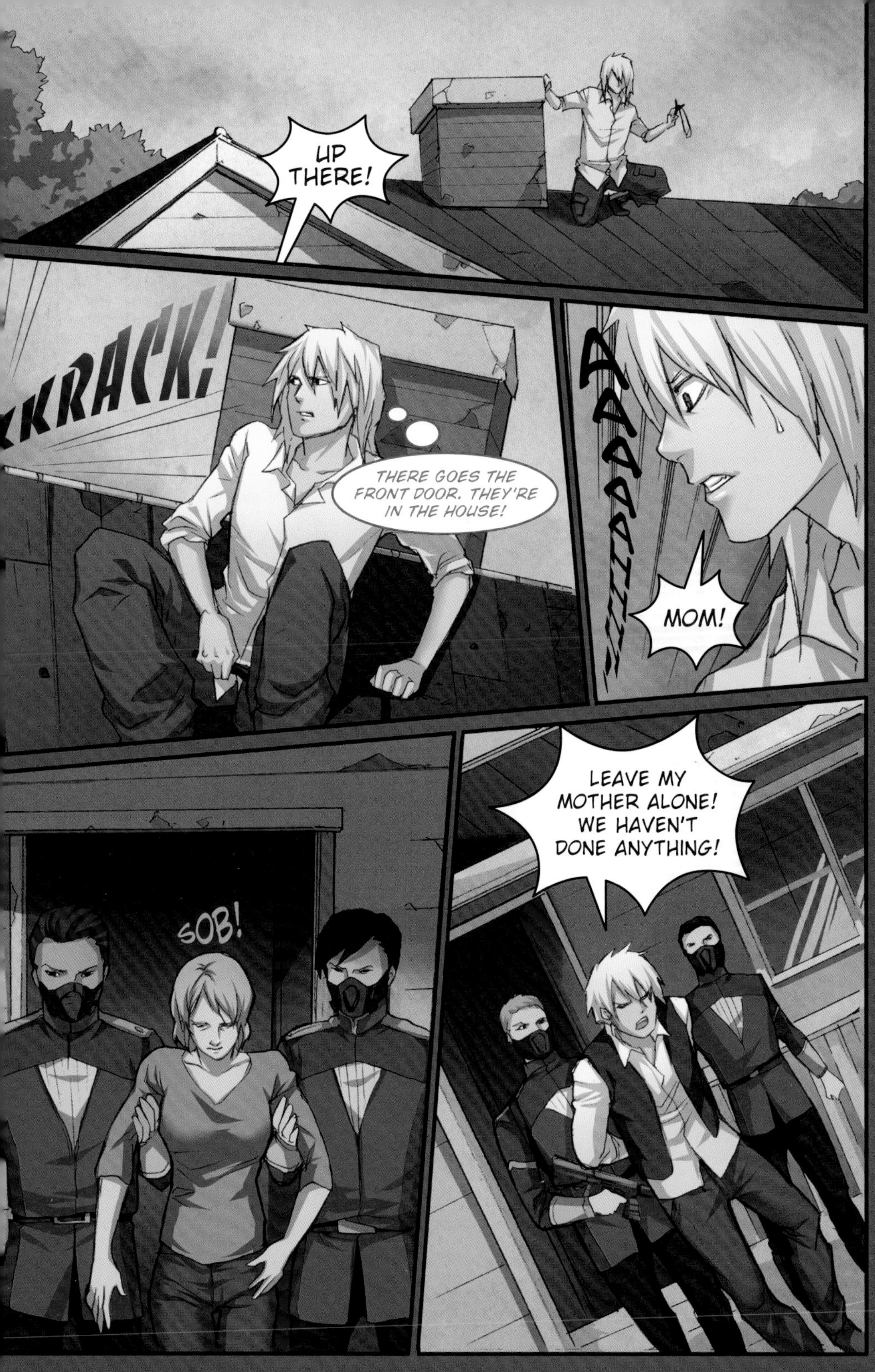
UP THERE!
KKRACK!
THERE GOES THE FRONT DOOR. THEY'RE IN THE HOUSE!
AAAAAHH!
MOM!
SOB!
LEAVE MY MOTHER ALONE! WE HAVEN'T DONE ANYTHING!

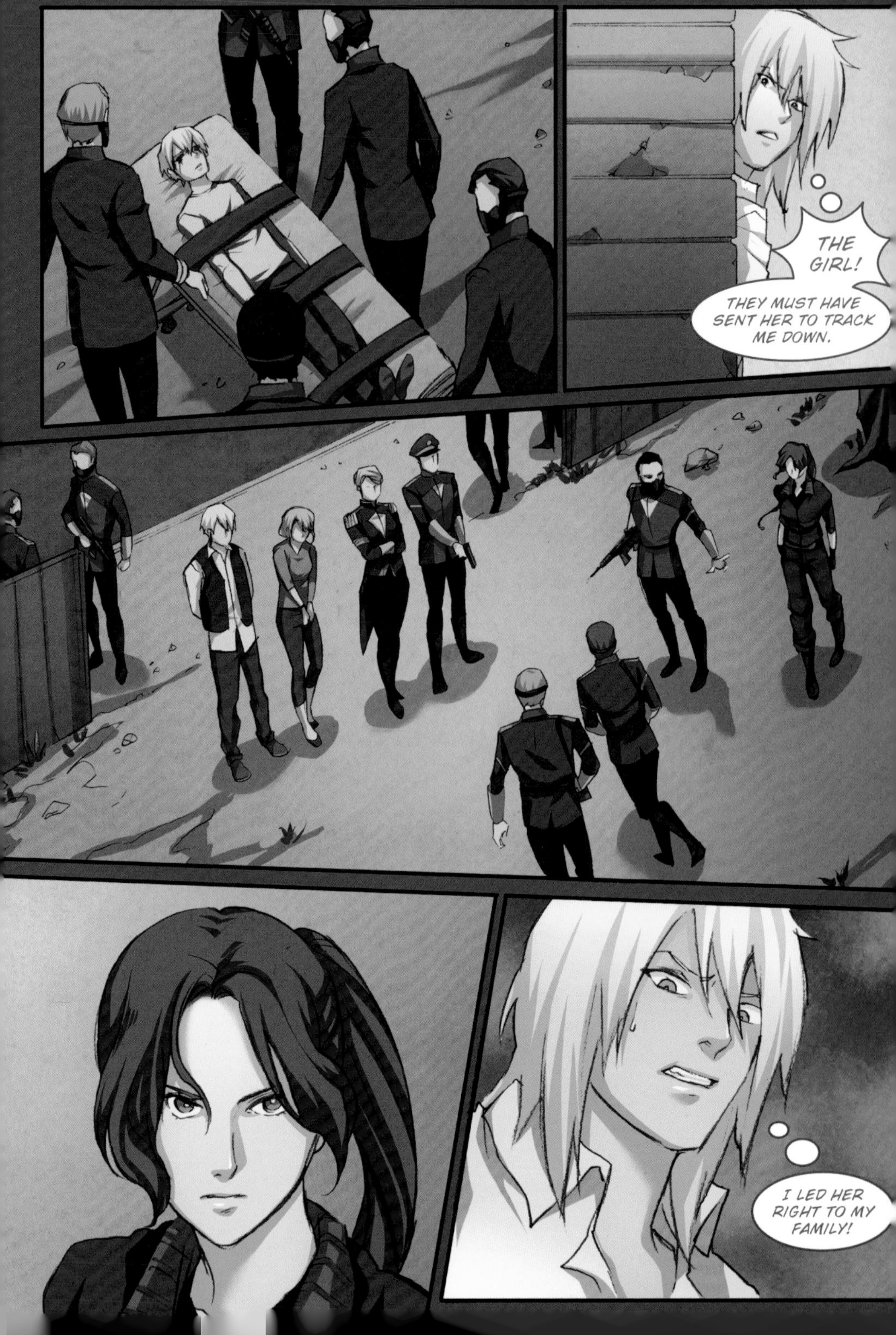
THE GIRL!
THEY MUST HAVE SENT HER TO TRACK ME DOWN.
I LED HER RIGHT TO MY FAMILY!

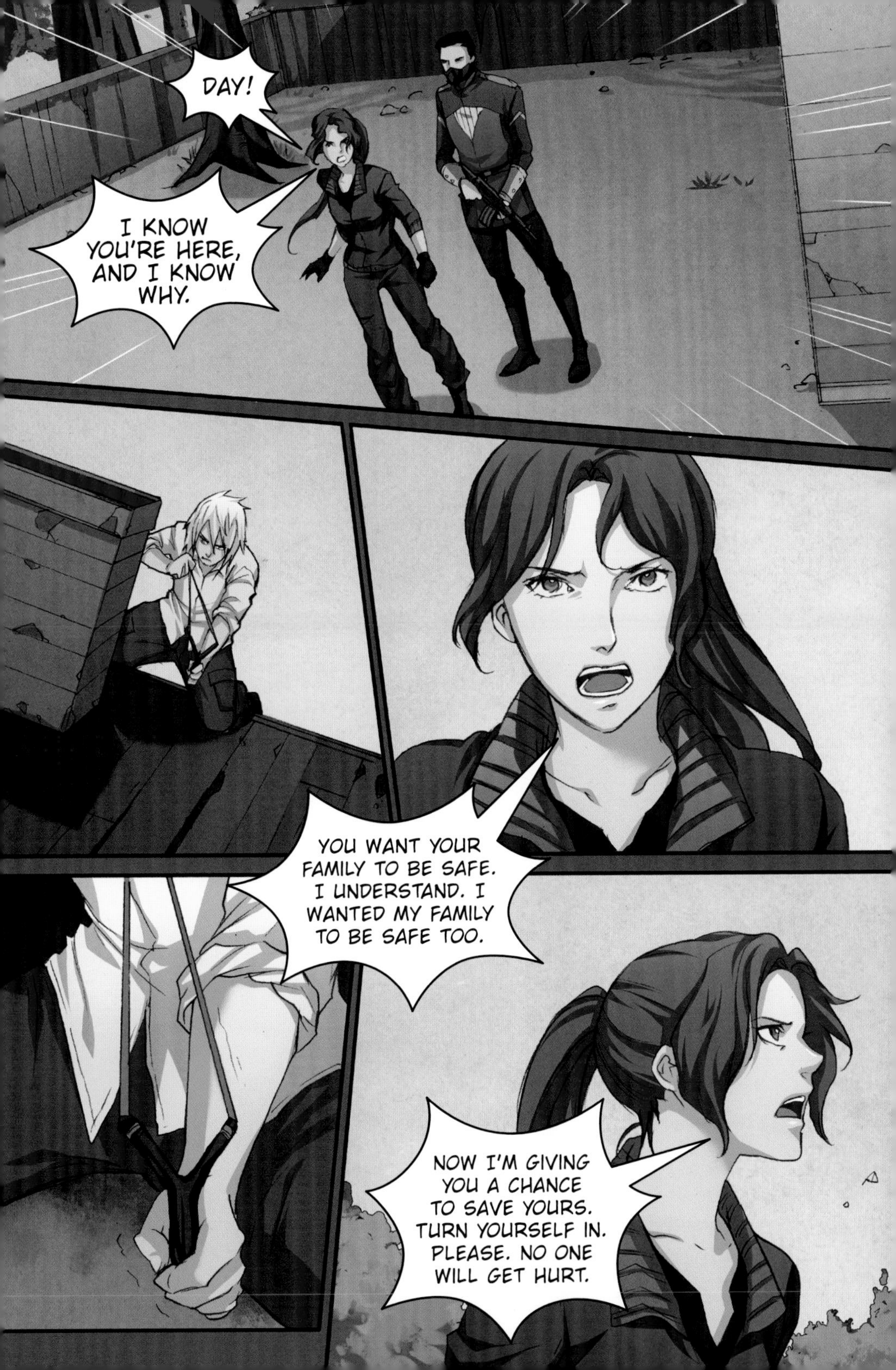
DAY!
I KNOW YOU'RE HERE, AND I KNOW WHY.
YOU WANT YOUR FAMILY TO BE SAFE. I UNDERSTAND. I WANTED MY FAMILY TO BE SAFE TOO.
NOW I'M GIVING YOU A CHANCE TO SAVE YOURS. TURN YOURSELF IN. PLEASE. NO ONE WILL GET HURT.

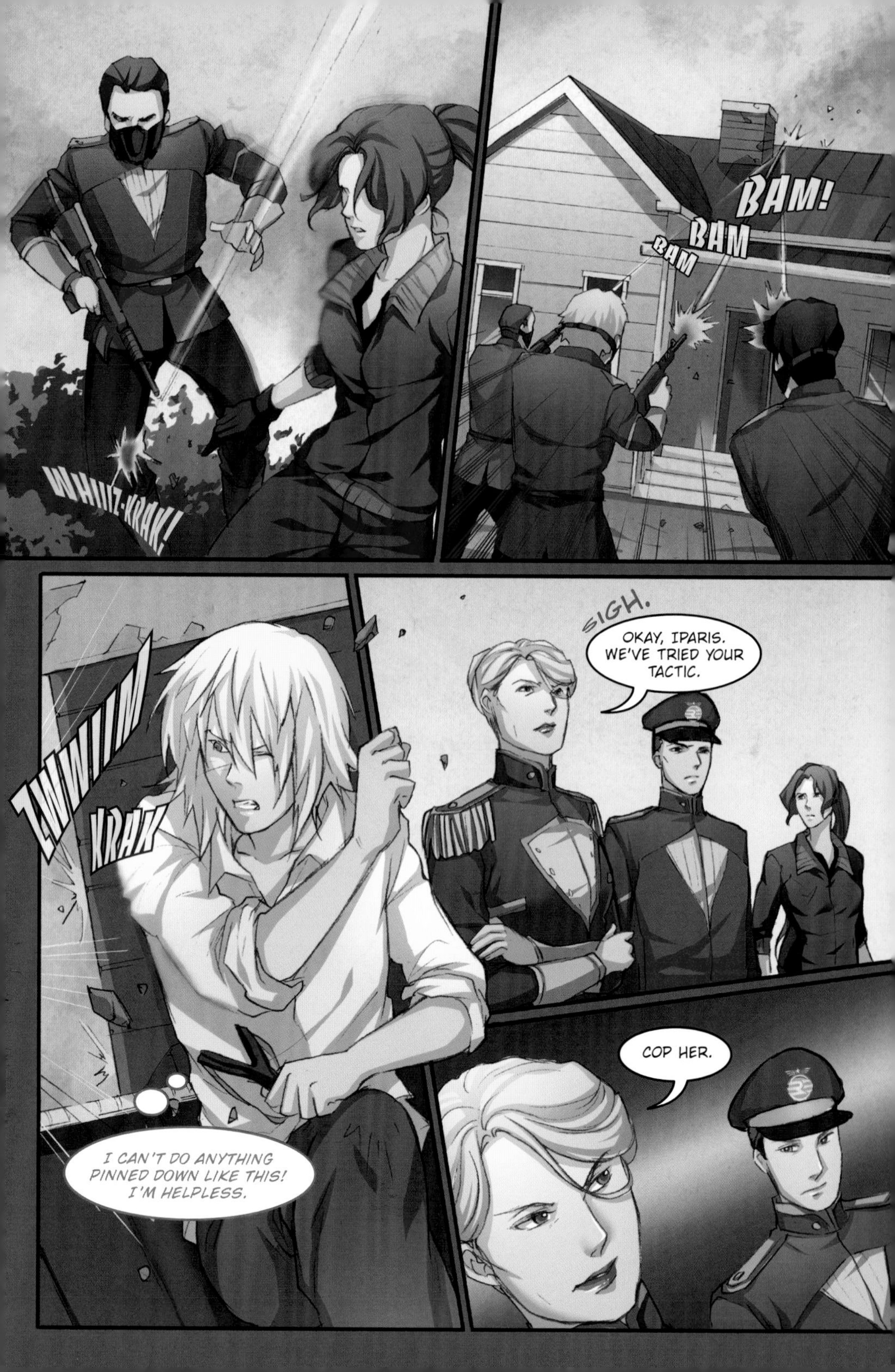
WHUZ-KRAK!
BAM
BAM
BAM!
ZWWIIM
KRAK
I CAN'T DO ANYTHING PINNED DOWN LIKE THIS! I'M HELPLESS.
SIGH.
OKAY, IPARIS. WE'VE TRIED YOUR TACTIC.
COP HER.

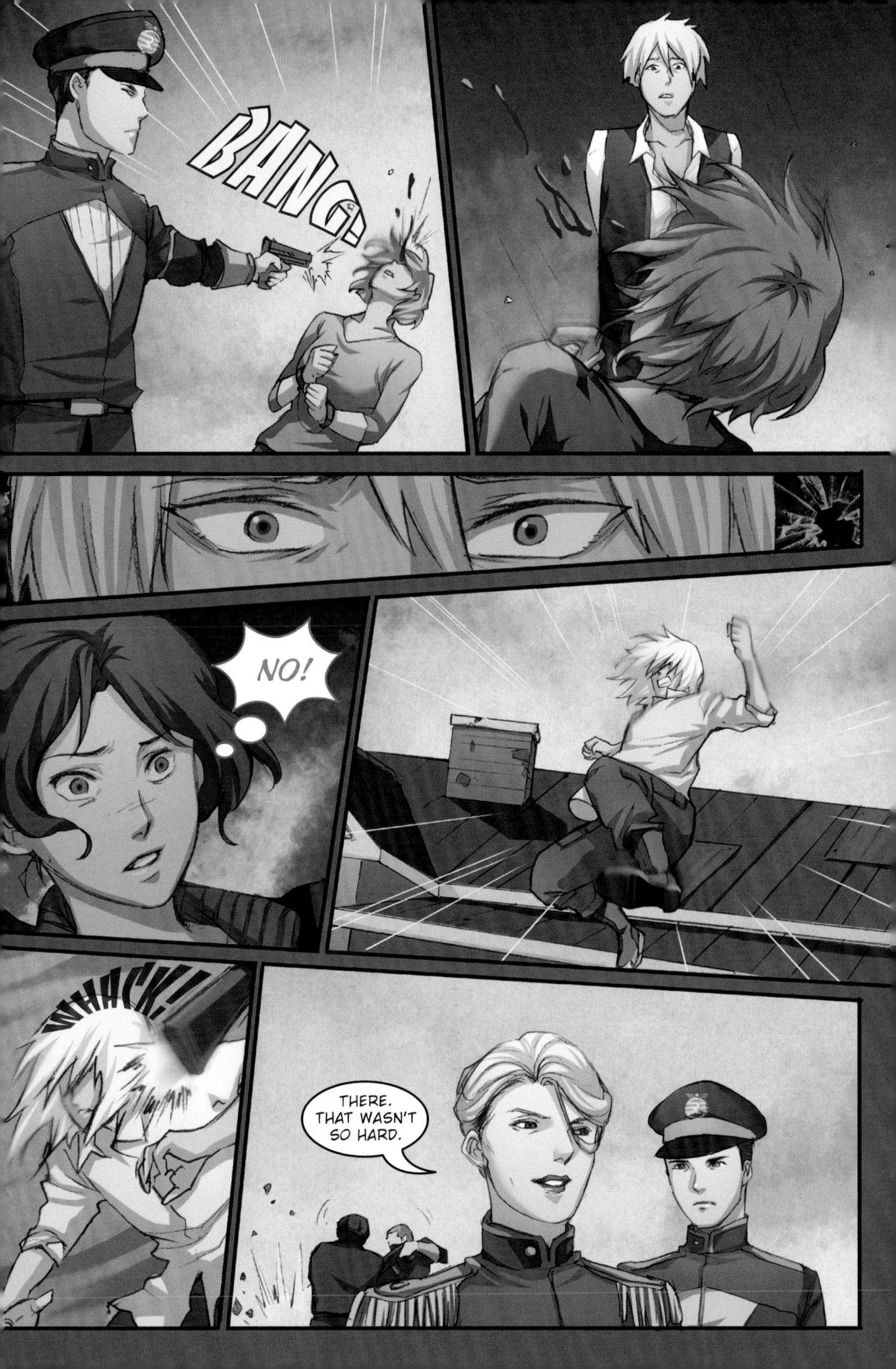
BANG!
NO!
WHACK!
THERE. THAT WASN'T SO HARD.

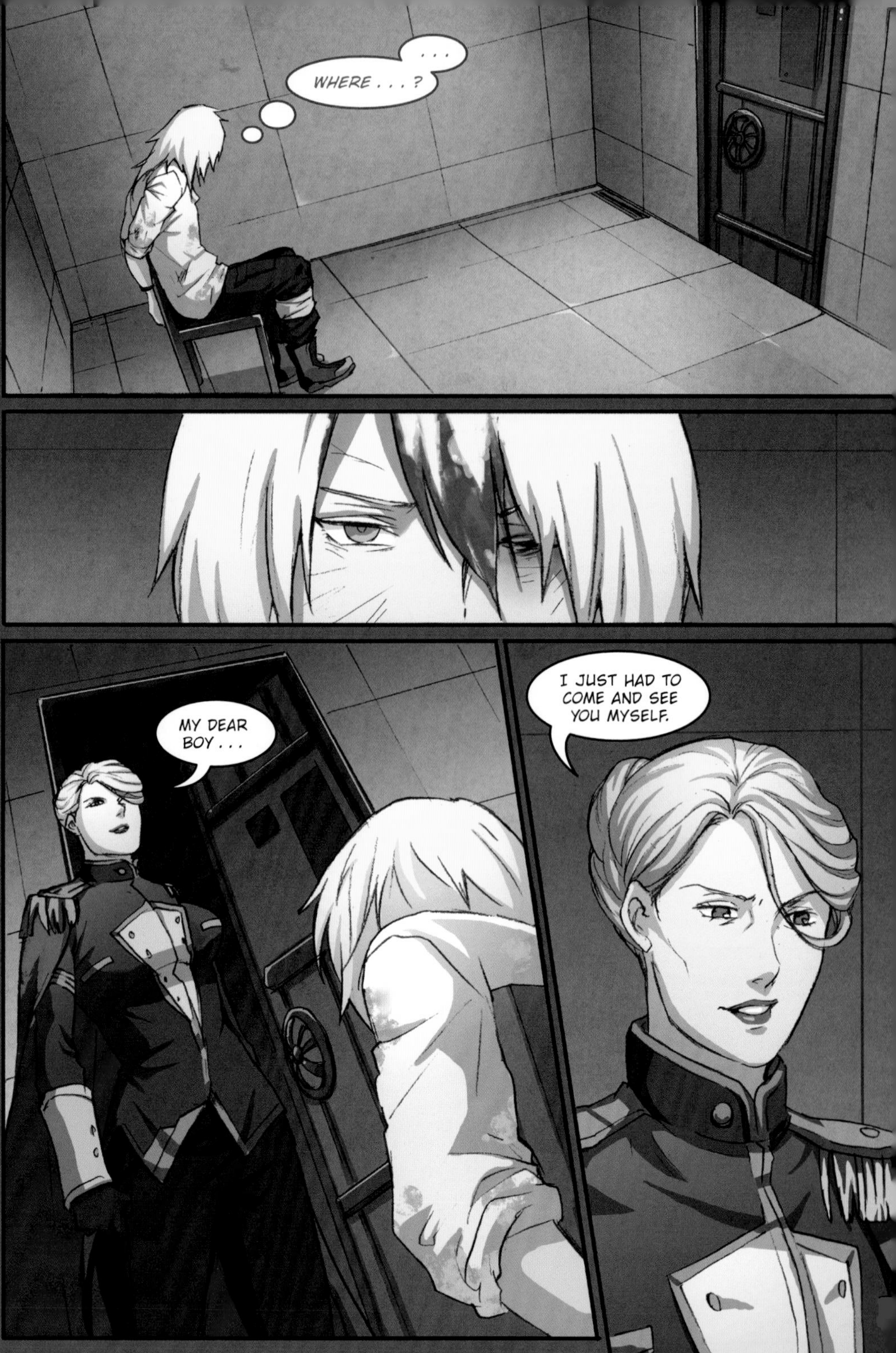
...
WHERE . . . ?
MY DEAR BOY . . .
I JUST HAD TO COME AND SEE YOU MYSELF.

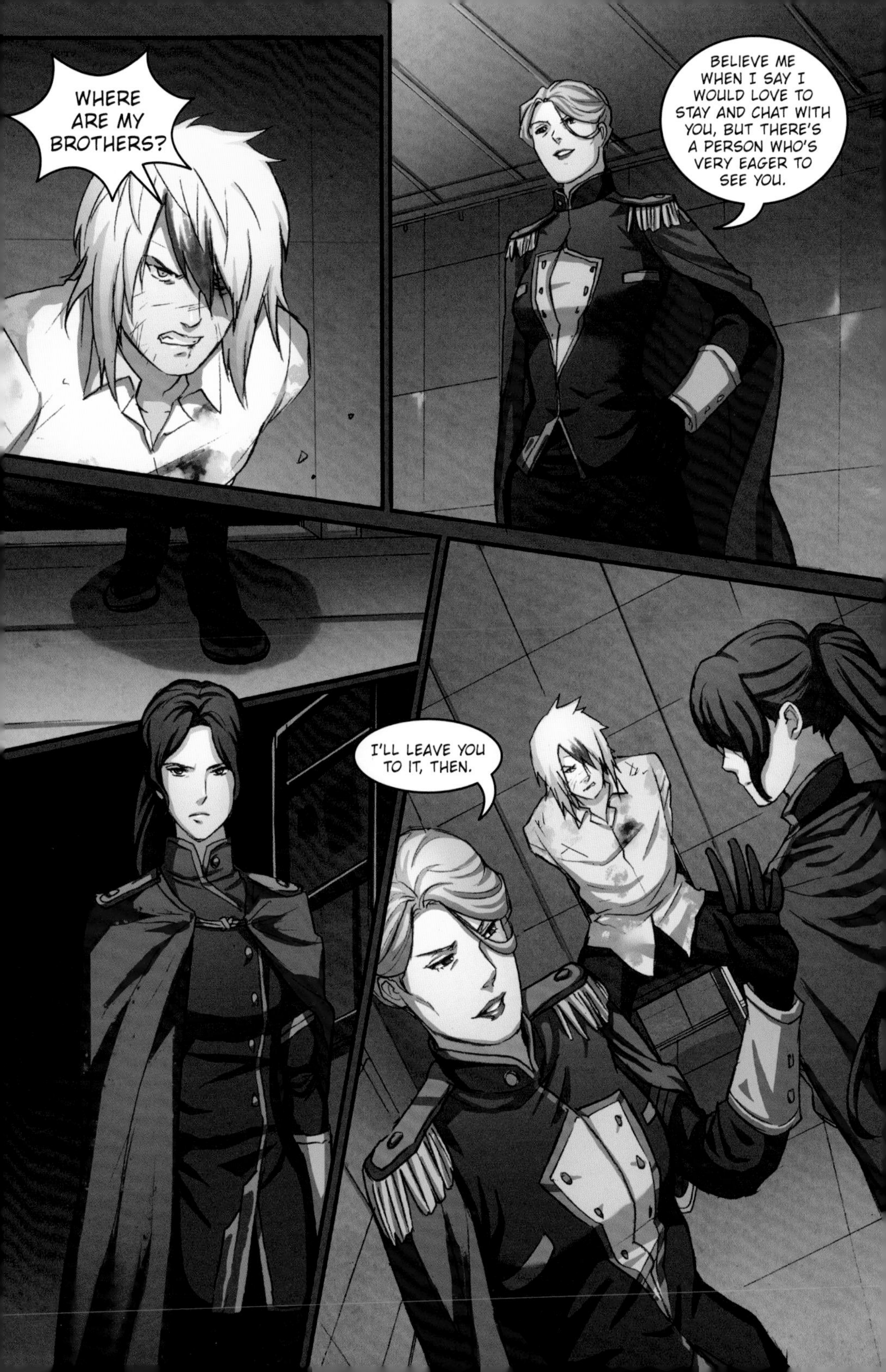
WHERE ARE MY BROTHERS?
BELIEVE ME WHEN I SAY I WOULD LOVE TO STAY AND CHAT WITH YOU, BUT THERE'S A PERSON WHO'S VERY EAGER TO SEE YOU.
I'LL LEAVE YOU TO IT, THEN.

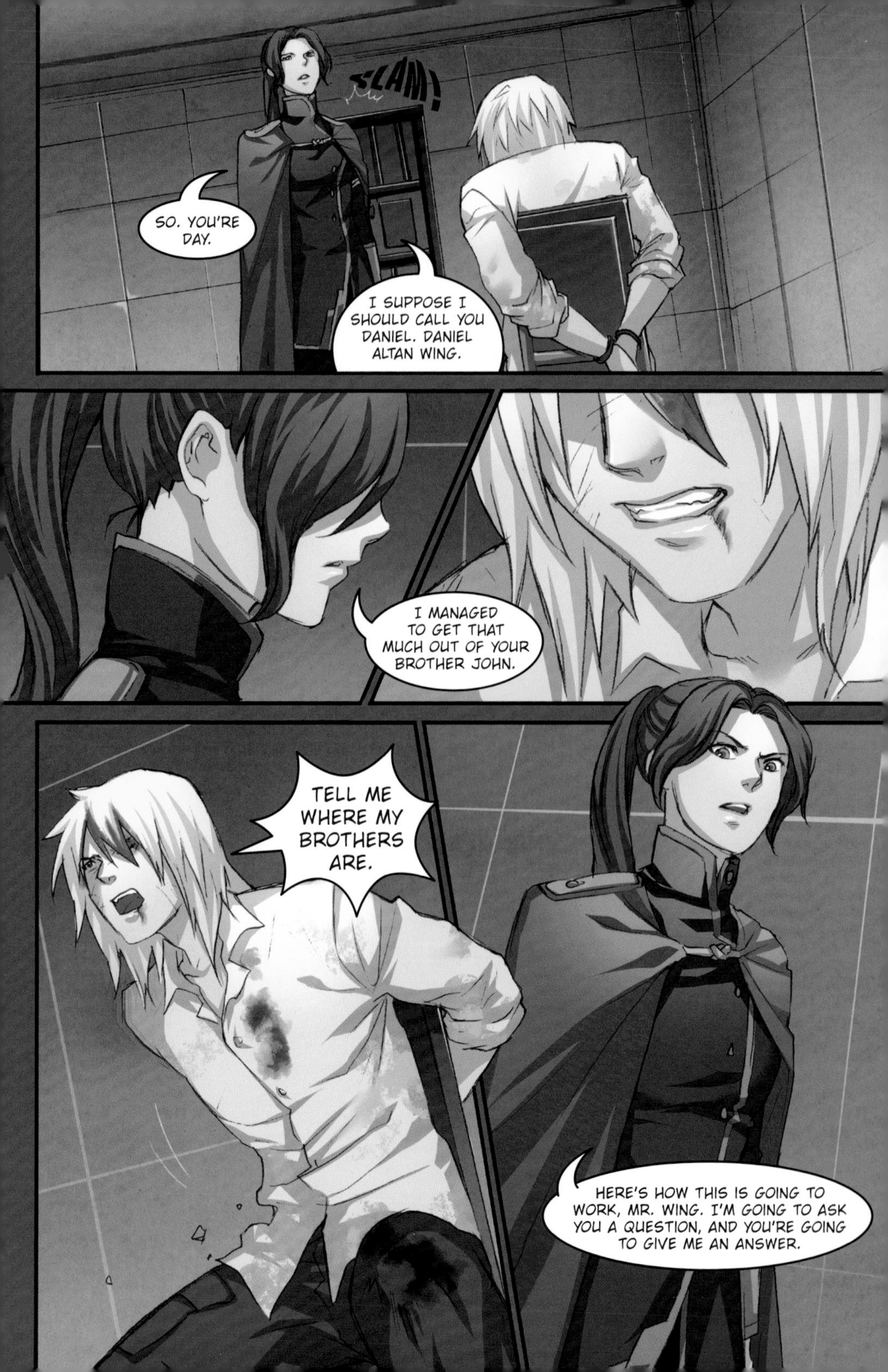
SLAM!
SO. YOU'RE DAY.
I SUPPOSE I SHOULD CALL YOU DANIEL. DANIEL ALTAN WING.
I MANAGED TO GET THAT MUCH OUT OF YOUR BROTHER JOHN.
TELL ME WHERE MY BROTHERS ARE.
HERE'S HOW THIS IS GOING TO WORK, MR. WING. I'M GOING TO ASK YOU A QUESTION, AND YOU'RE GOING TO GIVE ME AN ANSWER.

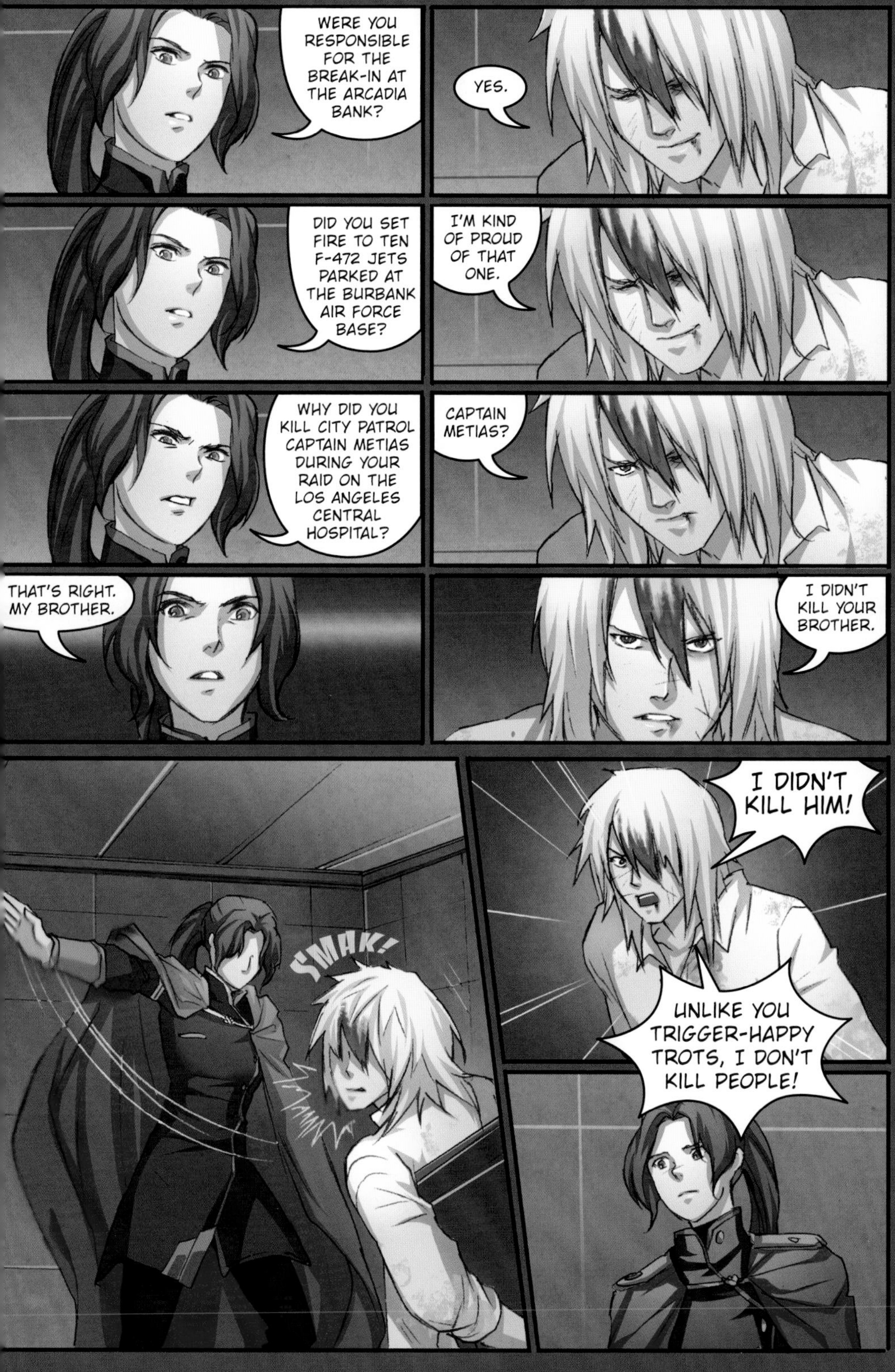
WERE YOU RESPONSIBLE FOR THE BREAK-IN AT THE ARCADIA BANK?
YES.
DID YOU SET FIRE TO TEN F-472 JETS PARKED AT THE BURBANK AIR FORCE BASE?
I'M KIND OF PROUD OF THAT ONE.
WHY DID YOU KILL CITY PATROL CAPTAIN METIAS DURING YOUR RAID ON THE LOS ANGELES CENTRAL HOSPITAL?
CAPTAIN METIAS?
THAT'S RIGHT. MY BROTHER.
I DIDN'T KILL YOUR BROTHER.
SMAK!
I DIDN'T KILL HIM!
UNLIKE YOU TRIGGER-HAPPY TROTS, I DON'T KILL PEOPLE!

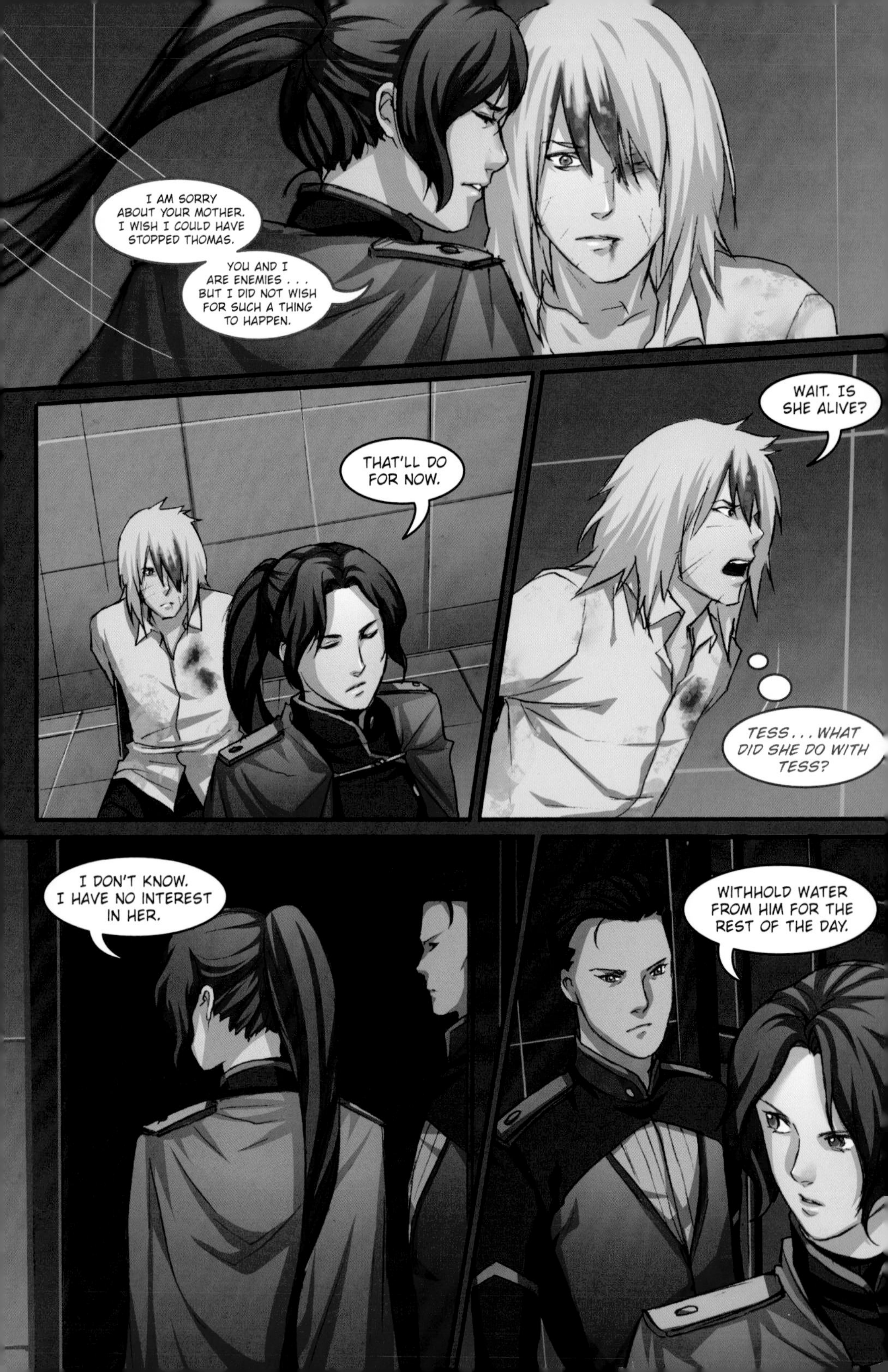
I AM SORRY ABOUT YOUR MOTHER. I WISH I COULD HAVE STOPPED THOMAS.
YOU AND I ARE ENEMIES . . . BUT I DID NOT WISH FOR SUCH A THING TO HAPPEN.
THAT'LL DO FOR NOW.
WAIT. IS SHE ALIVE?
TESS . . . WHAT DID SHE DO WITH TESS?
I DON'T KNOW. I HAVE NO INTEREST IN HER.
WITHHOLD WATER FROM HIM FOR THE REST OF THE DAY.

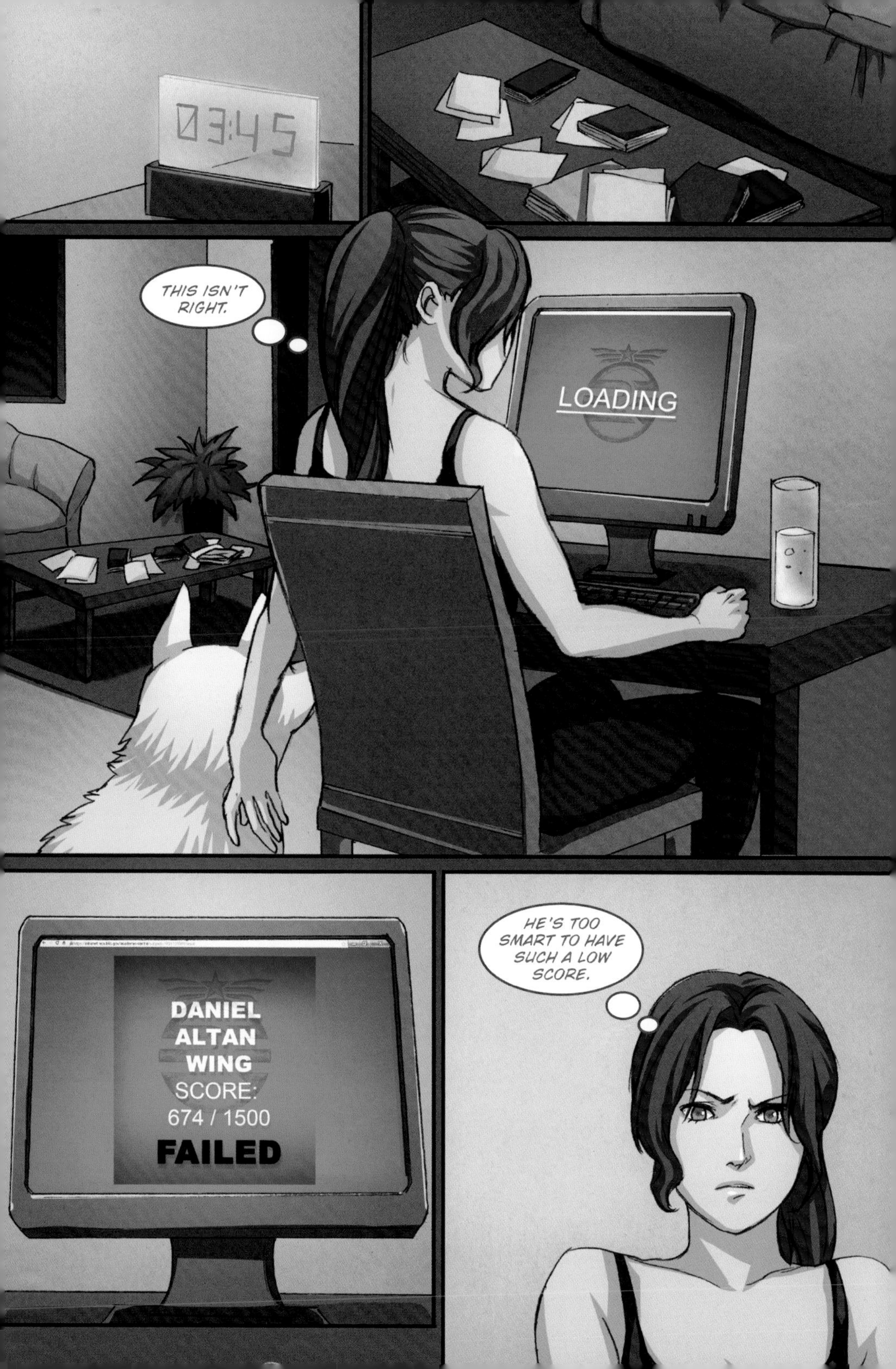
03:45
THIS ISN'T RIGHT.
LOADING
DANIEL ALTAN WING
SCORE: 674 / 1500
FAILED
HE'S TOO SMART TO HAVE SUCH A LOW SCORE.

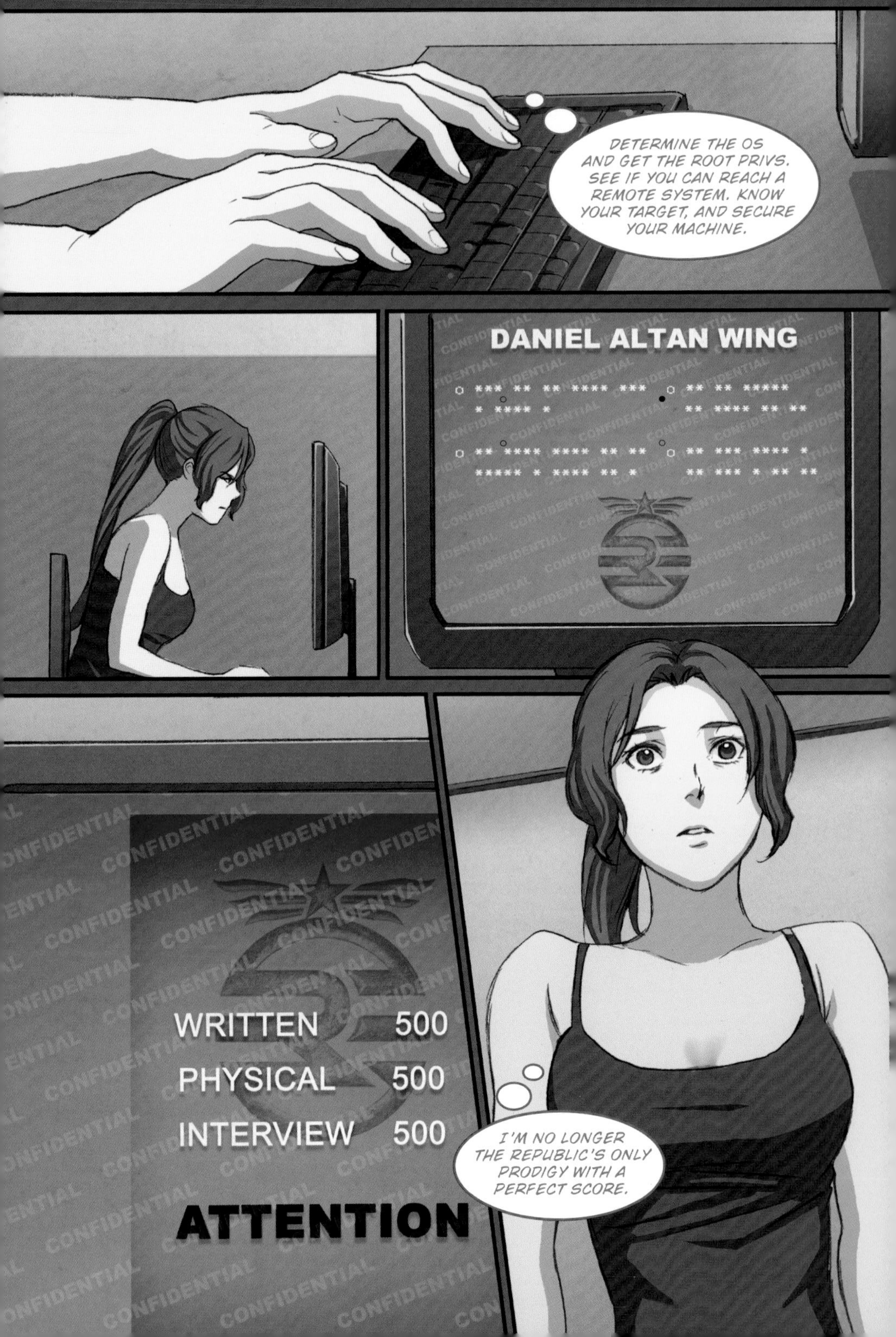
DETERMINE THE OS AND GET THE ROOT PRIVS. SEE IF YOU CAN REACH A REMOTE SYSTEM. KNOW YOUR TARGET, AND SECURE YOUR MACHINE.
DANIEL ALTAN WING
CONFIDENTIAL
WRITTEN 500
PHYSICAL 500
INTERVIEW 500
ATTENTION
I'M NO LONGER THE REPUBLIC'S ONLY PRODIGY WITH A PERFECT SCORE.

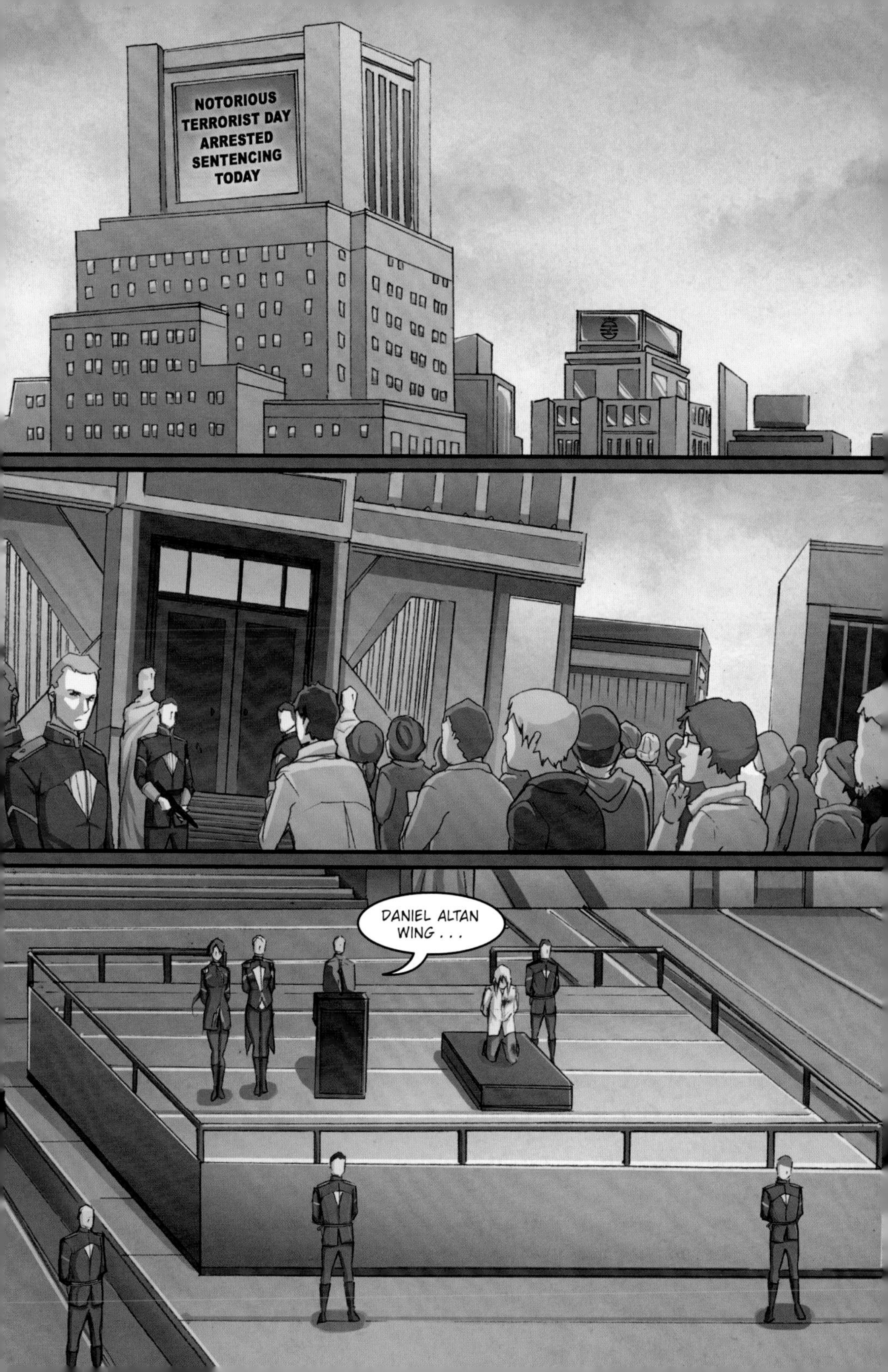
NOTORIOUS TERRORIST DAY ARRESTED SENTENCING TODAY
DANIEL ALTAN WING . . .

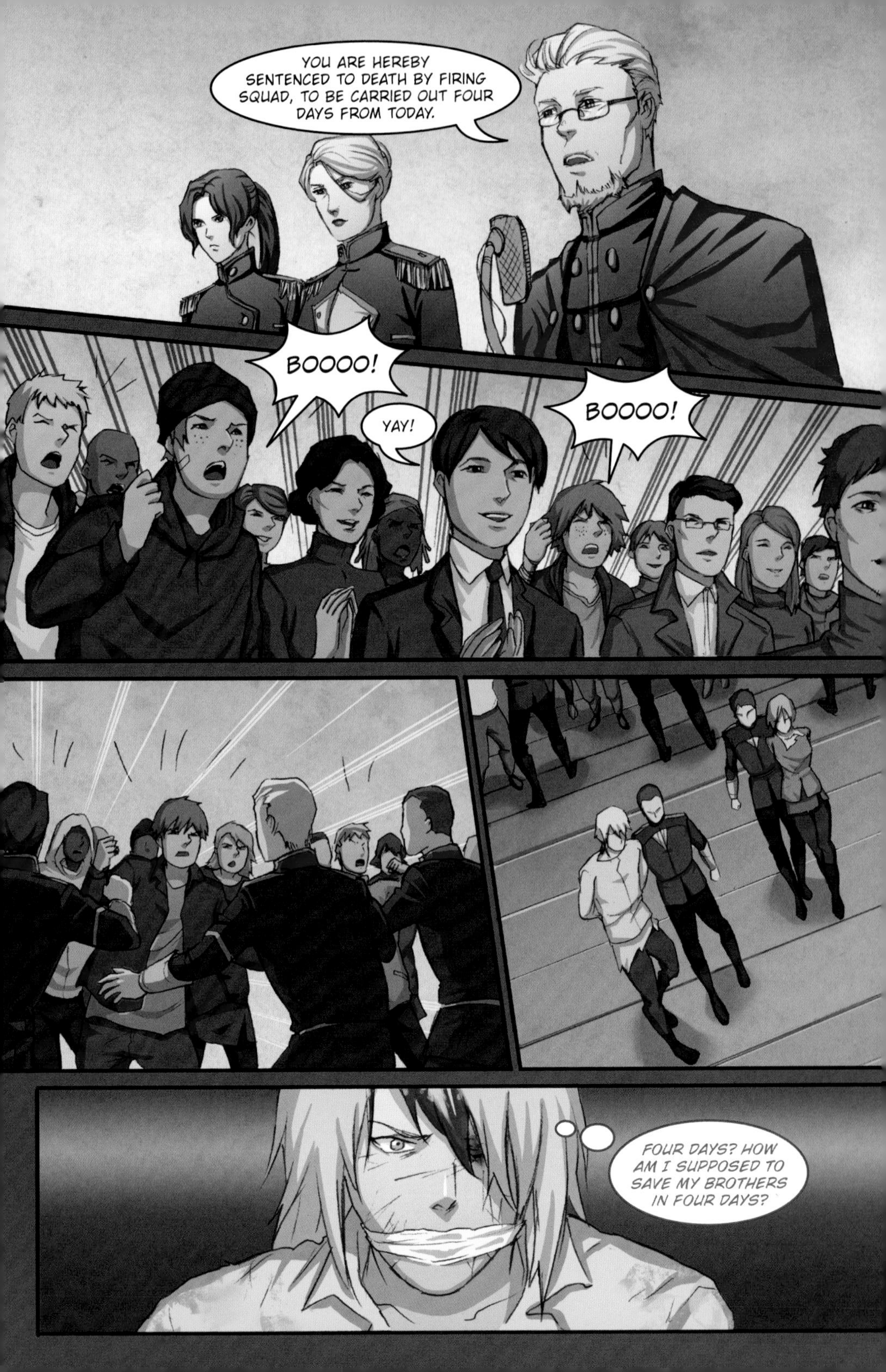
YOU ARE HEREBY SENTENCED TO DEATH BY FIRING SQUAD, TO BE CARRIED OUT FOUR DAYS FROM TODAY.
BOOOO!
YAY!
BOOOO!
FOUR DAYS? HOW AM I SUPPOSED TO SAVE MY BROTHERS IN FOUR DAYS?

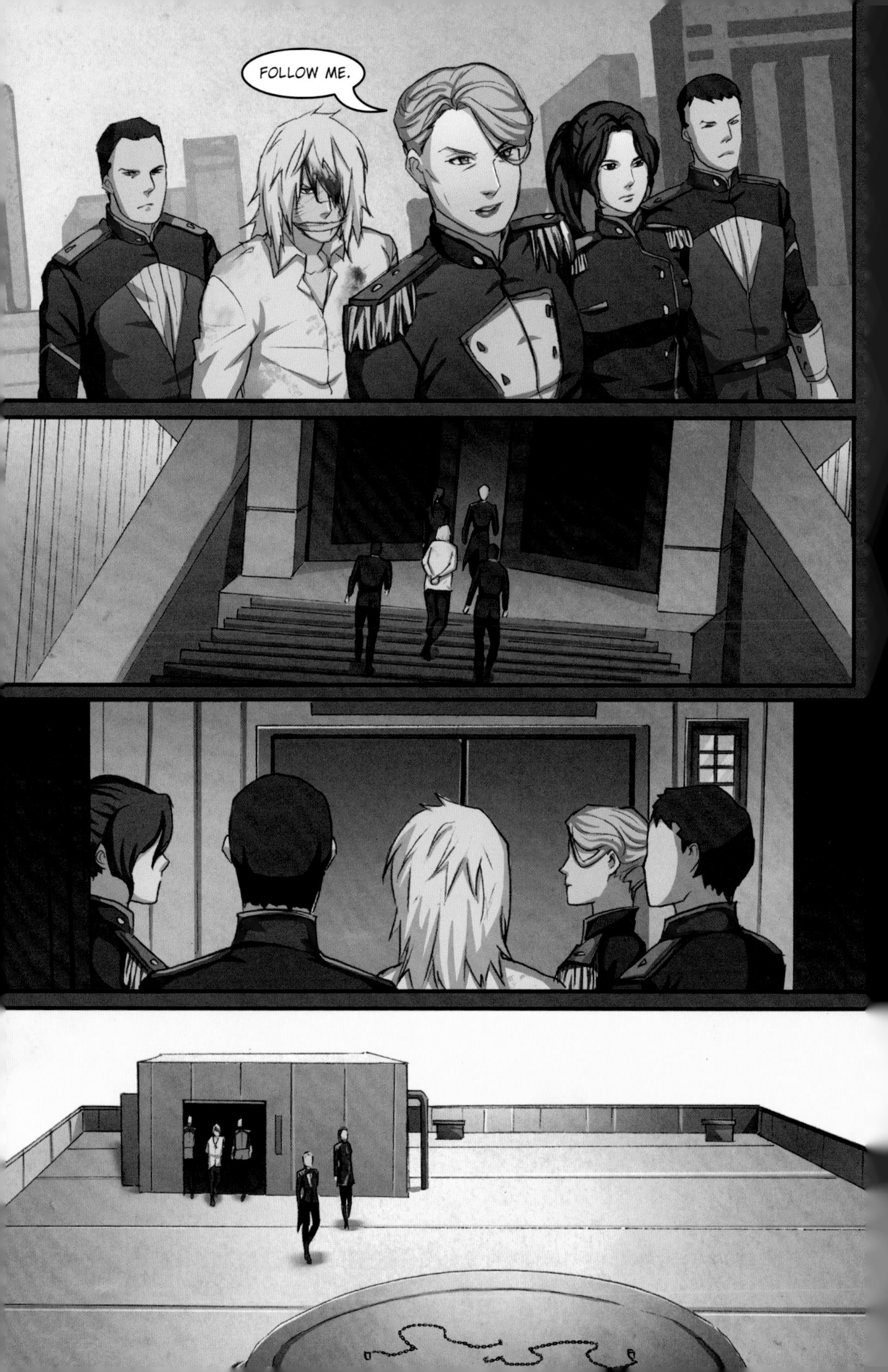
FOLLOW ME.

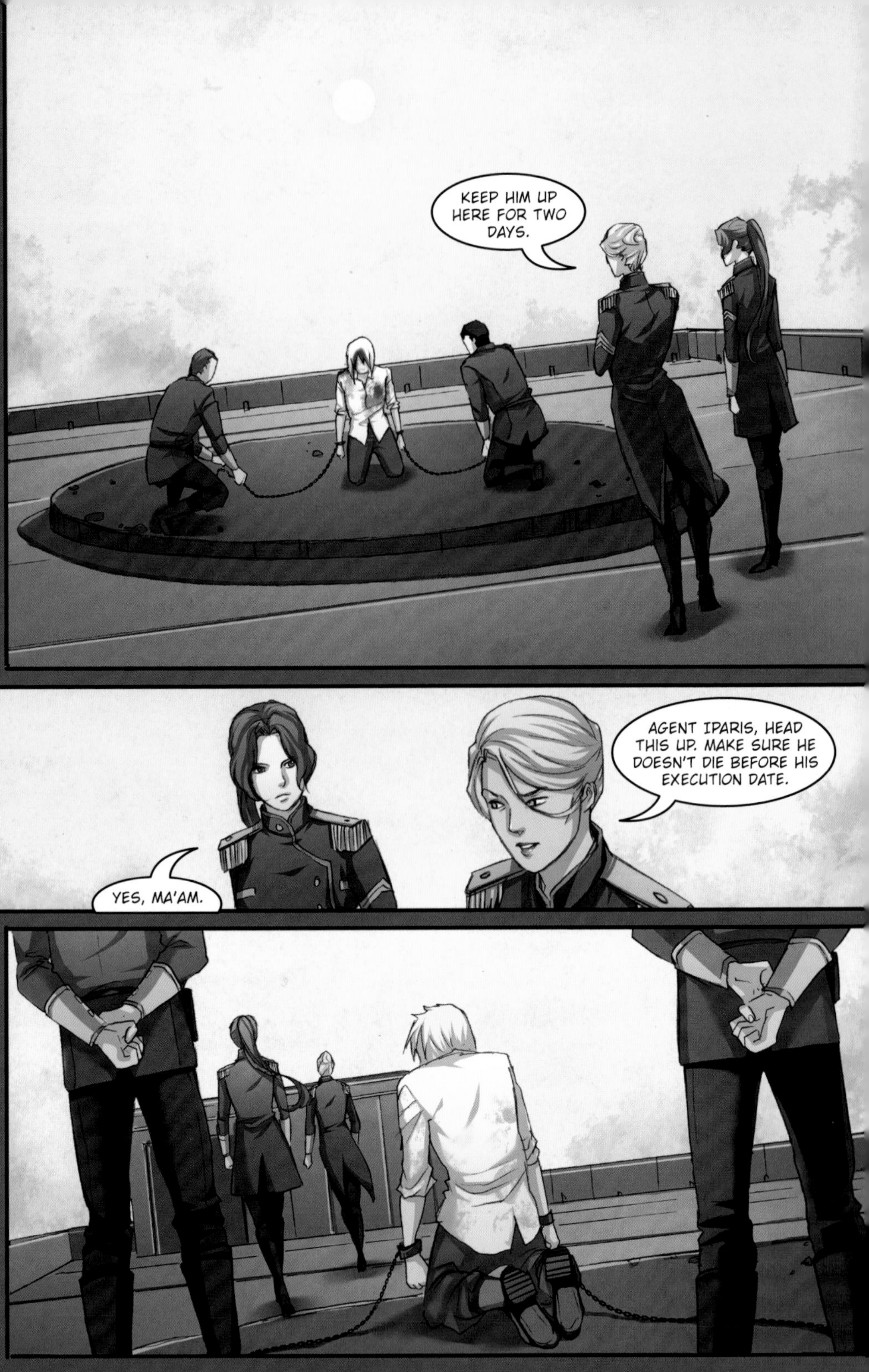
KEEP HIM UP HERE FOR TWO DAYS.
AGENT IPARIS, HEAD THIS UP. MAKE SURE HE DOESN'T DIE BEFORE HIS EXECUTION DATE.
YES, MA'AM.

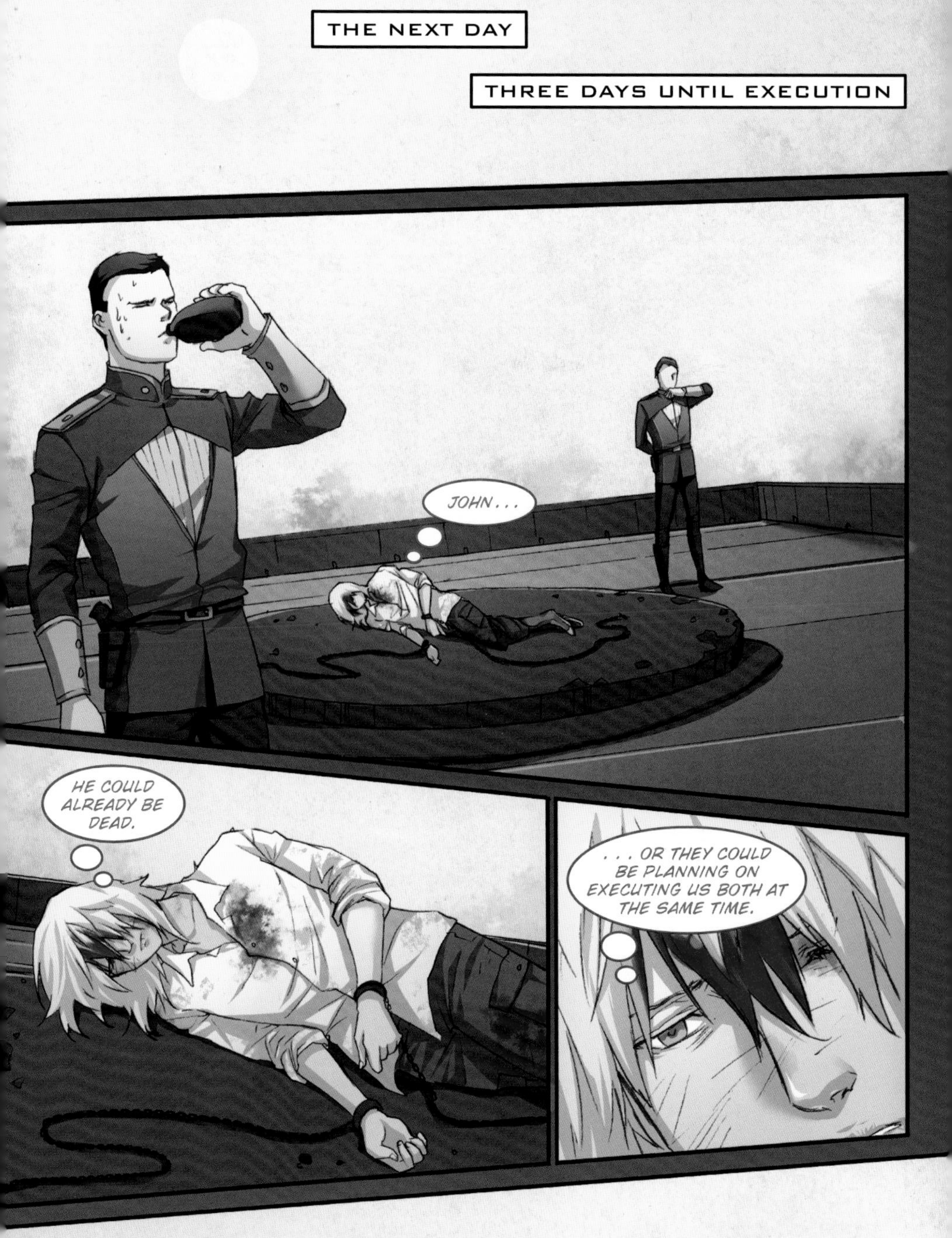
THE NEXT DAY
THREE DAYS UNTIL EXECUTION
JOHN . . .
HE COULD ALREADY BE DEAD.
. . . OR THEY COULD BE PLANNING ON EXECUTING US BOTH AT THE SAME TIME.

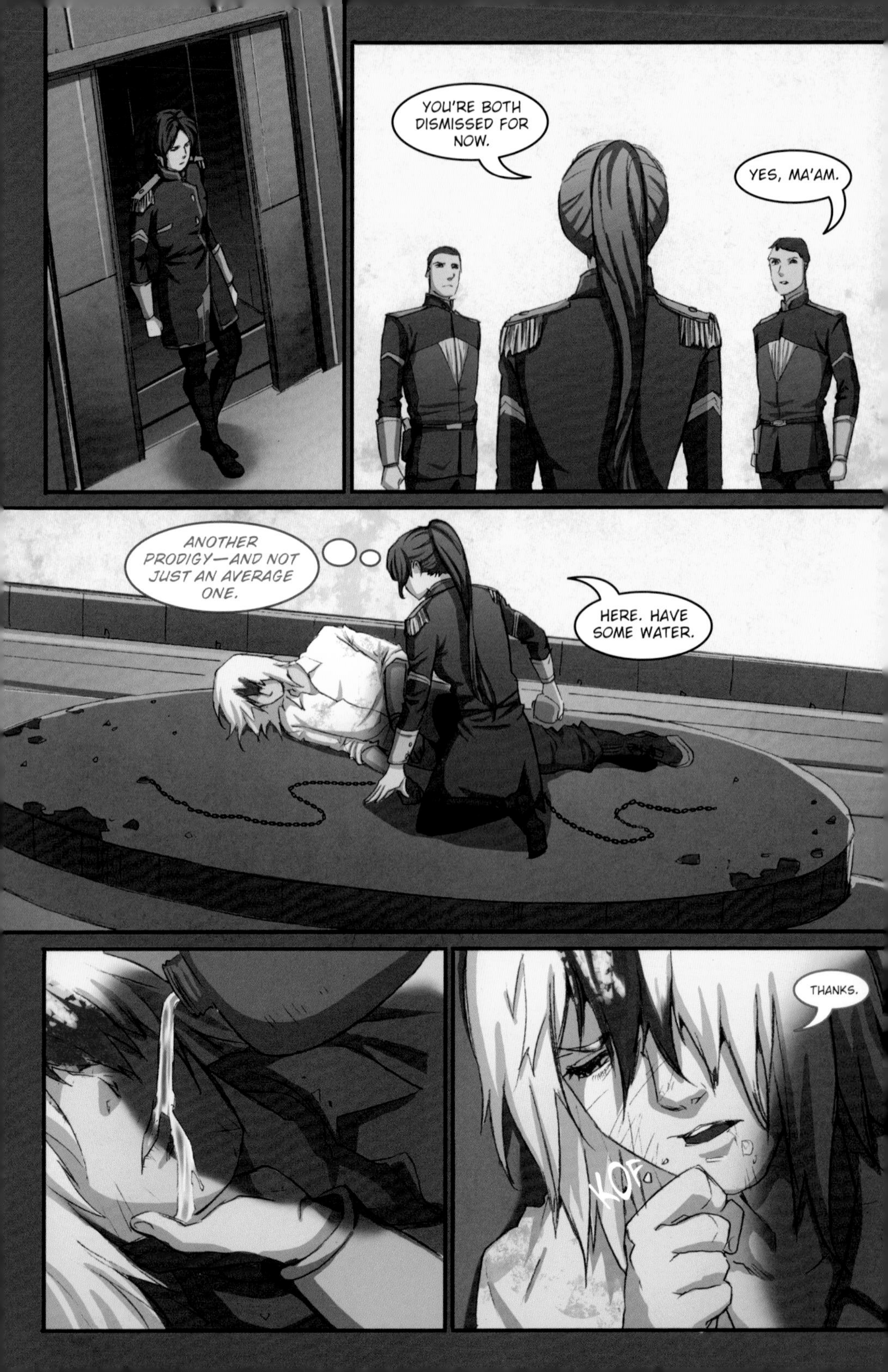
YOU'RE BOTH DISMISSED FOR NOW.
YES, MA'AM.
ANOTHER PRODIGY—AND NOT JUST AN AVERAGE ONE.
HERE. HAVE SOME WATER.
THANKS.
KOF

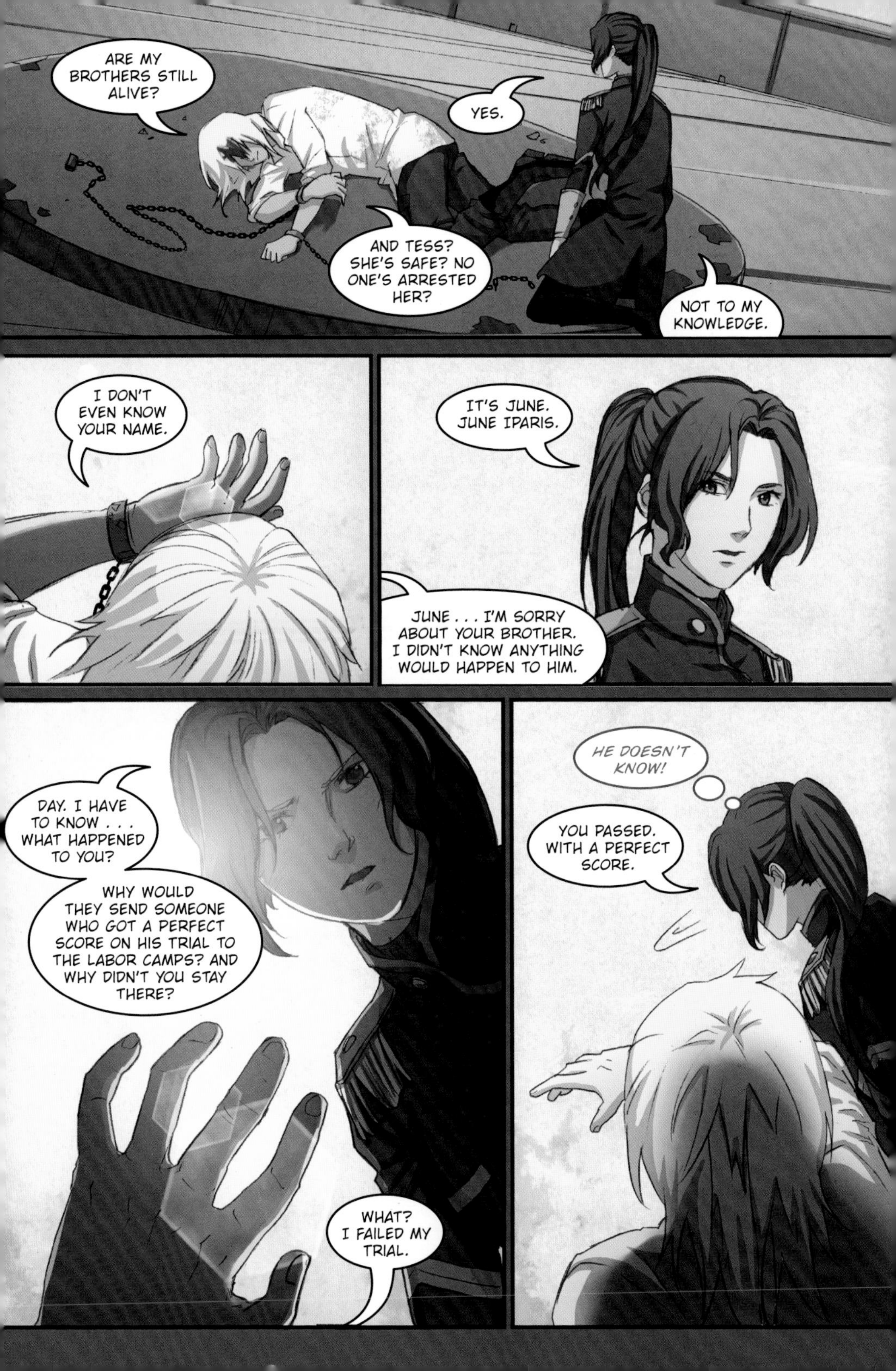
ARE MY BROTHERS STILL ALIVE?
YES.
AND TESS? SHE'S SAFE? NO ONE'S ARRESTED HER?
NOT TO MY KNOWLEDGE.
I DON'T EVEN KNOW YOUR NAME.
IT'S JUNE. JUNE IPARIS.
JUNE . . . I'M SORRY ABOUT YOUR BROTHER. I DIDN'T KNOW ANYTHING WOULD HAPPEN TO HIM.
DAY. I HAVE TO KNOW . . . WHAT HAPPENED TO YOU?
WHY WOULD THEY SEND SOMEONE WHO GOT A PERFECT SCORE ON HIS TRIAL TO THE LABOR CAMPS? AND WHY DIDN'T YOU STAY THERE?
WHAT? I FAILED MY TRIAL.
HE DOESN'T KNOW!
YOU PASSED. WITH A PERFECT SCORE.

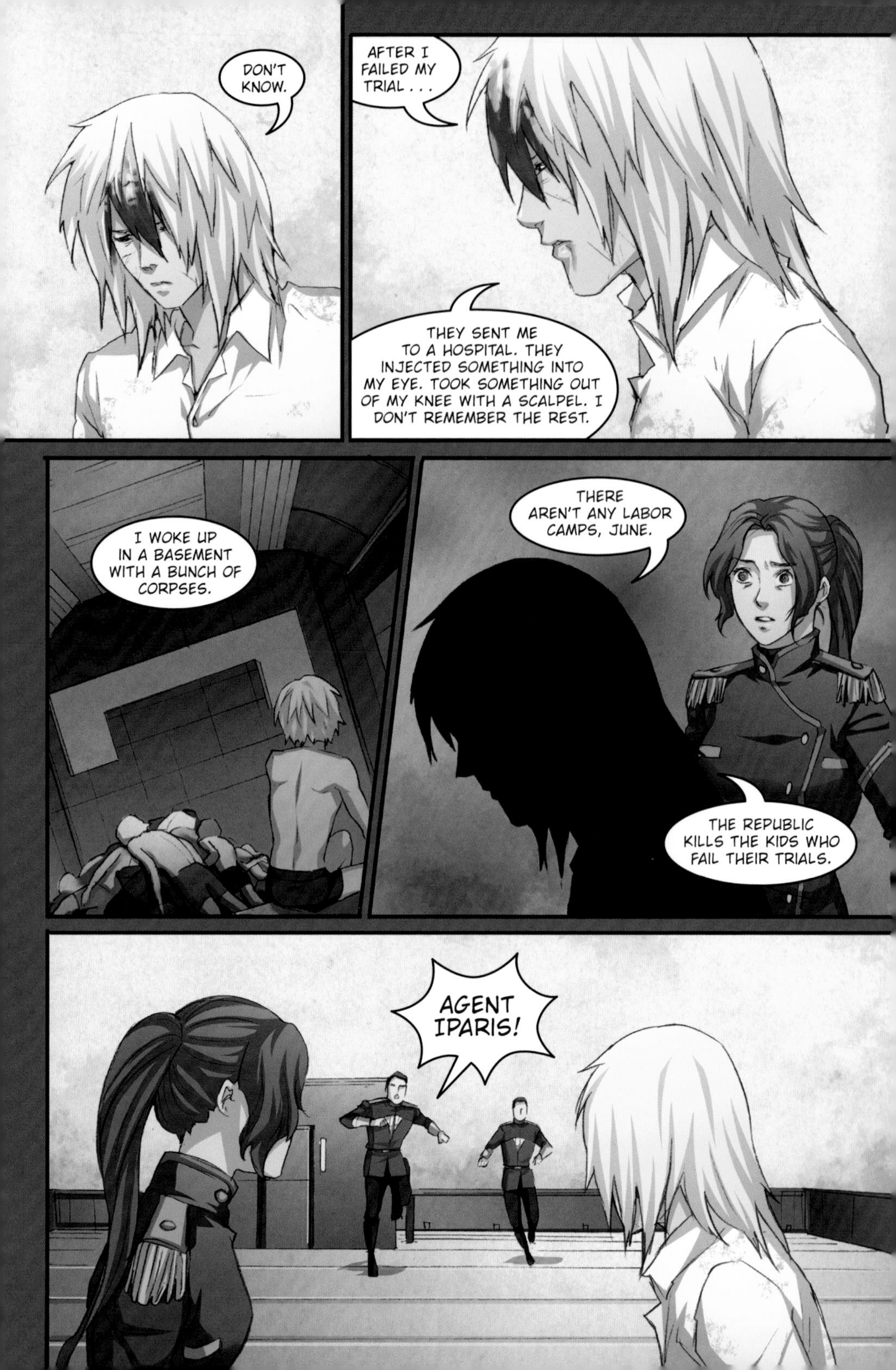
DON'T KNOW.
AFTER I FAILED MY TRIAL . . .
THEY SENT ME TO A HOSPITAL. THEY INJECTED SOMETHING INTO MY EYE. TOOK SOMETHING OUT OF MY KNEE WITH A SCALPEL. I DON'T REMEMBER THE REST.
I WOKE UP IN A BASEMENT WITH A BUNCH OF CORPSES.
THERE AREN'T ANY LABOR CAMPS, JUNE.
THE REPUBLIC KILLS THE KIDS WHO FAIL THEIR TRIALS.
AGENT IPARIS!

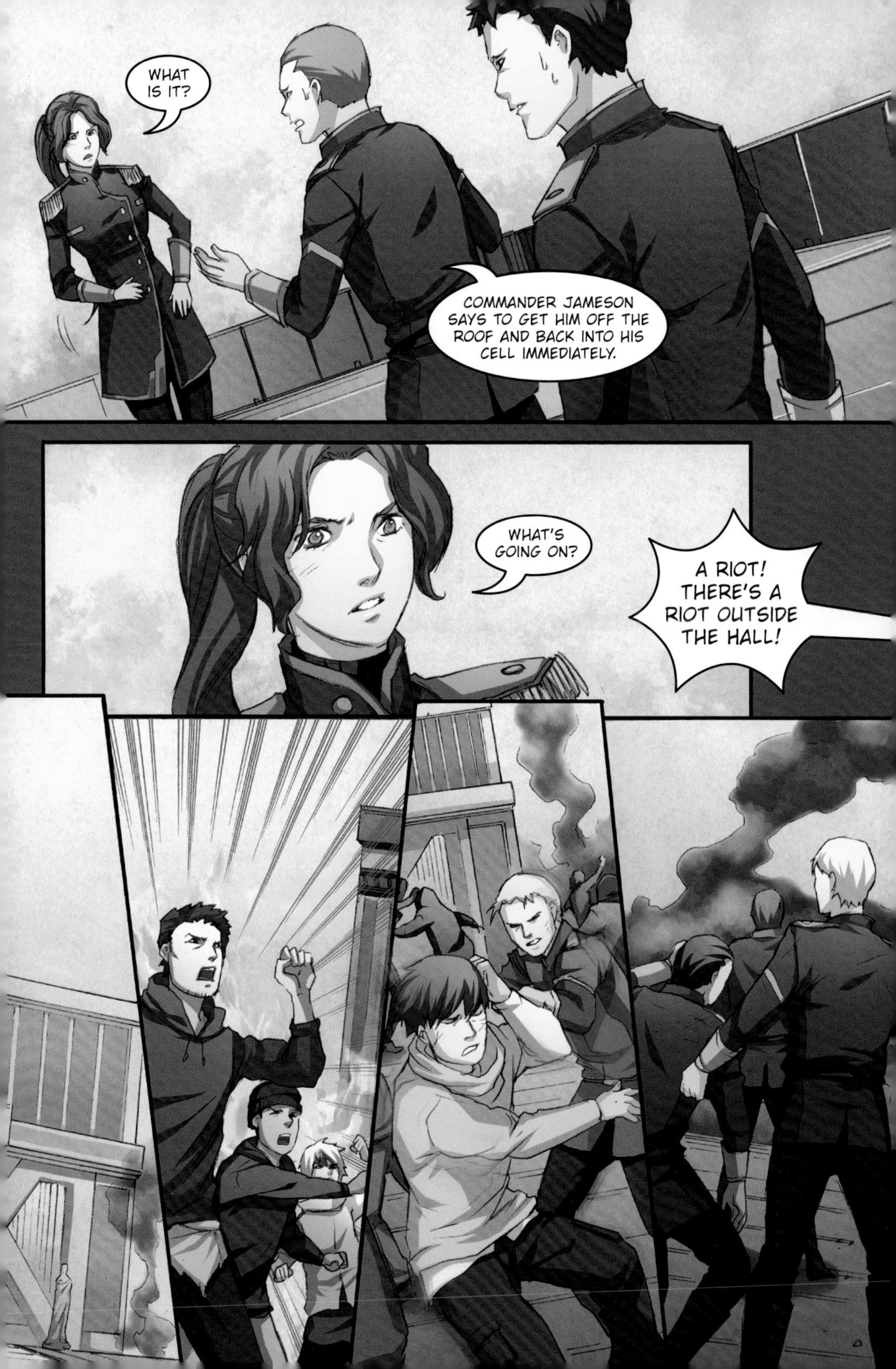
WHAT IS IT?
COMMANDER JAMESON SAYS TO GET HIM OFF THE ROOF AND BACK INTO HIS CELL IMMEDIATELY.
WHAT'S GOING ON?
A RIOT! THERE'S A RIOT OUTSIDE THE HALL!

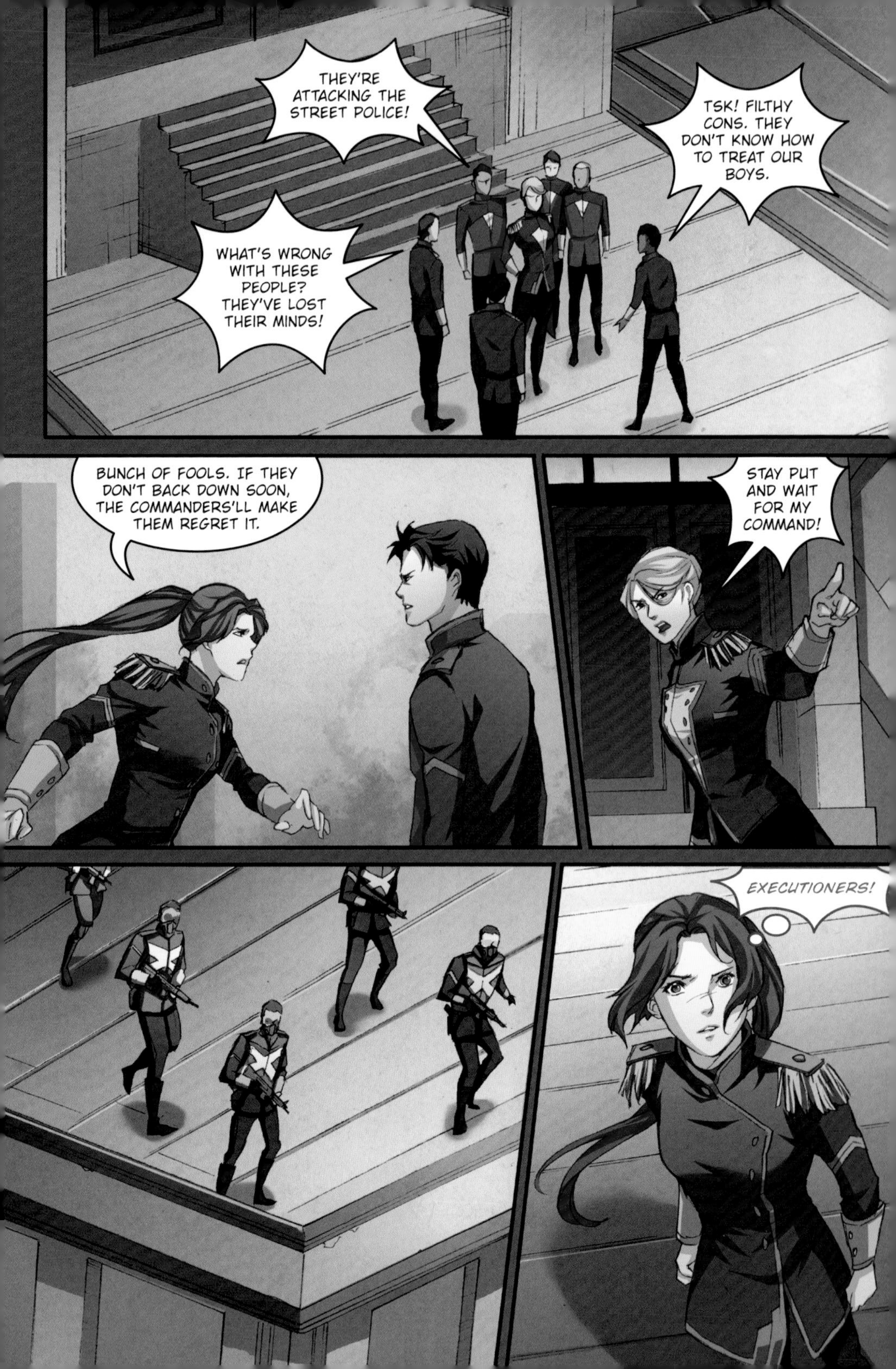
THEY'RE ATTACKING THE STREET POLICE!
TSK! FILTHY CONS. THEY DON'T KNOW HOW TO TREAT OUR BOYS.
WHAT'S WRONG WITH THESE PEOPLE? THEY'VE LOST THEIR MINDS!
BUNCH OF FOOLS. IF THEY DON'T BACK DOWN SOON, THE COMMANDERS'LL MAKE THEM REGRET IT.
STAY PUT AND WAIT FOR MY COMMAND!
EXECUTIONERS!

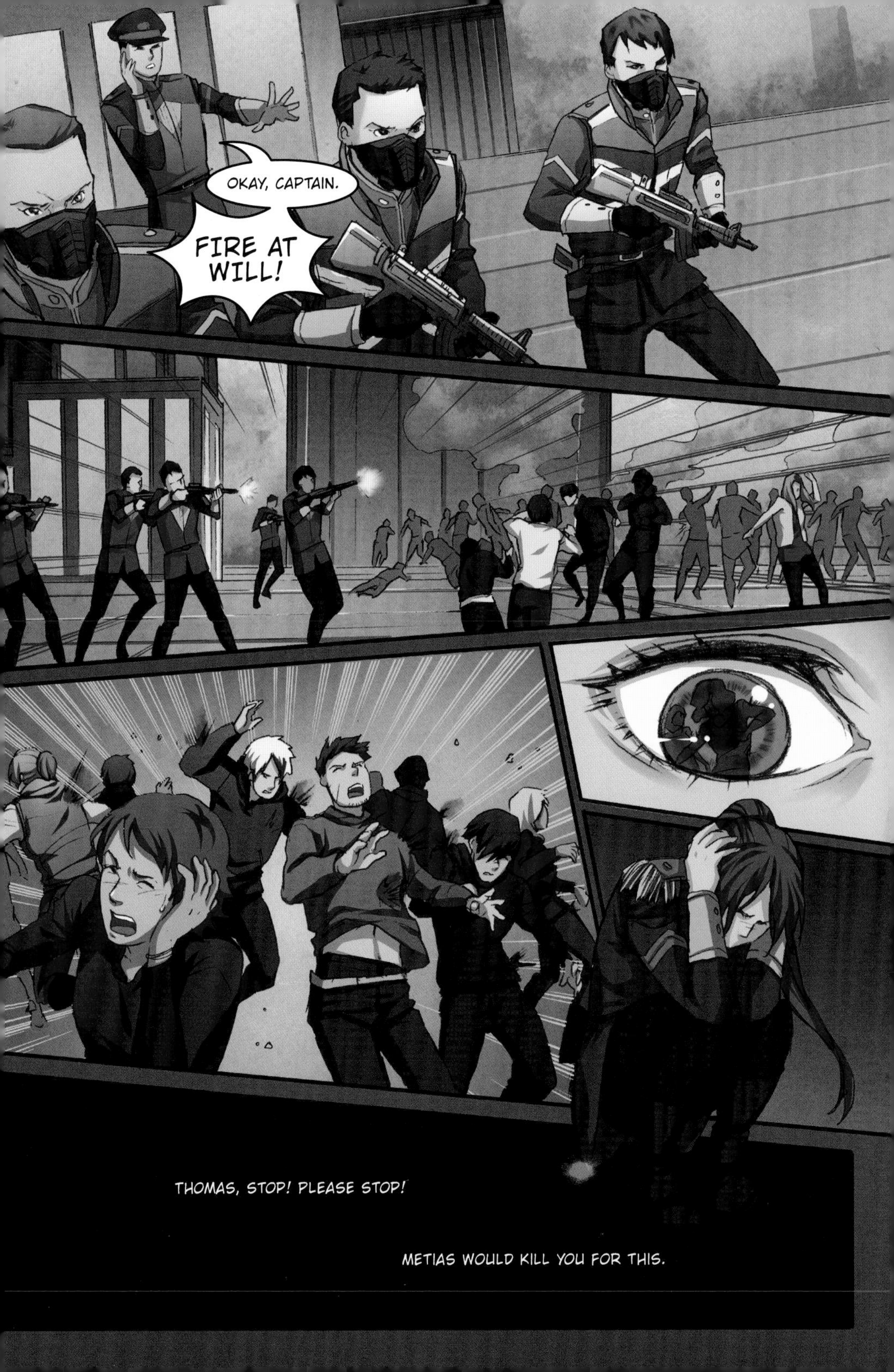
FIRE AT WILL!
OKAY, CAPTAIN.
THOMAS, STOP! PLEASE STOP!
METIAS WOULD KILL YOU FOR THIS.

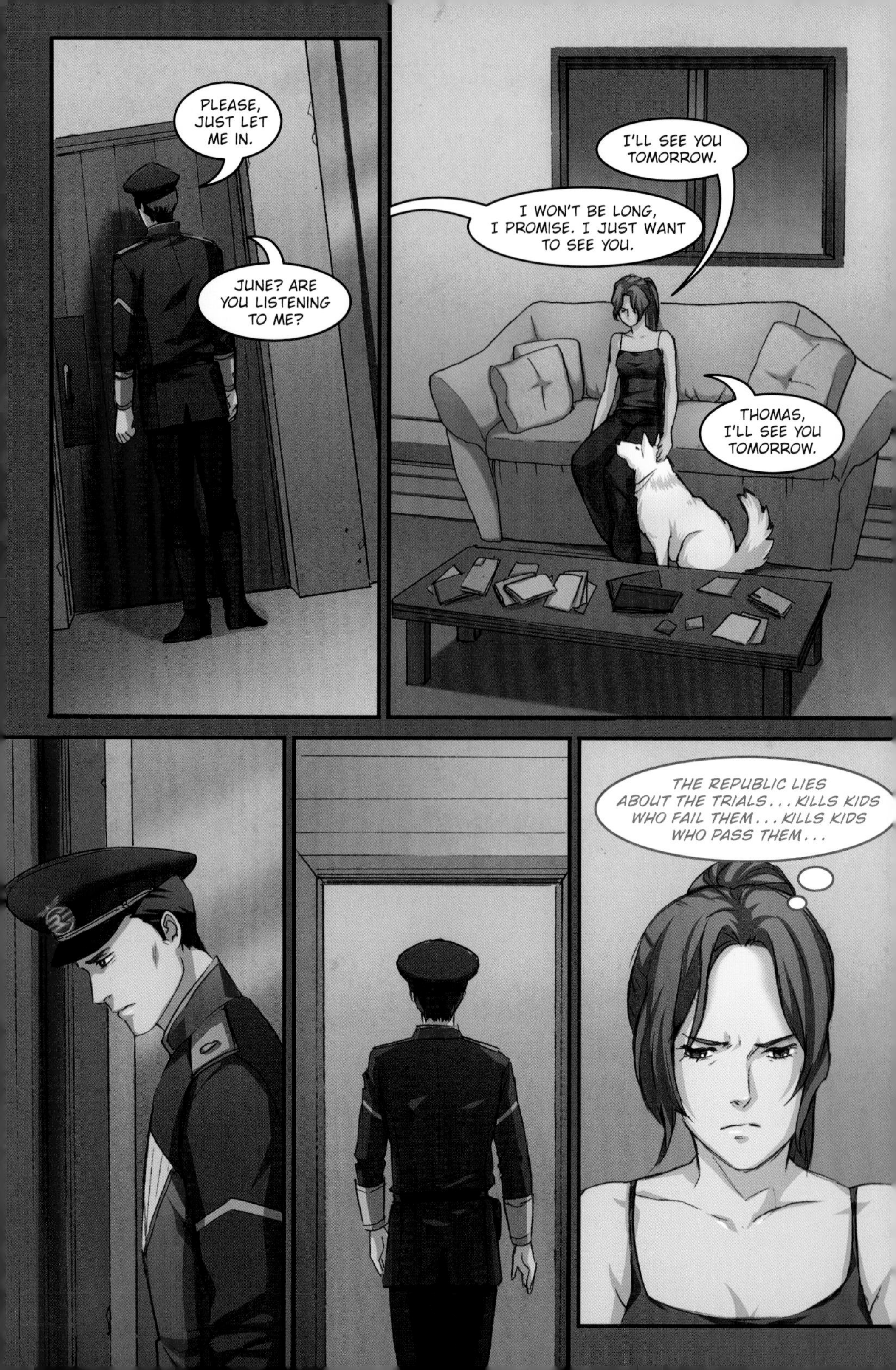
PLEASE, JUST LET ME IN.
JUNE? ARE YOU LISTENING TO ME?
I WON'T BE LONG, I PROMISE. I JUST WANT TO SEE YOU.
I'LL SEE YOU TOMORROW.
THOMAS, I'LL SEE YOU TOMORROW.
THE REPUBLIC LIES ABOUT THE TRIALS . . . KILLS KIDS WHO FAIL THEM . . . KILLS KIDS WHO PASS THEM . . .

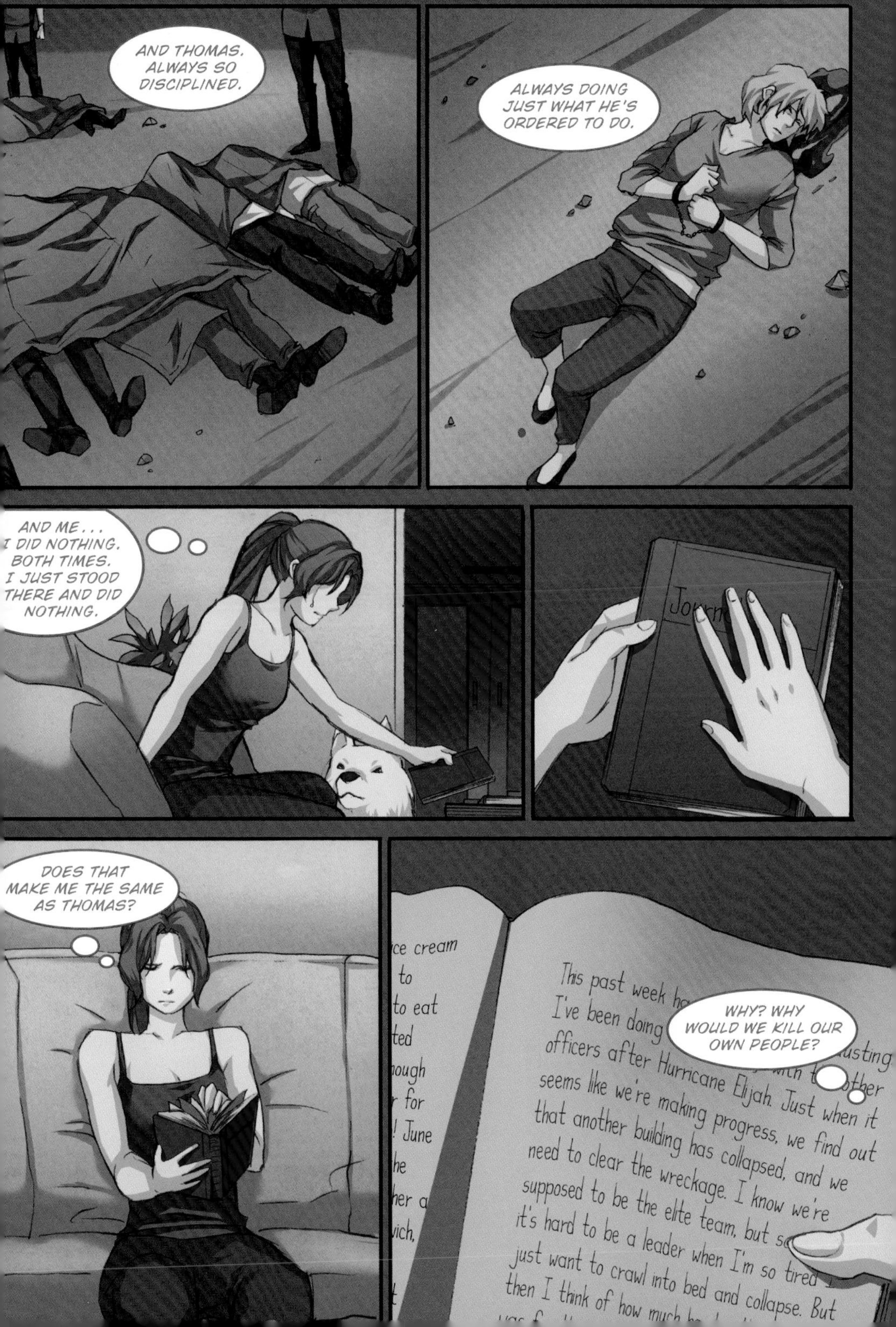
AND THOMAS. ALWAYS SO DISCIPLINED.
ALWAYS DOING JUST WHAT HE'S ORDERED TO DO.
AND ME . . . I DID NOTHING. BOTH TIMES. I JUST STOOD THERE AND DID NOTHING.
Journ
DOES THAT MAKE ME THE SAME AS THOMAS?
ice cream
to eat
! June
This past week h
I've been doing
officers after Hurricane Elijah. Just when it
seems like we're making progress, we find out
that another building has collapsed, and we
need to clear the wreckage. I know we're
supposed to be the elite team, but s
it's hard to be a leader when I'm so tired
just want to crawl into bed and collapse. But
then I think of how much h
WHY? WHY WOULD WE KILL OUR OWN PEOPLE?

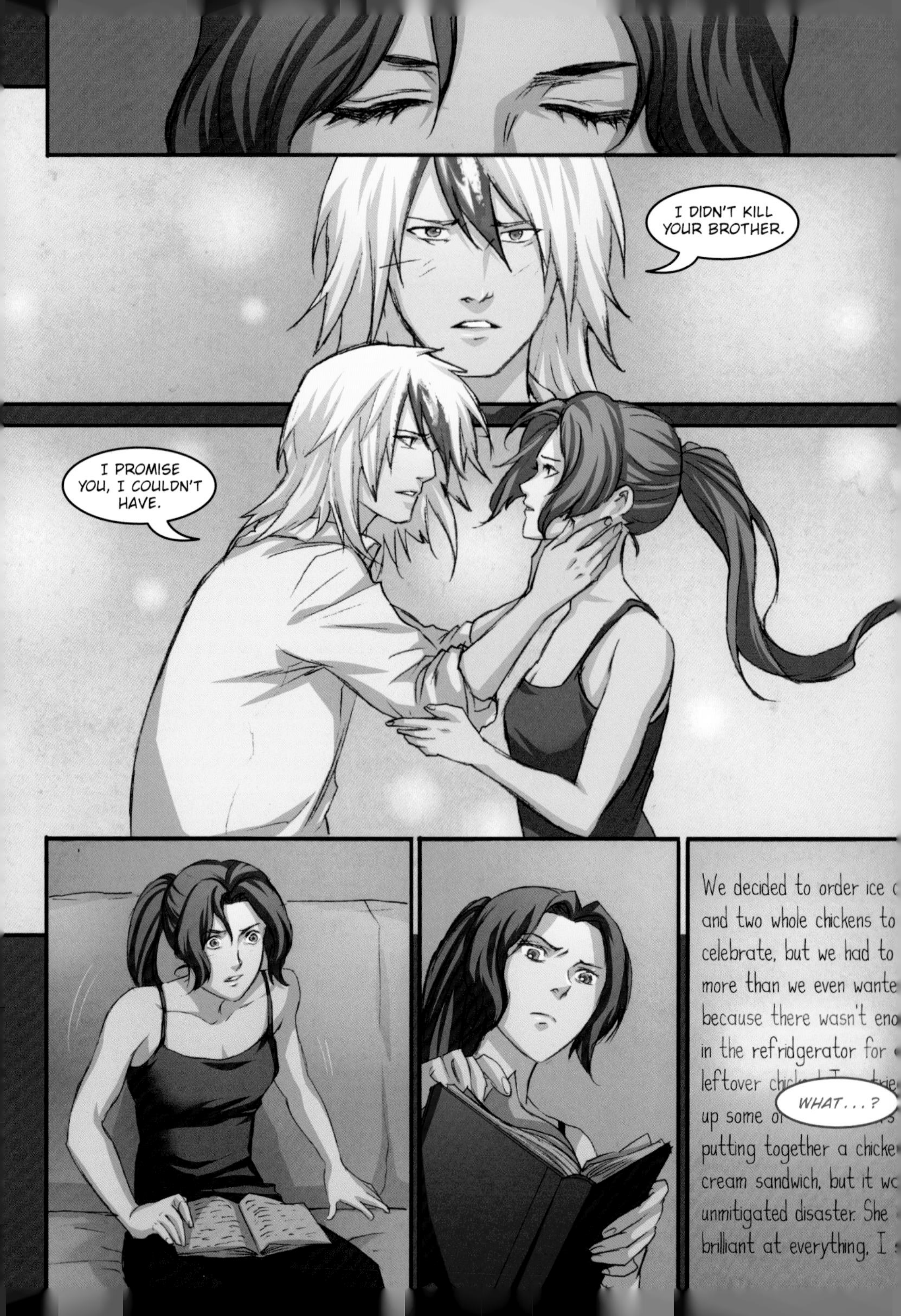
I DIDN'T KILL YOUR BROTHER.
I PROMISE YOU, I COULDN'T HAVE.
We decided to order ice
and two whole chickens to
celebrate, but we had to
more than we even wante
because there wasn't eno
in the refridgerator for
leftover chi
up some o
putting together a chicke
cream sandwich, but it w
unmitigated disaster. She
brilliant at everything. I
WHAT . . . ?

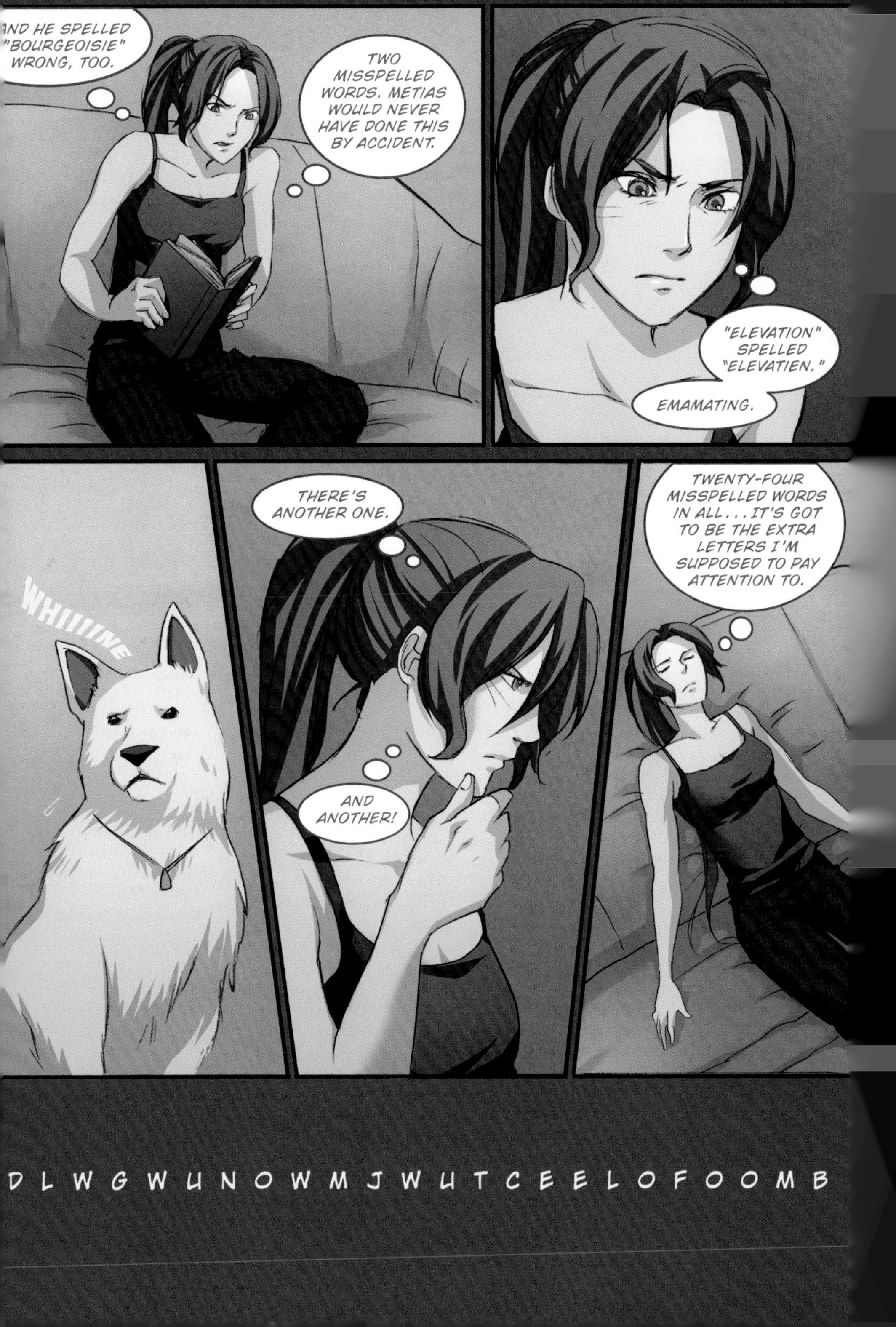
AND HE SPELLED "BOURGEOISIE" WRONG, TOO.
TWO MISSPELLED WORDS. METIAS WOULD NEVER HAVE DONE THIS BY ACCIDENT.
"ELEVATION" SPELLED "ELEVATIEN."
EMAMATING.
WHIIIINE
THERE'S ANOTHER ONE.
AND ANOTHER!
TWENTY-FOUR MISSPELLED WORDS IN ALL . . . IT'S GOT TO BE THE EXTRA LETTERS I'M SUPPOSED TO PAY ATTENTION TO.

D L W G W U N O W M J W U T C E E L O F O O M B

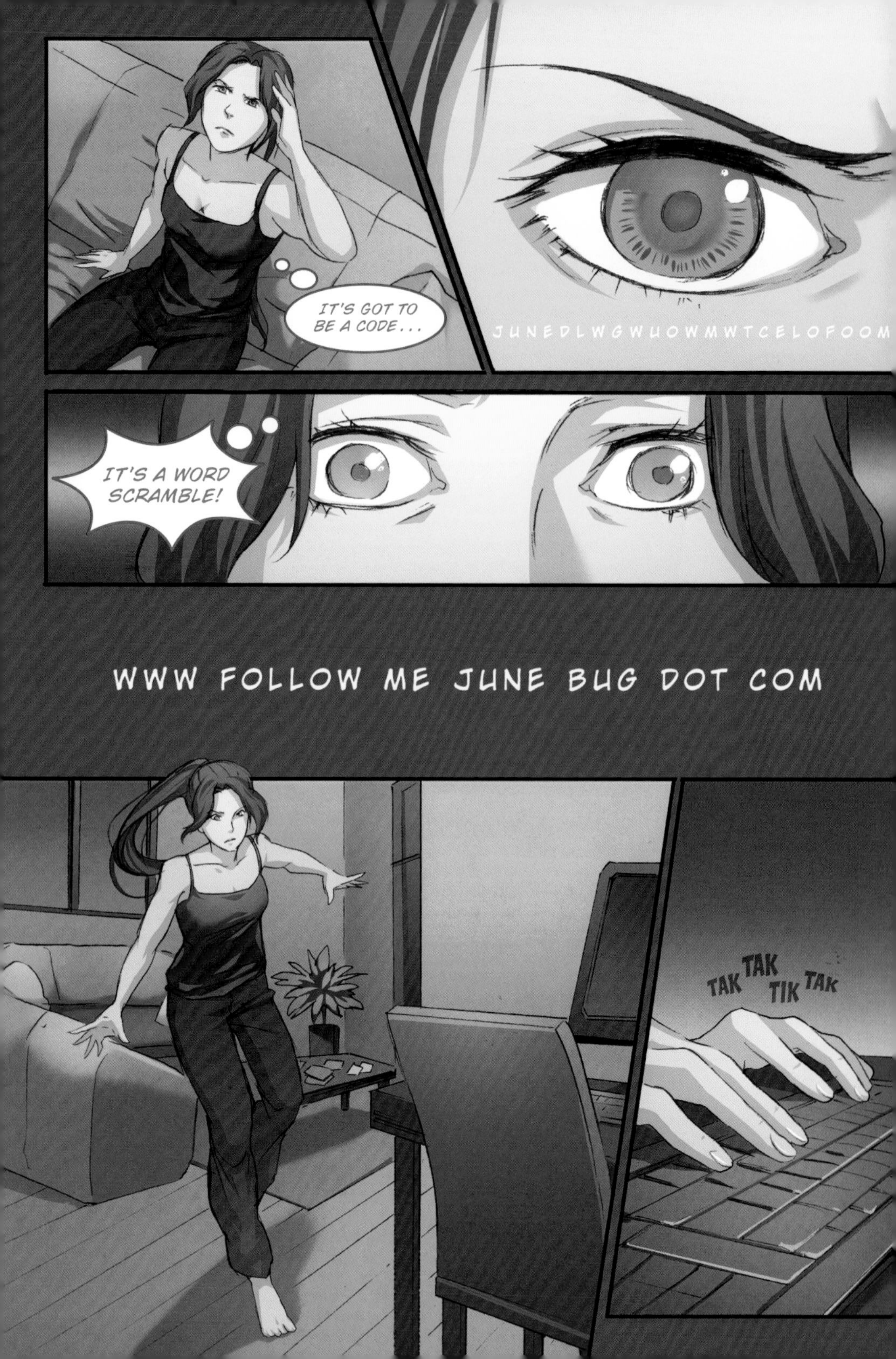
IT'S GOT TO BE A CODE...
JUNEDLWGWUOWMWTCELOFOOM
IT'S A WORD SCRAMBLE!
WWW FOLLOW ME JUNE BUG DOT COM
TAK TAK TIK TAK

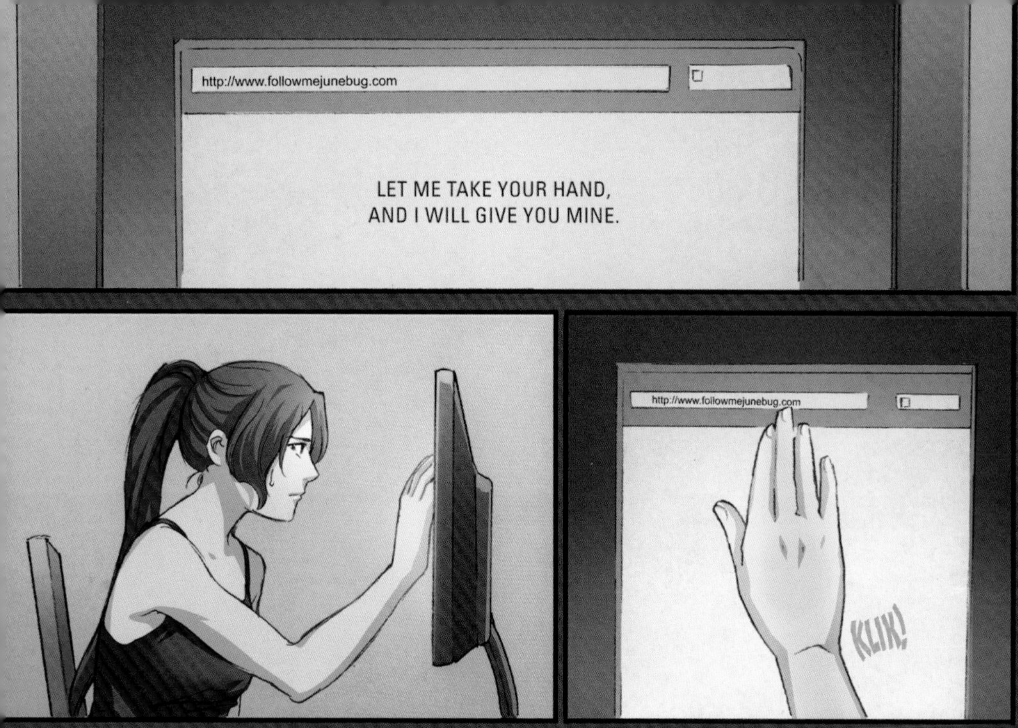
http://www.followmejunebug.com
LET ME TAKE YOUR HAND,
AND I WILL GIVE YOU MINE.
http://www.followmejunebug.com
KLIK!

JULY 12

This is for June's eyes only. June, you can delete all traces of this blog by pressing your right hand against the screen. Today I discovered that Dad tried to resign the day before he and Mom were killed in a car wreck.

SEPTEMBER 15

Who knew the deceased civilians database was so difficult to hack? There's something behind our parents' deaths, and I'm going to find out what it is.

NOVEMBER 17

You asked me why I seemed so out of it today. Today I found a report on our parents' car accident. Except it wasn't an accident. They were murdered by the Republic because Dad found out the plague viruses are released intentionally, by the government. That's why they always have the right vaccines ready and waiting to go. That's why the plague always hits the poor sectors first and hardest. Dad discovered this and wanted to resign, and that's why he and Mom are dead. They were murdered.

NOVEMBER 26

Thomas knows. He knows what I suspect. He said he'd keep it a secret. I think I can trust him.

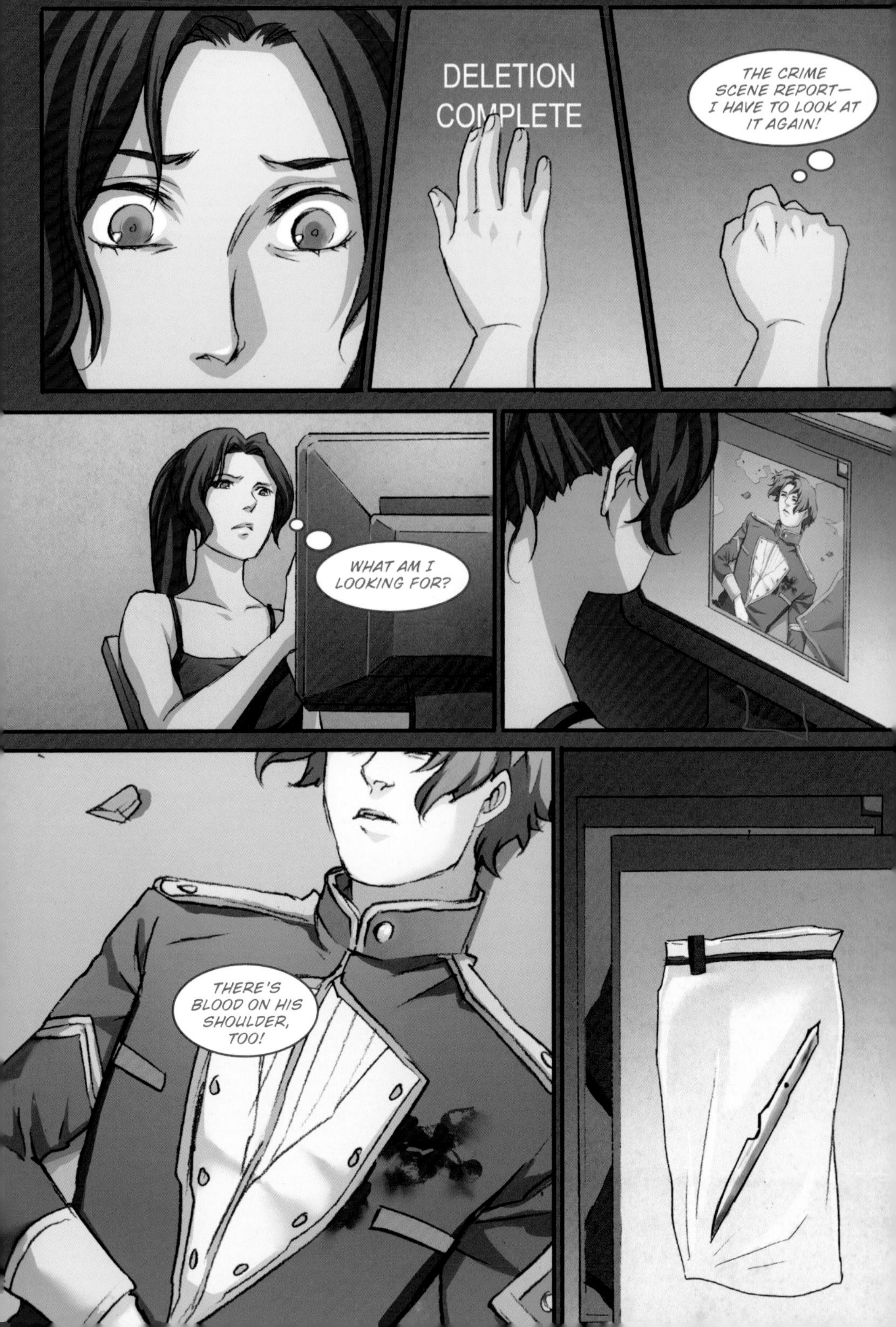
DELETION COMPLETE
THE CRIME SCENE REPORT— I HAVE TO LOOK AT IT AGAIN!
WHAT AM I LOOKING FOR?
THERE'S BLOOD ON HIS SHOULDER, TOO!

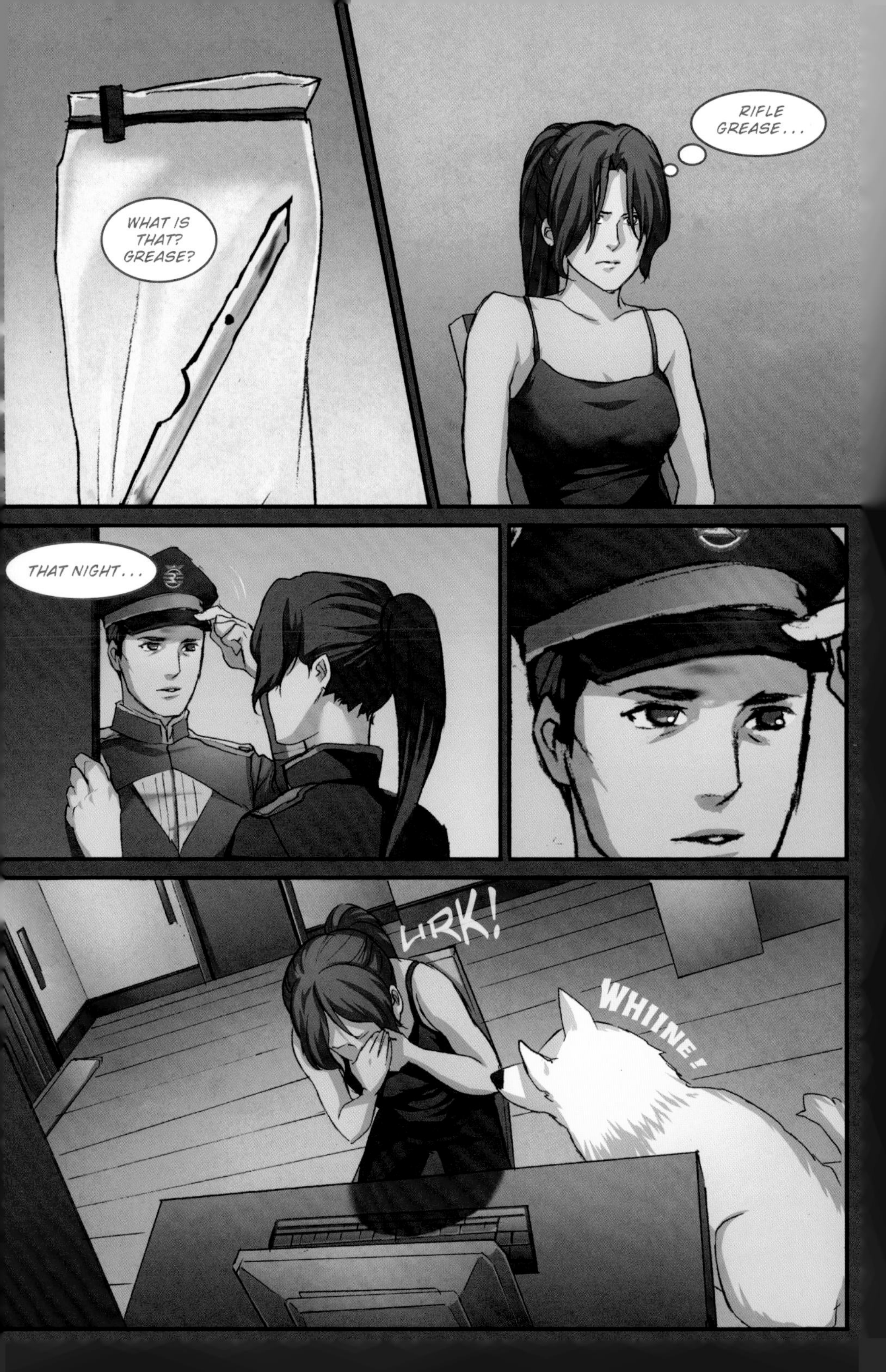
WHAT IS THAT? GREASE?
RIFLE GREASE . . .
THAT NIGHT . . .
URK!
WHIINE!

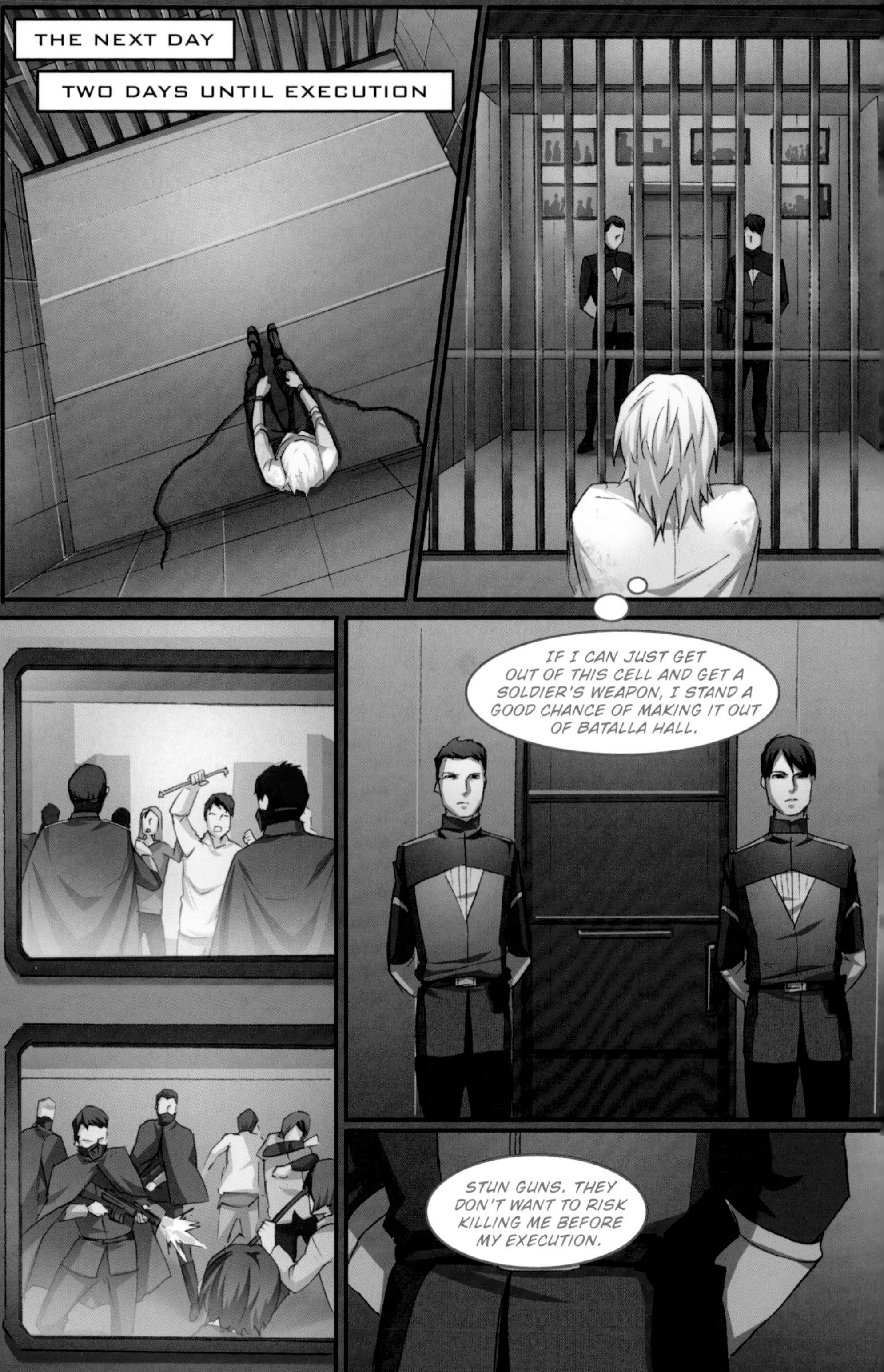
THE NEXT DAY
TWO DAYS UNTIL EXECUTION
IF I CAN JUST GET OUT OF THIS CELL AND GET A SOLDIER'S WEAPON, I STAND A GOOD CHANCE OF MAKING IT OUT OF BATALLA HALL.
STUN GUNS. THEY DON'T WANT TO RISK KILLING ME BEFORE MY EXECUTION.

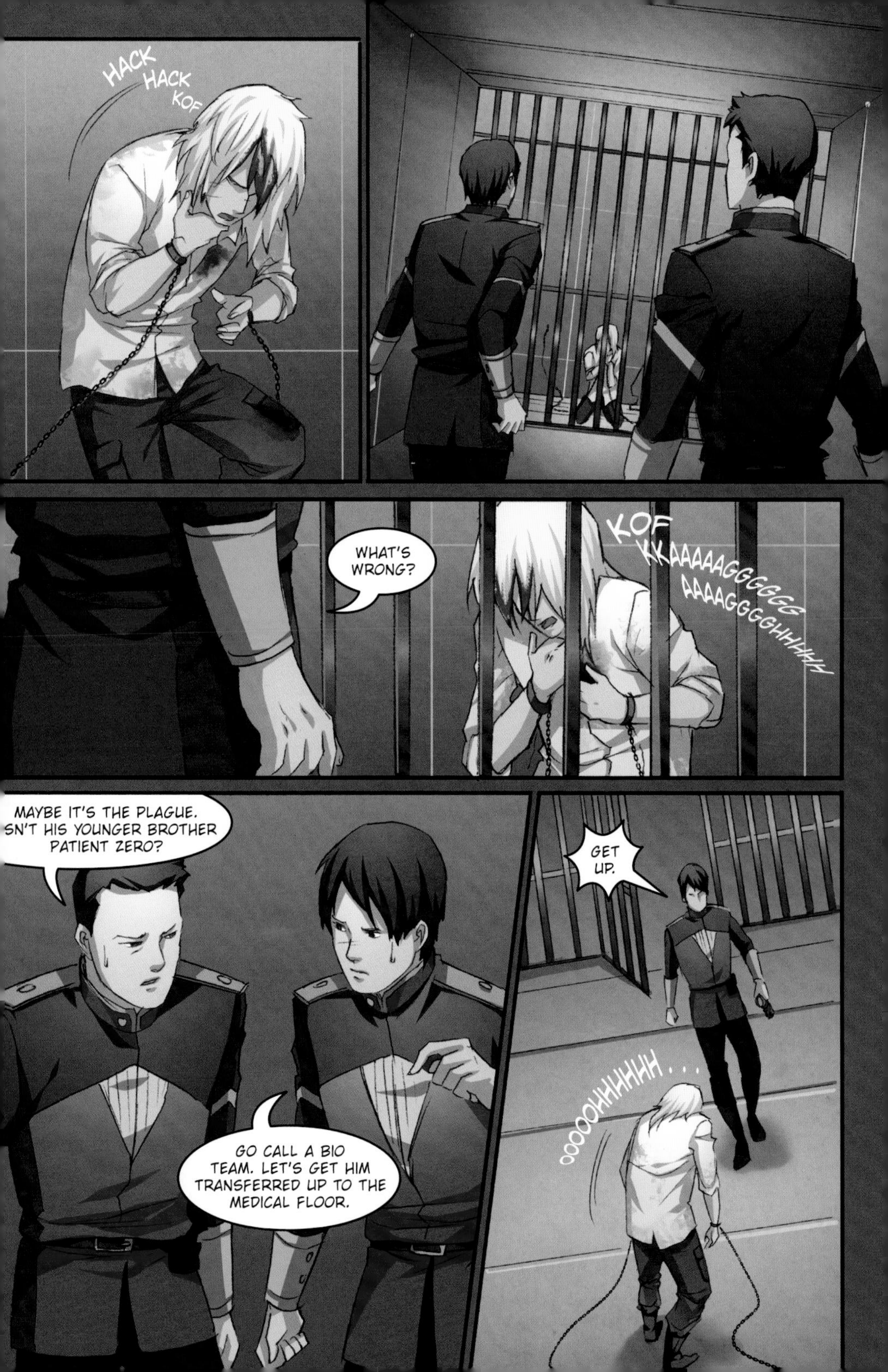
HACK
HACK
KOF
WHAT'S WRONG?
KOF
KKAAAAAAGGGGGG
AAAAGGGGHHHHHH
MAYBE IT'S THE PLAGUE. SN'T HIS YOUNGER BROTHER PATIENT ZERO?
GO CALL A BIO TEAM. LET'S GET HIM TRANSFERRED UP TO THE MEDICAL FLOOR.
GET UP.
OOOOOHHHHHH . . .

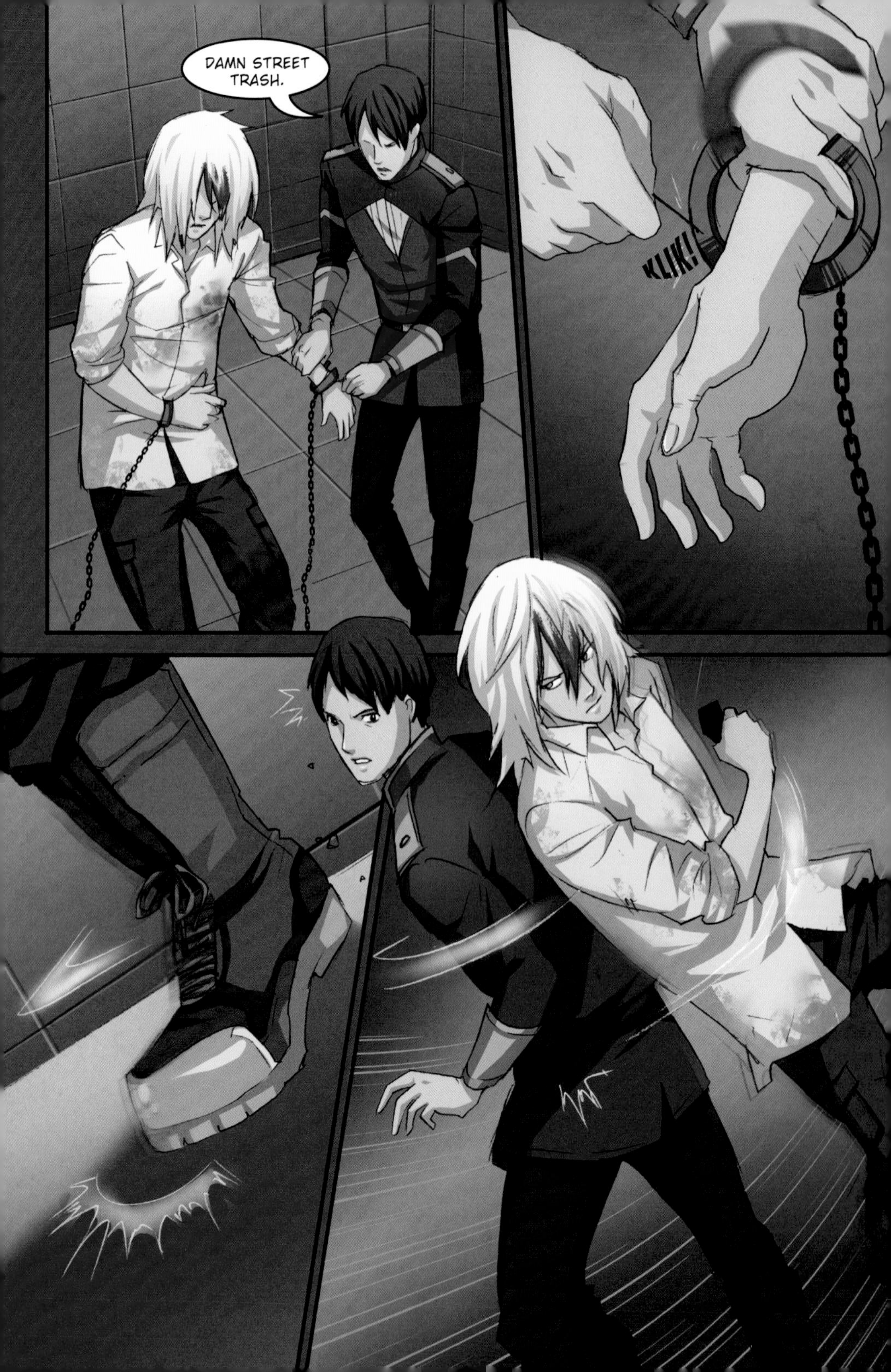
DAMN STREET TRASH.
KLIK!

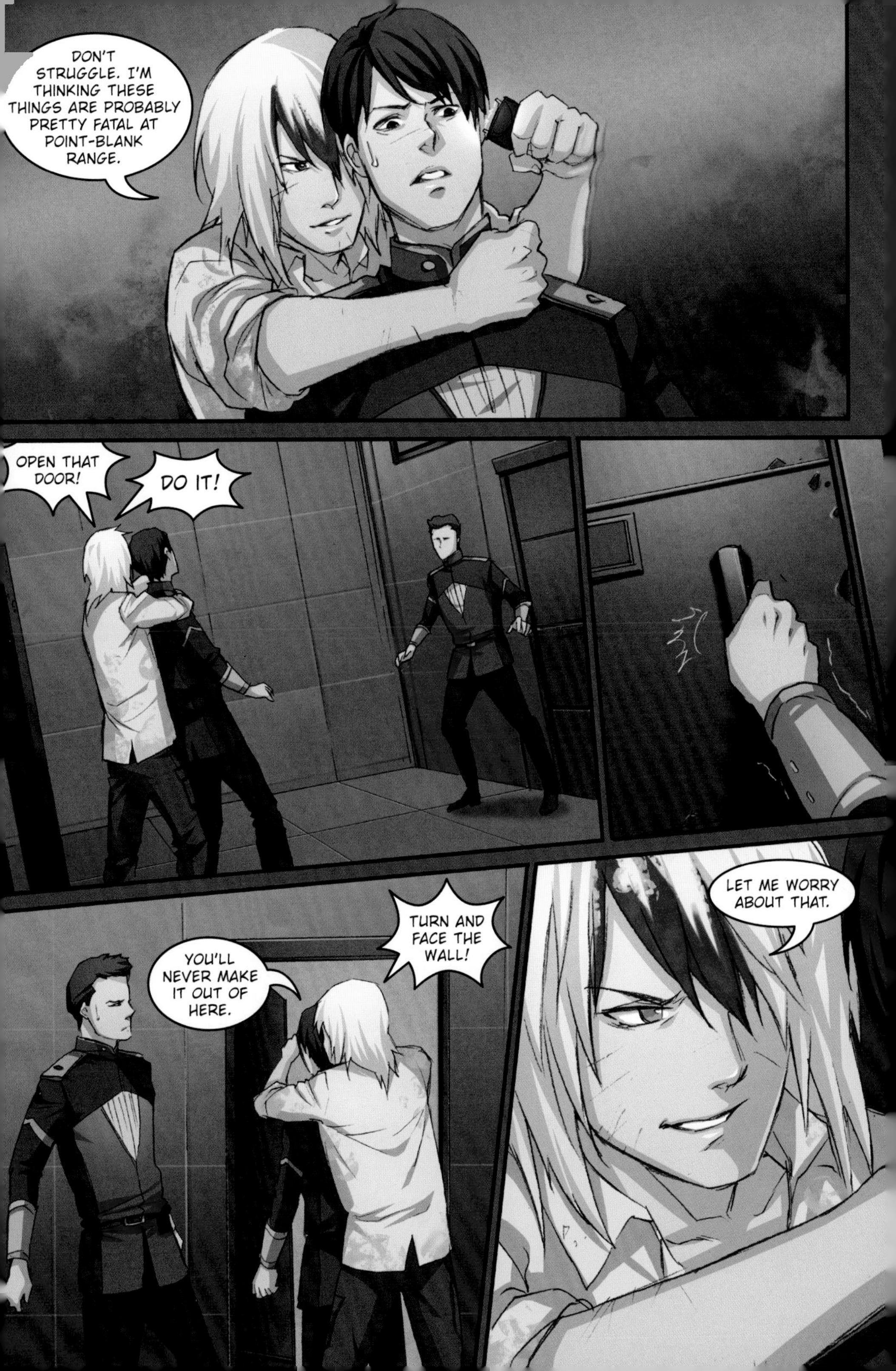
DON'T STRUGGLE. I'M THINKING THESE THINGS ARE PROBABLY PRETTY FATAL AT POINT-BLANK RANGE.
OPEN THAT DOOR!
DO IT!
TURN AND FACE THE WALL!
YOU'LL NEVER MAKE IT OUT OF HERE.
LET ME WORRY ABOUT THAT.

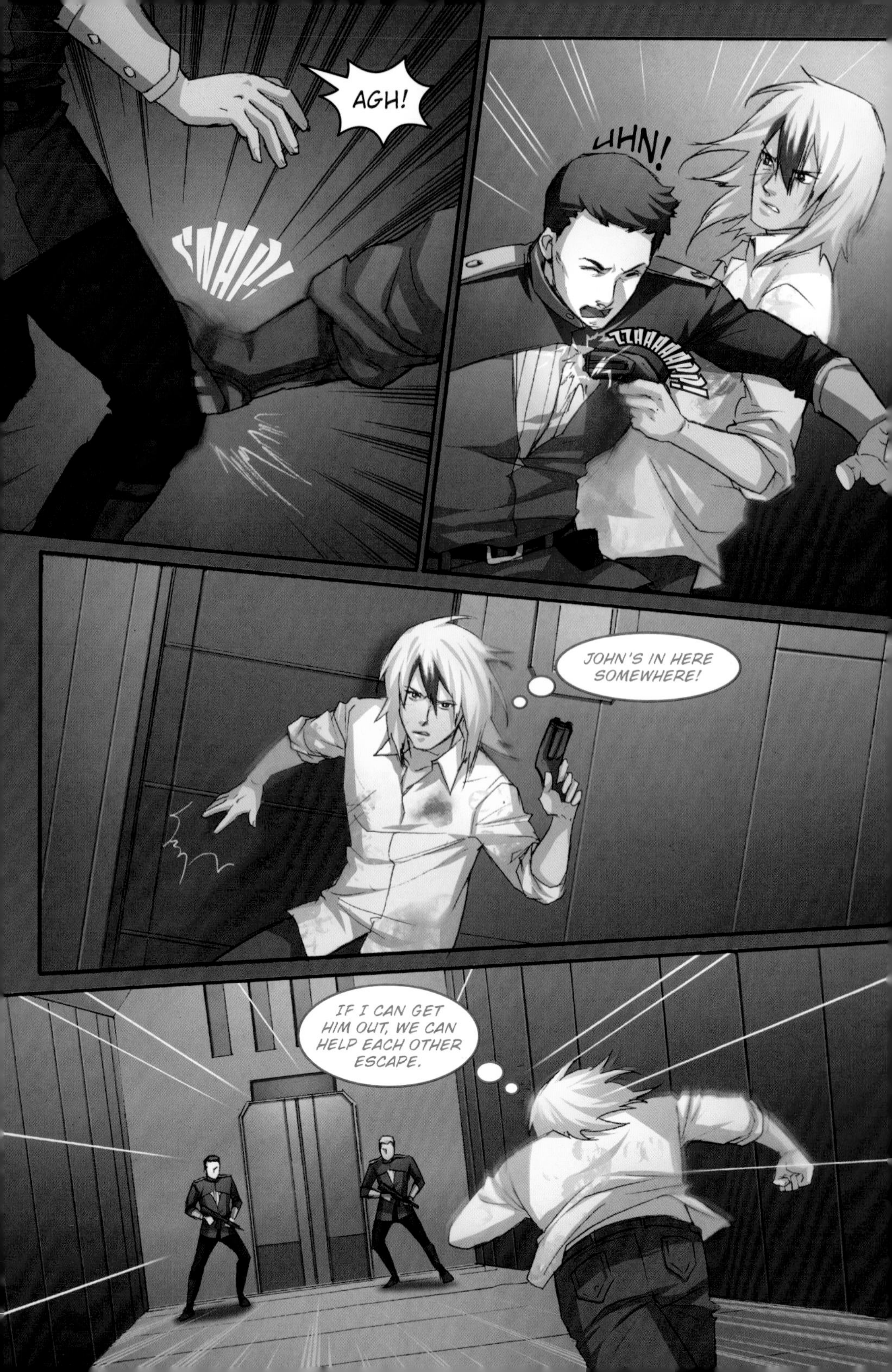

AGH!
SNAP!!
UHN!
ZZAAAAAPP!!
JOHN'S IN HERE SOMEWHERE!
IF I CAN GET HIM OUT, WE CAN HELP EACH OTHER ESCAPE.

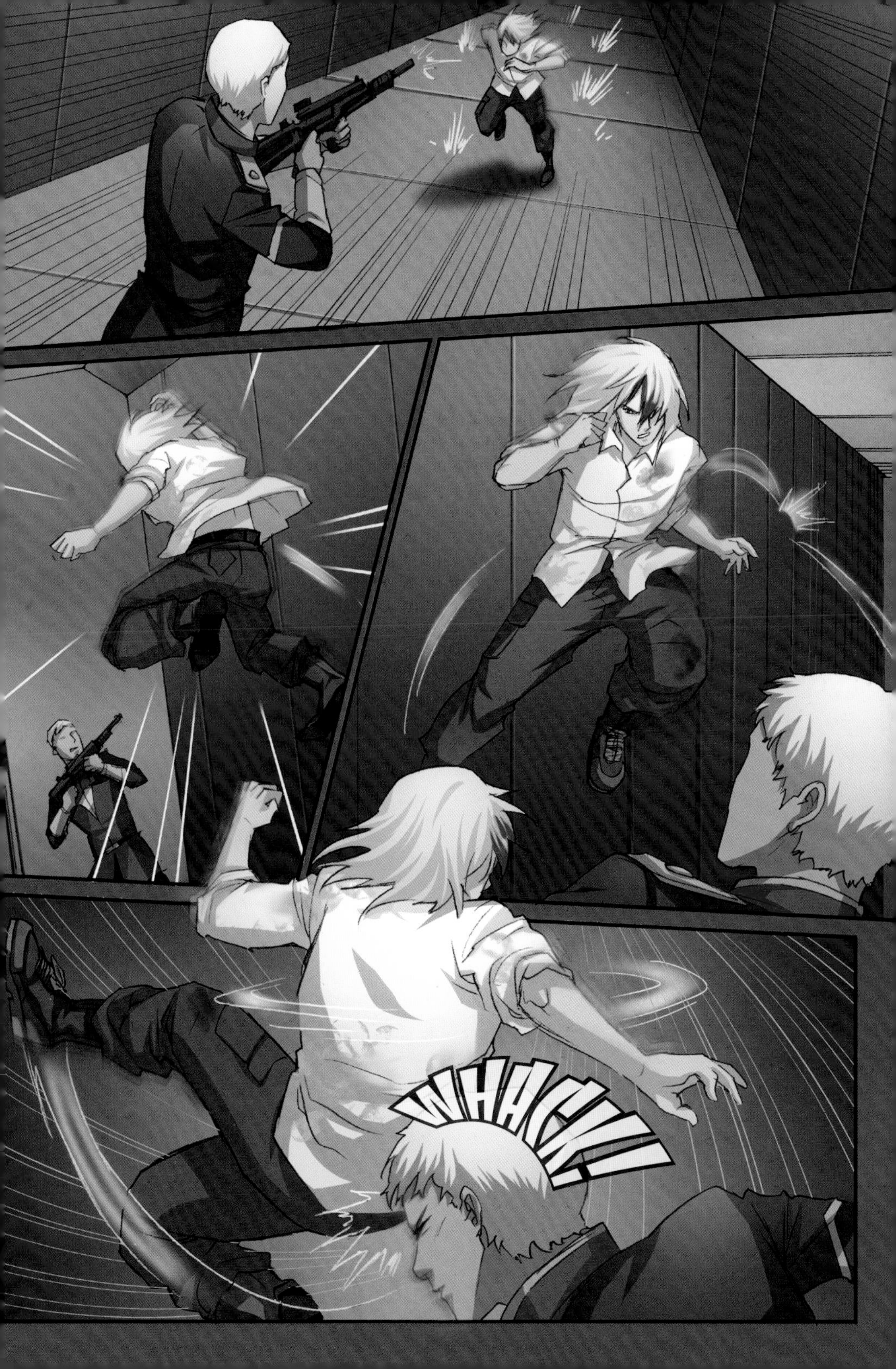
WHACK!!

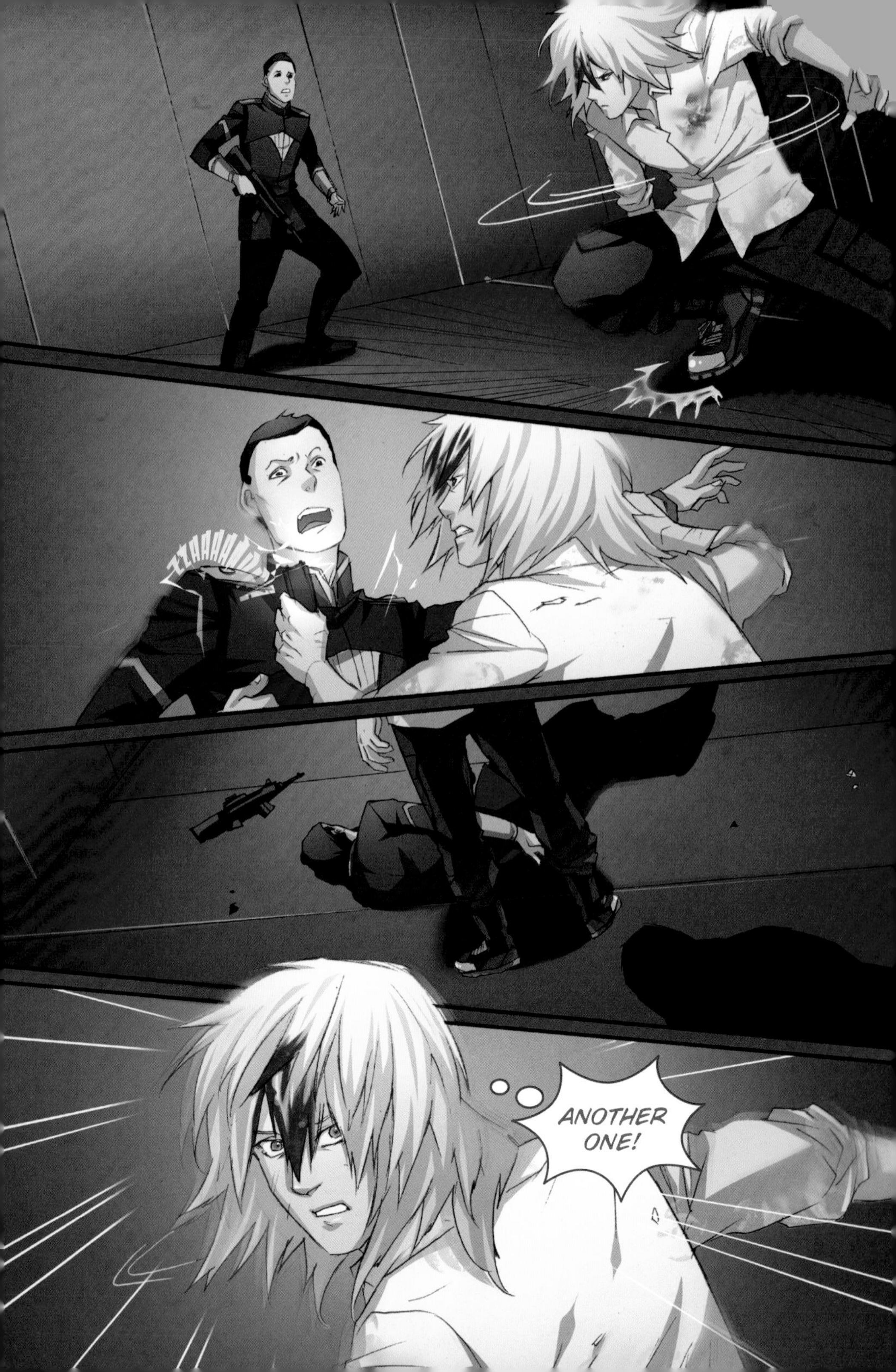
ANOTHER ONE!

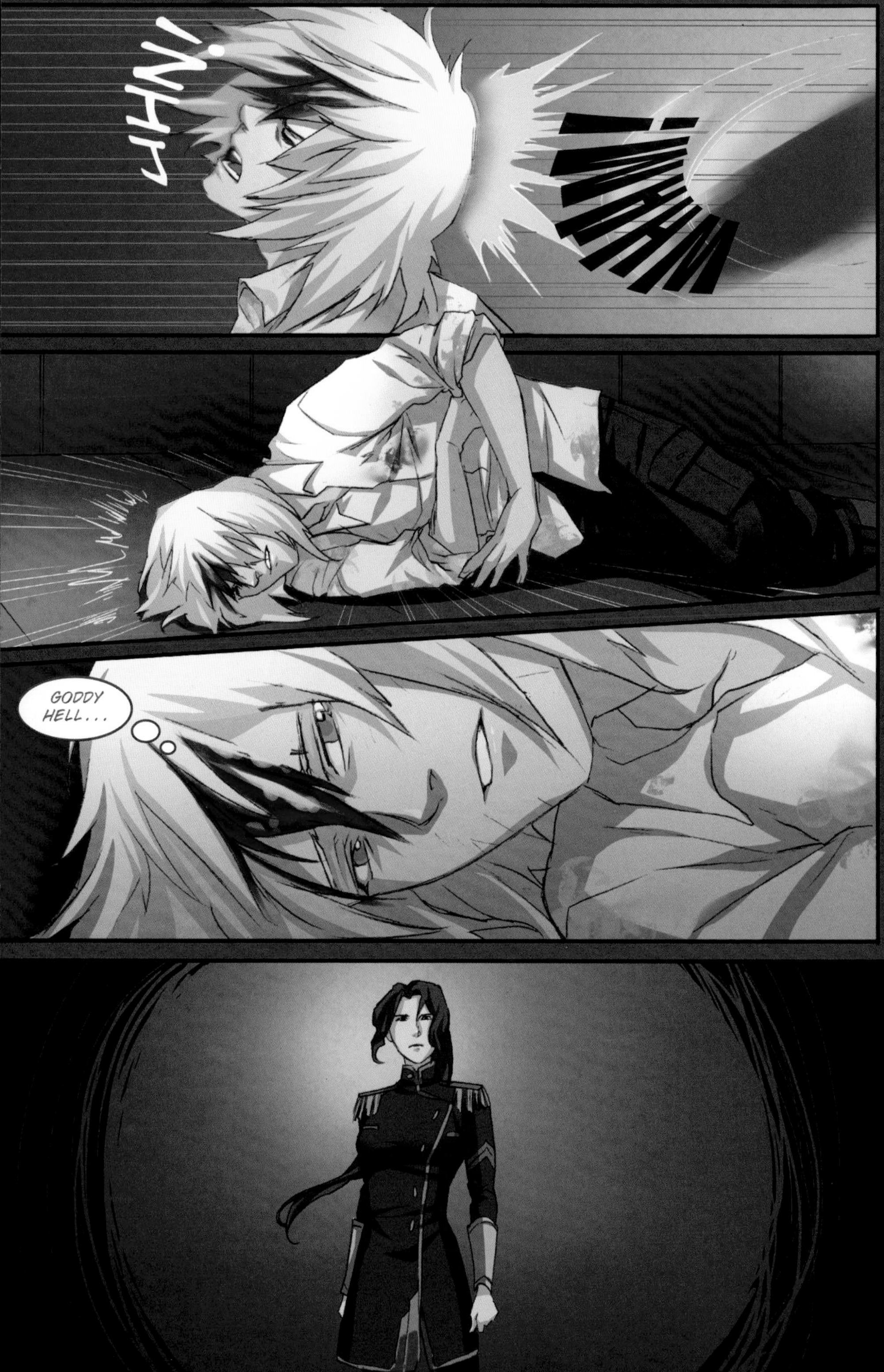
UHHN!
WHAM!!
GODDY HELL...

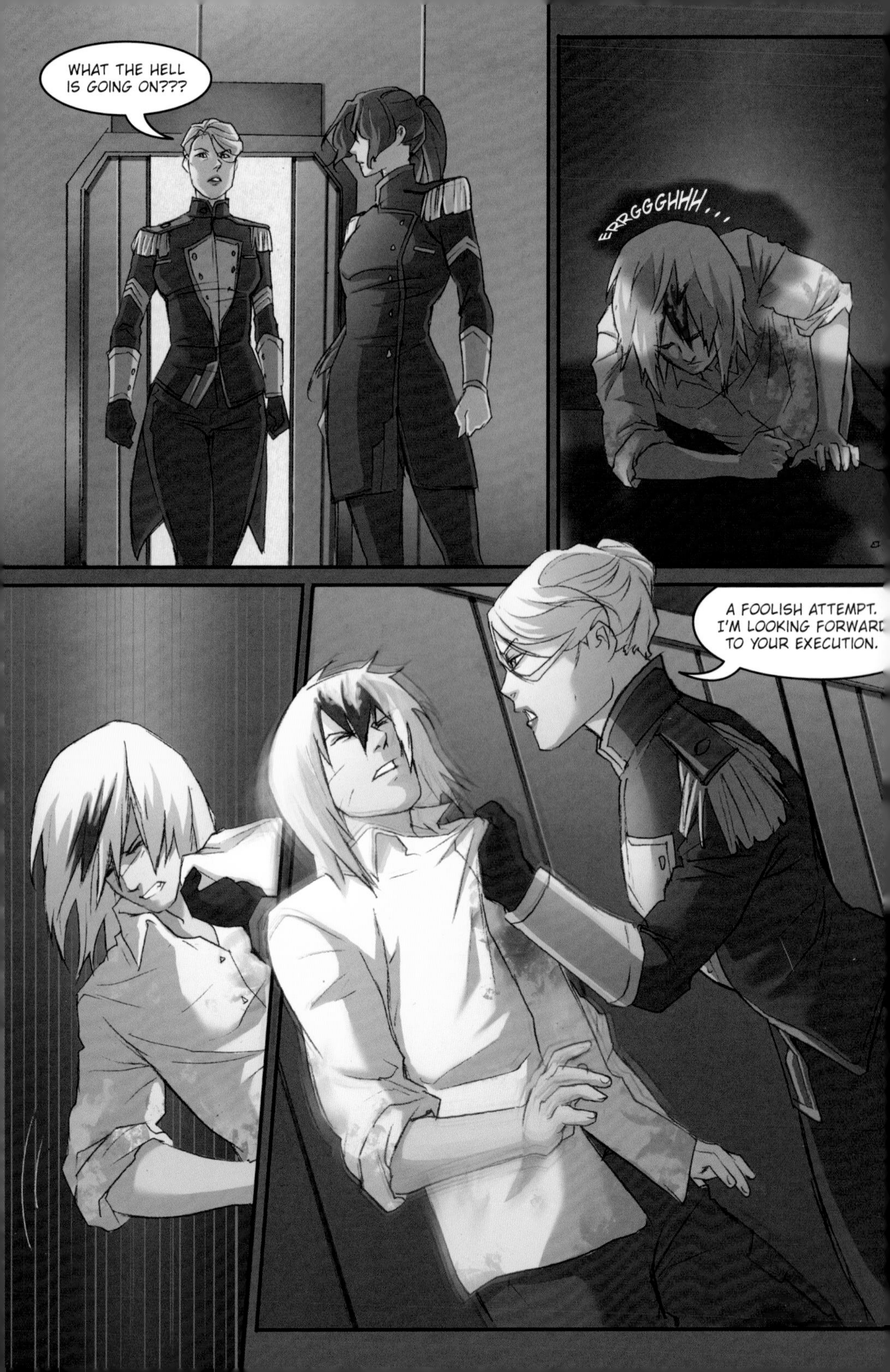
WHAT THE HELL IS GOING ON???
ERRGGGHHH...
A FOOLISH ATTEMPT. I'M LOOKING FORWARD TO YOUR EXECUTION.

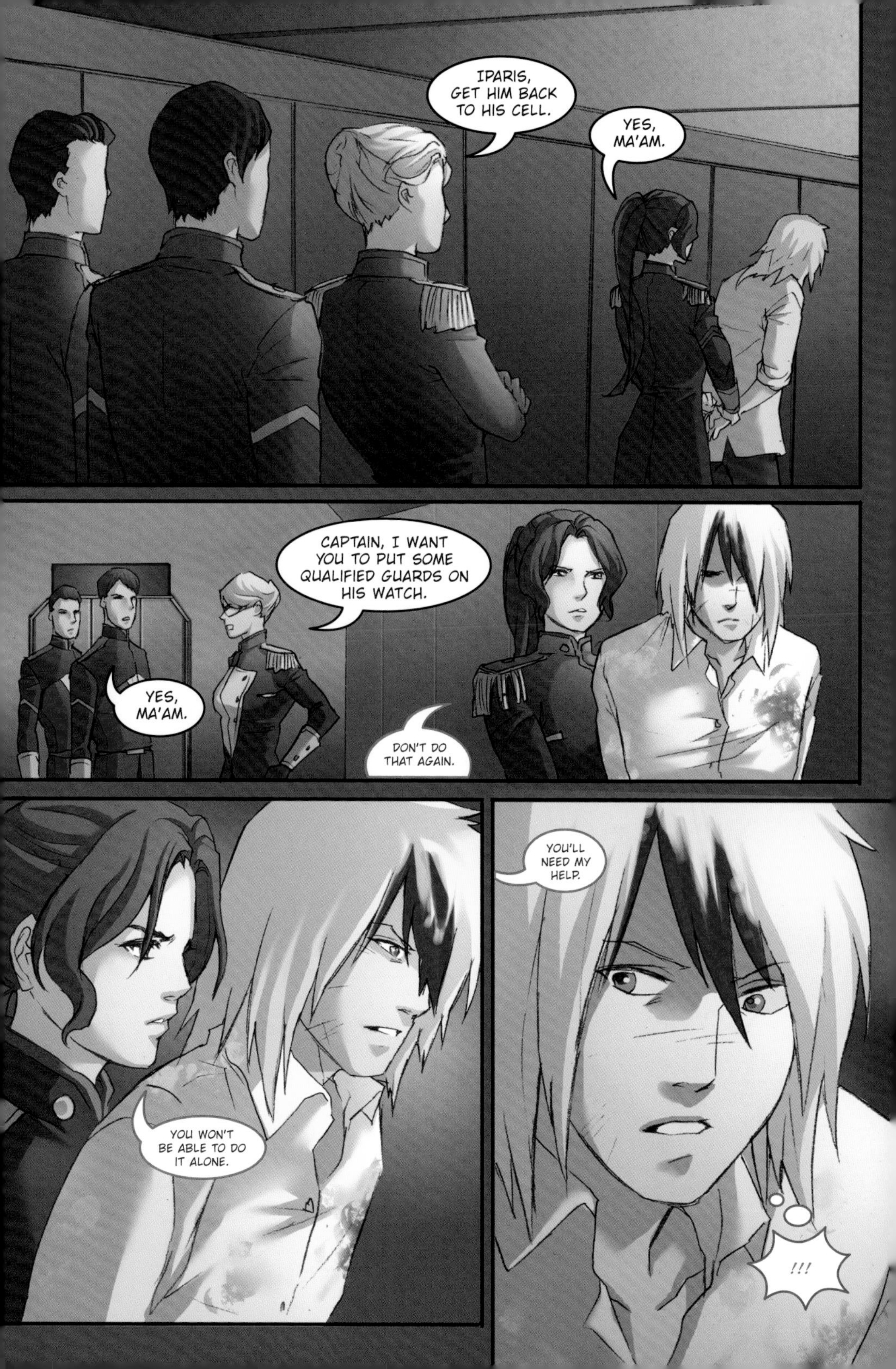
IPARIS, GET HIM BACK TO HIS CELL.
YES, MA'AM.
CAPTAIN, I WANT YOU TO PUT SOME QUALIFIED GUARDS ON HIS WATCH.
YES, MA'AM.
DON'T DO THAT AGAIN.
YOU WON'T BE ABLE TO DO IT ALONE.
YOU'LL NEED MY HELP.
!!!

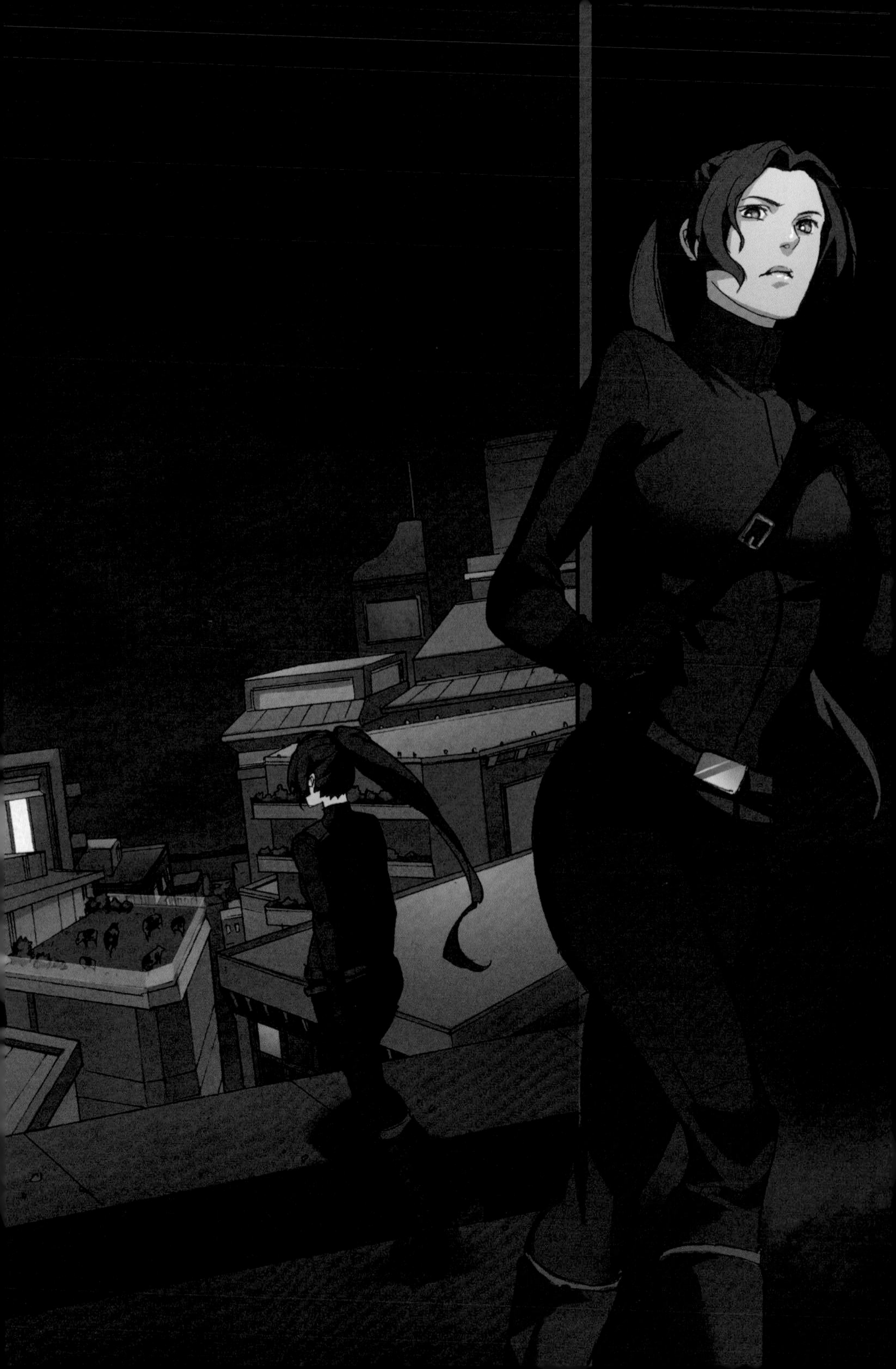

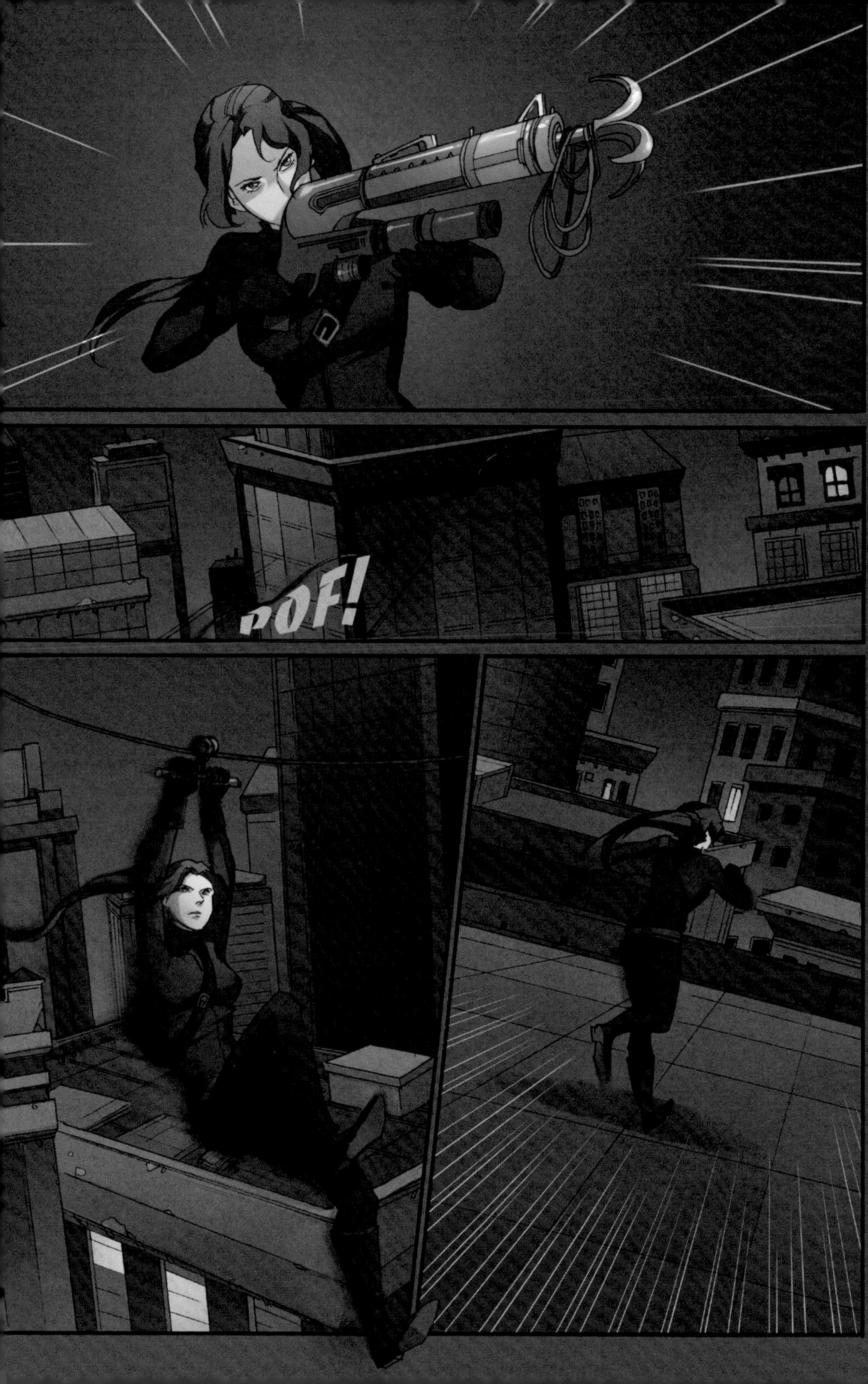
POF!

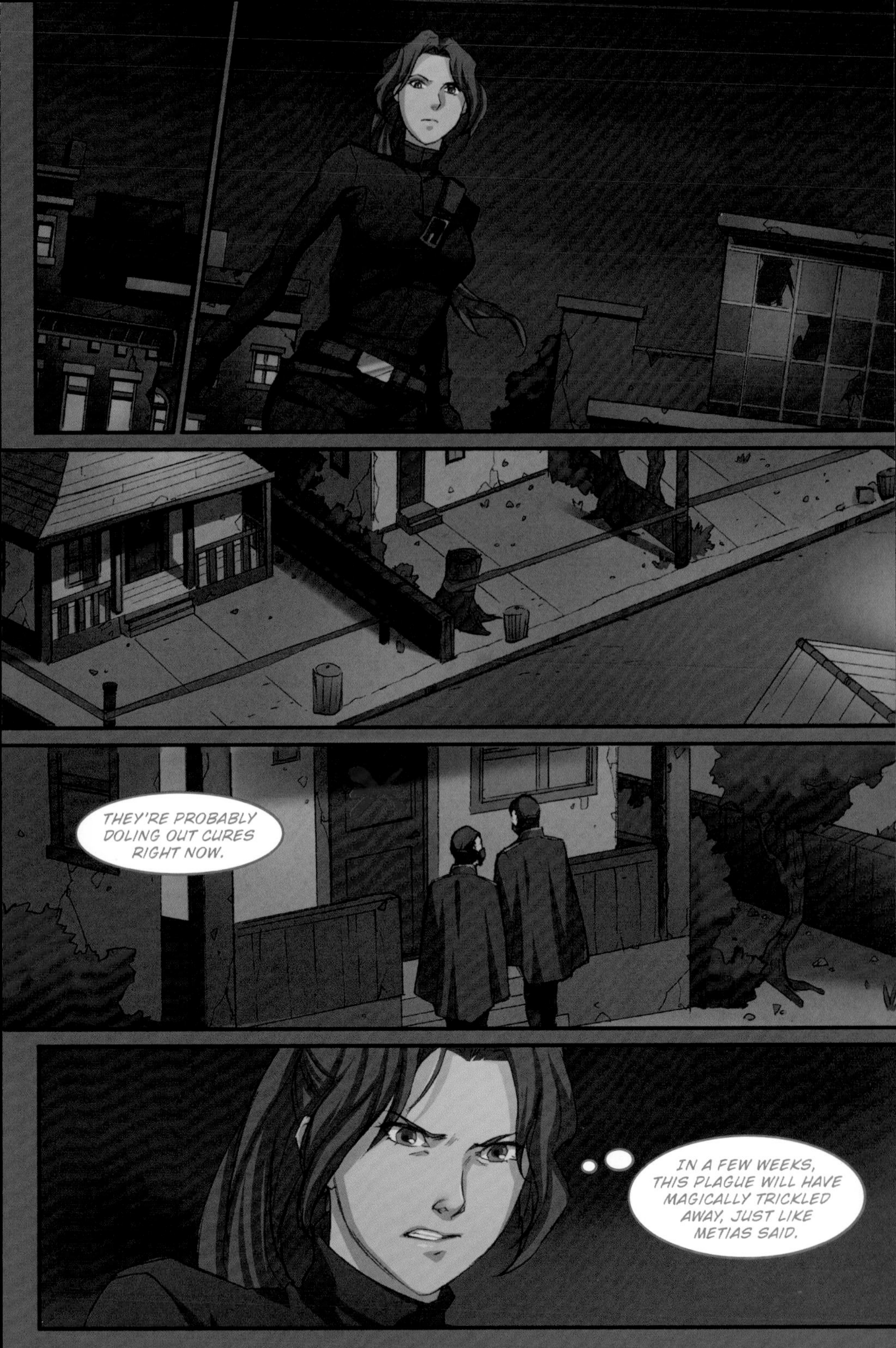
THEY'RE PROBABLY DOLING OUT CURES RIGHT NOW.
IN A FEW WEEKS, THIS PLAGUE WILL HAVE MAGICALLY TRICKLED AWAY, JUST LIKE METIAS SAID.

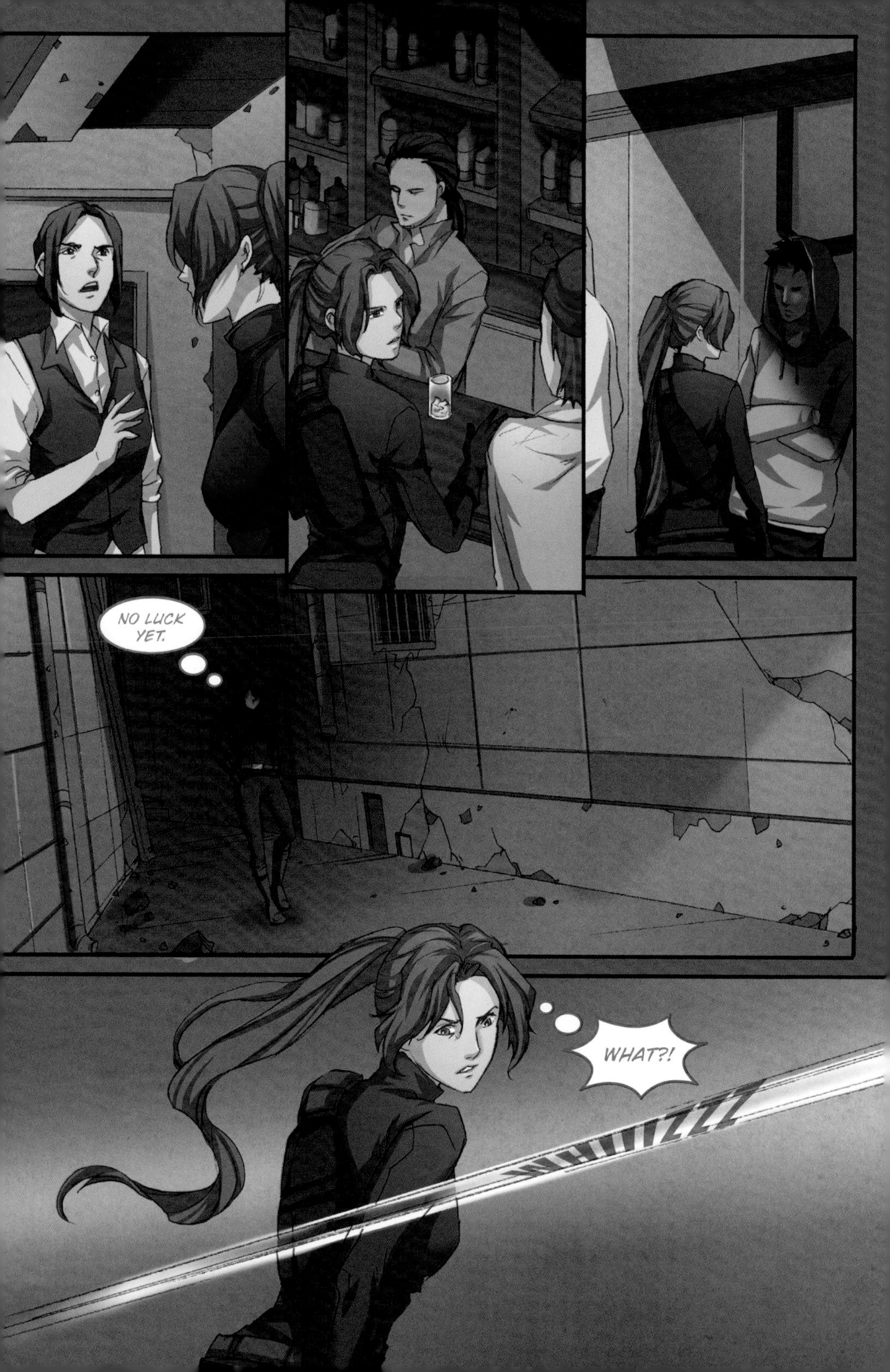
NO LUCK YET.
WHAT?!
WHUIZZZ

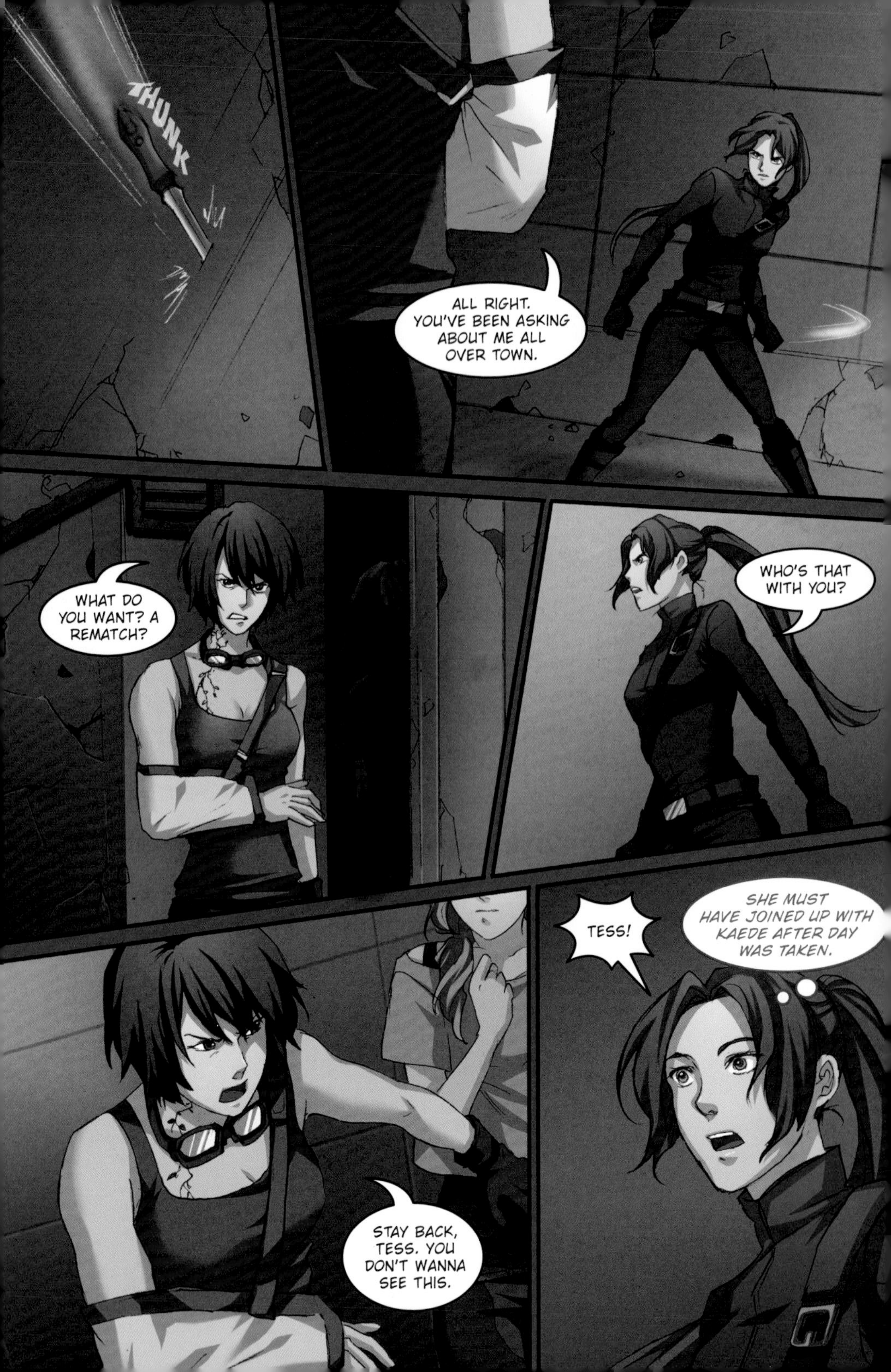
THUNK
ALL RIGHT. YOU'VE BEEN ASKING ABOUT ME ALL OVER TOWN.
WHAT DO YOU WANT? A REMATCH?
WHO'S THAT WITH YOU?
STAY BACK, TESS. YOU DON'T WANNA SEE THIS.
TESS!
SHE MUST HAVE JOINED UP WITH KAEDE AFTER DAY WAS TAKEN.

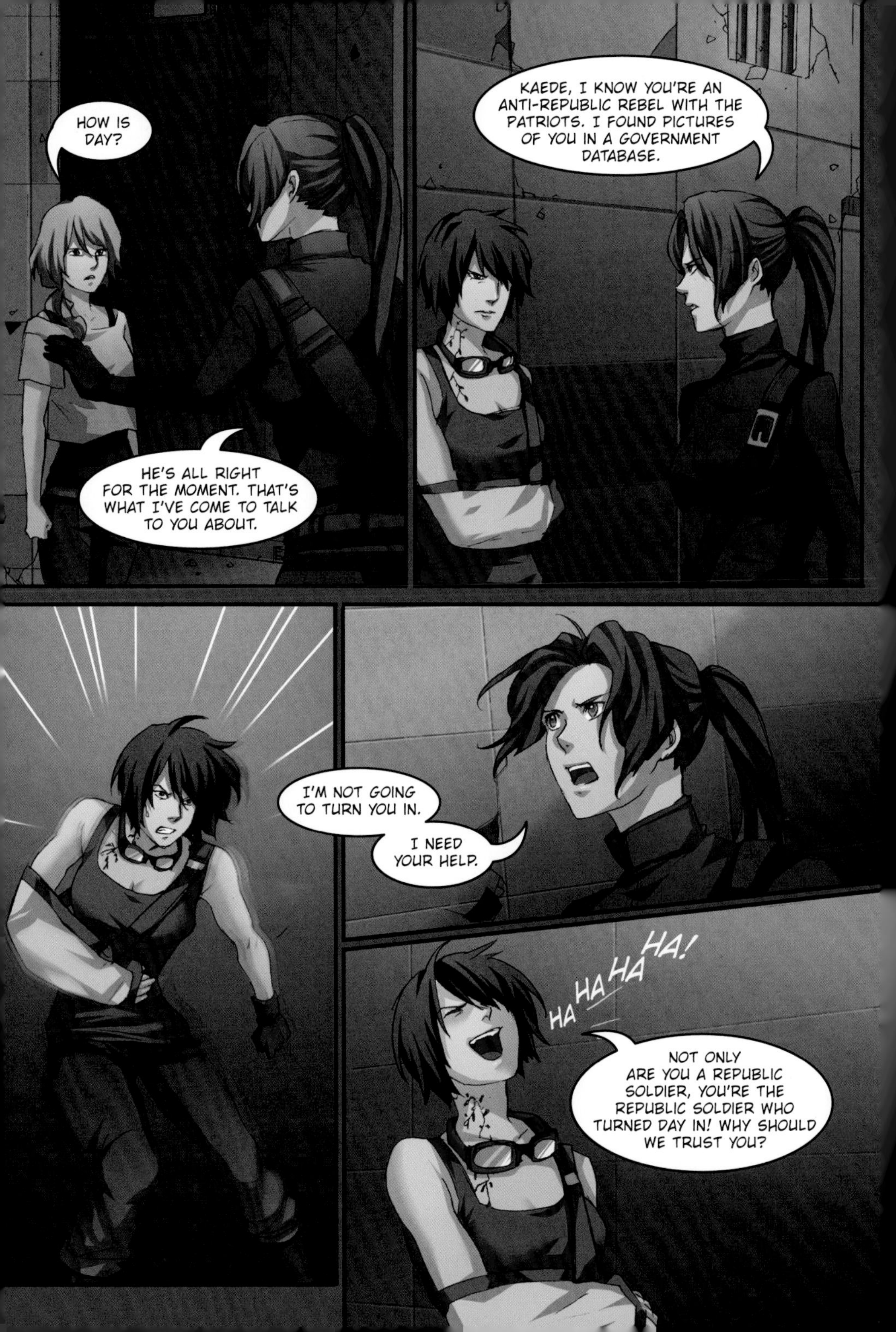
HOW IS DAY?
HE'S ALL RIGHT FOR THE MOMENT. THAT'S WHAT I'VE COME TO TALK TO YOU ABOUT.
KAEDE, I KNOW YOU'RE AN ANTI-REPUBLIC REBEL WITH THE PATRIOTS. I FOUND PICTURES OF YOU IN A GOVERNMENT DATABASE.
I'M NOT GOING TO TURN YOU IN.
I NEED YOUR HELP.
HA HA HA HA!
NOT ONLY ARE YOU A REPUBLIC SOLDIER, YOU'RE THE REPUBLIC SOLDIER WHO TURNED DAY IN! WHY SHOULD WE TRUST YOU?

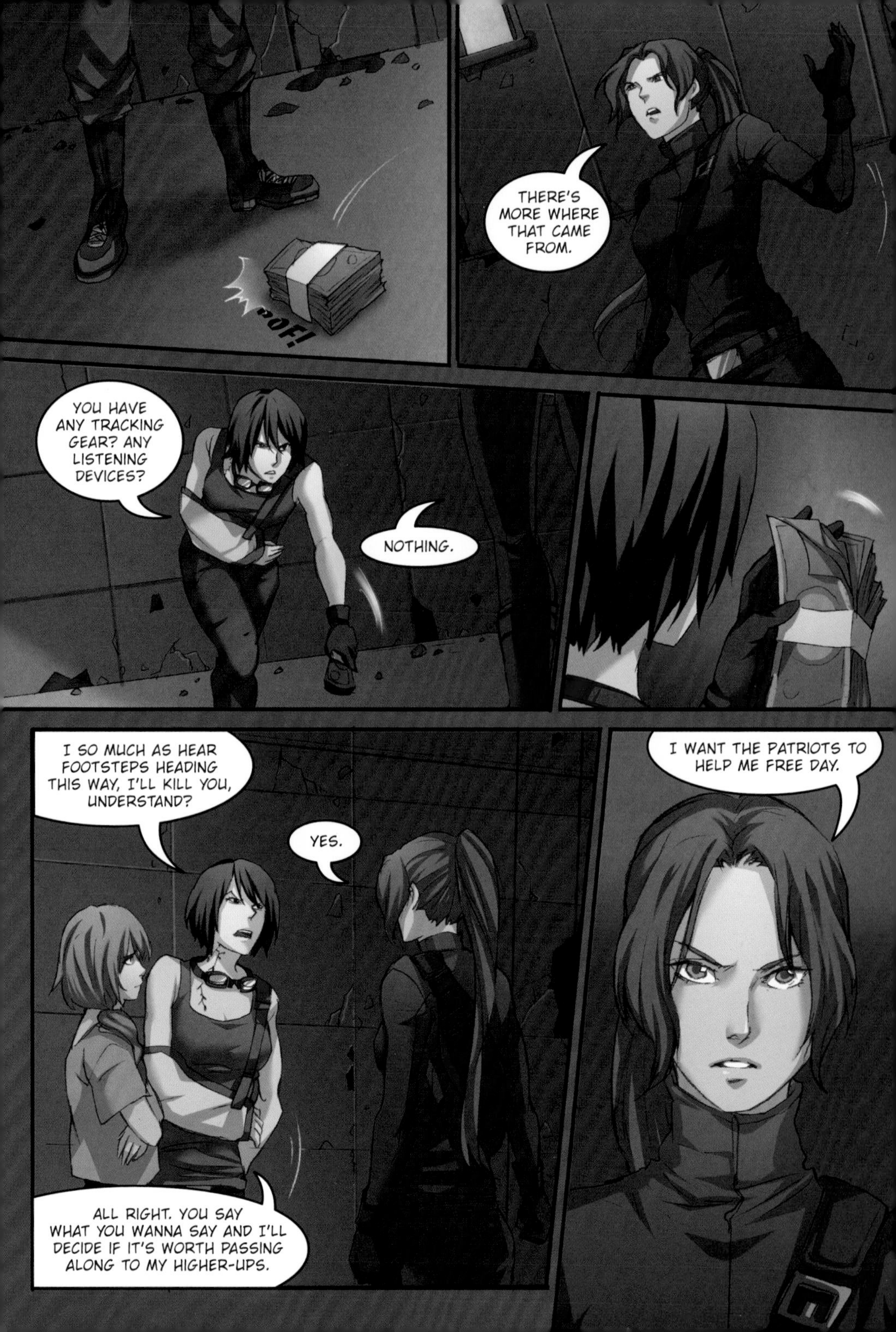

POF!
THERE'S MORE WHERE THAT CAME FROM.
YOU HAVE ANY TRACKING GEAR? ANY LISTENING DEVICES?
NOTHING.
I SO MUCH AS HEAR FOOTSTEPS HEADING THIS WAY, I'LL KILL YOU, UNDERSTAND?
YES.
ALL RIGHT. YOU SAY WHAT YOU WANNA SAY AND I'LL DECIDE IF IT'S WORTH PASSING ALONG TO MY HIGHER-UPS.
I WANT THE PATRIOTS TO HELP ME FREE DAY.

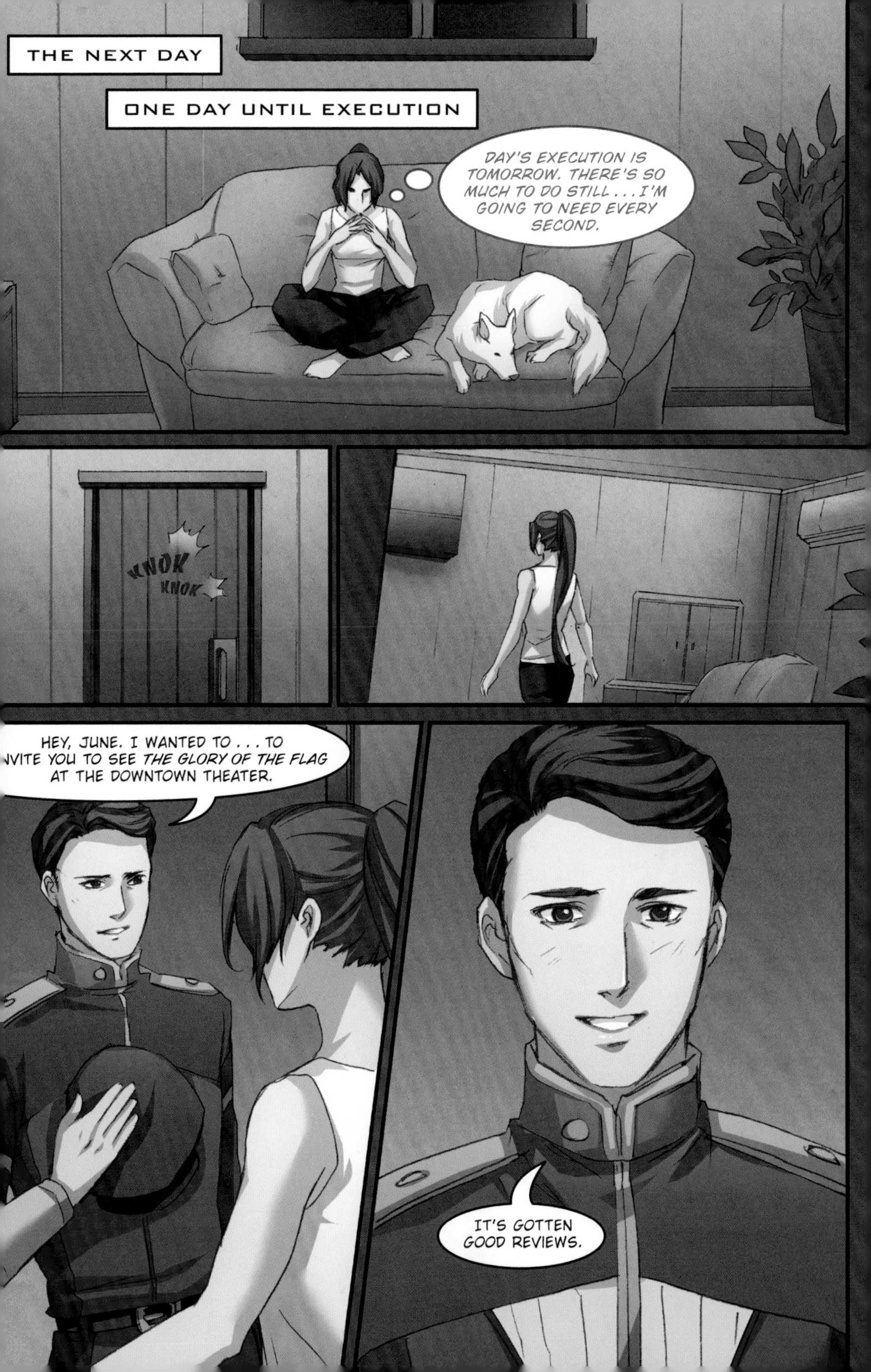
THE NEXT DAY
ONE DAY UNTIL EXECUTION
DAY'S EXECUTION IS TOMORROW. THERE'S SO MUCH TO DO STILL . . . I'M GOING TO NEED EVERY SECOND.
KNOK KNOK
HEY, JUNE. I WANTED TO . . . TO
NVITE YOU TO SEE *THE GLORY OF THE FLAG*
AT THE DOWNTOWN THEATER.
IT'S GOTTEN GOOD REVIEWS.

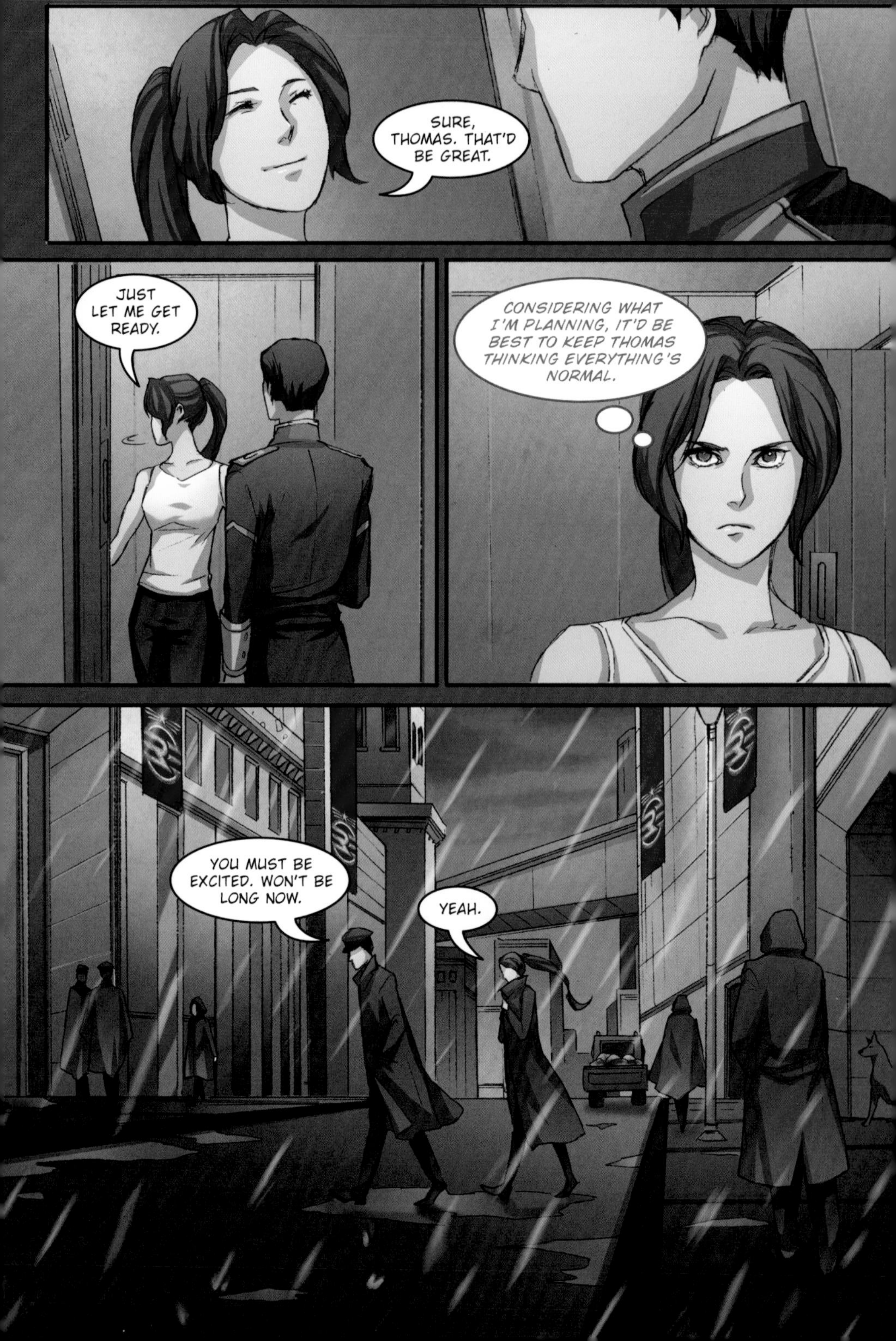
SURE, THOMAS. THAT'D BE GREAT.
JUST LET ME GET READY.
CONSIDERING WHAT I'M PLANNING, IT'D BE BEST TO KEEP THOMAS THINKING EVERYTHING'S NORMAL.
YOU MUST BE EXCITED. WON'T BE LONG NOW.
YEAH.

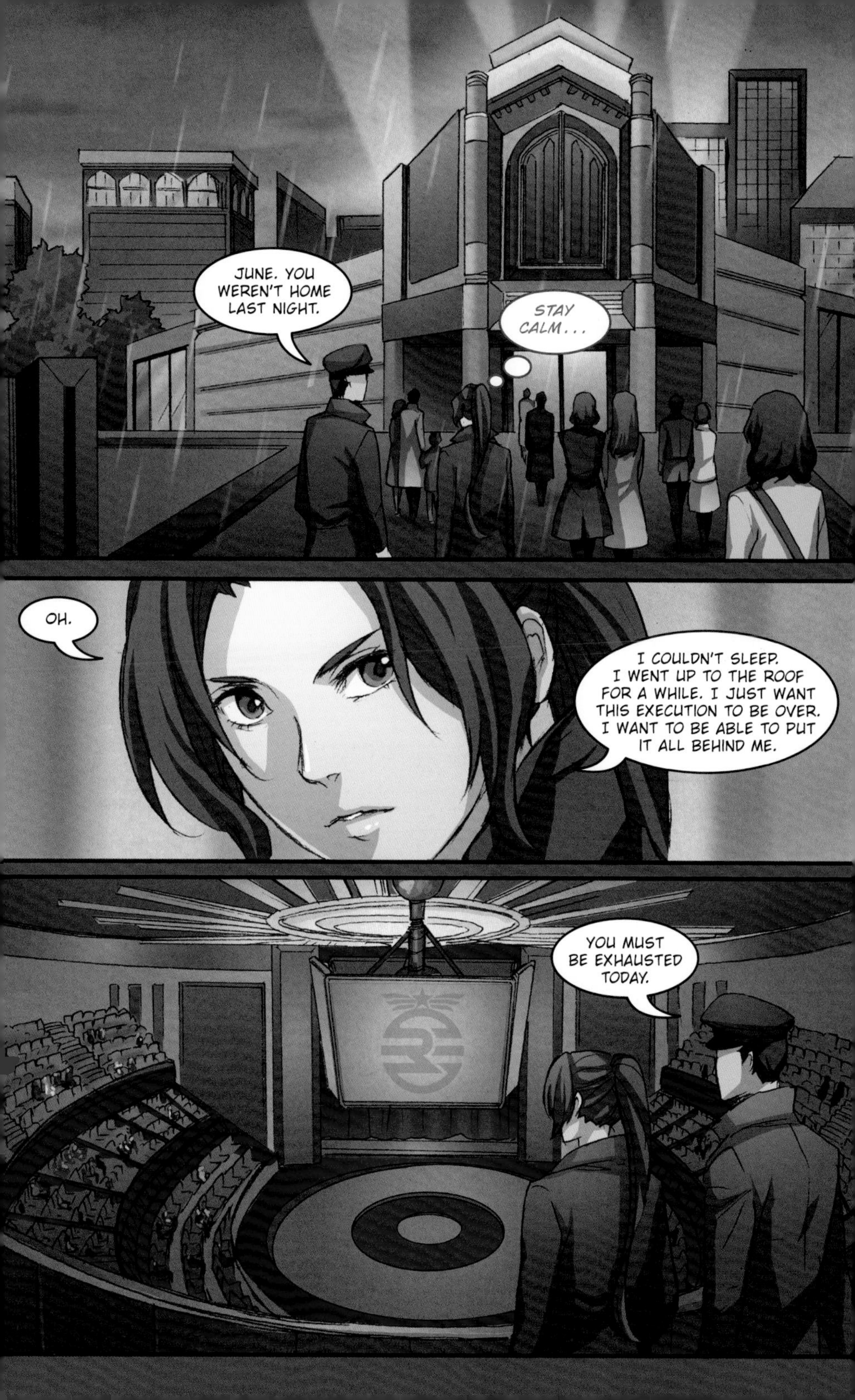
JUNE. YOU WEREN'T HOME LAST NIGHT.
STAY CALM . . .
OH.
I COULDN'T SLEEP. I WENT UP TO THE ROOF FOR A WHILE. I JUST WANT THIS EXECUTION TO BE OVER. I WANT TO BE ABLE TO PUT IT ALL BEHIND ME.
YOU MUST BE EXHAUSTED TODAY.

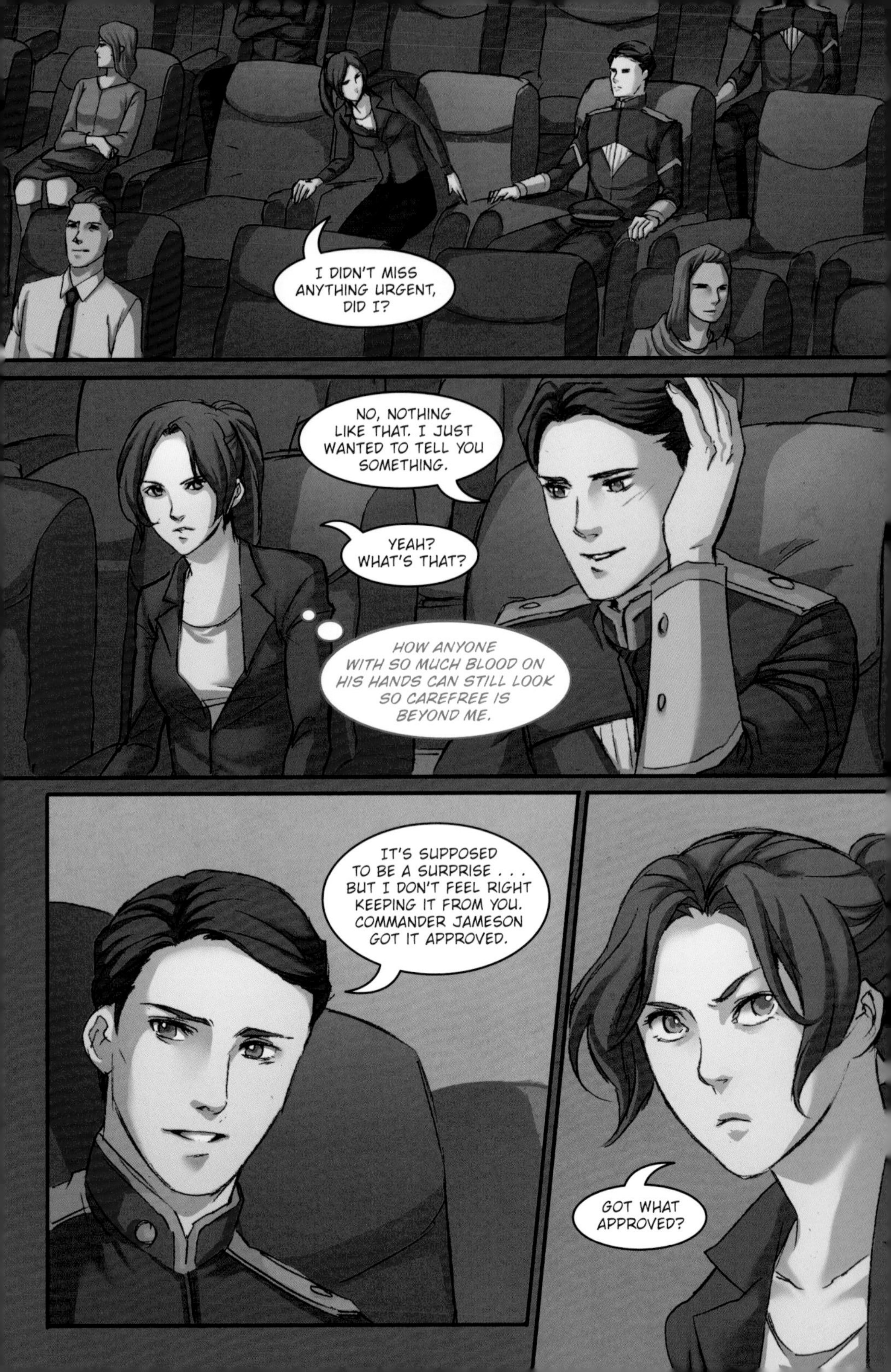
I DIDN'T MISS ANYTHING URGENT, DID I?
NO, NOTHING LIKE THAT. I JUST WANTED TO TELL YOU SOMETHING.
YEAH? WHAT'S THAT?
HOW ANYONE WITH SO MUCH BLOOD ON HIS HANDS CAN STILL LOOK SO CAREFREE IS BEYOND ME.
IT'S SUPPOSED TO BE A SURPRISE . . . BUT I DON'T FEEL RIGHT KEEPING IT FROM YOU. COMMANDER JAMESON GOT IT APPROVED.
GOT WHAT APPROVED?

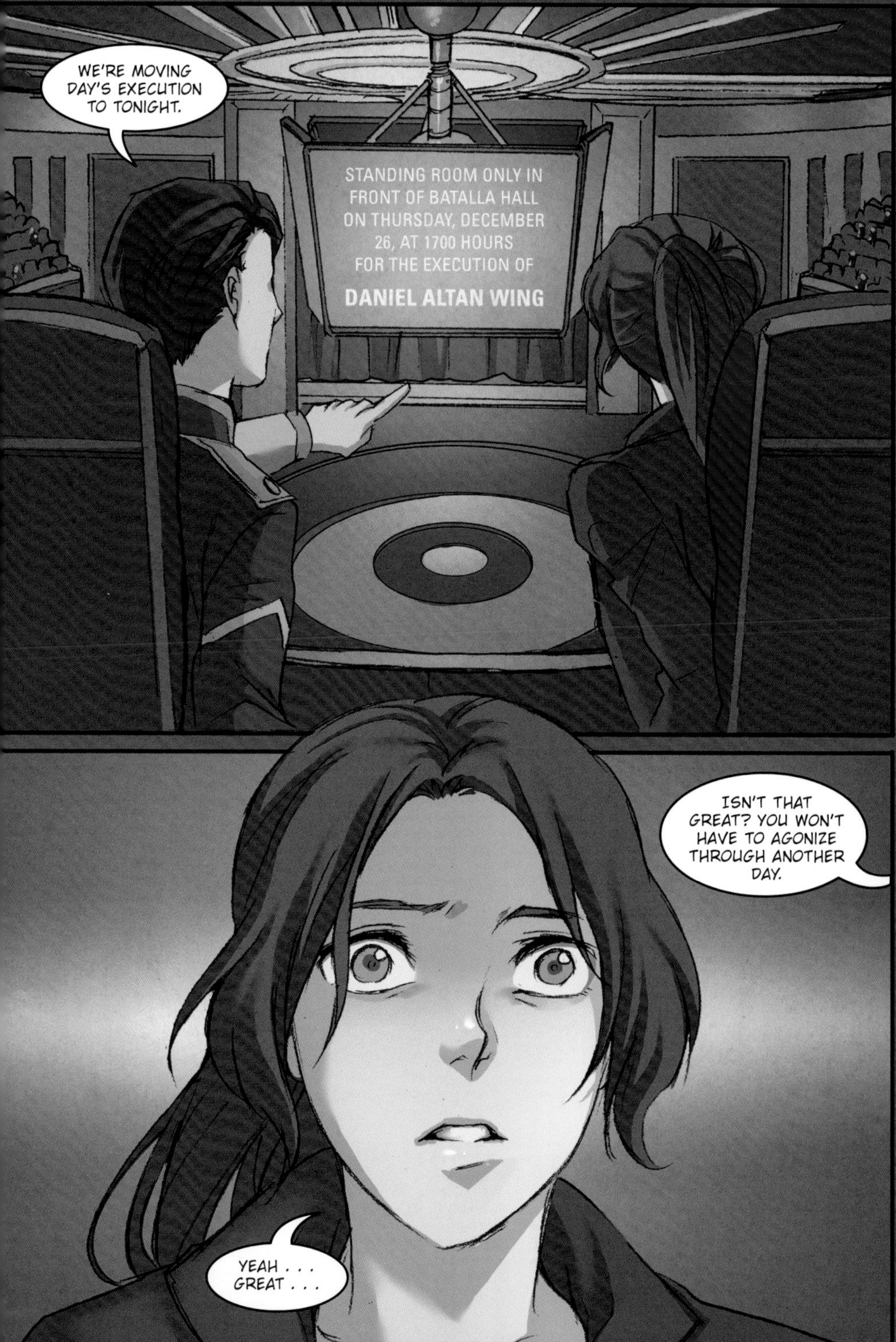
WE'RE MOVING DAY'S EXECUTION TO TONIGHT.
STANDING ROOM ONLY IN FRONT OF BATALLA HALL ON THURSDAY, DECEMBER 26, AT 1700 HOURS FOR THE EXECUTION OF
DANIEL ALTAN WING
ISN'T THAT GREAT? YOU WON'T HAVE TO AGONIZE THROUGH ANOTHER DAY.
YEAH . . . GREAT . . .

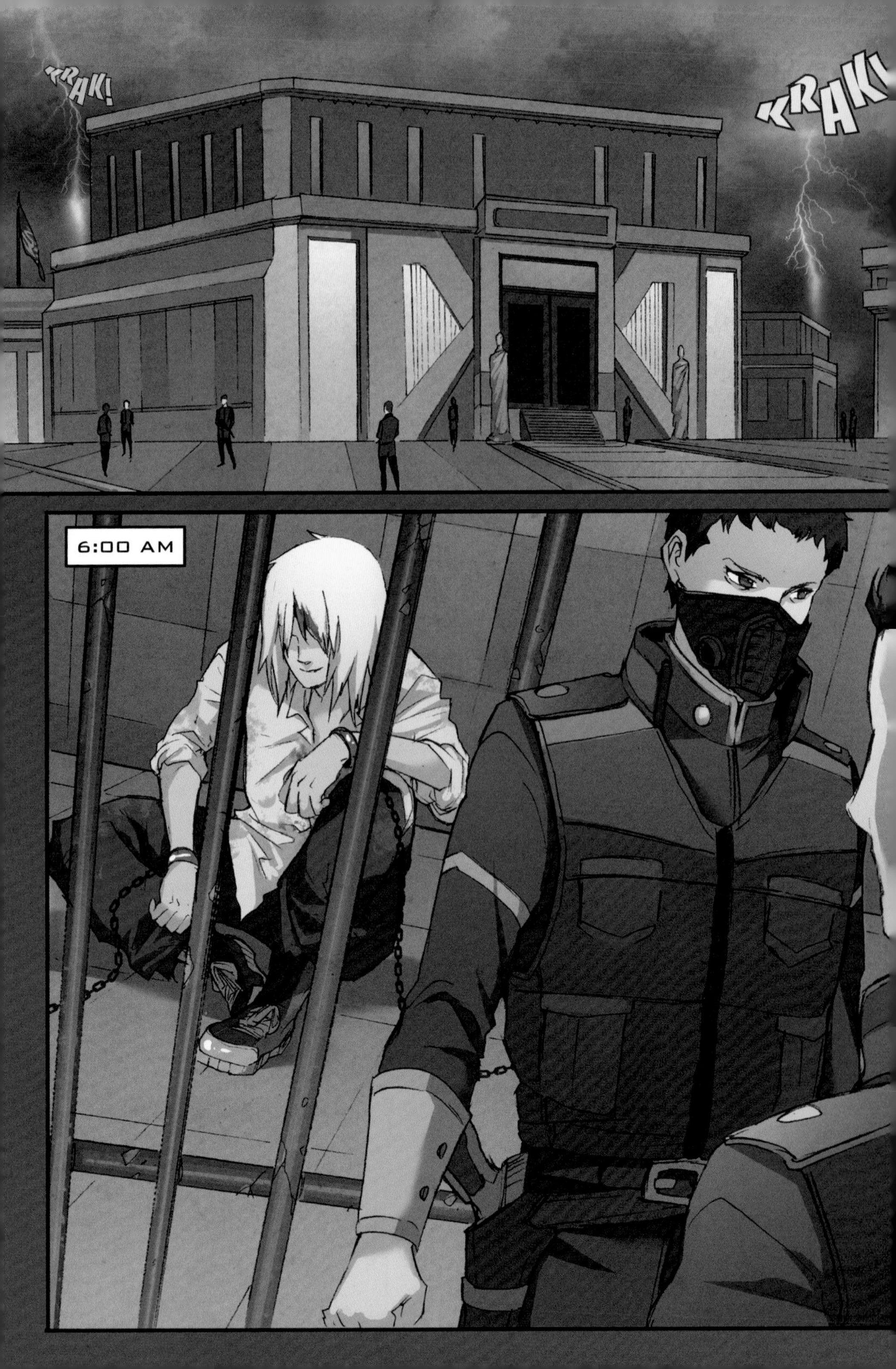

KRAK!
KRAK!
6:00 AM

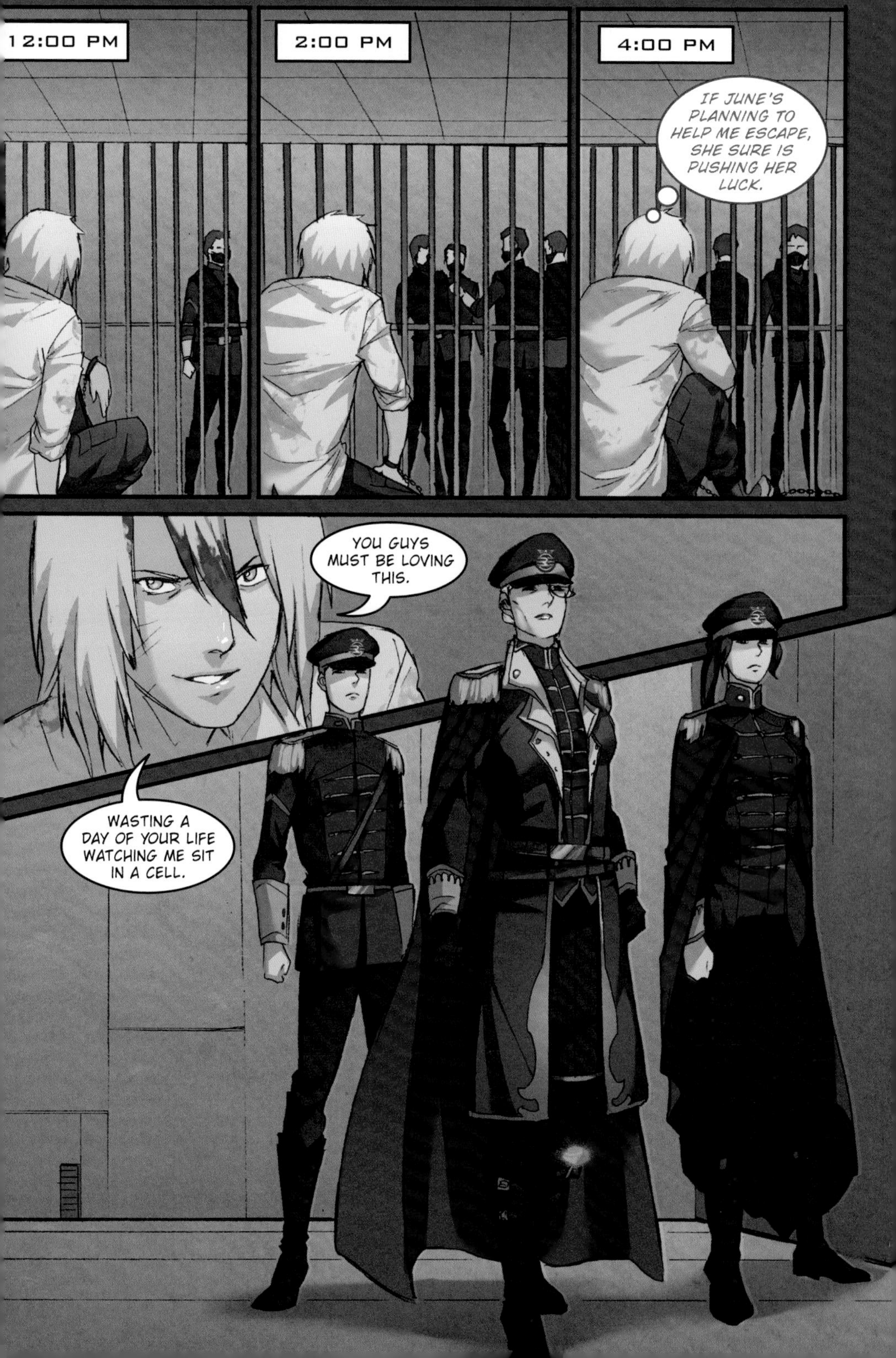
12:00 PM
2:00 PM
4:00 PM
IF JUNE'S PLANNING TO HELP ME ESCAPE, SHE SURE IS PUSHING HER LUCK.
YOU GUYS MUST BE LOVING THIS.
WASTING A DAY OF YOUR LIFE WATCHING ME SIT IN A CELL.

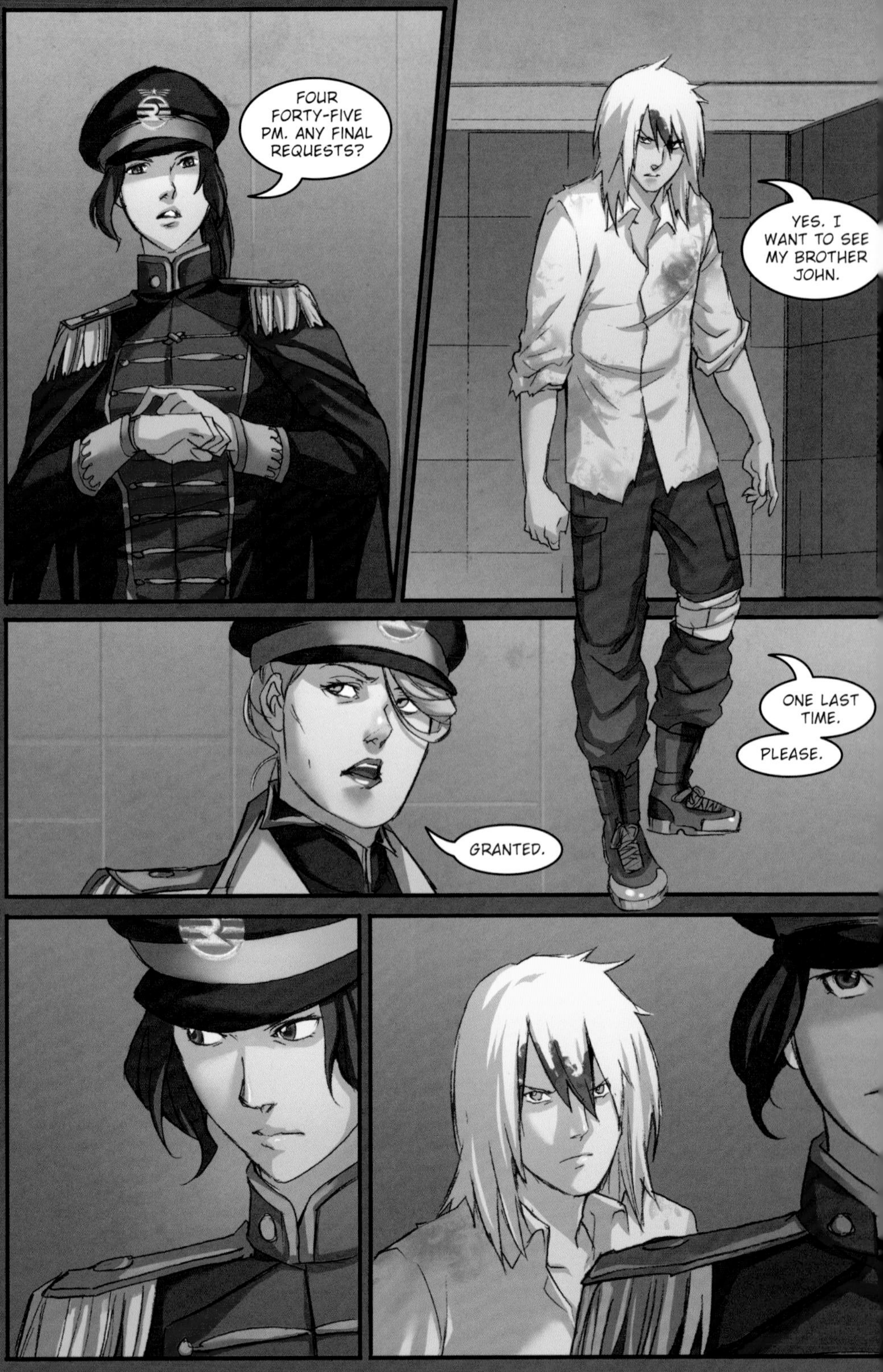
FOUR FORTY-FIVE PM. ANY FINAL REQUESTS?
YES. I WANT TO SEE MY BROTHER JOHN.
ONE LAST TIME.
PLEASE.
GRANTED.

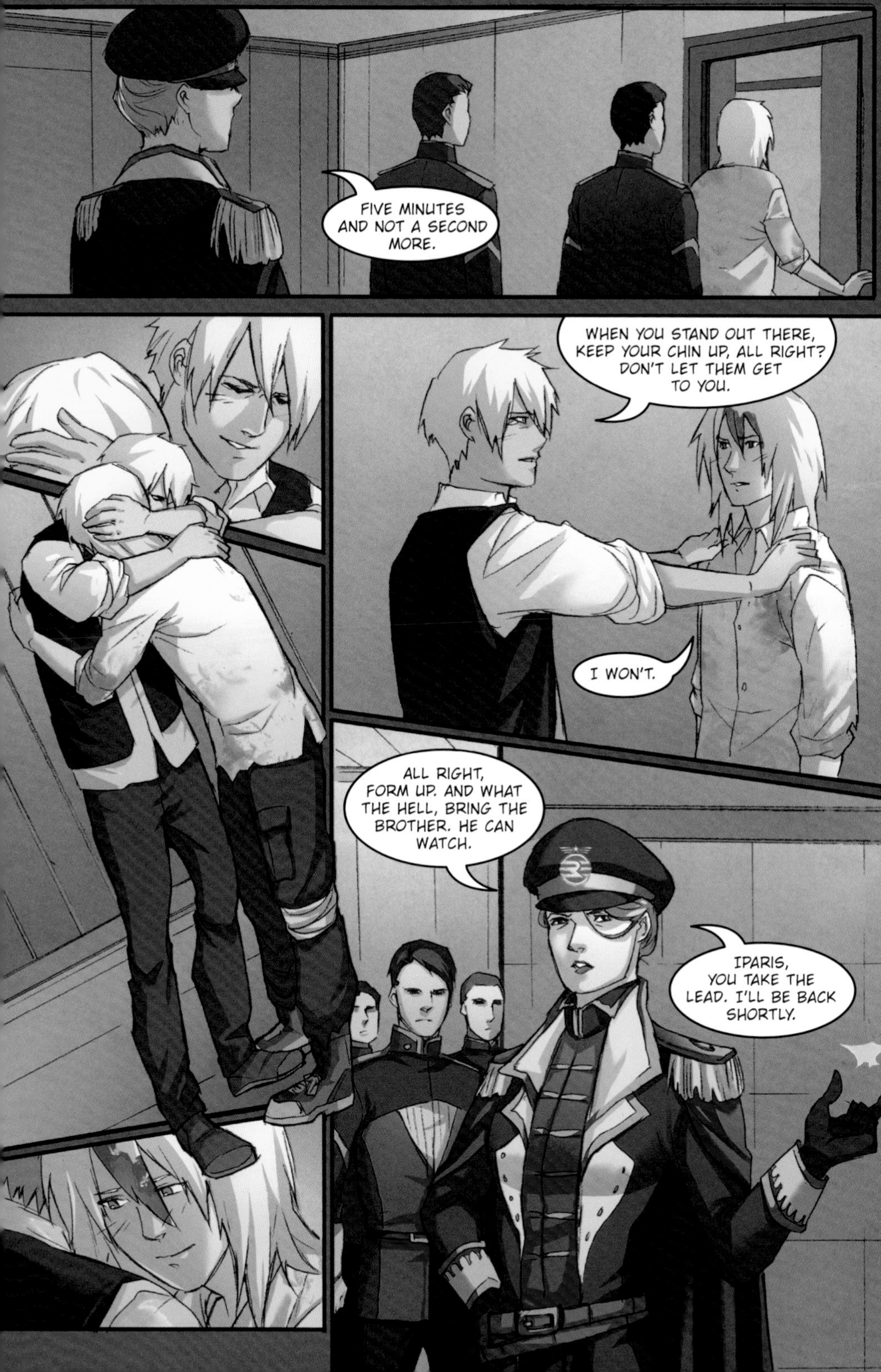
FIVE MINUTES AND NOT A SECOND MORE.
WHEN YOU STAND OUT THERE, KEEP YOUR CHIN UP, ALL RIGHT? DON'T LET THEM GET TO YOU.
I WON'T.
ALL RIGHT, FORM UP. AND WHAT THE HELL, BRING THE BROTHER. HE CAN WATCH.
IPARIS, YOU TAKE THE LEAD. I'LL BE BACK SHORTLY.

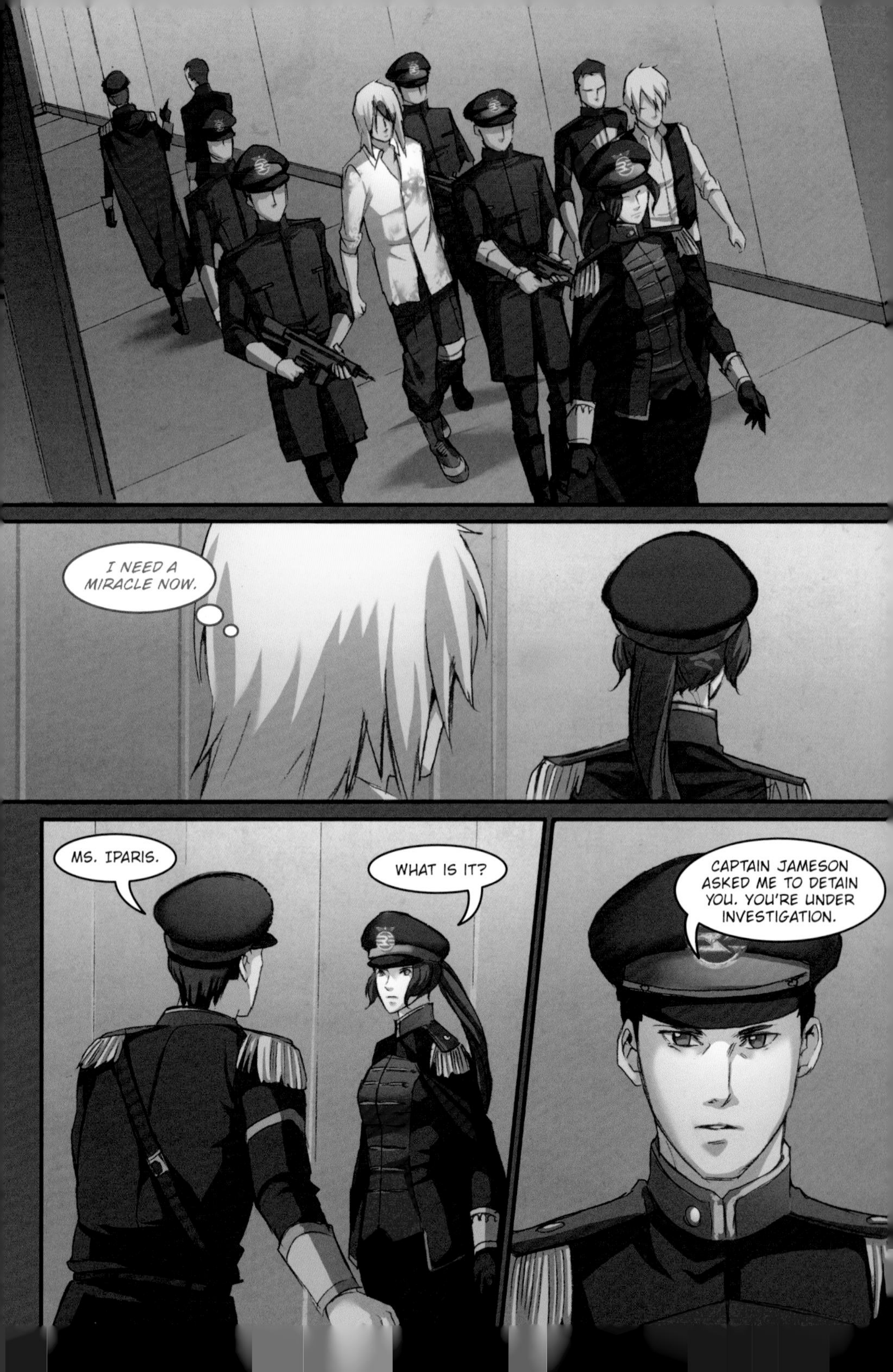
I NEED A MIRACLE NOW.
MS. IPARIS.
WHAT IS IT?
CAPTAIN JAMESON ASKED ME TO DETAIN YOU. YOU'RE UNDER INVESTIGATION.

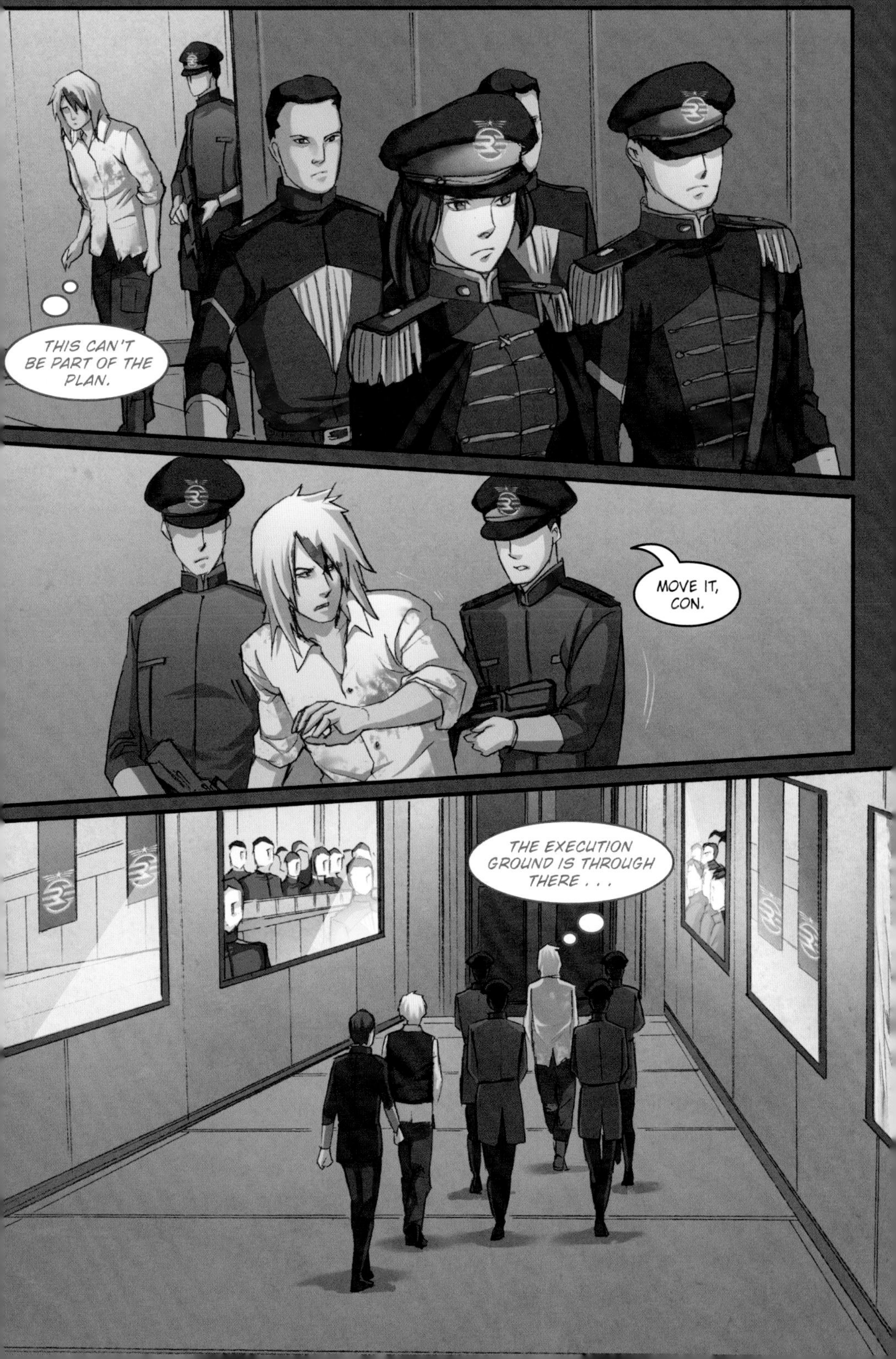
THIS CAN'T BE PART OF THE PLAN.
MOVE IT, CON.
THE EXECUTION GROUND IS THROUGH THERE . . .

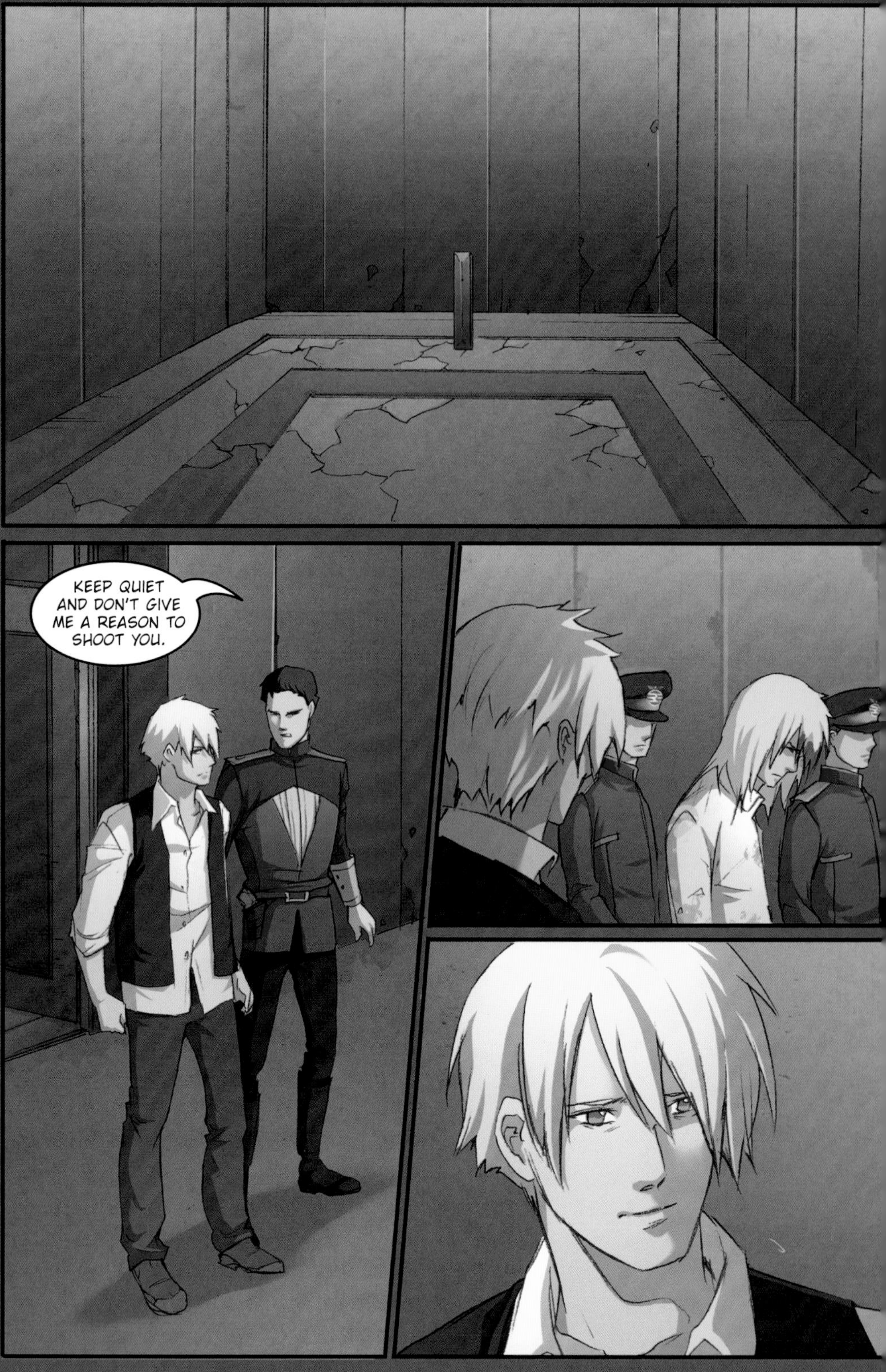
KEEP QUIET AND DON'T GIVE ME A REASON TO SHOOT YOU.

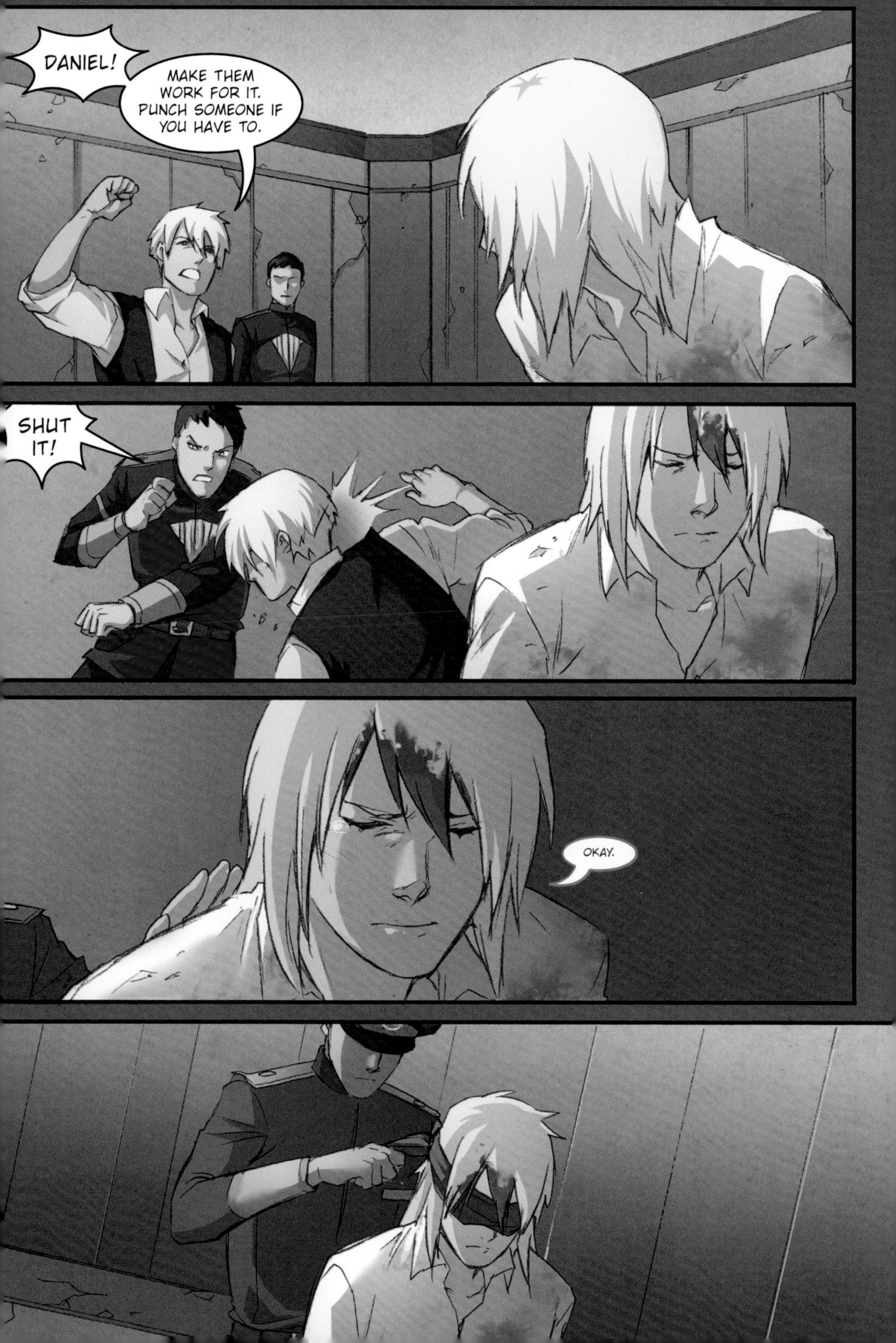
DANIEL!
MAKE THEM WORK FOR IT. PUNCH SOMEONE IF YOU HAVE TO.
SHUT IT!
OKAY.

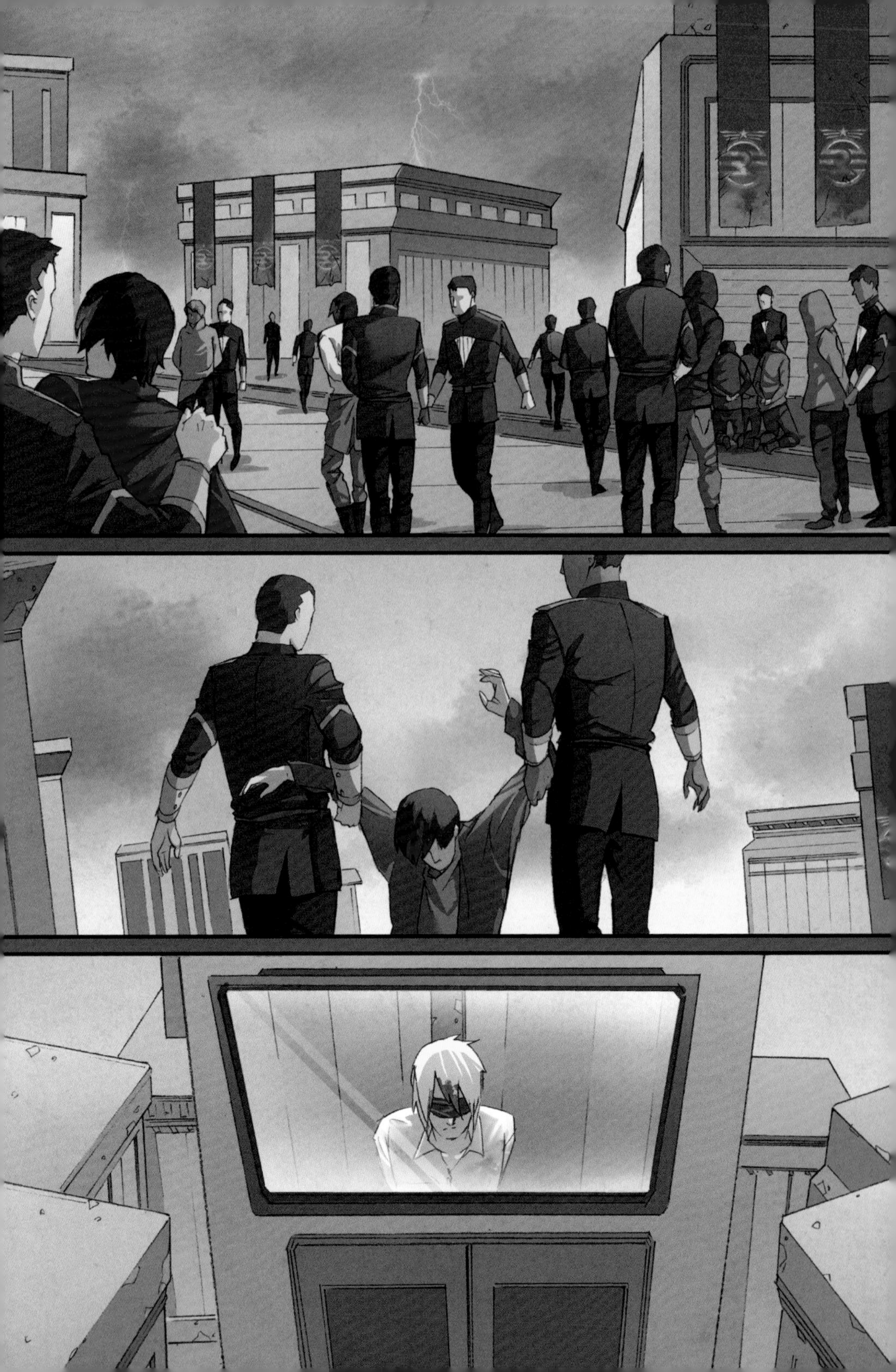

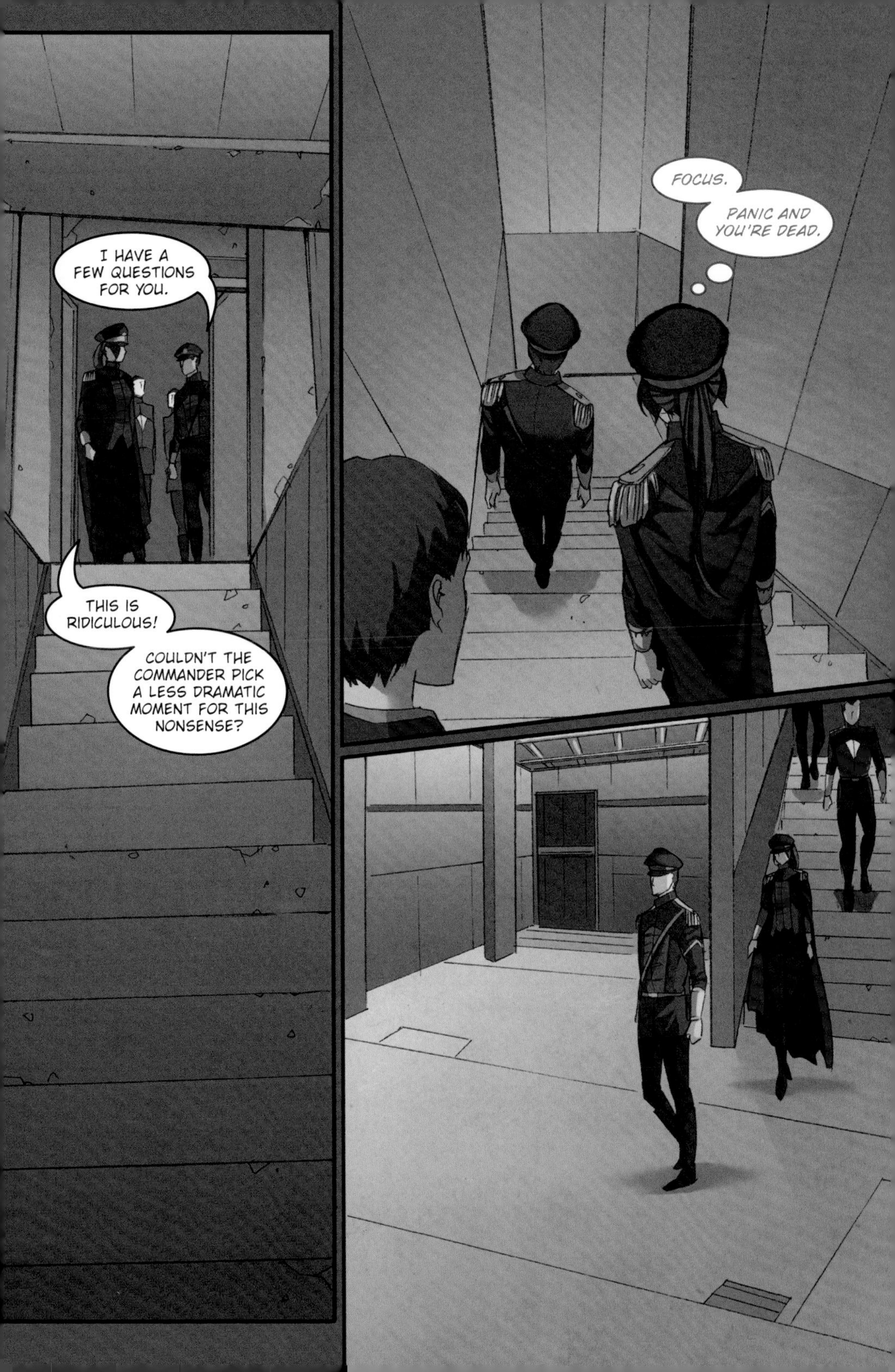
I HAVE A FEW QUESTIONS FOR YOU.
THIS IS RIDICULOUS!
COULDN'T THE COMMANDER PICK A LESS DRAMATIC MOMENT FOR THIS NONSENSE?
FOCUS.
PANIC AND YOU'RE DEAD.

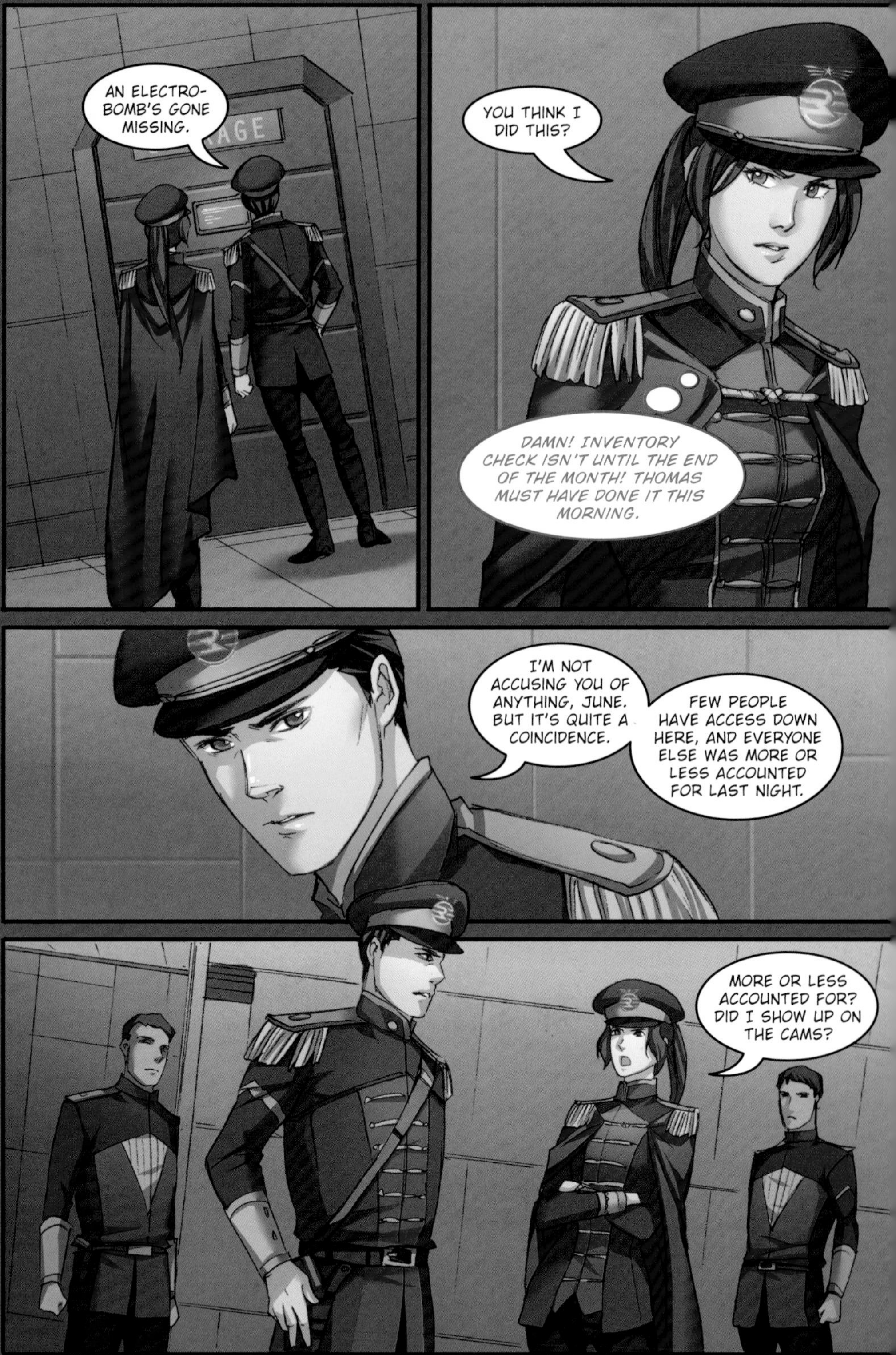

AN ELECTRO-BOMB'S GONE MISSING.
AGE
YOU THINK I DID THIS?
DAMN! INVENTORY CHECK ISN'T UNTIL THE END OF THE MONTH! THOMAS MUST HAVE DONE IT THIS MORNING.
I'M NOT ACCUSING YOU OF ANYTHING, JUNE. BUT IT'S QUITE A COINCIDENCE.
FEW PEOPLE HAVE ACCESS DOWN HERE, AND EVERYONE ELSE WAS MORE OR LESS ACCOUNTED FOR LAST NIGHT.
MORE OR LESS ACCOUNTED FOR? DID I SHOW UP ON THE CAMS?

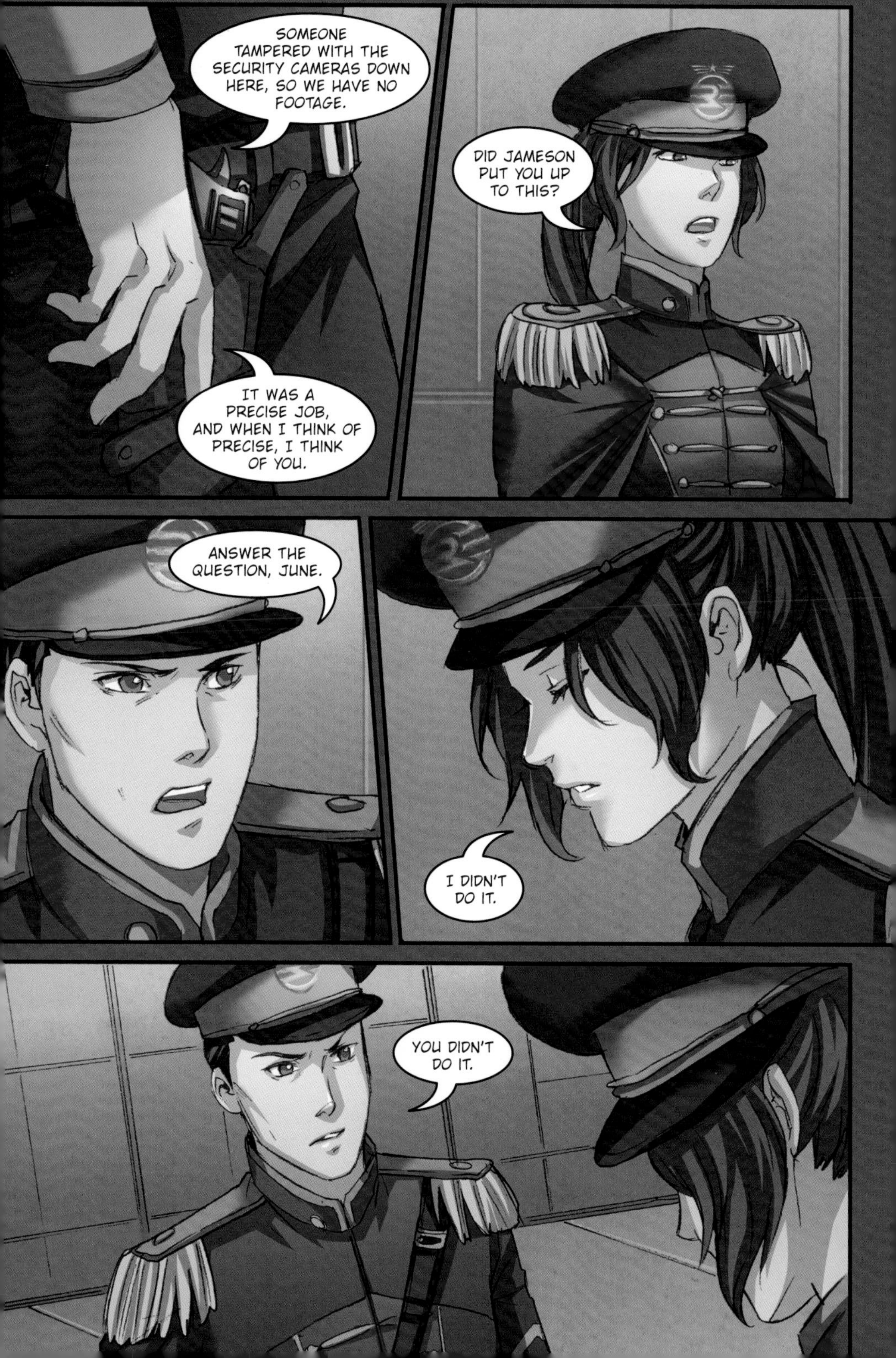
SOMEONE TAMPERED WITH THE SECURITY CAMERAS DOWN HERE, SO WE HAVE NO FOOTAGE.
IT WAS A PRECISE JOB, AND WHEN I THINK OF PRECISE, I THINK OF YOU.
DID JAMESON PUT YOU UP TO THIS?
ANSWER THE QUESTION, JUNE.
I DIDN'T DO IT.
YOU DIDN'T DO IT.

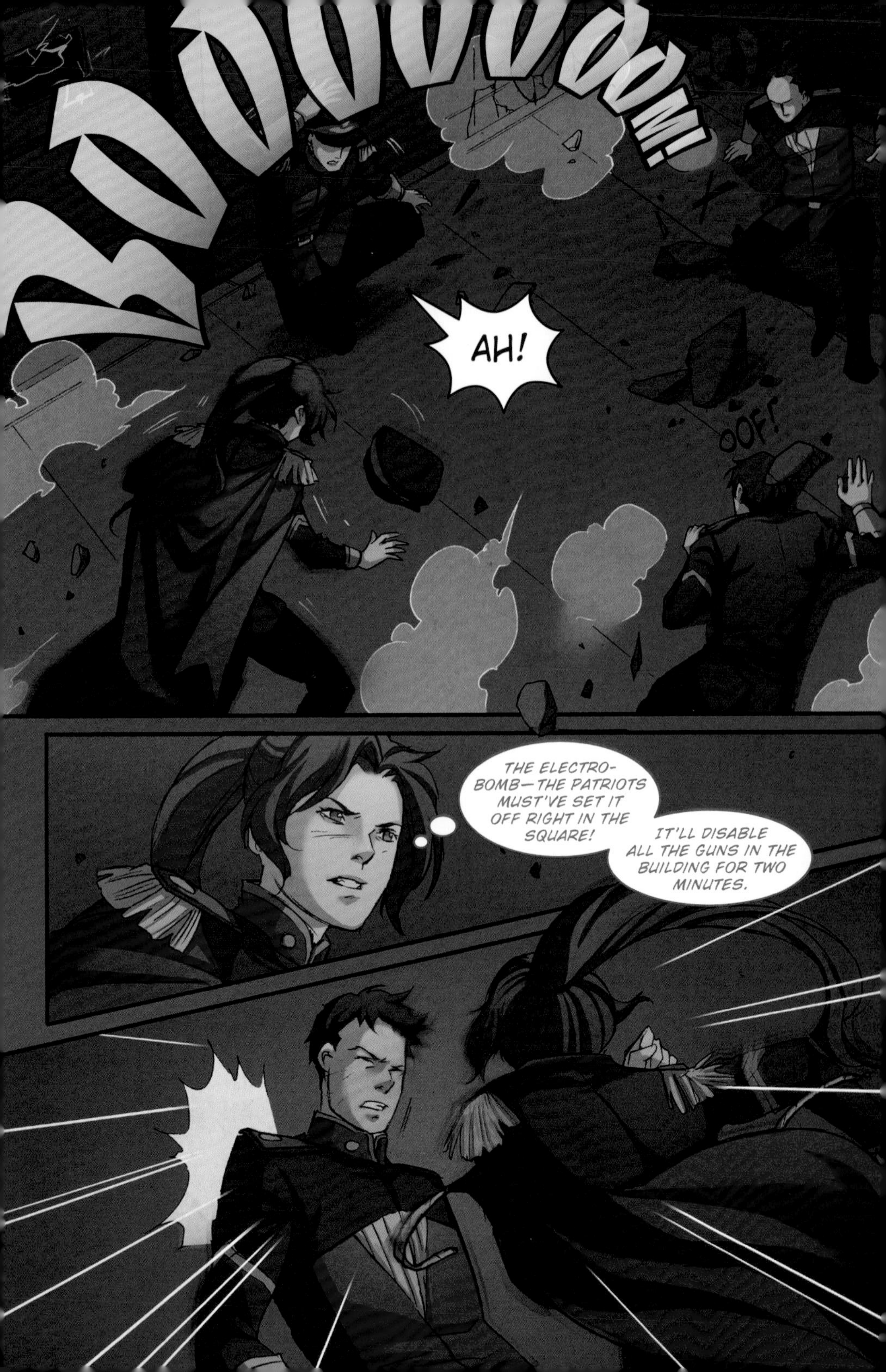
BOOOOOOOOM!
AH!
OOF!
THE ELECTRO-BOMB—THE PATRIOTS MUST'VE SET IT OFF RIGHT IN THE SQUARE!
IT'LL DISABLE ALL THE GUNS IN THE BUILDING FOR TWO MINUTES.

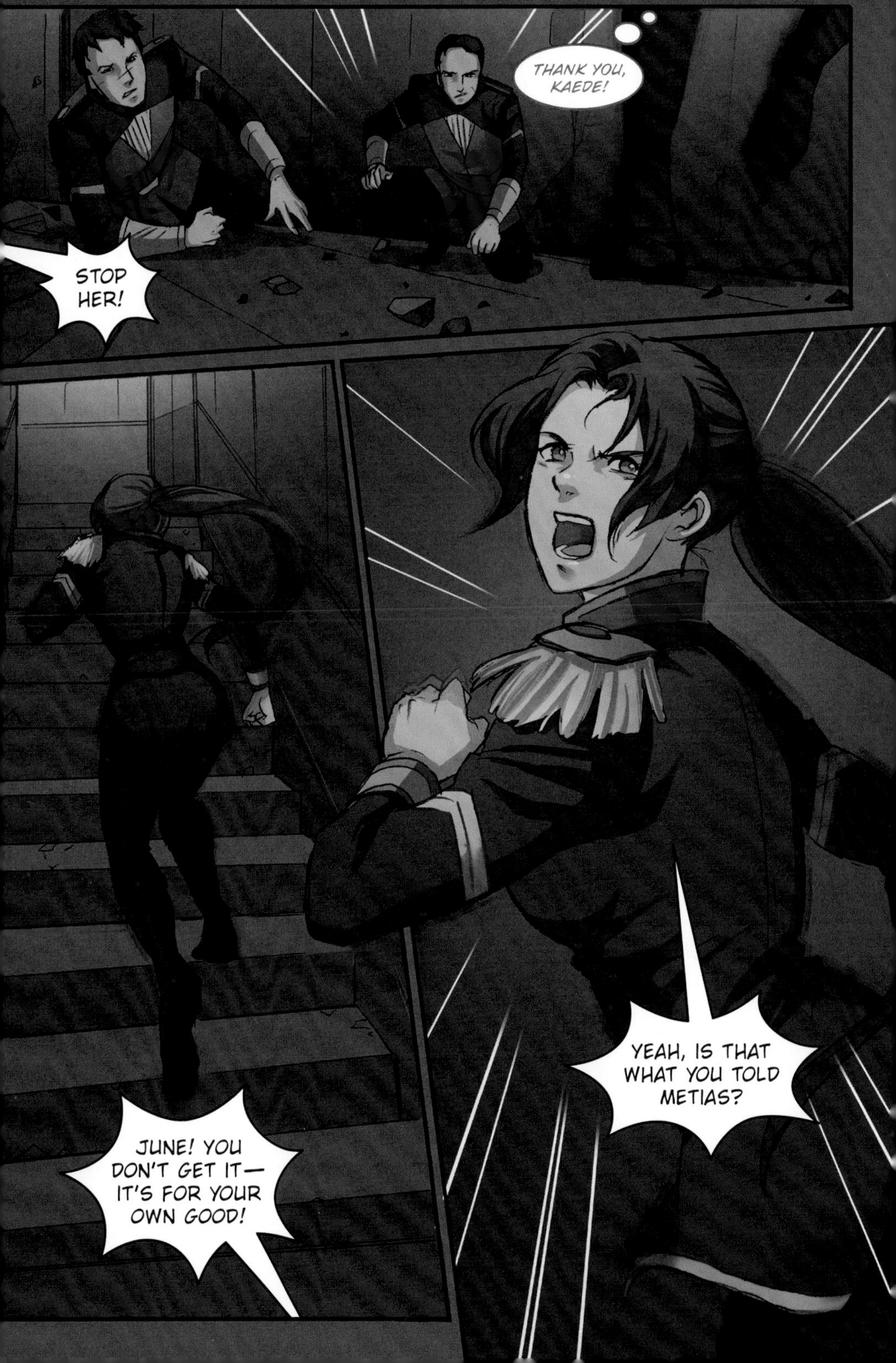
THANK YOU, KAEDE!
STOP HER!
JUNE! YOU DON'T GET IT— IT'S FOR YOUR OWN GOOD!
YEAH, IS THAT WHAT YOU TOLD METIAS?

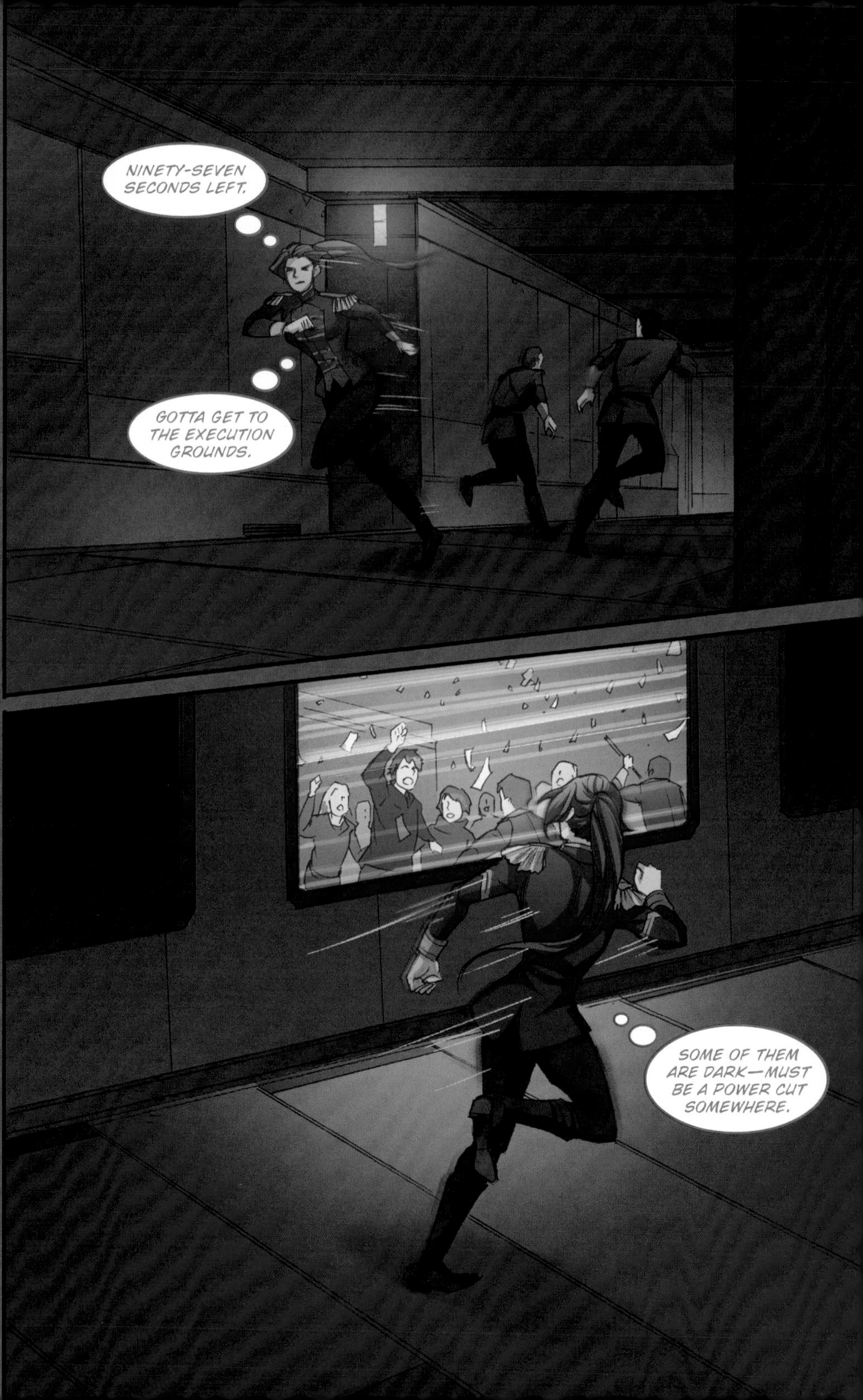
NINETY-SEVEN SECONDS LEFT.
GOTTA GET TO THE EXECUTION GROUNDS.
SOME OF THEM ARE DARK—MUST BE A POWER CUT SOMEWHERE.

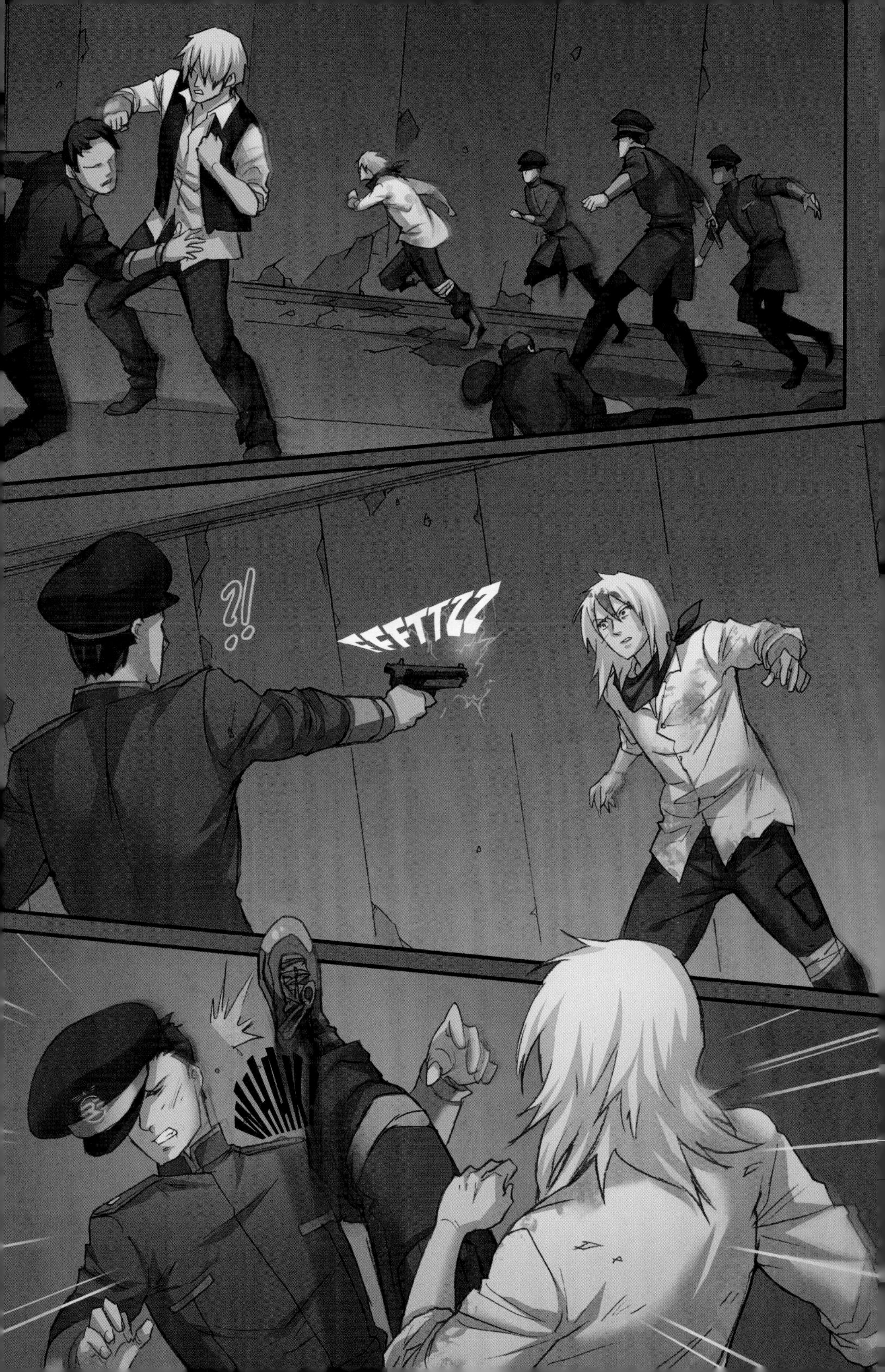
?!
FFFTTZZ
WHAK

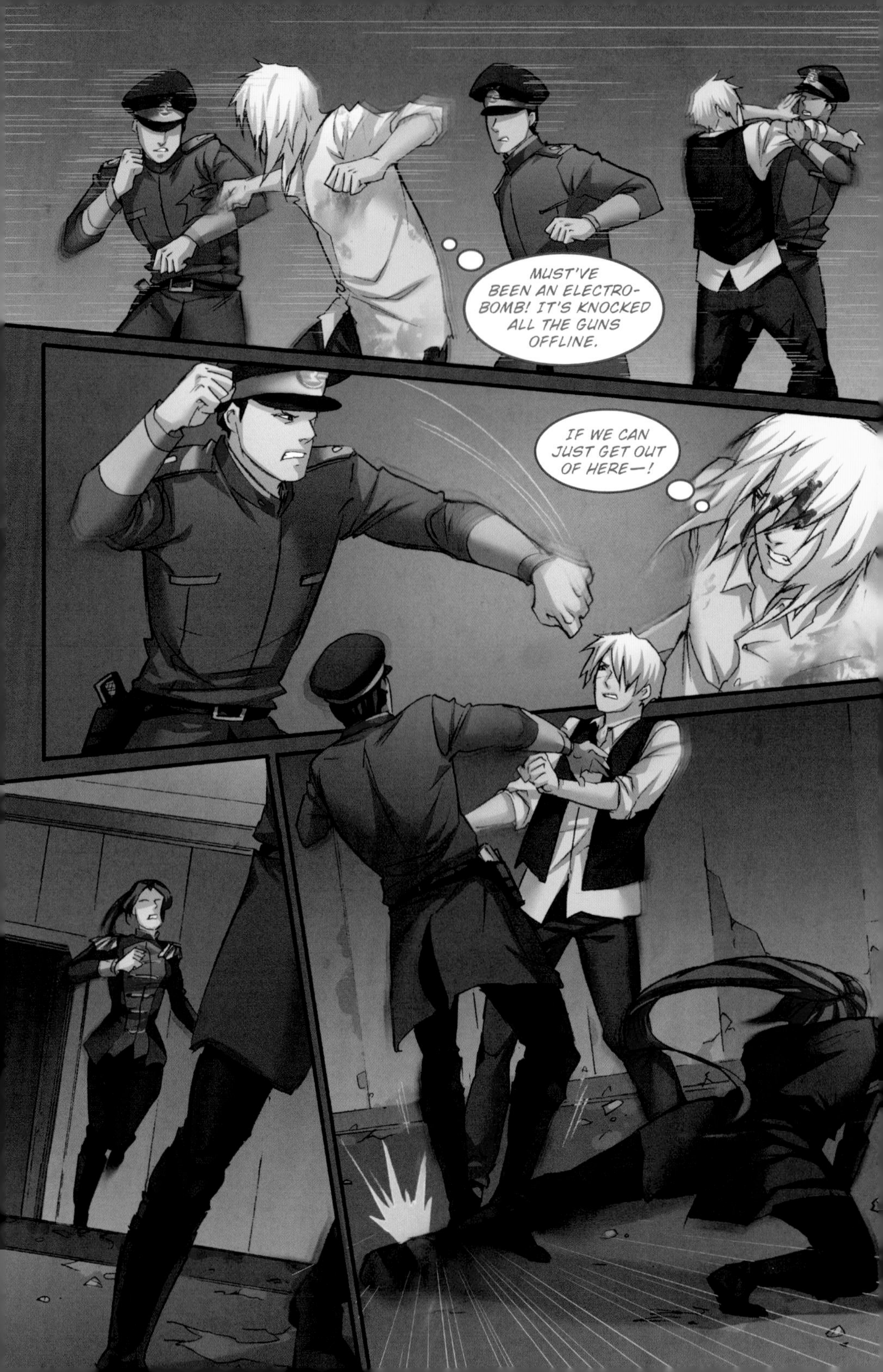
MUST'VE BEEN AN ELECTRO-BOMB! IT'S KNOCKED ALL THE GUNS OFFLINE.
IF WE CAN JUST GET OUT OF HERE—!

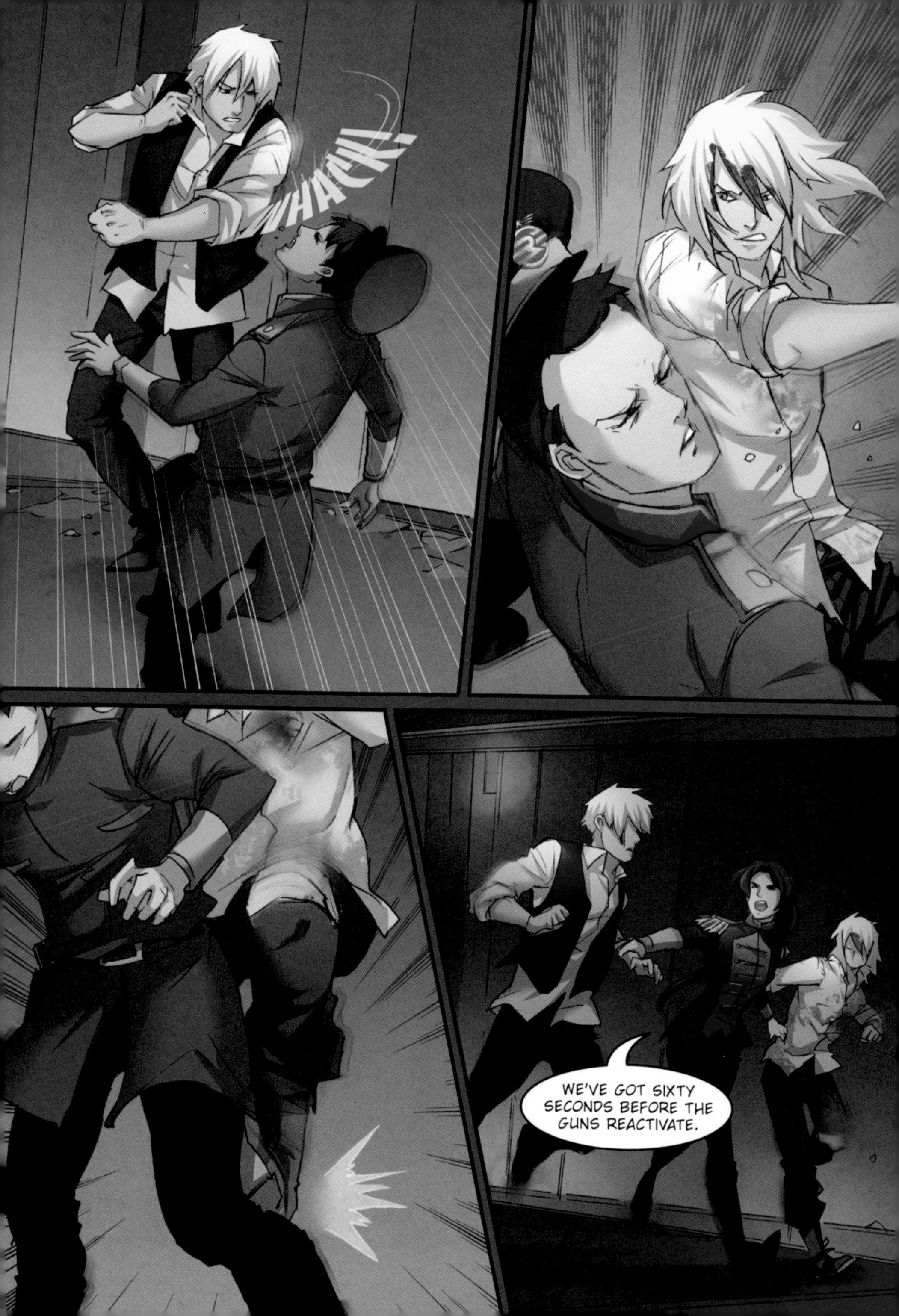
WHACK!
WE'VE GOT SIXTY SECONDS BEFORE THE GUNS REACTIVATE.

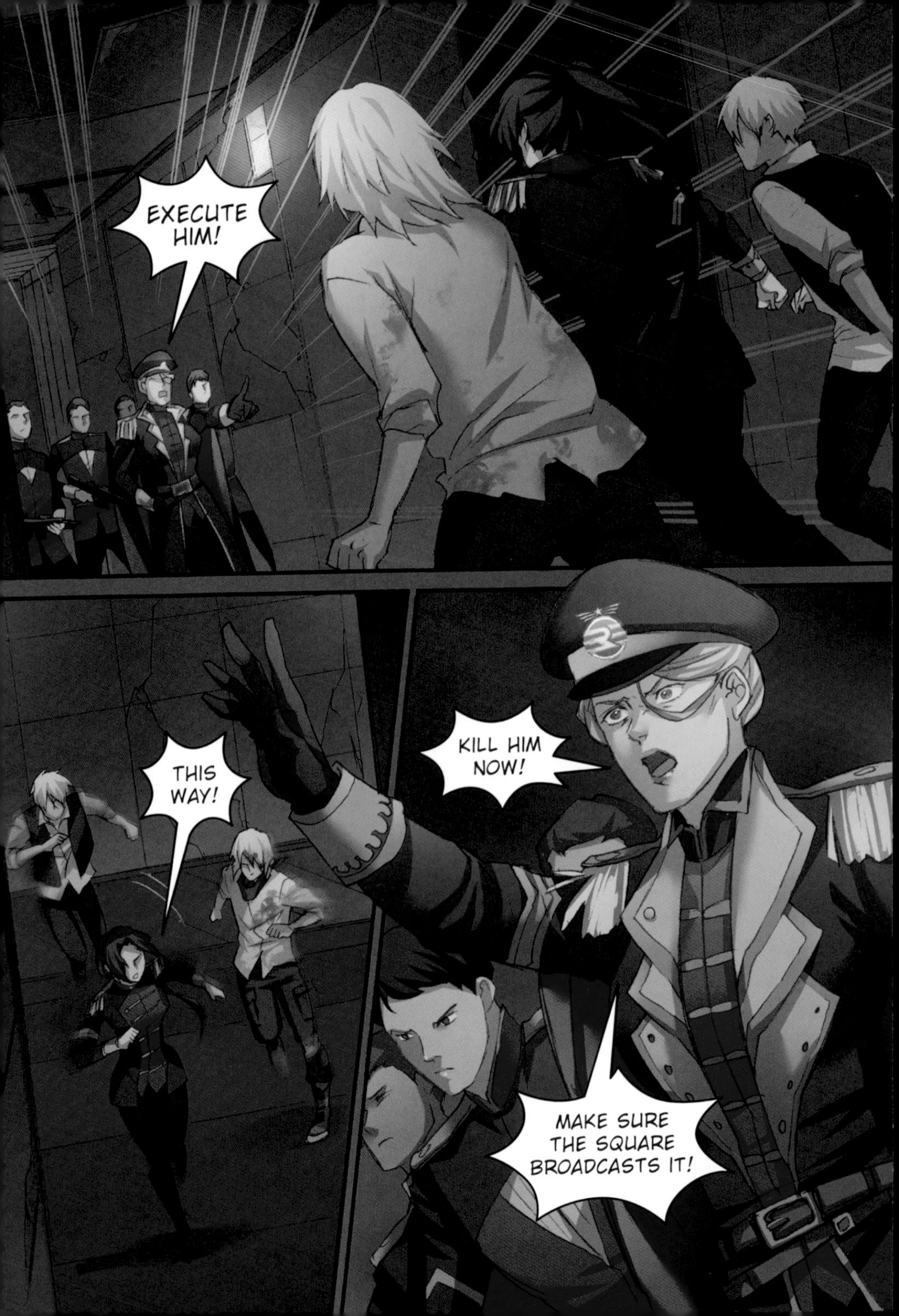
EXECUTE HIM!
THIS WAY!
KILL HIM NOW!
MAKE SURE THE SQUARE BROADCASTS IT!

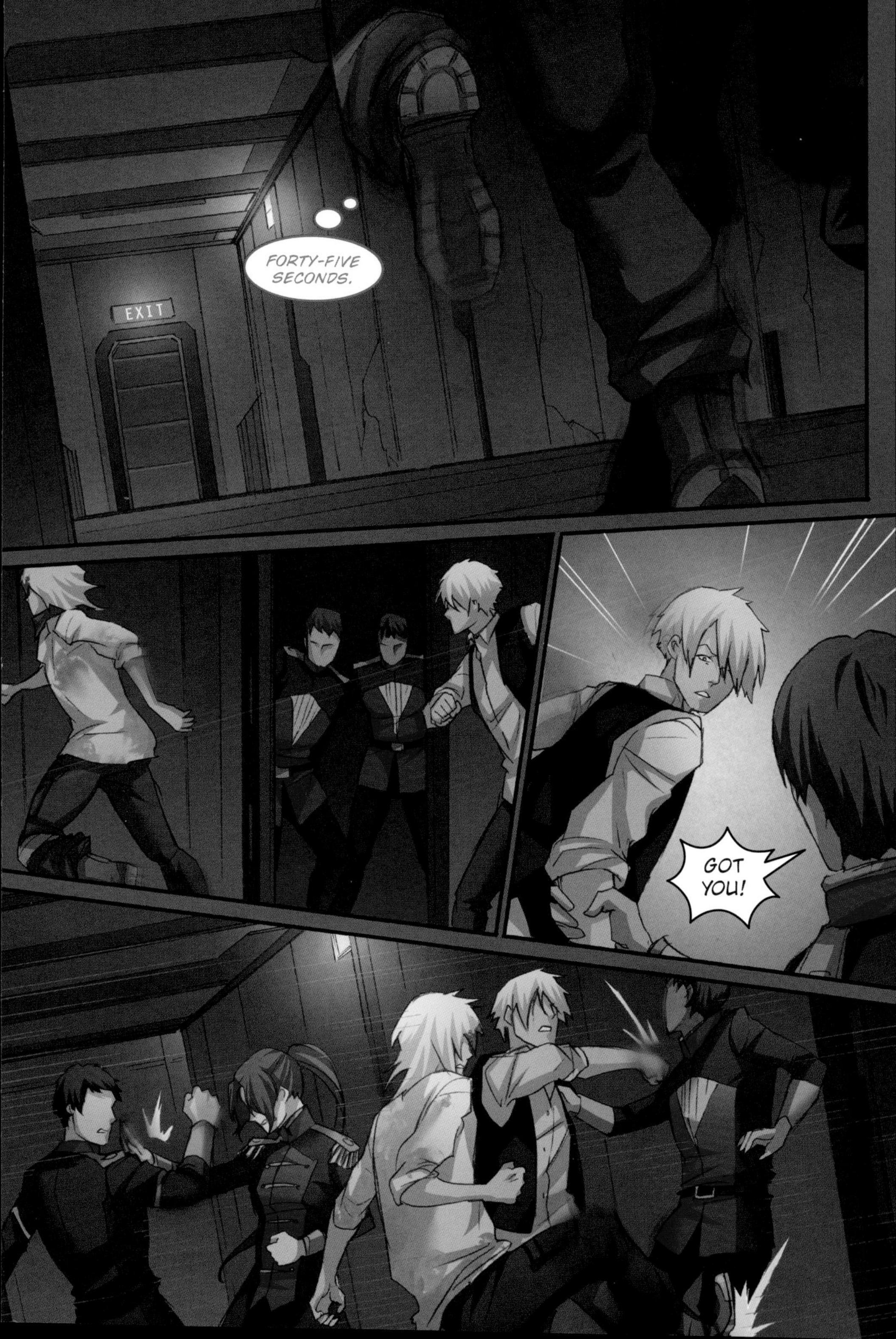
FORTY-FIVE SECONDS.
EXIT
GOT YOU!

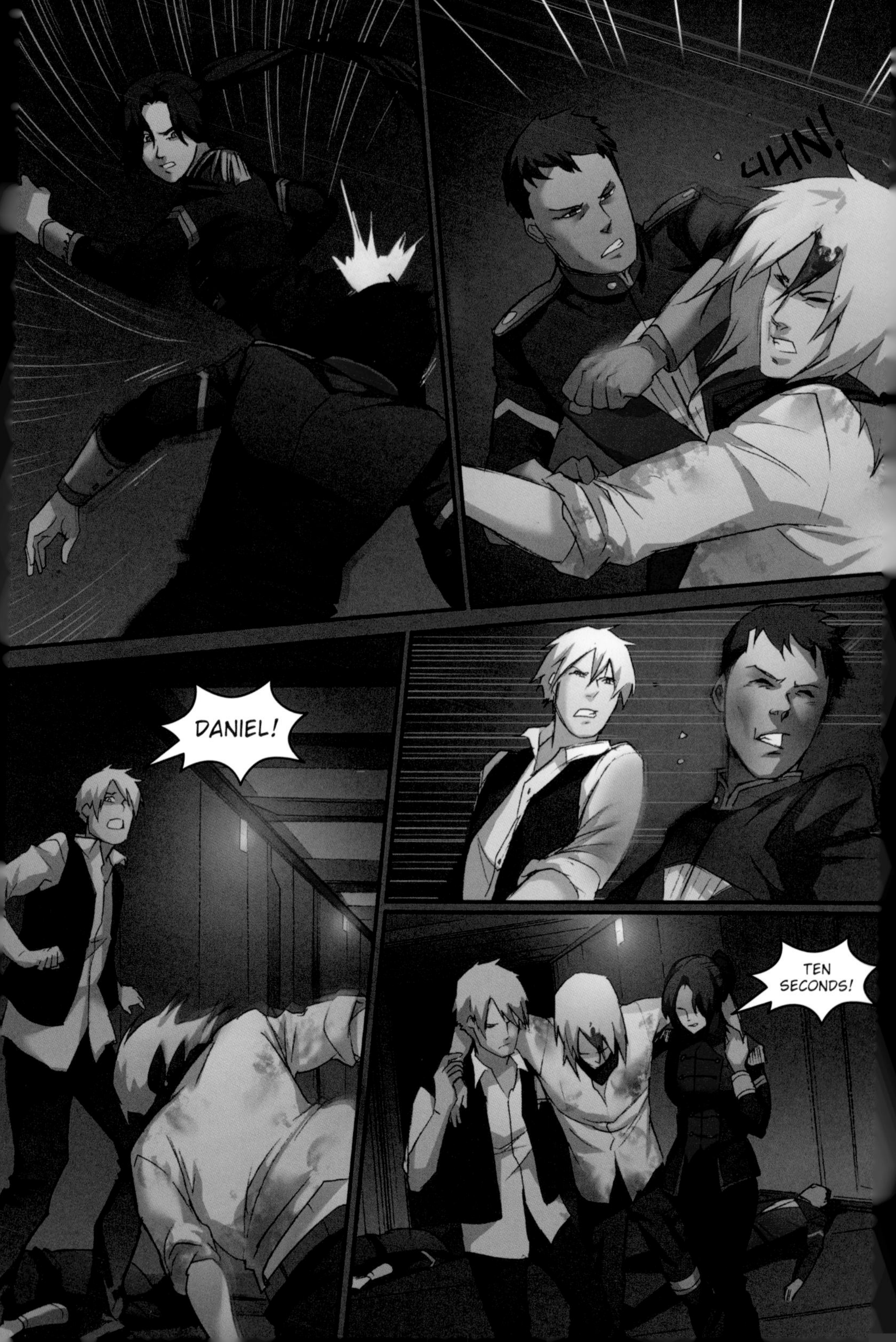
UHN!
DANIEL!
TEN SECONDS!

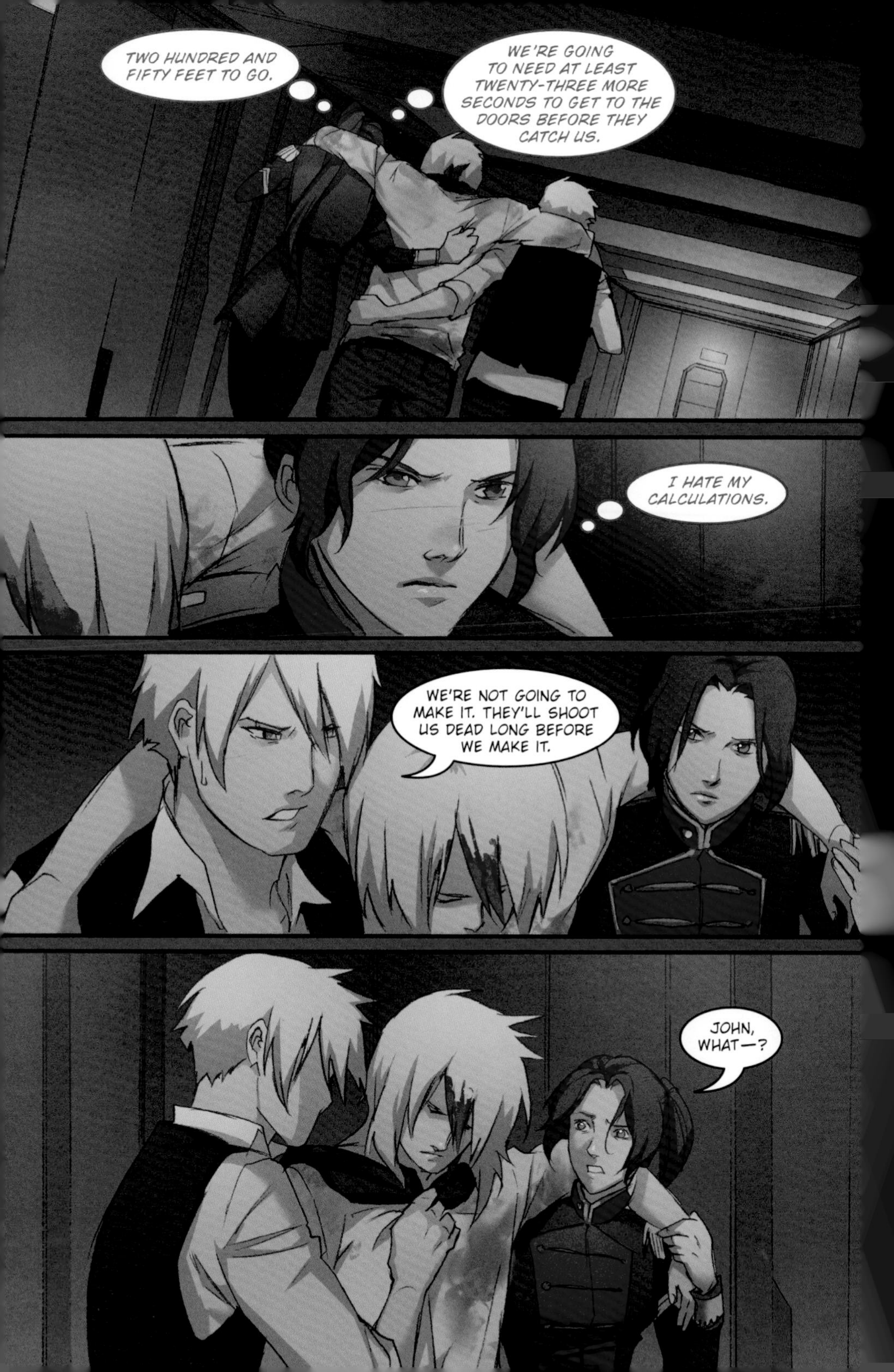
TWO HUNDRED AND FIFTY FEET TO GO.
WE'RE GOING TO NEED AT LEAST TWENTY-THREE MORE SECONDS TO GET TO THE DOORS BEFORE THEY CATCH US.
I HATE MY CALCULATIONS.
WE'RE NOT GOING TO MAKE IT. THEY'LL SHOOT US DEAD LONG BEFORE WE MAKE IT.
JOHN, WHAT—?

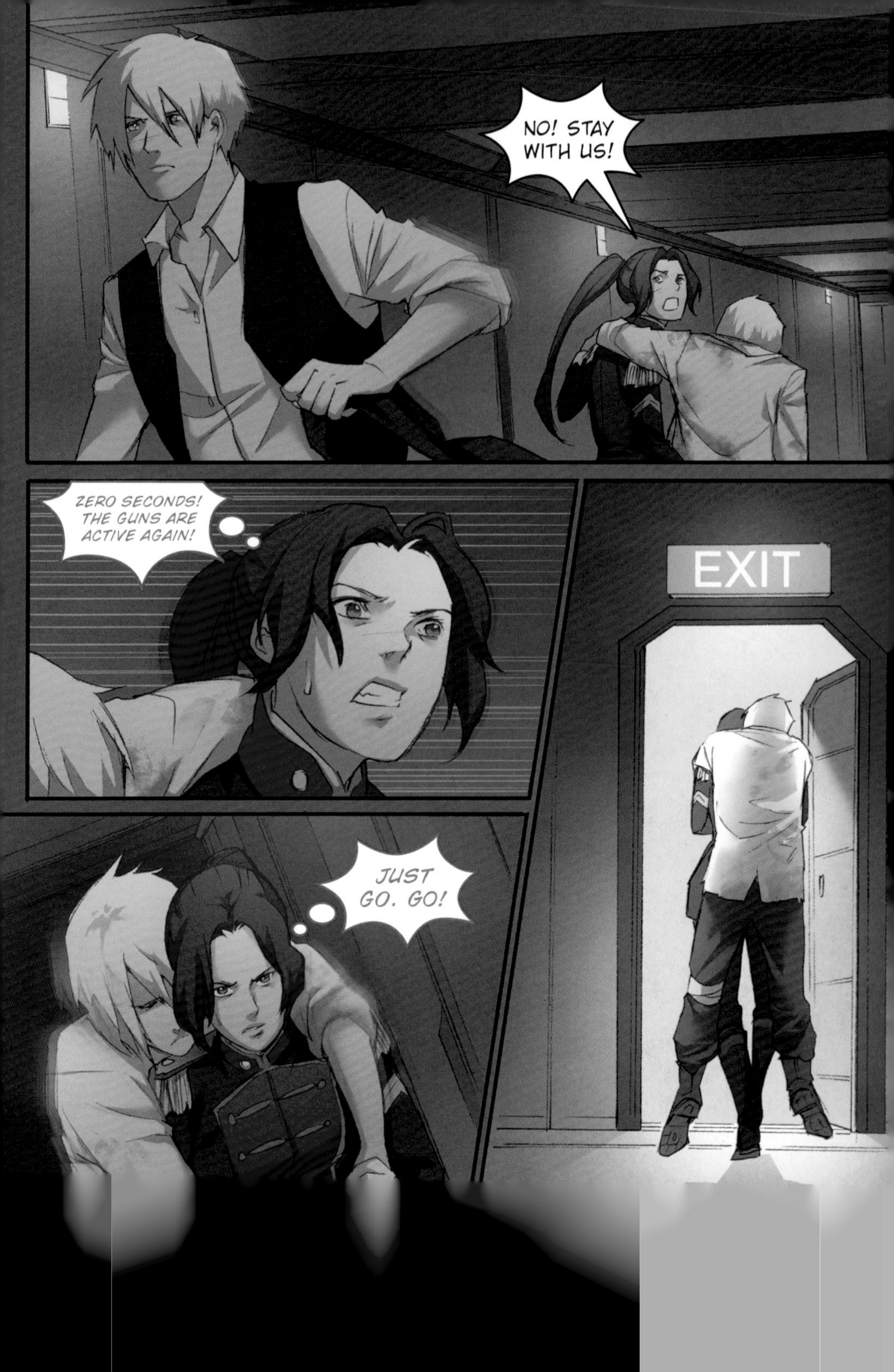
NO! STAY WITH US!
ZERO SECONDS! THE GUNS ARE ACTIVE AGAIN!
JUST GO. GO!
EXIT

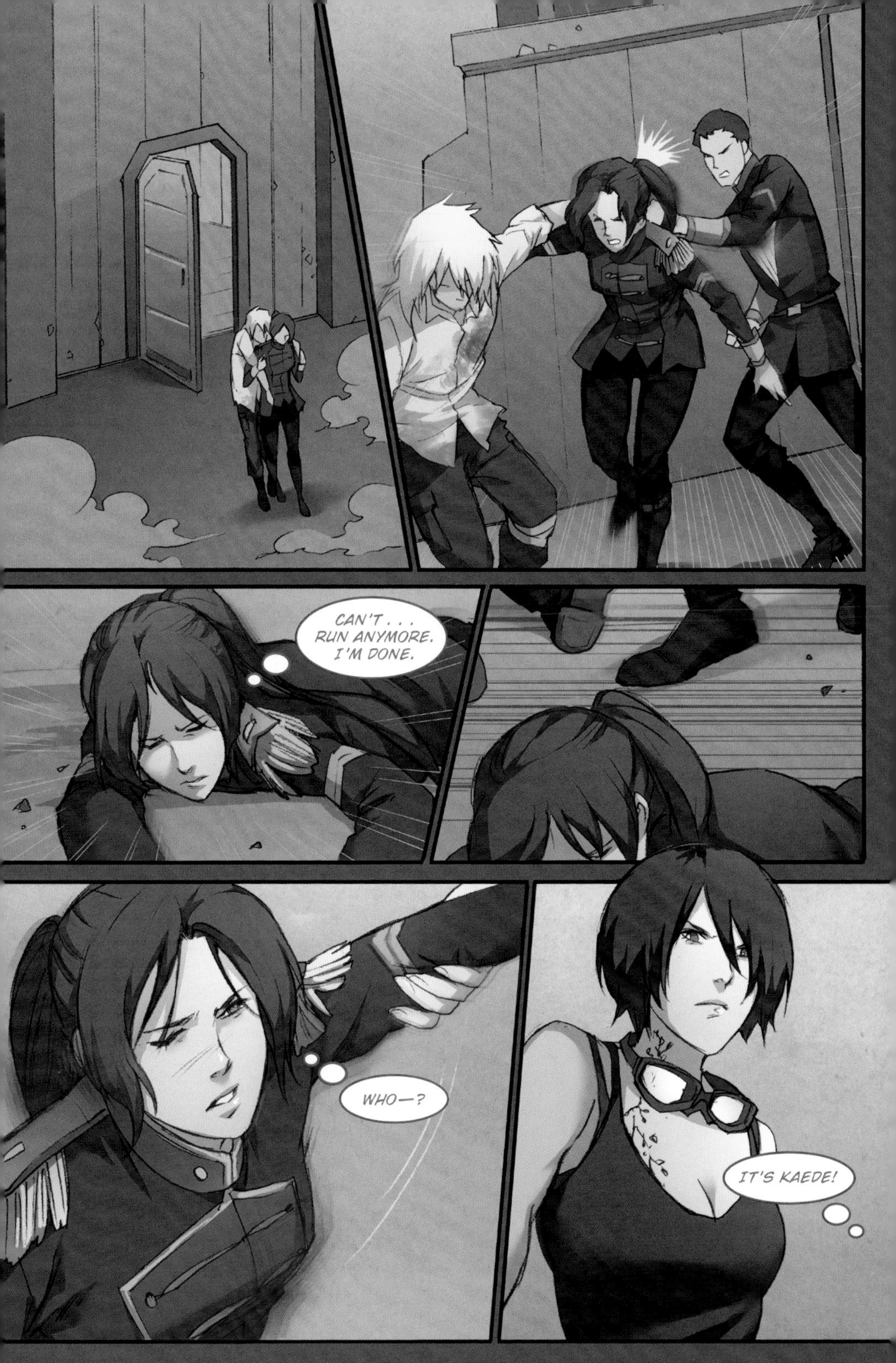
CAN'T . . . RUN ANYMORE. I'M DONE.
WHO—?
IT'S KAEDE!

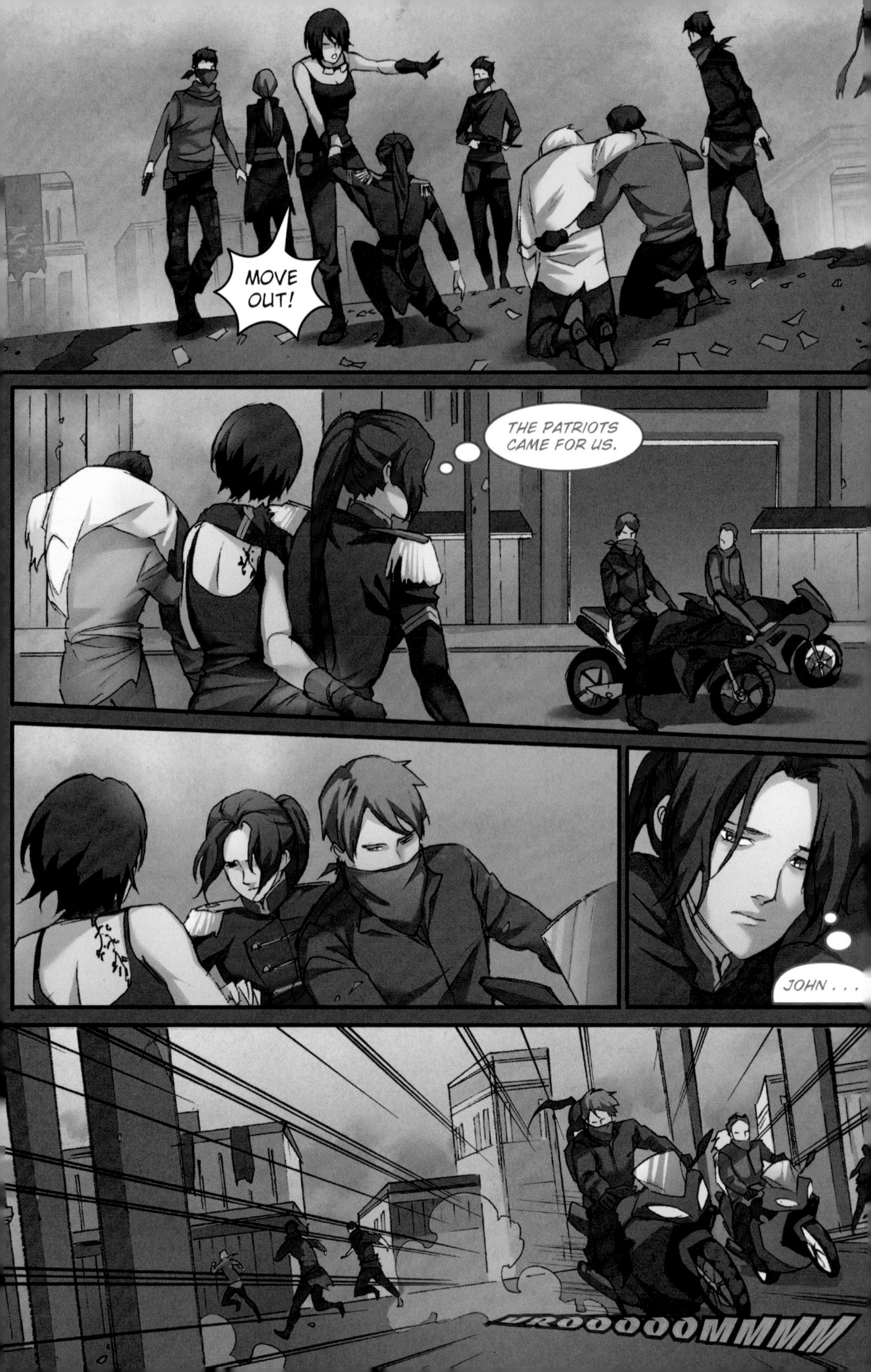
MOVE OUT!
THE PATRIOTS CAME FOR US.
JOHN . . .
VROOOOOOMMMMM

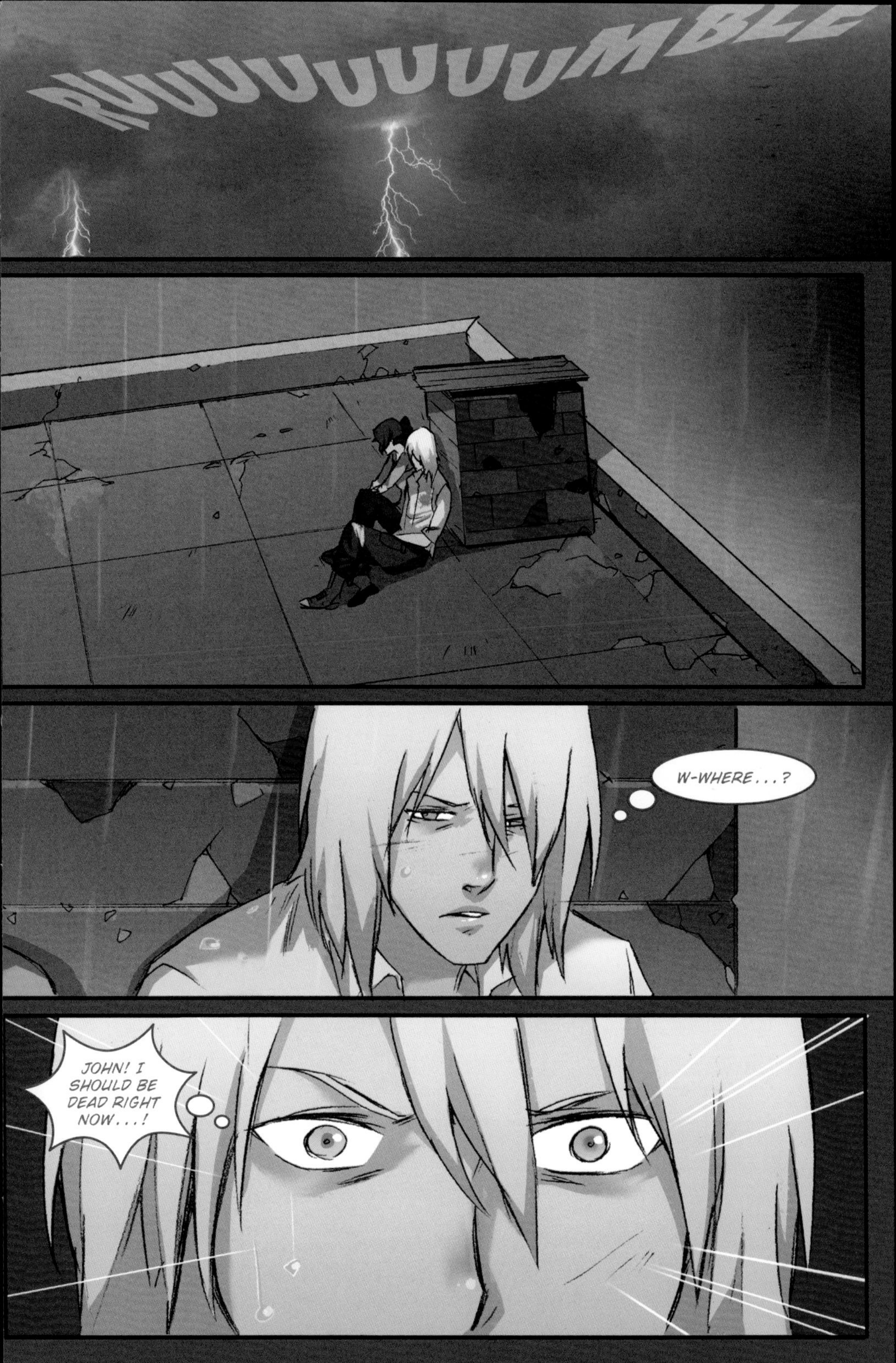
RUUUUUUUUMBLE
W-WHERE...?
JOHN! I SHOULD BE DEAD RIGHT NOW...!

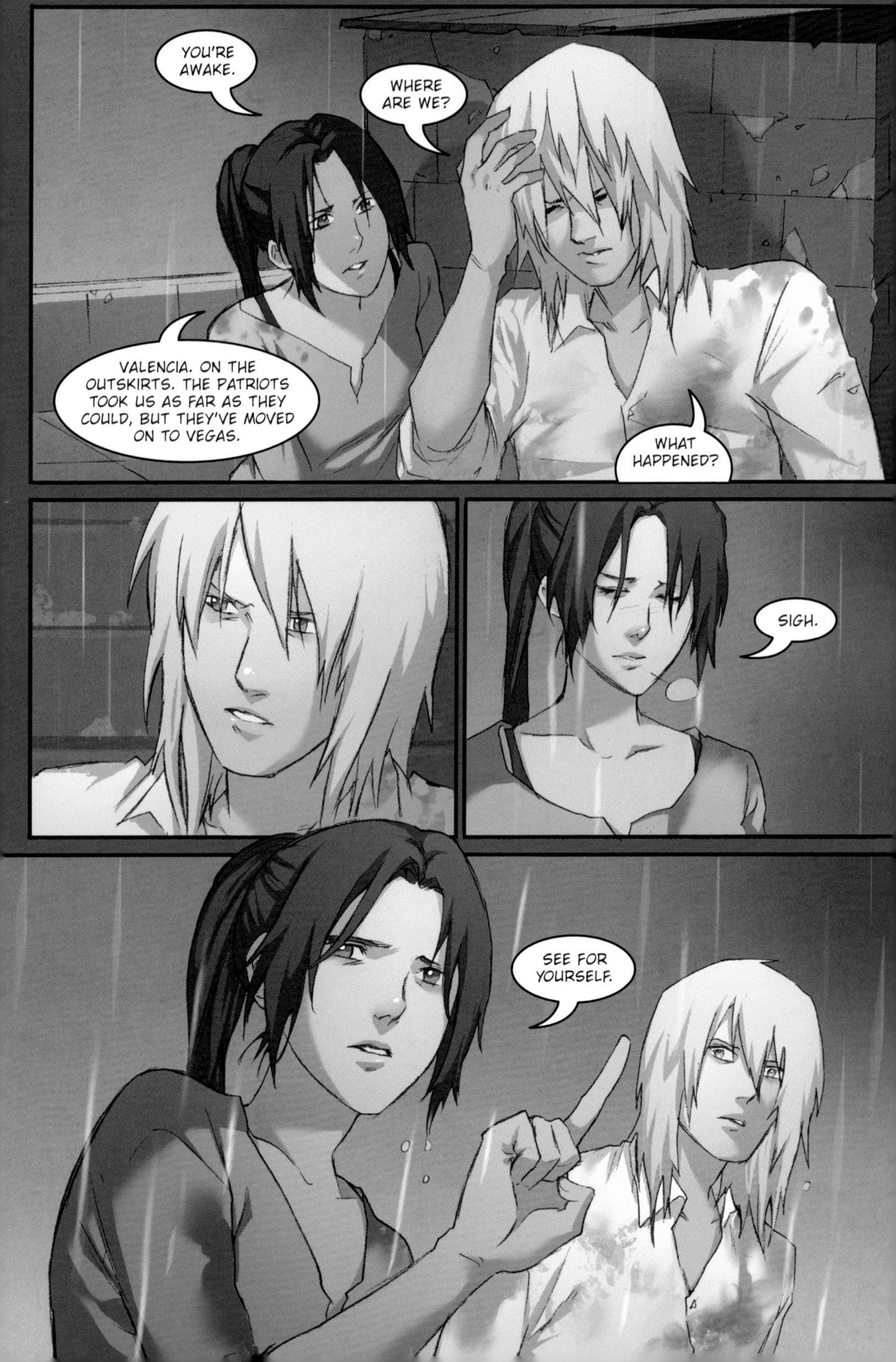
YOU'RE AWAKE.
WHERE ARE WE?
VALENCIA. ON THE OUTSKIRTS. THE PATRIOTS TOOK US AS FAR AS THEY COULD, BUT THEY'VE MOVED ON TO VEGAS.
WHAT HAPPENED?
SIGH.
SEE FOR YOURSELF.

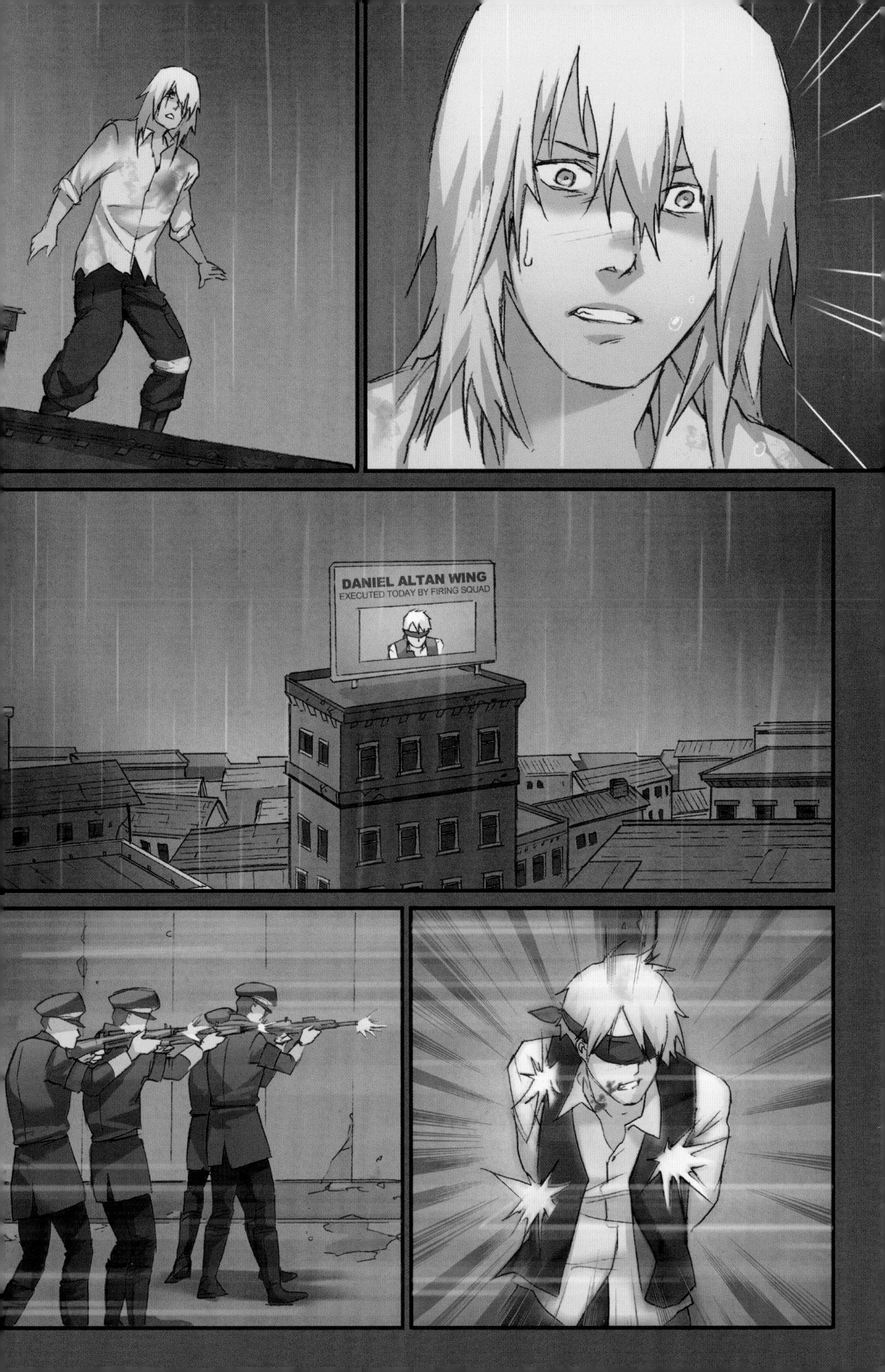
DANIEL ALTAN WING
EXECUTED TODAY BY FIRING SQUAD

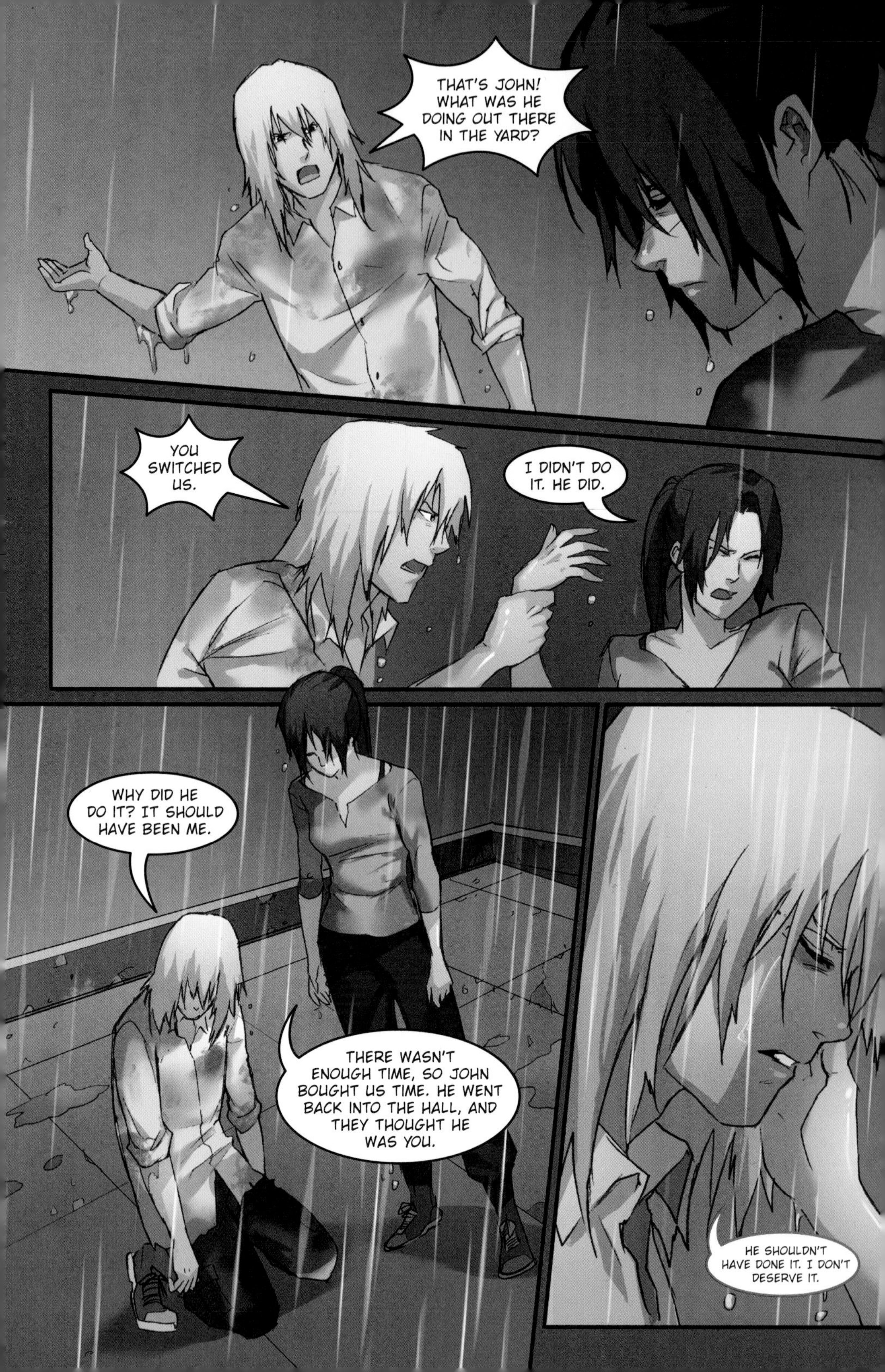
THAT'S JOHN! WHAT WAS HE DOING OUT THERE IN THE YARD?
YOU SWITCHED US.
I DIDN'T DO IT. HE DID.
WHY DID HE DO IT? IT SHOULD HAVE BEEN ME.
THERE WASN'T ENOUGH TIME, SO JOHN BOUGHT US TIME. HE WENT BACK INTO THE HALL, AND THEY THOUGHT HE WAS YOU.
HE SHOULDN'T HAVE DONE IT. I DON'T DESERVE IT.

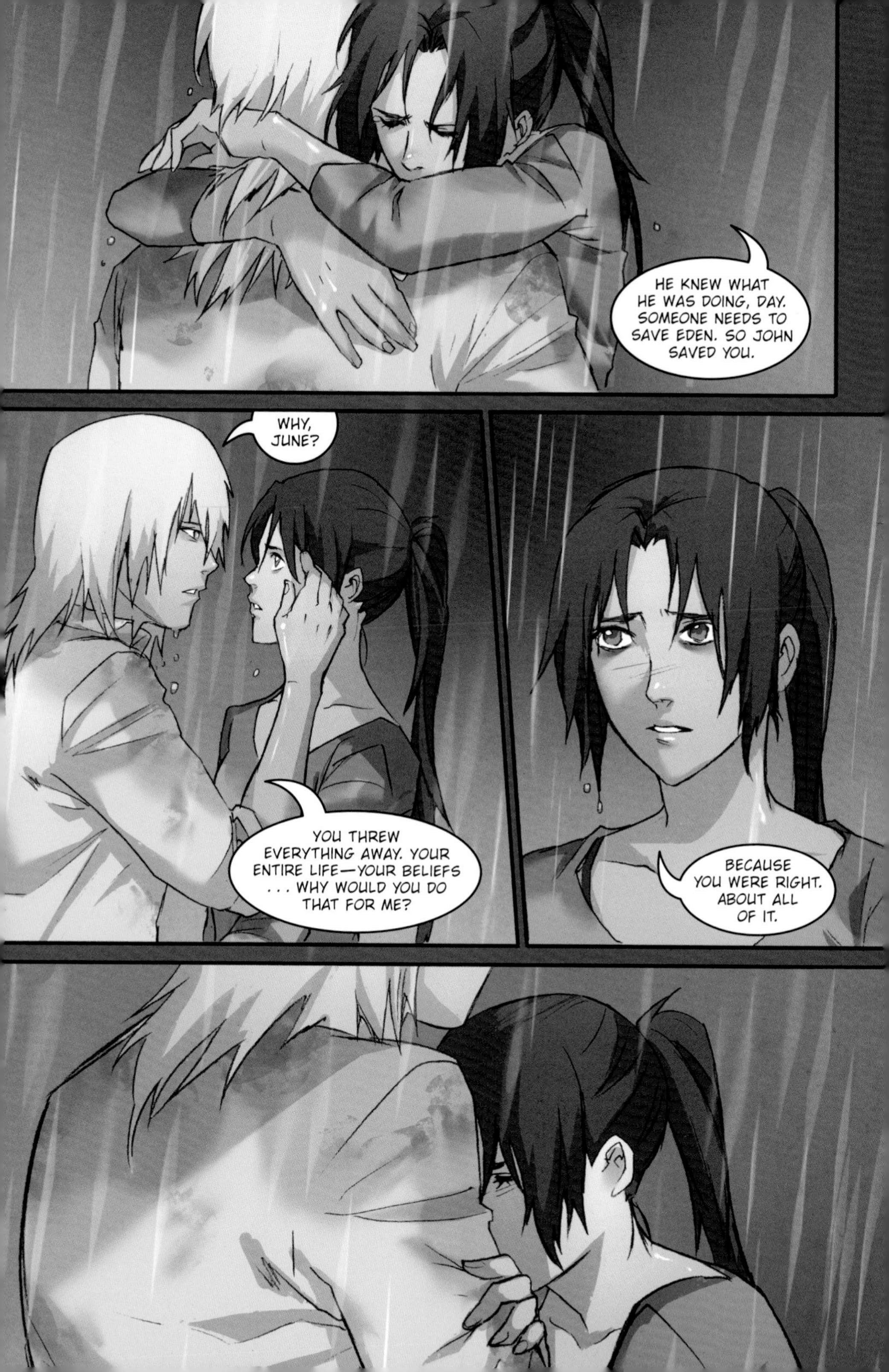
HE KNEW WHAT HE WAS DOING, DAY. SOMEONE NEEDS TO SAVE EDEN. SO JOHN SAVED YOU.
WHY, JUNE?
YOU THREW EVERYTHING AWAY. YOUR ENTIRE LIFE—YOUR BELIEFS . . . WHY WOULD YOU DO THAT FOR ME?
BECAUSE YOU WERE RIGHT. ABOUT ALL OF IT.

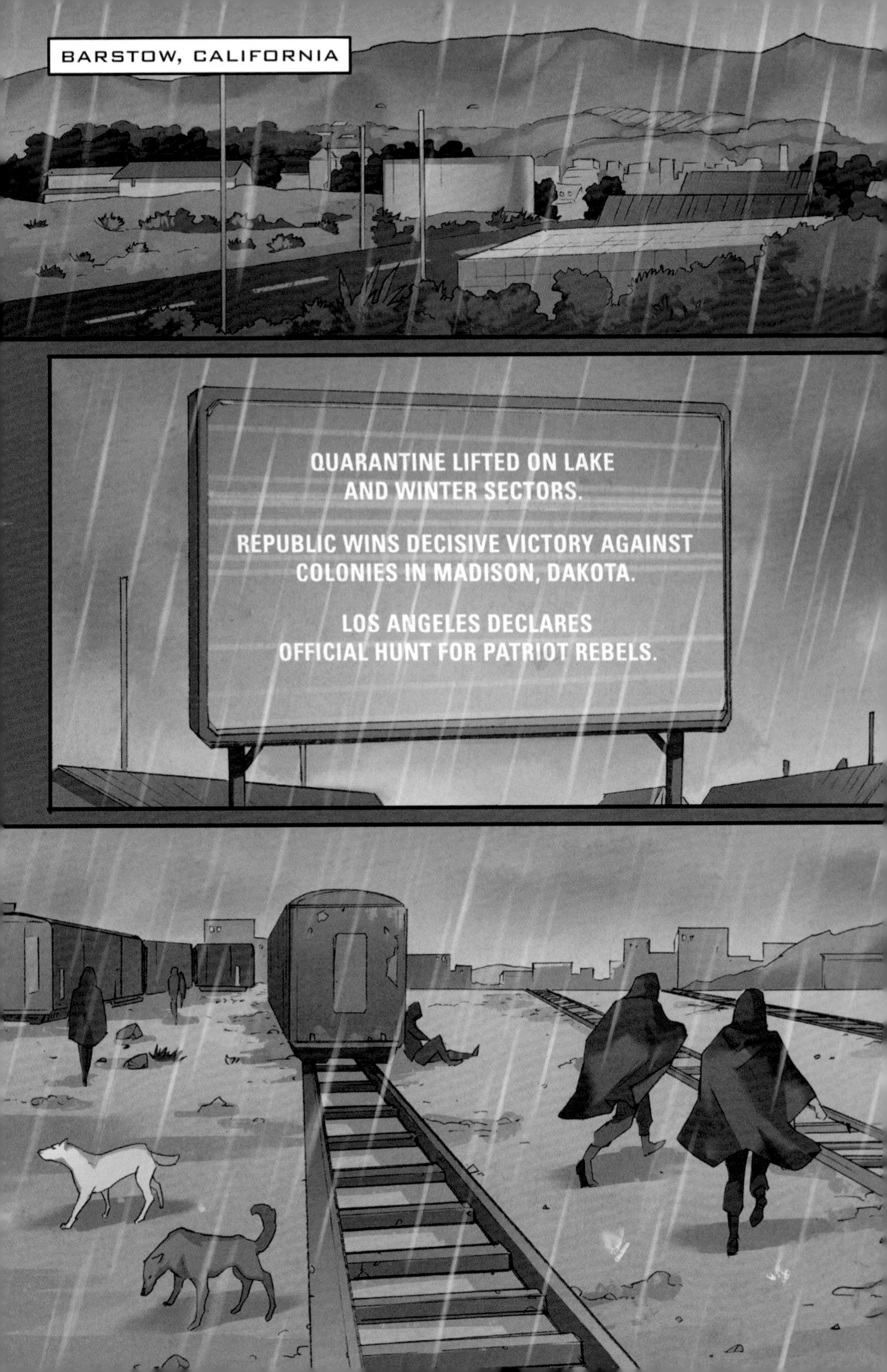
BARSTOW, CALIFORNIA
QUARANTINE LIFTED ON LAKE AND WINTER SECTORS.
REPUBLIC WINS DECISIVE VICTORY AGAINST COLONIES IN MADISON, DAKOTA.
LOS ANGELES DECLARES OFFICIAL HUNT FOR PATRIOT REBELS.

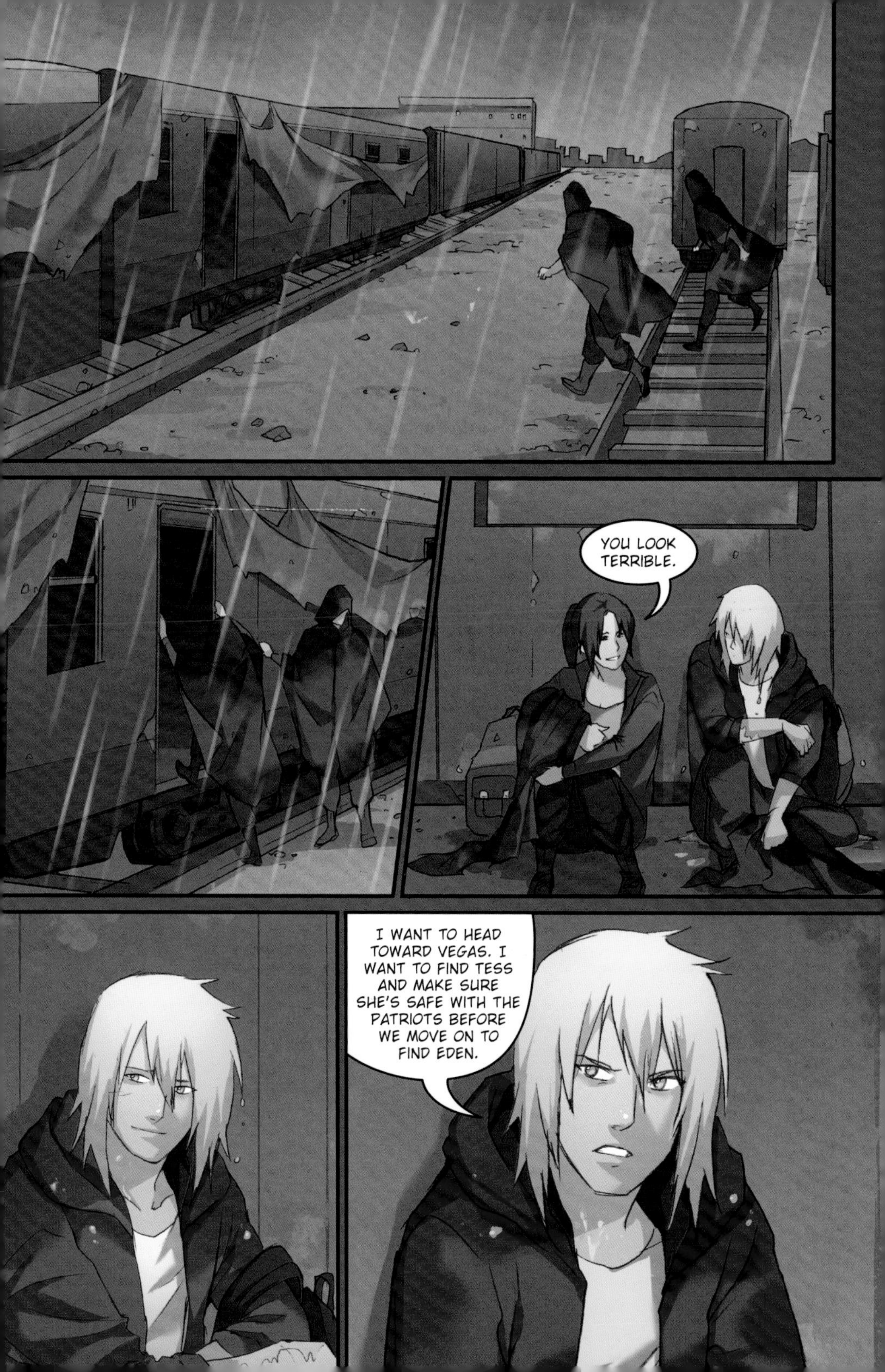
YOU LOOK TERRIBLE.
I WANT TO HEAD TOWARD VEGAS. I WANT TO FIND TESS AND MAKE SURE SHE'S SAFE WITH THE PATRIOTS BEFORE WE MOVE ON TO FIND EDEN.

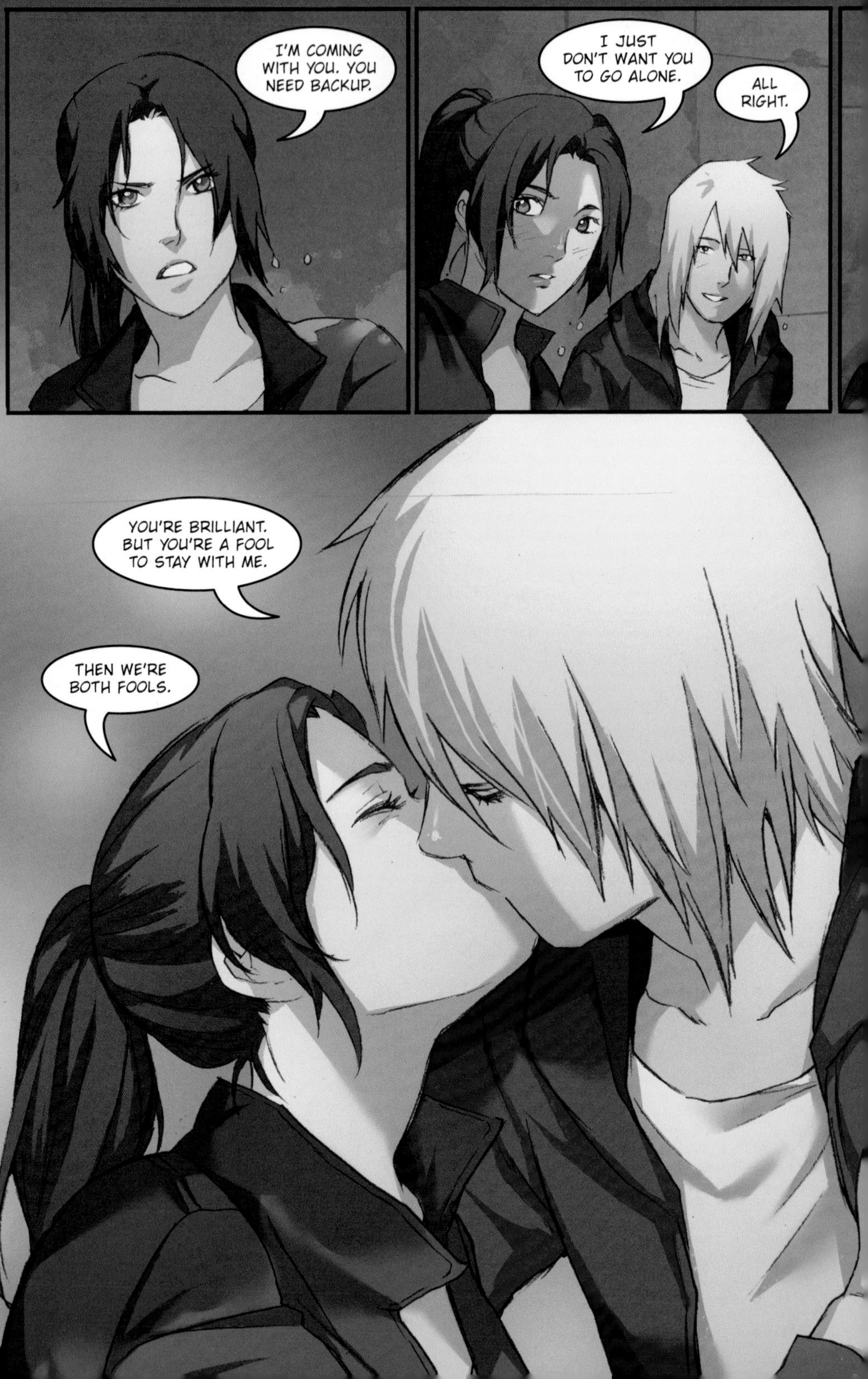
I'M COMING WITH YOU. YOU NEED BACKUP.
I JUST DON'T WANT YOU TO GO ALONE.
ALL RIGHT.
YOU'RE BRILLIANT. BUT YOU'RE A FOOL TO STAY WITH ME.
THEN WE'RE BOTH FOOLS.

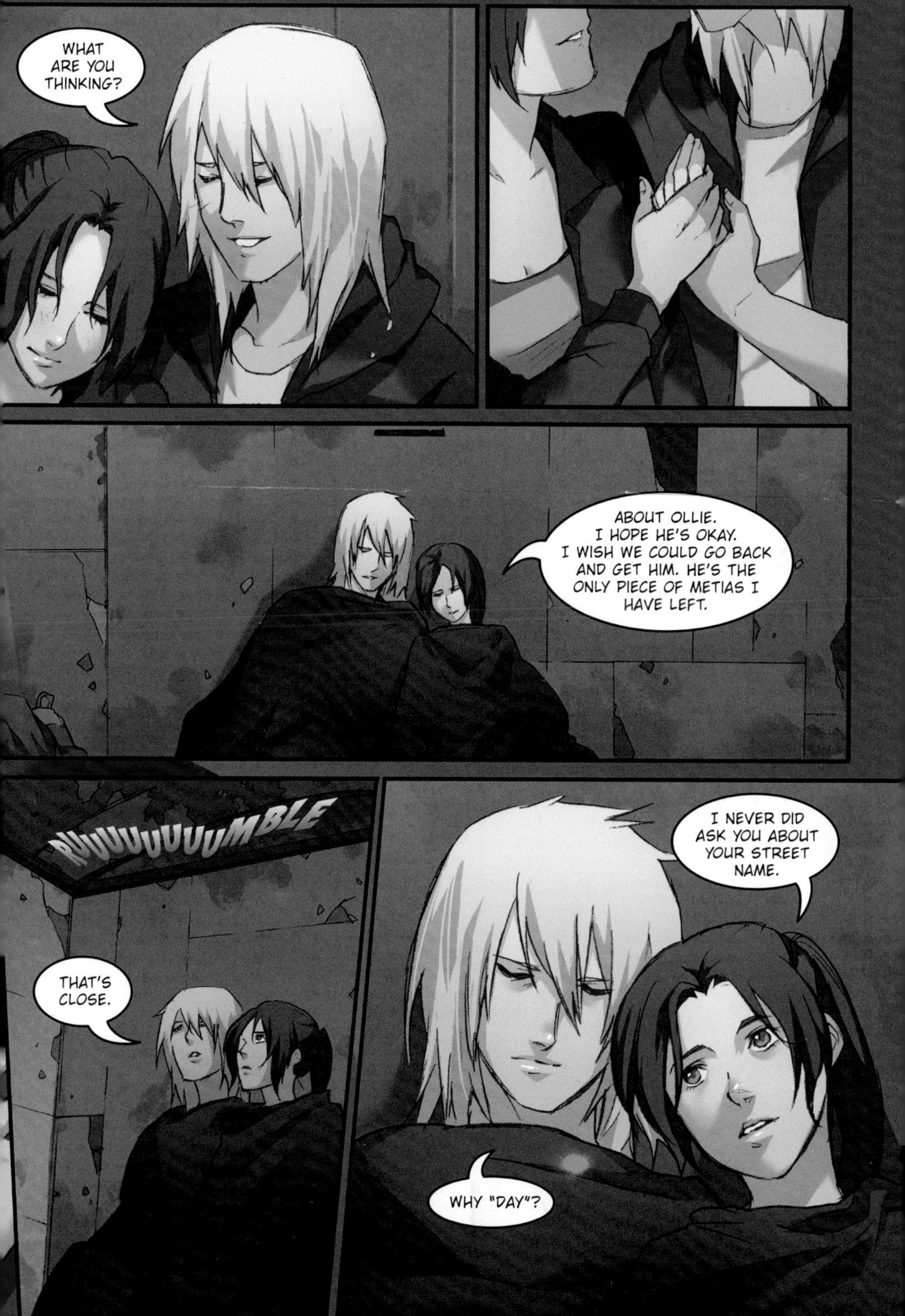
WHAT ARE YOU THINKING?
ABOUT OLLIE. I HOPE HE'S OKAY. I WISH WE COULD GO BACK AND GET HIM. HE'S THE ONLY PIECE OF METIAS I HAVE LEFT.
RUUUUUUUUMBLE
THAT'S CLOSE.
I NEVER DID ASK YOU ABOUT YOUR STREET NAME.
WHY "DAY"?

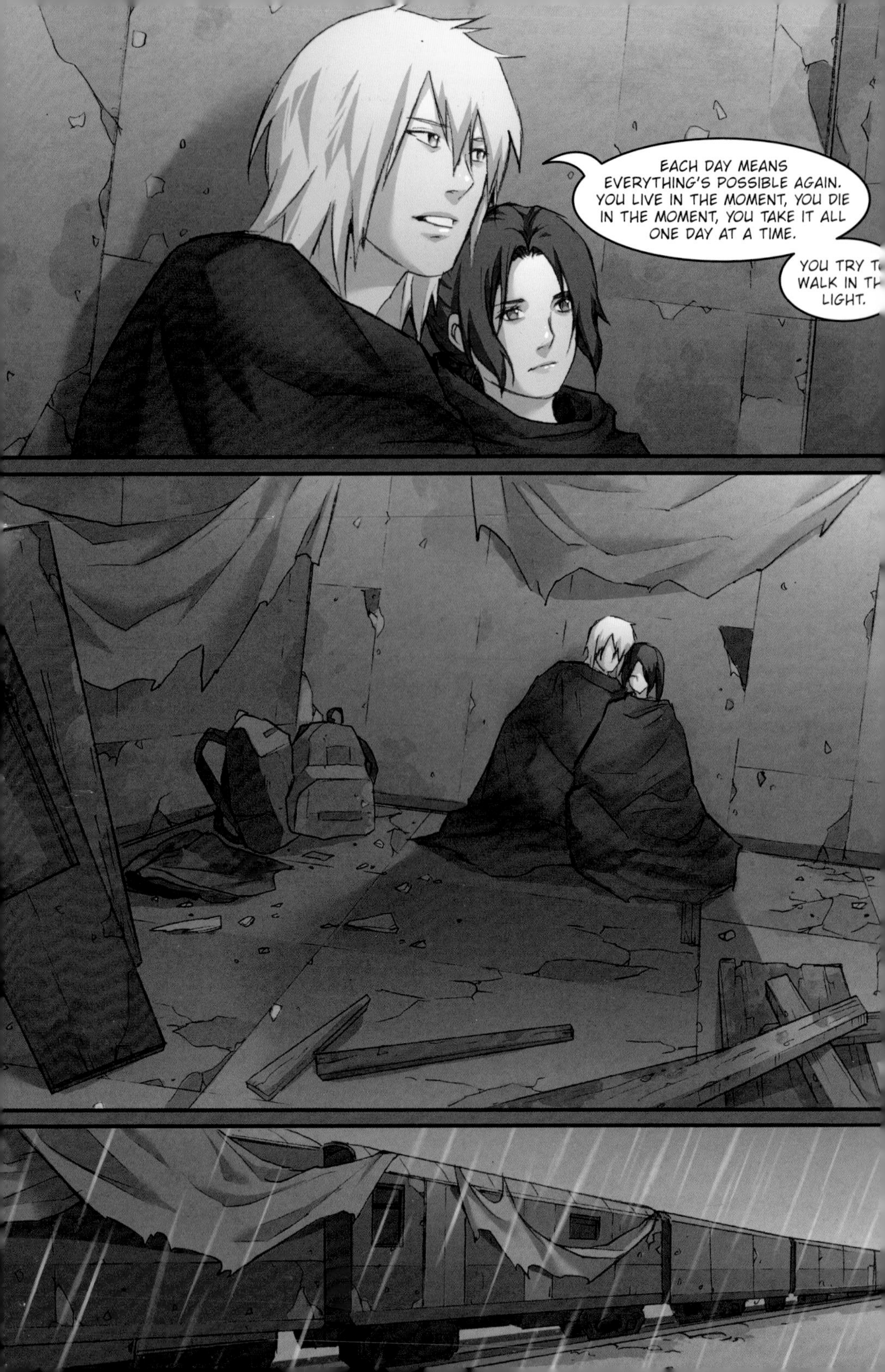
EACH DAY MEANS EVERYTHING'S POSSIBLE AGAIN. YOU LIVE IN THE MOMENT, YOU DIE IN THE MOMENT, YOU TAKE IT ALL ONE DAY AT A TIME.
YOU TRY T WALK IN TH LIGHT.